THE ABSOLUTION OATH

The Absolution Oath

The Immortal Cities Saga: Book One

Edited by E. A. Wyatt LLC

Printed in the United States of America

First Edition: 2025

ISBN (Paperback): 978-1-969052-00-2

Printed by IngramSpark

THE ABSOLUTION OATH

THE IMMORTAL CITIES SAGA
BOOK ONE

E. A. WYATT

For my mother, my ride or die, and a ruthless reader who read this book and said
something along the lines of:
"Yeah, I think you've got something here."

For my father, my cheerleader, who believes in me and everything I do to an
unparalleled degree.

WOEFUL WOODS
NORTHERN FOREST
INFINITY MOUNTAINS
FARMLANDS
CHARPH
FALDONIAN MOUNTAINS
SOLTAN LAKE
SORBIS
WOODLANDS
COASTAL PLAINS
INNER CITY
OUTER CITY
RIDGE WOODS
RIVER SORBIS
FIVE RIVER
MISUNDRE
AZURE BAY
POSTERN WATERFALLS
LINOLAY BEACH
THE SOUTHERN PLAINS
WHITE SEA
VIVINMOOR
KINGDOM OF SOLTA
1 - Selene's House
2 - Valentine Manor
3 - Temple of the Maste
4 - Hotel Solta
5 - Capitol Building
6 - Protector Headquart

Valentine Ancestry

Part I

CHAPTER ONE

14.SEVEN.4004

Sitting in the cushioned chair at the centuries-old oak desk, I placed a sheet of Cole's monogrammed stationery on the leather desk pad and pulled a pen from the center drawer. Taking care to date and address the letter, I wrote the words haunting me:

I once thought I knew what I wanted.

What followed was every thought, every feeling, and every truth that had helped me come to find those words, actualized in the black ink flowing freely as the words poured out of me.

Everything I couldn't bring myself to say aloud.

The pen skittered across the white page until it was a mess of scribbles with just enough room to sign my name. I blew on it, waiting for the ink's sheen to fade, and folded it in half twice before slipping it inside the book I'd been reading. Free, for the time being, from myself.

Returning the pen, I stood and left Cole's office, wandering down the hall of his apartment to the old mahogany console table situated between the two doorways to the sitting room, brought in solely to display the only picture in the apartment—a golden framed photo of Cole and me in the manor's garden—and my innocuous little hiding place.

Because no one ever paid any mind to accent furniture, and certainly no one bothered to figure out how to open the stubborn drawer.

A simultaneous lift, right shift, and tug on the handle, and it slipped right out. I tucked the book away for safekeeping, deciding I'd determine what to do with the letter later.

Emotional decisions were best made after at least a few hours of consideration.

And there was no real decision to be made anyway. I'd burn it. I always did.

Fingering the key dangling from my neck, I collapsed onto the couch before the sitting room window and stared out at the valley Valentine Manor sat within, letting my gaze drift across the pristine green lawn to the Ridge Woods at the edge, saturated in the deep orange glow of the setting sun.

Here, it was easy to think there was nothing but green, that the manor was the most blissfully isolated place in the kingdom, but it was an illusion. From this part of the home, if you knew where to look, a sliver of the wrought iron gate the people of Sorbis liked to crowd—hoping to get a glimpse of a member of the royal family—poked out, reminding you where you really were, and what this place really was...

"You are in here," a voice said, breaking me from my stupor.

I turned from the slowly darkening world to the doorway, where Cole, the Crown Prince of Solta and my Bidden, stood smiling, a rogue square of sunlight casting a sheen on his perfectly combed black hair and setting his jade green eyes ablaze. He slipped out of the dark blue suit jacket he wore to work every day and draped it across the armchair closest to him.

Undoing the button at the throat of his white button-up, he crossed the room to me. "I almost didn't believe the Protectors outside my parents' apartment when they said you weren't in there."

I gathered myself together in just enough time for him to fall on the seat beside me. "I'm surprised as well. I thought you weren't going to be back tonight."

The emerald cufflinks at his wrists caught and tossed the light as he propped his elbow on the back of the couch and peered down at me. "Yes, well, it didn't take as long as expected, so I have the rest of the night off." Pulling my legs into his lap, he ran a finger along my bare calf, making the skin pebble. "Pleasantly surprised as I am, why are you here and not with my mother? I was beginning to think nothing but sleep or death could tear you from her side."

"Master Guardian Norris wanted to try a new treatment in private." Dropping my gaze, I took a breath. "He berated me today—said I wouldn't look twenty-three much longer if I continued to worry like I do."

"Is that why I caught you staring dolefully out the window?" he teased. "He isn't wrong, doll. Extreme, yes, but you shouldn't be spending every free waking hour worrying about something you have no control over and can do nothing about."

I waved him away in frustration, grateful at least for a moment to feel something besides the aching emptiness in my chest. "Immortals forbid I worry about someone I love."

He grabbed my flailing hand, bringing my fingers to his lips. "I worry about her too, but I've accepted I am no Elder, and the best outcome for her won't be by my doing. Norris is doing everything he can to help her."

I bit my tongue, fighting the urge to correct him. As the Master Guardian of Skill and the attendant to the king, his mission was solely to keep the queen alive by any means necessary, so the Pledge the king had made to her wouldn't affect him. It didn't even matter if he kept her alive in a proper state.

"I know," I nodded. Anything less would prolong the lecture on why I shouldn't worry. "How was Misundre?" I asked—suddenly and gratefully remembering where he'd been. A perfect subject change, so I might forget what I really wanted to. "What did your brother say?"

The sudden hope I had faltered at Cole's frown.

He sucked in a sharp breath through his teeth. "He isn't coming."

"You're not serious?" I waited a moment, searching his face, hoping it was a joke. "You're serious." Heat lashing every nerve in my body, I leapt from my spot on the couch. "That impudent little shit. His mother could be," *is* corrected a whisper-soft voice in my head, "dying, and he won't honor the only request she's made of him in twenty-some years." I started to pace the room. "All I hear is Damien this, Damien that—what is wrong with him?"

Cole reached for me, but I yanked away. "There's no reason to be upset," he said, scooting to the edge of the couch. "I expected no less. My brother made it clear when he left how he felt about Sorbis and our father—doll, come back and sit with me."

How was I supposed to sit?

"She's going to be crushed." The grief might even push her over the edge. My fists clenched and unclenched at my side, tears of rage and fear stinging my eyes. "Take me to him. I'll make him regret that."

Moving to his feet, he grabbed my waist, pulling me to his chest. So close I could see my gold eyes reflected in his. "Relax. As delightful as it'd be to watch you rip into him, it'll do no good. My mother will expect a rejection." His fingers sent shivers through me as he lifted the hem of my dress and leaned to brush his lips along my ear, planting a desperate kiss on my neck. "Let's stop talking about this. Why don't I have the kitchen prepare dinner, and you spend the night."

"Cole," I managed. "You know we can't."

He made a low growl in his throat. "You don't know we can't, we haven't tried."

Gently, I pushed my hand against his chest, putting space between us. "We performed a verbal bond. I would say we know. I can do dinner," I conceded, "but I need to go home. Tomorrow starts my work week."

Sighing, he turned his attention to wrapping a strand of my long brown hair around his finger, and I worked to slowly let out the breath I'd been holding. "You know I like having you close, and we've barely seen each other the last couple of weeks. Julien can take you in the morning."

The use of the inclusive "we" made me want to raise my eyebrows. We hadn't seen each other through no fault or choice of my own.

His free hand cupped my chin, bringing me to look at him. "You know one of the perks of being my Bidden is you don't have to work —especially not in the worst, dirtiest area." Distaste contorted his face. "All you need is one word from me."

My stomach twisted at the thought of him reducing my hours again. "That's not necessary. I enjoy my work."

Cole's frown deepened. "I know."

"I'm starting to see a real and positive shift in the community."

Watching his thumb trace my lower lip, he said, "You should at least have protection with you. The commoners have been very vocal about their disappointment in my family and the Alliance Council recently."

"That's incredibly unnecessary. No one has ever expressed harm toward me."

Inhaling slowly, he lifted his gaze back to mine. "Have you given any more thought to moving in with me?"

I swallowed, my throat suddenly parched. "If I move in with you, the Alliance Access and everyone in the city will speculate about our being betrothed." And my status as their future queen.

"Is that such a big deal? Everyone knows how I feel about that and how I feel about you."

My knees softened, threatening to give way. This wasn't happening now. He was not about to do this now. "I thought we agreed we'd talk about that when the time came. There's so much going on—"

He pressed his index finger to my lips, silencing me. "We did, and I know now isn't an ideal time for either of us to have that conversation, but I want you to start thinking about it more…seriously. Getting a real notion for it." His green eyes glittered. "Because I want to make time for that conversation soon." Dropping his hold, he put his back to me and stretched his arms out wide. "As for tonight, you'll stay here, and I'll send for dinner," he said, mid-yawn. "I'm feeling like a nice steak, rare, and a large slice of chocolate cake. And of course I'll request a garden salad for you."

Relieved, I didn't even care he'd made up my mind for me. "That sounds lovely."

CHAPTER TWO

15.SEVEN.4004

I woke with a start—bedsheets tangled around my legs and my silk nightgown soaked in sweat.

In the manor. In my bed. Hand to my chest, I breathed, trying to ease my racing heart. Just another bad dream. Everything was okay.

After a minute, the pounding in my ears and chest slowed enough for me to make out the gentle snores on the other side of the cracked door, joining my room to Cole's. I exhaled the softest sigh of relief. I hadn't woken him. Good. At least the nightmare wouldn't end in coddling.

Sliding from the bed, I kept my ear locked on that snore, listening for changes as I tiptoed around my room, collecting my robe from the back of an armchair and locating my satin slippers right where I left them—neatly placed at the center of the door to the hall, ready to go.

The light charms in the hall activated as I cracked the door, giving me pause. When the snore didn't falter, squeezing out, I quietly shut it, heading for the front door and my next obstacle.

Protectors, standing guard to either side of the door in their red battle uniforms, nodded at me as I stepped out between them. All well and good until one of them came forward, setting the ends of his red cloak swirling around his ankles.

Hugging my arms to my waist, I pulled my robe tighter. "Is

something wrong?"

The sharp blue eyes of Protector Olick—one of the older, kinder Protectors—looked down at me from behind his helmet. "His Highness, Prince Cole, has asked that one of us accompany you should you leave the apartment after sunset."

Get caught sleeping in the garden once…

Tilting my head, I let my eyelids droop. "Please, I'm only going to the kitchen for a cup of lavender tea. An escort isn't necessary."

"I'm afraid orders are orders, my lady."

I delivered a flawless, bone-tired sigh. "Truly half an hour at most. There's nothing like having someone hover over you while you try to relax with a cup of tea. Let me enjoy it in peace. Please."

Olick considered me carefully, and I waited, not daring so much as to breathe should the slightest motion crack my guise.

Grumbling, he stepped back into position. "Thirty minutes and not a second more, or I will come looking for you."

I bowed my head in acknowledgment and moved along, careful to keep my step sleepy—even throwing in a yawn. Anything to help sell the lie.

Telling him the kitchen meant I would have to take a less direct path to my real destination, and thirty minutes meant I needed to move quickly. Luckily for me, the Hidden Halls made the last part easy, and an entrance was coming up.

I turned the corner into the next hall, ready to drop the facade, but a staff member coming from the opposite direction, a broom and dustpan in hand, followed by two patrolling Protectors, kept my step slow. I could feel the seconds fading as, reaching the hidden door, I stopped at the window, pretending to admire the full moon high overhead.

Please hurry them along. Please, no one else, I prayed silently to the

Immortal Idols.

A prayer ignored because an eternity passed while I waited for the staff member's shuffling and the hard thud of the Protector's boots to fade.

Three...two...one...

I performed a quick check in each direction—clear—and darted for the inconspicuous stretch of wall separating two paintings of former kings of Solta, passing through into a musty, narrow, stone corridor that ran parallel to the main hall and was lit by a finger-thin strip of ever-burning green light overhead.

The Hidden Halls were a remnant of Cole's great-great-grandfather, the Immortal Valentine, who had a thing about not wanting to see the staff. Quincy—my oldest friend and Cole's youngest brother—and I had stumbled upon them while playing as kids years ago, and judging by the webs haunting most of the turns, the spiders and I were the only ones using them now.

Running as fast as my stupid slippers allowed, I navigated the smooth stone floor of the halls without a thought, like a dance performed a thousand times. A left after five luminous hallways. Down two turns of a spiral stone staircase and into the open once more for as long as it took to push through the heavy wooden back doors of the rear foyer.

Right into the moonlit courtyard of the gardens.

I breathed a sigh of relief into the cool night air and inhaled the scent of blooming Olinda Roses—which opened and exuded their fragrance every night when the moon was at its highest—nearby, letting the smoky sweetness clear the lingering nightmare from my thoughts.

Running my hands over the ivy-covered lattice, I stepped into a dream and the most beautiful place in Sorbis.

A sea of white blooms nestled amongst black leaves reached their silver-tipped petals skyward, mirroring the stars overhead. I brushed my fingers along the velvet soft flowers, mindlessly winding along the stone path to the center of the garden where the Eternal Tree stood.

It wasn't much to look at compared to the trees of the Ridge Woods, which stood five times taller and had trunks three times as thick, but grandeur wasn't its draw.

The story went that the Immortal Valentine had performed the Eternal Pledge—a life bond represented by the exchange of Pledge Tokens—with his lover Olinda on that spot, and the tree had grown from their exchange of love. It was the only tree the groundskeepers never tended, as it never grew or lost its leaves, and as such, it was forbidden to touch it. And animals never bothered it. I'd watched birds fly for its canopy seeking the secrets amidst its green leaves, squirrels dash toward it looking for a place to call home, and beetles make their way to burrow themselves into the cool earth it sank its roots into. All of them were turned away as if an invisible shield kept them back.

Strong. Untouchable. Perfect. The tree was as much a symbol of their love as the Olinda Roses were a symbol of the woman herself—always described as someone who came alive at midnight. Lost in the mystique of it, I didn't notice that I wasn't alone until I was standing at the end of the stone path leading to the Eternal Tree.

"I shouldn't be here. I shouldn't be here," a voice muttered. "Why did I come?"

A sudden chill froze everything within me.

Pacing erratically under the tree, half concealed in the canopy's shadow, was a figure clad in heavy black boots and a knee-length black trench coat—a man, by the size of them.

Cole had warned me this might happen last time after the Protectors had found me asleep on the bench my knees were presently brushing up against—the only thing separating me from this stranger—and I'd stupidly informed him he needn't worry because I walked the gardens alone all the time and hadn't experienced any trouble. *It doesn't happen often, but delusional or unhappy people have managed to bypass the Protectors at the gate and the wards around the property*, he'd chided.

This wasn't just someone delusional or unhappy, though. The gardens were on the far side of the manor—this was someone delusional or unhappy with knowledge of the grounds.

"Immortals, I shouldn't be here," he groaned, a hand going to his head.

And clearly out of his mind on some kind of illicit recreational elixir.

Dangling from his twitching right hand was a glowing cigarette he tapped, sending the ash to the dirt. The absolute nerve… Forgetting myself, I opened my mouth—ready to give this disrespectful man a piece of my mind—and just as quickly remembered myself as I spotted the dark sack at his feet where something rope-like spewed from the opening.

My stomach twisted sharply.

His hand reached once more to his head. "What am I doing?"

Keeping my eyes on the stranger—because no way was I putting my back to him—I tiptoed backwards, desperate not to make any noise. If I could get back to the rear foyer doors, I'd be fine. I'd carefully and with as much composure as I could muster, make my way back to the apartment, climb into bed, and pretend to sleep.

Because Immortals knew I would never be able to sleep after this.

This stranger would never know I was here, and the next patrol would find and take care of him. I only needed to walk the path through the garden in reverse.

I could do that.

The hammering in my chest came to a dead stop as with my next step back, my slippers earned their name on the slick stone, sending me backward. I caught myself, but not before my hip brushed a rose bush, causing a sharp rustling.

Fuck. Stupid fucking slippers.

Startled, the man turned quickly, the heel of his boot digging into the dirt. I didn't need to see his face to know his eyes had settled on me.

The unguarded back door and Hidden Halls were now off the table.

If I wanted a chance of getting out of this, I needed to get the attention of the Protectors immediately, meaning my best bet now would be running for the front lawn.

"Hello," he said, carefully.

In an attempt to hide my shaking, I tucked a strand of hair behind my ear. "You must be lost," I said, my voice breaking on lost, betraying me. "The main road is about a ten-minute walk that way." I pointed toward the foot-worn path going up the hill. "I'll go get Protectors and have them escort you to the road. A Runner will be happy to phase you wherever it is you meant to go."

The man laughed. "That's cute, thanks, but I kind of live here." He took a long drag of his cigarette and flicked it at the white stone bench. The shadows on his face shifted as he took a step toward me. "I'm—"

I didn't give him a second to finish the sentence, whirling to run before he could get closer—getting whatever lead I could.

"Hey, wait," he called. The thump of his footsteps in the grass behind me sent a surge of power to my legs.

Fuck. Good job, Eden.

I only needed to get around the south side of the home to the front lawn, and the Protectors at the main gate would see me and do something about this.

"Stop, please," he said.

Did he really think I'd be such an easy target? Passing under Cole's and then my bedroom window, their drapes drawn shut to the world outside them, my thoughts went to Protector Olick standing outside the apartment's door, expecting me back from the kitchen at any moment. A fresh sense of despair crashed through me.

No matter how this ended, I'd never walk the manor or its grounds alone from dusk to dawn again, even for tea.

I broke onto the front lawn, awash in moonlight. Across the expanse of deep green, I made out the speck of light marking the guardhouse at the main gate.

Why was it so far away?

"Seriously," my pursuer groaned, his voice close behind me. Running up the hill had helped close the lead I'd started with.

"Help," I screamed as loud as my air-hungry lungs would allow. "Help, please."

Let them have heard.

"I'm not going to hurt you," the man panted. Too close now.

"What's going on out there?" a voice boomed. It'd come from the front door of the manor. Yes, good, so much closer than the gate. I only needed to last a little longer.

"Over here!" I cried. My legs started to slow in defense of the burn tearing through my muscles.

The sound of weapons clinking together and boots smashing stone called back in response. Yes, yes, run. So close. Thank the Immortals. This was it. Come on, come on.

Long, cool fingers encircled my wrist, triggering an explosion of dry heat in my stomach. I spun so quickly, fist raised, sure I'd strike my pursuer. To my chagrin, he grabbed my other wrist before the strike passed the halfway point.

Shrinking away from me, he laughed. *He laughed.*

Moonlit strands of wavy black hair fell into the bemused green eyes staring down at me from a tan face. My frantic heartbeat momentarily slowed, seized by a strange sense of familiarity.

"I didn't mean to scare you. I'm—"

Orbs of light appeared overhead, casting the yard in an unnaturally white glow, tearing his attention away.

This was it. With all my remaining energy, I reared my leg back, ramming my knee as hard as I could where it'd hurt. The air left his lungs with a sharp whoosh, his grip on me releasing instantly as he fell to one knee.

"Over here," I rasped, running by him.

Electricity filled the air, prickling the hair on my arms. My heart dropped, taking my hope along with it.

Battle magic.

They were preparing to attack. Of course they were. An intruder at the manor in the middle of the night, and they didn't know I was out here—that I was the one screaming for help.

"Wait, don't it's me—"

"Eden?" Cole shouted. My name was followed by the frantic cry of, "Your Highness, it isn't safe."

"Cole," I cried, not even caring about the slight touch of anger in his voice.

"Your Highness, stay back," another voice reprimanded.

"Eden, where are you?"

Bursting into view of the front door, I barely avoided a blast of magic as I ran up the stairs. Cole was halfway down the steps, wearing only a white t-shirt and dark blue sleeping shorts, when his frantic eyes found me.

Throwing myself against him, he squeezed me tight to his chest. "I wake up to screaming and find you gone, and then all this commotion.

What are you doing out here alone? Why isn't a Protector with you?"

The confession came out like vomit. "I was only getting a cup of tea, but then I decided a walk would be nice, and then this demented man started chasing me—"

His brows knitted together. "And you didn't pass a single Protector on the way out of the manor?"

"I—"

A darkness to rival the night flashed across his eyes. "What have I told you about walking alone at night?"

"I know, I just need—"

"I asked you to walk with a Protector if you insist on these night strolls. We'll talk about this later." He turned his attention to the tall bushes along the stairs where the Protectors had disappeared. "What's going on here?"

"A misunderstanding," came a sigh.

I shifted in Cole's hold to see what was going on, expecting to see the stranger dragged behind the Protectors in cuffs. Instead, he strolled forward, rubbing his leg, followed by them, their heads bowed.

"One my balls will never forget. I guess father made good on his threat to have all photos of me removed." His gaze momentarily flicked to me.

Cole straightened, his hold on me shifting to my waist. "Damien."

What.

I looked between them. The brother who'd renounced his title and vowed never to come back. The same brother who'd refused his mother's request just that morning—this was him?

I wanted to slap myself for not seeing the resemblance, but looking between the two—aside from black hair and bright green eyes, the two looked nothing alike. Not like Cole and Quincy, who took after their father—strong brow, square jaw, straight hair, tall and lean. What I'd come to expect a Valentine to look like.

The familiarity I felt…

I'd believed none of Queen Lupine's children took after her, but looking at him, there were her sharp cheekbones and pointed chin. Shaggy hair, finger-combed back from his face and skin several shades darker than his brothers—no doubt due to countless hours in the Misundran sun, and the dark blue—not black—jacket he wore was close to bursting around his arms and chest, hard with muscle.

Smiling, he held up his hands and said rather flatly, "Surprise."

"You changed your mind," Cole said, sounding less than happy.

Damien stopped on the stairs, two steps below us. "I did." He glanced over his shoulder at one of the Protectors. "I left my bag at the Eternal Tree. Could you please retrieve it for me?"

The Protector looked to Cole for permission.

Cole's eyes didn't leave his brother. "Did you forget they don't answer to you anymore?"

"No…but I didn't think you'd deny the request."

The brothers stared at each other, both unmoving but for Cole's thumb gliding slowly along the curve of my waist.

To my knowledge, telepathy wasn't a skill of the Immortal Valentine or Faldone—lineage both men shared—but even having been raised by their mother, I knew there were secrets I didn't know about the family. And some exchange I wasn't privy to was undoubtedly happening.

Damien dropped his gaze and inclined his head slightly, conceding.

What agreement had been made?

Relaxing next to me, Cole nodded for the Protectors to go. "What were you doing in the gardens?" he asked his brother.

Damien gestured broadly. "Reacquainting myself with the place before I made myself known."

"Well, you made quite the entrance. You were always good at that," Cole said. "I guess I shouldn't be surprised your change of heart happened in the middle of the night, though it is less than ideal."

"I came when I was ready," he said, tone clipped. He shifted his eyes to me, making my breath catch. "Are you going to introduce me?"

Cole stopped stroking my waist. "Didn't work in an introduction when you were chasing her across the lawn?"

"I tried, but I guess I look worse than I thought."

"As much as I'd love to agree, she has nightmares and an overactive imagination."

My blood prickling, I said, "You don't have to patronize me."

A flicker of amusement warmed Damien's eyes, and Cole's grip tightened slightly.

"This is Eden Alexander, my Bidden," Cole said.

"Ah, mother's mortal ward. My Uncle Heath mentioned you. It's a pleasure to meet you." He held a golden-brown hand out to me. The same one that'd been wrapped around my wrist a moment ago.

I looked from the offering to his eyes, his mutterings at the tree echoing in my head. "I'm glad you changed your mind about coming. Lupine's been talking about you endlessly. She was so hopeful you'd come. I didn't know how she'd handle the news of your decision not to."

Something like regret flashed across his face as he retracted his hand. "Can I see her now?"

Cole cleared his throat. "While mother will be overjoyed to see you, it is the middle of the night, and rest is crucial for her. Your visit can wait until morning. I know you have your apartment at Vermillion—"

"Actually, I was hoping I could stay here for the duration of my visit. There's no need to put Mari out. That is if father will allow it."

Cole shifted against me. "Father hasn't stayed at the manor since mother informed him of her pregnancy, so he won't be an issue. It's too late to have a guest room made up, though, so you can stay in the spare room in my apartment."

Now, it was me tensing. An offer to stay in his apartment.

Where we slept.

The corners of Damien's mouth tugged down, clearly not loving the idea either. "Is there something wrong with my old room?" he asked.

At that moment, the Protectors returned carrying the big black bag I'd seen by the Eternal Tree, the rope—the sleeve of a sweater—still dangling freely.

"Our father turned it into Master Guardian Norris's quarters after you left." Cole put his back to his brother, pulling me with him. "Now let's continue this inside. I've had enough of the chill."

CHAPTER THREE

15.SEVEN.4004

I lay in bed helplessly wide awake, listening to Cole's gentle snoring, wondering how he could sleep so soundlessly after the night's events, let alone the commotion on the other side of the door.

After being escorted back to the apartment by two Protectors, Cole and Damien had gone somewhere to talk. A quick conversation because barely any time passed before I heard the door to Cole's room open and the bed shift as he settled in once more. As for Damien, hyper-aware of his presence, I heard every move he made, and I wasn't the only one who couldn't sleep.

His boots struck the floor with a vengeance. *Stompstompstomp.* Pause. *Stompstompstompstompstomp.* The door to the apartment opened and abruptly closed, providing the briefest reprieve from his tyrannical stomping, and then all too soon it was back, accompanied by the discordant sound of glasses colliding against one another and liquids sloshing. The gentle heat of magic pulsed through the walls, followed by a sharp gasp of relief as he presumably gulped down the elixir he'd made.

It had to be close to sunrise when the apartment finally fell silent. For a handful of moments, sleep caressed me like a teasing lover, only to be scared away by the five o'clock alarm charm Cole used. Groaning, he crawled out of bed, and it was his shuffling about for the next thirty minutes that kept me alert. It ended with a kiss on my cheek as I feigned sleep, and I marked an hour until my wake-up call.

That was my last thought before I sat straight up, my heart pounding my chest. What time was it?

I couldn't have…Surely I wasn't… I scrambled to the drapes and threw them back.

Recoiling away from the bright mid-morning light, I ran to the closet only to remember I didn't have any regular clothes at the manor, and there was no longer time to go home as planned. Pulling on yesterday's yellow dress and grabbing my bag, I flew out the door.

No real sleep. No time to change. No time to shower. No time to even look in the mirror.

I burst into the main hall, stumbling upon Elodie, the staff member who attended Cole's apartment, moseying about.

The same Elodie I'd left a note for requesting a wake-up call.

"Why didn't you wake me?" I exclaimed, half-crazed.

Elodie stared after me, alarmed. "The door, miss. I thought you'd changed your mind."

Walking away as fast as was considered proper, I dared one glance back and saw what she referred to hanging from the hook at the center of the door. A pale wooden *Do Not Disturb* sign that'd never left its place on the back of the front door glared at me from its new position between the two Protectors.

Damien Valentine.

I took a steadying breath and moved on. There'd be time to handle that later.

Late. I was late. And late as I was, the walk from the manor to the estate's private path pained me. As the future king of Solta's Bidden, I set a standard for Soltan etiquette. Even when all I wanted to do was sprint, I had to stay poised and unhurried for the people who might see me—at the gate beyond and from the many windows of the manor.

At the private path, shrouded by trees, that changed. Running now would only provide me seconds, but if I were any later, I might die.

With shaking hands, I removed the Valentine family signet ring—a simple silver piece bearing the Immortal Valentine's signature concentric circle insignia—from the side pocket of my bag and worked it on. One finger to the cool metal was all it took to summon Julien, and breaking through to the other side of the property's protection ward, I had my finger at the ready.

In a blink, the Valentine family's personal Runner appeared, one step short of being trampled. A purposely placed strand of dark blue hair divided his scowl. "Yes?"

"I'm late," I exclaimed, grabbing his elbow.

Before I could take a breath, the birdsong calm of the valley and the mossy smell of the Ridge Woods became the bustle of hawkers selling goods, shoes smacking cobblestones, and the smell of freshly baked lemon bread.

"Your sweaty hands soiled my shirt," the Runner sneered.

Fighting the nausea phasing always gave me and lacking the patience to deal with his mood, I cut down the path to the brick building looming ahead, calling back over my shoulder, "I'm sorry, Julien. I'll have it laundered."

Huge and made of solid wood, it took my entire body weight to force open the front door to Selene's House.

Silence and the colluding smells of molding clay and orange wood polish greeted me. Well-worn wooden floors groaning under my feet, I hurried past the stairs leading to the dormitories and down the white-walled halls covered in the children's newest crayon drawings, to the kitchen where I supported Selene House's chef, Forrest, doing anything and everything but cooking—something he insisted on doing himself.

Fifty-two orphaned children between the ages of six months and sixteen, plus ten full-time attendants, called the two-story building on a self-sustaining farm home. By this time—ten in the morning, according to the grandfather clock I'd passed—every child over four would be attending lessons at the nearby school, and the younger ones would be with an attendant in the craft room.

Through the narrow window of the swinging doors leading to the kitchen, I peeped a young woman standing between two worn wooden tables. She wore a pristine white apron over a black cap-sleeved dress, and her magenta hair in a low ponytail at the base of her neck.

Rho's fierce lilac eyes hooked me as soon as I pushed inside. "You're so late," my best friend crooned.

Sighing, I tossed my bag aside and threw on one of the aprons hanging on a nail by the door. "I know, I know. I'm sorry."

"I've known you for eight years, and you've never been late."

I patted the pockets of my pants for a hair tie, remembering as I did that I was neither wearing pants nor did I have pockets.

Rho slipped an orange ribbon from her apron's pocket and passed it to me. "You being late was a bad sign. Your being unprepared is a sign that the Immortals are coming back to end all of life in Solta. What's wrong?"

"I hardly slept," I said, gathering up my unbrushed hair. "Cole returned from his trip to Misundre early and asked me to stay the night with him at the manor. It only got worse from there, I—"

Eyes glittering, Rho leaned closer. "So, the rumors are true?"

Soaping up my hands, I passed them through the ice-cold water surging forth from the faucet. "Rumors?"

She handed me a towel. "Damien Valentine has returned to Sorbis."

"There are rumors already?"

She tottered her head. "More or less. I did hear gossip in the street, but Cole sent Julien to Grayden's apartment super early this morning, and having spent the night, I was privy to the exchange. He wouldn't shut up about it—it was Damien this and Damien that. Right before he ran out the door, just for shits, I told him he gives pussy-splitting dick, and what does he say?" She lowered her voice to her version of a baritone. "'Damien's back, I have to go.'" She tucked a missed strand of hair behind my ear. "He ran out so quickly—as giddy as if there were a sale at his favorite leather shop. I knew they were cousins and they were close, but nothing like that."

Close to Grayden. I'd known that, but after the events of last night and this morning, hearing it was another tick against him.

"I don't know what's so great about him," she added.

I looked up, surprised. "You know him?"

She cocked an eyebrow. "I did live in Misundre for the first sixteen years of my life. I don't know him personally, but I know of him well enough. Classic philanderer. He's been messing around on Violet for years. Watch yourself around him. You're a snack ready to be eaten."

Sleeping with Alliance Council member Violet of Misundre, that was like ten more ticks against him. Son or not—this was who Lupine had thought it was pivotal to see? "I'm his brother's Bidden."

Tapping a long nail on the table, she raised her eyebrows suggestively. "From what I've heard, that's never stopped one of the brothers."

I nodded, ready to move on. "What does Forrest need from us today?"

She motioned over her shoulder to bowls of cleaned berries. "I did it all."

Peering around her more fully, I spotted a pile of ears of corn and a large bowl of potatoes. "What's that?"

Her face fell flat. "Thank you, Rho, for doing the worst of the work when I failed to show up on time," she mimed, ending her show with a sigh. "There's still corn to shuck and de-kernel and potatoes to dice," she jabbed her thumb over her other shoulder, "and there's that."

That was every dirty dish from dinner the previous night and breakfast that morning. "You did the worst of the work?"

She shrugged, turning her attention to the vegetables. "Let's get these to Forrest, and then we'll start that mess."

Filling the space beside her, I nudged her elbow. "Thank you, Rho, for carrying my load. I'll make it up to you."

Mischief turned the corners of her mouth as she grabbed for the corn. "Oh, I know."

Dumping the potatoes onto the counter, I asked, "What's Forrest making today?"

Rho worked her nails under a husk and ripped. "You know I don't ask questions."

Leaning back, I spotted the chef—who'd been working here since the Savior Selene had appointed him herself at opening some sixty years ago—through the small glass window, standing over a giant stock pot, slowly scraping in a bowl of seasoned cubed beef.

"Looks like stew."

"Hm," she grunted. "So, Damien Valentine is why you're late for the first time in your life?"

I should have known that conversation wasn't over. The knife I held sliced smoothly through the potato. "Yeah. He made quite the entrance, too. I stumbled upon him at midnight, under the Eternal Tree, muttering to himself."

Collecting the diced chunks, I tossed them into a bowl.

Rho grimaced. "Muttering to himself? Sounds like he's lost touch with reality. Misundre will do that to you—it's the heat." She leaned over an inch, lowering her voice. "Why were you up at that time anyway? Is everything okay? One of your nightmares?"

Stomach turning at the mention, I nodded my head.

"Do you want to talk about it?"

Smiling, I reached for the next potato. "No, but thank you."

She nodded her reluctant acceptance—it was the answer I always gave her. "Do you need me to pick you up some more of the darkness elixir?"

My hand slipped on the knife, narrowly missing my knuckles. "Not so loud, Rho," I hissed, quickly assessing all the doors.

"You're being paranoid. There's no one around."

Maybe, but the last thing I needed was the Alliance Access publishing a salacious article about my deteriorating mental health and an elixir addiction—which was precisely how they would describe my nightmares and the use of an elixir to treat them.

"None of that pout face. I have something that'll cheer you up." She reached under our work table and pulled forth a rainbow-colored box. "I was waiting for you to ask about our side project. The candy shop finally contributed something today."

I'd forgotten. My heart swelled at the sight of the candy store's logo.

Finally.

In addition to our kitchen duties, when we started working here, we took it upon ourselves to build relationships with the community, hoping that one day they'd stop seeing the orphanage as a financial burden and recognize the value of supporting these children throughout their growth.

And slowly, they did.

It wasn't consistent or even notable at times—donating enough of anything for fifty children was a big request—but it was better than it had been.

I'd been chipping away at the candy store owner for a while.

Lifting the lid revealed an assortment of hard candy, enough for each child to have at least two pieces. This was going to be great.

"How many blow jobs did this cost you?" she asked.

I grabbed the first thing I could—lucky for her, it was a piece of potato and not the knife—and threw it at her. "Rho!"

"Immortals, you're so serious," she chuckled, dodging it. "Would it be so bad? The shop owner's son is cute—in a mortal farmhand way— and he's always looking at you like he'd like to take you to the back room and give you a different kind of sugar."

My skin burned hot. "That's not funny. I'm Bidden to Cole."

"Yeah, yeah, and verbally bound to have no sex with him until after you've been blood bound and made queen. Which can't happen until you reach the Immortal Age, which is still a year and a half away for you, and by that time, it'll have been almost three years for you without sex. I'd die."

She reminded me of this fact at least once every time we worked together.

Putting her back to the counter, she stared at me intently, lowering her voice to a whisper. "In all seriousness—minus the dreams—you are okay, aren't you? You haven't said much about it, but I can see Lupine's situation is weighing on you."

Thankfully, my surprise at her question got lost in the intensity with which I diced.

"It's been a lot, but I'm fine." Throwing the last diced potato into the bowl, I met her lavender gaze, smiling. "I appreciate your concern, really."

She nodded once. "If you ever need to or want to talk, you know you can come to me."

"I know."

"Perfect, then…" She grabbed the bowl full of diced potatoes from the table and slid the corn over, smiling devilishly. "In exchange for this morning."

I laughed and rolled my eyes, not really minding. I liked the work.

"Oh, one more thing," she leaned close, whispering. "The elixir?"

I didn't look away from the corn I shucked. "Yes, please."

CHAPTER FOUR

15.SEVEN.4004

Wanting to work in silence to clear my mind and thinking the dishes wouldn't take any amount of time, once the vegetables were finished, I insisted Rho take the rest of the day off to make up for the morning. Hesitant at first, she took one look at the pile and left.

She was the smart one.

Running my permanently pruney hands down the skirt of my dress, for the second instance that day, I moved across Valentine Manor's lawn at a proper speed in a race against time—and Immortals, I swear it was laughing at me as the sun set at breakneck speed, casting its burnt orange glow across the valley.

Bounding up the stairs of the main entrance, I quietly cursed the Immortal Valentine for limiting the manor to two points of entry, as I was only now halfway to the king's apartment and headed in the same direction I'd just come. I knew it was due to security, but given the size of the manor, having entrances at the middle of the home in the front and back only was a waste of time.

But what need an Immortal care for time? That was for the rest of us, and I had—glancing out the window—at most, an hour before Master Guardian Norris gave Lupine her elixirs for the night.

Nearing the turn leading to the king and queen's apartments, I entered an indecent half-jog. In this part of the home, the windows remained covered, and at King Elias's request, the lights were kept low—spaced at such a distance that between where one light covered and the next, there was an equally sizable gap of darkness. Combined with the dark green peeling wallpaper, the creaky floorboards, and legends about the home being haunted, the staff avoided coming down here unless necessary, so odds were no one would see me.

The Protectors flanking the apartment door came into view a moment later, looking as serious as I knew they were bored. Nodding to them, I saw myself in.

I wasn't superstitious, but if any part of the manor was haunted, it was *this* hollow place. In each room, dust-covered white sheets concealed most of the furniture, and the lights blinking on as I walked through were a faint greenish-yellow, teasing things in the darkness more than erasing shadows. The smell of metal clung to the warm air, and thanks to soundproofing charms Master Guardian Rei had affixed to each space, the sounds I made were the only ones I heard.

I burst into the shadowy, sparsely decorated master bedroom, finding Lupine—the woman who was like a mother to me—sitting upright in her bed of blankets, grinning as she cradled her very pregnant stomach. In the flickering light of the fire—the only light in the room—I could make out a touch of pink in her sunken cheeks and a glimmer in her eyes, making her look more alive than she had in months.

The vise around my heart eased slightly. Maybe there was hope.

"I'm so sorry I'm late," I exclaimed.

Her lightly matted dark purple hair, chopped at chin-length for easy care during her treatment, flitted about as she waved me in. "Eden, my girl, come in."

I made a mental note to have a staff member come in and wash it. "It was such a busy day, and I was late to work. I've been late all day, but I'm here now. It's been—"

A flicker of motion from the other side of the room stopped me short.

On the sofa by the bed, seated closest to his mother, was Damien—his scooting over a seat what had caught my attention—cloaked in a monochrome black ensemble of a thick sweater, pants, and a wool coat. Half his ink-black hair had been finger-combed back out of his face, and his bright green eyes were trained on me.

I'd forgotten about him in my rush. Which was ironic, considering he'd been the source of it. Of course, he'd be here. Lupine was why he'd come.

I tucked a loose strand of hair behind my ear. "You have company. I didn't know you had company." As badly as I'd wanted to talk to her, I couldn't help but be happy the person she'd wanted to see so desperately was here with her. "I can go."

"Nonsense," Lupine exclaimed. "Come in. I've been waiting for you to join us. I wanted to introduce you. This is my son Damien." She turned to him. "Damien, you remember your tutor, Charlotte Alexander? This is her daughter and my ward, Eden."

Uncertain about any more dealings with Damien for the day, I had half a mind to insist I could come back later. Tomorrow evening, my thoughts corrected grimly. I gave him a simple nod and offered Lupine a smile. "We met last night." Passing the blazing red fireplace, I shifted my bag to my hands. "It was actually because of him that I was late to work this morning."

"Damien," Lupine admonished.

Taken aback, Damien looked from me to his mother. "Now, that's not fair. I have no idea what she's talking about."

Skirting the corner of the bed, I fell onto the sagging, worn cushion beside him. "So, you didn't put the do not disturb sign on the apartment door, effectively blocking my wake-up call?"

A v formed in the space between his brows. "I did do that…I'm sorry, I wasn't aware."

I tugged the ribbon free from my hair, shaking it loose. "I realized it wasn't intentional after I calmed down."

Damien looked back at his mother. "See, not intentional."

"You probably deserved a scolding for something." She clapped her hands together. "Now, since my two favorite people are here and we don't have long, we'll have to get right to it. I have something for us to celebrate your return, Damien, and I am overdue for celebration."

We both watched Lupine extract a small, dingy glass bottle from deep amidst the mound of pillows behind her. Inside, a shimmering dark purple elixir sloshed about, making my stomach turn.

Breki.

She gestured for Damien to take it, making the large emerald ring enrobed in gold on her middle finger—the Pledge Token King Elias had given her—glitter.

He didn't move an inch, staring at it like one might stare at a snake. "What is that?"

She rolled her eyes. "Real breki. I had my attendant bring it to me the other day in preparation for your return. Skittish girl—you would have thought I'd asked her for a dagger to slit my wrists. I knew I needed to start sooner if I was going to enjoy myself before I fall asleep, so take turns among yourselves."

My jaw slackened.

If anyone had caught the girl, not only would she have lost her job, she would have faced the wrath of Master Guardian Norris and the king, which could have meant anything. And recreational elixir or not, Lupine didn't know how breki—the strongest legal recreational elixir —would interact with everything the Master Guardian gave her. It very well could have been as harmful as a dagger to the wrist.

"Lupine," I said. "You should not—"

She clicked her tongue, silencing me. "I'm fine. The girl is and will be fine. None of that mothering tonight. As the one needing to loosen up the most, the first drink goes to you."

Leaning forward to shift a pillow, she tossed it toward me, giving me no choice but to catch it.

Despite the blistering heat of the room and its presence under Lupine's pillows, the glass of the bottle was ice cold. It made a soft popping sound as the cork released, and a plume of salty anise hit me like a punch to the face, burning its way up my nose and drying out the back of my throat.

I'd tried breki once before at a high society event. Good breki was terrible. Whatever this was had been found in a puddle of piss in the Shadow Market District and labeled breki.

"Enough of that," Lupine said. "It won't bite. Sting a bit, but what elixir doesn't?"

"Most of the ones you want to drink," Damien muttered.

Raising the bottle to the queen, her indigo eyes glowing in anticipation, I said, "To your health, Lupine," and turned to Damien, who watched the bottle's position inches from my lips warily, "and to your visit."

I barely swallowed before I started coughing as the salty elixir assaulted everywhere it touched. "Immortals, that is the worst thing I've ever tasted."

Lupine grinned. "A lot more potent as well."

I half threw the bottle at Damien, desperate to be rid of it. Lupine nodded her encouragement at him.

He sniffed once and drank a mouthful, swallowing it without so much as a wince. "That tastes like a skills student's first attempt at breki."

The queen waved us away. "Neither of you likes it. You've made your point. You'll change your mind in a minute when it starts to take effect. Pass it back to Eden. We don't have long."

I took another drink, controlling my reaction better now that I knew what to expect. Having already burned my mouth and throat, the sting on the second drink was more of an itch. "I know we're supposed to be celebrating, but I'm only taking two more gulps, and that'll have to suffice for your celebration. I can't have a repeat of this morning tomorrow."

"Where do you work?" Damien blurted, his emphasis on the word work indicating he, like most, was surprised I did.

Passing him the bottle, I stared right into his green eyes so I could witness his reaction to the answer fully. "Selene's House."

Choking, Damien clutched his chest. "The orphanage in the farmlands?"

That never got old.

Plucking it back before he could drop it, I drank again. "That's the one."

"She's doing great work, too," Lupine beamed. "In the nearly eight years she's worked there, she's transformed not just the orphanage but the area."

I thumbed the cork hanging off the bottle. "I wouldn't say transformed, and it isn't just me."

"Don't be so modest. All the relationships you've helped build in the community, the drastic decrease in post-departure suicides. Not to mention the children adore he—"

"What is this?" a nasally voice barked.

Damien's left hand, resting on his leg, balled into a fist.

In the doorway to the bedroom stood the stout, rat-eyed Master

Guardian of Skill, his arms lost in the folds of his blue robes.

Eyes spotting the bottle in my hand, Master Guardian Norris snarled, sending spittle flying, and the folds of liver-spotted skin under his chin swaying. "The queen should be getting ready to rest for the evening, not enduring your drunken antics. Get out. Now."

"I don't—" Damien started.

I placed my hand on his rigid forearm, hoping it'd stay him. The urge to challenge him itched under my skin as well, but acting on it had never gotten me anywhere I wanted to be.

"Don't," I said, the word loud enough for only him to hear. Getting to my feet, I leaned over the mound of blankets covering Lupine and placed a kiss on her cool cheek. "Stay strong. I'll see you tomorrow evening."

How quickly the exuberance burning inside of her had reduced to stoicism, I thought as her bony hand patted my cheek. "I'll be fine. Come when you can. Have a good night, my darling." Finish the bottle, she mouthed.

Damien was right behind me. "Get some rest. I'll see you in the morning," I heard him say as I grabbed my bag and put my back to the room, keeping my head down as I passed the Master Guardian.

In the hall, I didn't slow, wanting to put as much distance between myself and the monster as possible. I shivered as I failed to not think about the things he did and then hated myself, as was routine, for leaving Lupine alone with him.

"Hey, Eden," Damien called, powering toward me. "Wait up."

I threw a glance over my shoulder but kept moving. Not even a sudden reappearance of the Immortal Idols would stop me. "Yes?"

He caught me at the door to the main hall, nodding at the Protectors as he mirrored my stride but not saying anything again until we were out of earshot.

"What was that back there?" he asked, his voice low and fiery. "Both you and my mother accepted his order without a second's hesitation."

"It was time for Lupine's treatment. I could tell you were going to challenge Master Guardian Norris, and that never ends well."

"That I was. He has no power to give orders."

"Yes, but he has power vested in him by the king over others, which allows him to control you." I glanced up at him. "In this case, he has power over Lupine's health and the administration of her care and could bar you from seeing your mother, which would make returning here pointless and Lupine very sad."

He fell silent for a second and then said, "Would you like to have dinner?"

I dared another glance, surprised by the swift change in topic and his sudden shift in demeanor. "I, uh, can't. I need to get home."

"You don't live here?"

"Not full-time. Not since I turned sixteen." Anticipating the next question, I said, "I only stay here when Cole is home and I don't work, or he asks me to. I have work tomorrow, and there's been no request, so home I go."

"As the prince's Bidden, I'm surprised the Alliance Council allows that."

A question as much as a statement. I shrugged, turning right down the sparsely lit corridor, now enduring injections of silver moonlight streaming in through the panel windows.

"I'll walk you out then," Damien volunteered.

Curious, I stopped abruptly and looked up at him, realizing when my eyes landed on his chest that he was a good half a head taller than either of his brothers. Craning to look higher, I noticed a sheen to the green of his eyes that made them...glow brighter than Valentine eyes normally did.

Breki wasn't the only thing running through him.

Rho's earlier warning about Damien echoed in my thoughts. "That really isn't necessary."

"I don't know. Didn't you hear? There were sightings of a demented man chasing a woman last night," he teased.

He'd heard that.

"You were talking to yourself."

"Some may call that thinking out loud."

Remembering the breki clutched in my hand, I took a swig, appreciating the courage it instilled in me to ask things like: "Why do you really want to walk with me? Are you hoping for an apology for kicking you in the dick?"

His eyes widened a fraction. "Because it's the gentlemanly thing to do, though an apology wouldn't hurt."

"Hm, it really isn't necessary. It's a short walk to the manor's wards from the private path." I slipped the silver ring from my bag and held it up. "Julien's pretty fast. I'll be alright."

I started, but Damien moved to block me, running a hand through his wavy black hair. "Okay, fine. I didn't know you existed until a day ago, and since then, I've heard your name mentioned nonstop. As someone close to my mother, I'd like to know who you are."

It was his reference to his mother, rather than his family, that kept me from leaving him standing there without an answer. Another drink —that was four, right? —and I pressed the bottle into his chest.

"Fine, but it's going to be a conversation because estranged son or not, the feeling is mutual, except I've been suffering your name my entire life."

I waited for him to say something as we finished the stretch of the hall to the exit, but silence ruled the walk. Outside, the cool, moonlit summer night soothed me. I had to endure Julien once more, but I'd be in my own bed soon.

As I began to think he might have changed his mind, he said, "I'm sorry again about the door. And sorry about last night as well—I didn't mean to scare you. If you don't mind me asking, was I really so frightening?"

I snorted. "Feeling sensitive about being scary? I think it's fair to say that any shadowy figure, when you aren't expecting it, is scary. You don't need to keep apologizing, by the way. I shouldn't have bypassed the Protectors. My reaction is as much my fault." I brushed my fingers across the top of a bush decorating the manor's exterior. "Why, of all places, were you in the garden?"

"Reacquainting myself with the grounds," he said, repeating last night's answer.

I stopped short to look up at him, letting my skepticism at his answer play out across my face. "Strange place to start."

"What would you like me to say?"

"The truth. You're important to Lupine, and I would like to trust you, but I can't if you won't answer me honestly."

He straightened. "I know you heard me. You already know why I was there. I don't know why you need to hear it again."

"Maybe it was a test to see if you'd lie to me."

His nostrils flared.

"Relax, Damien. I'll let that one slide since the second most common thing I've heard accompanying your name is how much you hate Sorbis." A gentle breeze rustled a loose strand of hair, and I tucked it behind my ear. "I guess I don't understand—if you were so conflicted, why did you change your mind?"

Something sparked in those bright green eyes. "Because I care about my mother, and after Cole's visit yesterday, I knew I'd never forgive myself if," he swallowed, "if something does happen to her."

"It was so bad for you to come back."

"Was that supposed to be another question?"

I shook my head. "Just a sad thought." Going against my better judgment, I took the bottle of breki back from him and started toward the path again. "I'm glad you did," I threw over my shoulder. "Come and stay, that is. I haven't seen her remotely that happy in months. She almost looked like herself again."

Under the canopy of the trees, we became two black shapes on the shadowy path.

"I might not if you hadn't caught me," he sighed.

I smiled to myself. "Then I guess the fright of my life was worth it."

He huffed a laugh. "You asked me something, and I was honest. Now, I'd like to ask you something."

"Mostly honest," I corrected, reluctantly adding, "What?"

"Why were you out walking that late? Cole mentioned nightmares?"

I felt absently for the key at my throat. "I'd rather not talk about that."

"I don't know if anyone has told you, but trust is reciprocal."

Groaning, I waved him away. "I have the occasional nightmare, and then I can't go back to sleep, so I walk around to relax. There. I don't like talking about it. It's embarrassing."

"No more embarrassing than my trepidation returning here."

The path ending, we stopped once more outside the property's wards.

"To that," I said, slipping on the ring and returning the bottle. "I say we all have our fears, and at least you overcame yours." I sucked in a breath, mentally preparing for Julien's apathetic mood. "I'll see you tomorrow, probably. Have a good night."

He ran a hand through his hair. "Eden…I could take you home."

I arched an eyebrow.

Damien raised his hands defensively, the bottle of breki sloshing. "Just an offer. Now that I'm out here, I don't think I'll go back right now, and I've never used Julien to get anywhere, but I know he isn't the most pleasant to deal with."

I looked from the ring to him, weighing my options. Anyone would be better than Julien… "I guess if it wouldn't be too much trouble, I would appreciate a break from his complaining."

"None at all." Damien reached for me.

I snapped back as his fingers brushed my waist. "Whoa, what are you doing?"

"I have to touch you to phase you."

"Not on the waist. I'll hold your arm. Have you been to Union Square?"

He bristled. "You live on the outskirts of the outer city as well?"

Grabbing his elbow, I rolled my eyes. "You have the same look on your face that you did when I mentioned my work."

"I'm surprised, is all. Most of high society wouldn't step foot into that part of the city, let alone live there. You do both."

"I'm not high soci—"

There was no warning. Before my eyes, we were standing at the heart of a surprisingly empty Union Square, the statue of Valentine and Faldone making peace hovering high overhead.

Unprepared for the shift, my hand went straight from his arm to my stomach as I fell against the low brick platform elevating the statue.

Mixing breki and phasing, top ten worst choices of my life.

"What happened? Are you okay?" Damien asked. He started to reach for me, but I held up a hand, stopping him.

"I…need a minute. Phasing…always makes me…nauseous. I've been doing it…so much recently, then the breki…"

Hesitantly, Damien leaned against the spot next to me. "That wouldn't have happened if you'd gotten closer to me. The closer you are to me, the less time my magic—which isn't compatible with you—spends moving through you."

Taking a deep, steadying breath, I shook my head. "That sounds like a gimmick."

"How so?"

I squinted at him. "You're telling me you've never told a woman…you were trying to bed…to get closer when you phased to spare them?"

He shifted, jacket scraping the brick. "I am courteous, so it goes without saying I have. It'd only be a gimmick if it weren't the truth. And I wouldn't need one if it were that far along."

"I've never heard anything…about getting closer from anyone who's phased me."

He glanced at the sky, considering his next words. "How many people have phased you that have gone through the Academy? I learned that there."

I thought of Grayden and the couple of times he'd been asked to. "A handful."

He arched an eyebrow. "That would have cared to tell you that?"

"If this is true, I doubt those women know that. I can't believe it never occurred to you."

Adjusting to stare at me more fully, he said, "You know, if it was a gimmick, why would I use it on you, my brother's Bidden?"

I dropped my gaze. "No reason."

"Remember what I said about trust?"

Shifting forward, my hair fell into my face. "I'm sorry, what I'm about to say—it wasn't and isn't fair to you. My friend Rho told me I should watch myself around you." I tried to soften the words with a smile right as a wave of nausea hit. "She said she knew you from

Misundre. Called you a flirt and a philanderer."

Damien retracted as if slapped. "Rho as in Ole's kid Rhododendron?"

I nodded.

"Did she have an explanation for her accusations?"

"Something about your relationship with Alliance Council member Violet? That you sleep around despite your commitment to her or something along those lines. Honestly, the moment she mentioned Violet," I cringed, unable to hide my distaste, "I stopped listening."

"You have something against Violet?"

"I have something against anyone who sells lies about me to the Alliance Access."

He toed a loose chunk of brick. "It's hard to cheat on someone when you aren't in a relationship."

"I thought that might be a possibility, given her record," I sighed. "And Rho likes to gossip. I really shouldn't have listened. I don't like to judge someone based on gossip, but this morning, in my annoyance, I gave in to my baser nature." Feeling sheepish, I looked to him. "Will you forgive me?"

"There's nothing to forgive. It's easy to form an opinion about someone you don't or hardly know."

Something about the way he said it made me think he might be referring to me. And I almost asked him, but I knew I didn't want to know.

"How much further to your apartment?" he asked.

Grateful for the change in subject, I motioned to the building a hundred yards off to the right. "Just there."

"I won't have to carry you too far then."

Laughing, I straightened to standing. "You won't have to carry me at all. In one more moment, I'll be right as rain. Are you going to be okay?" I motioned at the breki, but it was the unnatural glow in his eyes that had grown brighter I referred to.

The corners of his mouth turned up in a huge grin. "Me? I wasn't the one who was almost sick on the walkway. I'll be fine, believe it or not," he flicked the glass of the bottle, making it ting, "I've had much worse than this."

"Because you were that skills student, weren't you?"

The smile reached his eyes. "I was." He stared at me like that long enough that heat bloomed in my cheeks, forcing me to look away. "Anyways, my elixiry Vermillion is not too far from here. I think I'll visit it, see how it's doing."

I nodded. "It's still one of the biggest elixiries in the city, you should be proud."

"You've been?"

"Many times, years ago." Taking a step away, I glanced once more at him. "Enjoy yourself, Damien. Thanks for bringing me home. Once again, have a good night."

"Goodnight, Eden," he said to my back.

The walk across the uneven gray stone of the square to my building lasted too long, as I was sure he watched me until I disappeared behind the building's privacy wards.

Up the four flights of stairs and safely inside my apartment, I released a breath I didn't know I'd been holding and collapsed on my bed.

CHAPTER FIVE

16.SEVEN.4004

Everything was right in the world the next day. No nightmares, no interruptions. Only solid, soundless sleep.

Rho didn't bring up Damien or my well-being, regaling me instead with details about her cute new neighbor as we cut onions and minced garlic. When we finished, with no requests from any of the other attendants, she rushed home, eager to cleanse herself of the stench before it soaked in.

Despite catching a whiff of myself on every warm summer breeze cutting through the streets, I took my time on the walk home, absently thumbing the vial in my pocket as I enjoyed how the sun, moving across a cloudless blue sky, felt on my skin. Rho had provided me with an entire vial of the darkness elixir, so at least in one way, everything would continue being right in the world for a while.

Lost in my reverie, I almost didn't notice the figure in an oversized tan coat beside the entrance to my building, casually watching people. I came to a stop, debating how bad I really needed to shower and change. Maybe I could head on to the manor. It wouldn't be the first time I visited Lupine in her bed smelling less than desirable, and it wasn't like I had plans to see Cole.

As if smelling my hesitation—more likely the onion and garlic as a gust of wind blew by—Rini Rain of the Alliance Access turned abruptly to me, her long blonde hair, pulled into a high ponytail, whipping an innocent passerby in the face in the process.

"Eden Alexander. Finally. I was beginning to think my source was wrong and you'd never come home," she grinned. Sauntering closer like a cat about to pounce on a mouse. "Or that I'd somehow missed you, which wouldn't have been good for you." She stopped a foot away, nose scrunched. "Immortals, why do you reek?"

Grateful for the Rini repellent, I folded my arms across my chest. "What do you want?"

Brown eyes gleaming, she stepped closer to me. "Interesting thing, I was in the company of Prince Damien last night. He brought me back to Valentine Manor—"

Bile touched the back of my throat. Is that what he thought of trust? Is that the fastest someone had ever broken trust? And Immortals, what was with his taste in women? "I have no interest in hearing about your escapades," I said.

"—to Prince Cole's suite," she continued, pretending like she hadn't heard me. She pulled a manila envelope from her coat and held it out to me. "This is for you."

Glancing at it, I shrank back. "What is it?"

She shoved it toward me. "Take a look. It isn't laced and it won't bite."

The fact that she needed to assure me of that made me want to touch it even less.

Reluctantly accepting it, I lifted the flap, catching a glimpse of the photo inside. The photo of us Cole kept on the entry table in his apartment at the manor.

I laughed. This was too good to be true. "I knew you were crazy, but I didn't think you were a fool. Stealing from the Crown Prince of Solta? Get ready to never write another story again. Now, get out of my face and away from my home."

I sidestepped her. A mistake.

Within reach, Rini pounced, sinking the long black nails of one hand into my upper arm and ripping the envelope away with the other. For the first time since I'd started seeing Cole, I regretted turning down protection.

"You aren't the queen yet, you bottom-feeder," she hissed, "and I won't stand for you talking to me like that. I don't know what insults me more, that you think you're above me or that you think I'd be so stupid." She came so close I could feel her breath on my face. "You haven't let me get to the best part. I gave you that picture so you'd know what I say next is true. I know your secret."

I glared at her, ready to knee her in the stomach and run if she got a hair closer. "What would that be?"

Her grin consumed the lower half of her face. "While I was snooping around, I stumbled upon a rickety little console table with a stuck drawer. It took some technique, but I eventually managed to get it open, and to my delight, inside was a little red book."

My heart came to a stop. And then it started to shrivel into nonexistence. There was no way…

"At first, I was so hopeful it was a diary, and I was rather bummed to see that it was a simple, boring book." She shook her head, emphasizing her next words. "But my oh my, do simple, boring things not have their surprises." Letting go of me, she brushed her knuckles along my cheek. "I'm willing to bet that letter was never supposed to be seen."

A wave of prickling heat moved through me, scorching my nerves and causing me to stumble slightly. What was happening?

"That's the reaction I was looking for—cute little hiding place by the way." She tapped a nail to her chin. "Now, here's how I see it. If you don't want it published in the Alliance Access for all to read, you're going to bring a million soltans to my home by midnight tonight, and in turn, I'll give you back the note and my memory of it. It'll be like this never happened."

My chest hurt, my lungs struggling to get air. This wasn't happening. But it was happening. She had me. And she knew she had me. And this was the end. "I don't have a million soltans."

She barked a laugh. "You're in bed with the royal family. I'm sure it won't be hard to attain." Backing away, she snorted, "And here I always thought this shitty apartment was a ruse for the commoners of Sorbis."

***

Putting on my best face, I walked through the halls of the manor to Cole's apartment, using everything I had to keep my body from shaking and silently praying to the Immortal Idols that, besides evidence stating otherwise, Rini Rain was pulling something out of her ass. I even managed a smile for the Protectors guarding the door as I eased it shut.

In the safety of the apartment, the pent-up anxiety was so bad I had to close my eyes and lean against the door for a few breaths. Please, please....

Opening my eyes, I slid them to the console table between the two doorways to the sitting room. There, the stupid golden frame lay, face down. Picking it up, my stomach sank as I confirmed the photo's absence. Clutching the table for strength, I worked out the drawer, revealing the worn red book. Right inside the cover, where the letter should have been, was nothing. Fingers shaking, I flipped to the next page. Then the next. And the next.

No. No. This couldn't be happening.

I took the book by each cover and shook as hard as I could. Ready to rip every page out if I had to. No whoosh of the crisp paper I'd poured my heart out on.

Head light, I sank to my knees.

Nononononono. There's no way. This isn't possible. What was I going to do? A million soltans or she was going to publish it. A million soltans or my life would be ruined. A million, when my account at the Reserve was lucky to have maybe fifteen thousand.

Lupine.

She was the only one who could tell me what to do. The only one who could help me, if she weren't so broken by what I'd done, she refused to.

Fighting for composure, I made my way to the King's suite, apprehension seizing every step. *It's tell Lupine, or the whole kingdom learns the truth by way of the Alliance Access.*

Entering the weakly lit room, I forced myself to swallow my fear. Three steps in, I spotted Lupine lying on her back, her head slack and her breathing slow.

My heart sank.

Maybe this was meant to happen.

Maybe Rini was meant to find the letter.

Maybe I should let it happen. It's what I wanted to some degree. Not like this, but—

Someone cleared their throat.

Startled, I stumbled a step back—the wooden floor creaking under my weight—locking eyes with Damien, who lay along the lounge in a black sweater and jeans, one leg dangling by the knee over the couch's arm, the other planted on the floor, casually fingering the pages of a book.

Searing heat spread down my spine. I shouldn't have to be questioning such matters under duress. This was his fault. He was the reason Rini Rain had the stupid letter.

Putting the book aside, he sat up grinning. Smiling like we were friendly. "Norris came early today, claiming she needed extra rest, but I came back—"

I turned and left before I could do something else I'd regret. Something that'd land me in the deepest cell of the Ground under Protector Headquarters. Halfway down the hall, the sound of his hard step joined my own.

"Eden, hey, wait," Damien called.

Hearing him say my name made me want to scream. If I were going to accept this fate, I wouldn't do it with him. I picked up my pace.

"Wait up." His voice was right behind me now. Immortals, he moved quickly. As evidenced by that first night. As evidenced by how quickly he bedded my living nightmare.

Don't you grab me, don't you dare grab—

His hand latched around my wrist.

Turning sharply, I swung. This time, he wasn't prepared, and I landed the punch in the center of his chest, knocking the wind from him. Every single finger on my hand popped, but rage blocked out the pain.

He released his hold of me.

"You have some nerve," I growled.

Rubbing the impact site, he wheezed, "What was that for?"

"Enjoy yourself last night?" I screeched, grateful for the hall's soundproofing. I could be as loud as I wanted. "The name *Rini Rain* sound familiar?"

He started to shake his head but stopped, realization dawning. "You have me followed?"

I rolled my eyes. "Why would I need to? She came to me today. She's the reporter who vilifies me—the one your lover, Violet, is always selling whatever lies she can. She stole something of mine when you brought her here."

He ran his fingers through his black hair. "I'm sorry, but to be fair, you didn't mention a name, and she never mentioned her work—but isn't that good news? If she stole something from the manor, Master Guardian Saier will arrest her himself. There's no need to be upset. Why haven't you mentioned it to Cole?"

I glared at him, nostrils flaring.

Surprise and understanding flickered in his eyes, absent of their unnatural glow today. "It's something you don't want him to know about."

A fresh wave of heat blistered my skin.

He straightened. "What did she take?"

"The photo of Cole and me. The one on the table in the entryway, along with a very personal…diary entry no one was obviously ever supposed to see. She's threatening to publish it if I don't give her what she wants by midnight tonight."

"What did it say?"

My heart plummeted into my stomach. "I…" I couldn't even say it, and tomorrow everyone would read it. I was going to be sick.

Surprise morphed into suspicion. "If this is something that involves my family, I need to know. Trust—"

"I don't want to hear about trust from you," I snapped. "Trust that if it were damaging to anyone in this family, I would tell Cole." I looked down. "It's about me, and I trusted my items were safe here." I took a breath to try and calm the sudden shaking racking my body. "And the only reason they weren't is because of you."

He winced. "What does she want?"

"What does everyone want?" I sighed. "Money, more than I have."

His smile returned, hope sparkling in his eyes. "That's it? I have money, Eden. Plenty of it. More than I know what to do with. How much do you need?"

I folded my arms over my chest. "I'm not borrowing your money. The last thing I need is to be indebted to you."

The light in his eyes flickered. "I would give you the money to make up for what I've done. You wouldn't be indebted. I don't work like that. How much does she want?"

"Try a million soltans."

He let out a low whistle. "Must be some diary entry if you'd even remotely consider paying that. It's done. I'll leave to get you the money now and be back within the hour."

He moved to go around me.

I reached out, putting a hand where I'd landed the blow. What was going on? "You're serious."

Damien looked down at my hand and then at my face. Holding my gaze, I saw my reflection in his eyes—saw the anger I felt, but more than that, the fear. "A million soltans is nothing to me. It certainly isn't worth pissing off the future queen of Solta." He nodded at my hand. "I need to go now before the Reserve closes."

My stomach twisted uncomfortably around the hope he offered. I looked back down the hall, where the firelight flickered in the darkened room. "What about Lupine?" I asked, looking for anything to say.

"As I was trying to tell you, my mother isn't going to be awake until the morning. She didn't sleep well last night, so Norris increased the intensity of her sleeping elixir."

I nodded my head absently.

"Meet me at the private entrance to the grounds in an hour," he said. "It's going to be alright. I give you my word."

***

Hugging my arms to my chest, I paced the stretch of grass before the private entrance, fueled by my hammering heart, which hadn't let up one beat since Damien's departure. Pivoting on my heel, I walked into a breeze carrying the warm smell of sandalwood, coming within a step of running smack into a figure dressed in black.

"You're late," I stammered.

"By a minute," Damien said, "but I was picking up something else I think you'll need, so I think you can forgive me." He fumbled around in his coat pocket. "How do we know she hasn't made copies? Or that now that she knows about the content of this mysterious diary entry, she won't just print her knowledge of it anyway?"

"She said she'd give me her memory of it."

He raised an eyebrow. "And you trust her to bring a valid memory elixir?"

The answer was a hard no, and my silence was enough for Damien.

He extended his hand to me, palm up. On display were two vials, one pearly blue vial of truth elixir and one smoke gray bottle of memory elixir. "That's what I thought. I know someone—the only person aside from myself—who can make the quality of elixir I would want to give her."

"You went to Shadow Market District?" I hissed. "The Council tracks the purchase of controlled elixirs." This nightmare only got worse.

"Believe it or not, I know how to practice discretion and be untraceable."

Having nothing nice to say in response, I rolled my eyes and returned to my pacing. Why had I believed, after what he'd done, that this was a good idea?

"Please, Eden. I gave you my word that everything was going to be alright," he sighed. From his other coat pocket, he pulled a brown drawstring purse out by its ties and offered it to me on the end of his pointer finger, coins clinking. "That might mean nothing to you, but it means something to me."

I looked from it to him and glared. He really wasn't helping his case. "This isn't funny. I need a million soltans, not four."

He tipped his chin. "Open it."

Skeptically, I yanked the drawstring bag open, revealing an endless well of green metal coins through the small opening. I lifted the bag to eye level. No, my eyes had not deceived me. I stuck my hand in, wondering if it was an illusion, but my fingers found metal after metal coin as my arm disappeared up to my elbow into nothing. And it weighed no more than a couple of coins and was no bigger than my palm.

Charms never ceased to amaze me.

"Why do you act like you've never seen a money pocket before? Surely, you've seen Cole or my mother use one."

I pulled the string closed and slipped the bag into my jeans pocket. "Maybe, but I've never paid much attention. I'm referred to as a leech on this family by high society enough. I stay out of Cole and Lupine's finances. I have what I have from work and what my parents left me. Your family's money is none of my business."

"It will be once you've bound yourself to my brother."

Nerves tickling my stomach, I held out my hand for the elixirs. "I'll think about that later. Thank you for this. I'd better get going."

Hand shooting up into his hair, he shifted his gaze. "Actually, things have changed. I do have a condition now. Something I do want from you."

I bristled.

"I want to go with you," he said quickly. "She took something of mine as well. I was ready to let it go, but since we're going to her anyway…"

I searched his face for signs of trouble but only found what looked like shame. "Fine," I ground out through my teeth. He'd save me from finding an explanation for Julien. "Rini lives up north by the lake, by the market in the art district."

"Always keep track of where your enemies live?"

"The art district was my favorite place in the city," I sighed. "Then she bought a home there a couple of years ago, and that was the end of that."

He clicked his tongue. "Got it. How are we doing this?"

"The same as the other night."

"As you wish."

I barely had hold of his elbow when the forest shifted to the park beside the market, and my stomach twisted in on itself.

Releasing my hold of him, I covered my mouth and ran behind the nearest tree. Collapsing to my knees in the dirt, I retched hard repeatedly, scaring away the people bartering produce at a stand a couple of feet away. Glad I'd forgotten lunch as the motion brought tears to my eyes. At least there was nothing to see.

Warm fingers deftly pulled my dark hair away from my face.

"Fuck, Eden." Damien dropped into a squat. His voice a whisper when he spoke again. "Just get close to me."

Slowing down, a layer of cold sweat coated my skin, my shaking arms keeping me upright. Breathe, I coaxed myself. In…out…in…out. Wiping at my eyes, my stomach slowly removed itself from my throat. Using the trunk of the tree, I pulled myself back to standing. "Let's just get this over with."

Rini's house, a gray home with a pristine white door, was the second house off Soltan Lake's promenade and a whole story taller than the rest of the houses around it. All I saw when I looked at it was every story she'd written about me since I'd turned sixteen, and the Alliance Council's media laws had stopped applying to me.

Head down so as not to draw any more attention to myself, I marched toward it, Damien silently following in my wake.

I slammed the side of my fist as hard as I could into the door, slightly peeved when it didn't so much as splinter. It swung open before I made contact the second time, like she'd been waiting by the door.

Rini stepped into view wearing a gold silk robe belted loosely at the waist and little else. "Eden Alexander, before the sun has set. You could have taken a shower, though you know. The smell of you in this heat is sensory assault." Her brown eyes looked from me to Damien, giving him an appreciative scan. "And Damien, good to see you again."

Damien's eyes narrowed at her. "You look different from what I remember."

Flipping her blonde hair back, she shimmied her shoulders. "Would it help if I did this?" Before my eyes, her long ash blonde hair deepened to a brown as deep as mine, and her brown eyes to a soft hazel.

"A shifter," he sighed, "the perfect reporter for the Alliance Access."

"I like to think so, too," she winked. Her attention fell to our empty hands. "Do you have what I asked for?"

I lifted the bag of coins from my pocket.

Her eyes grew twice the size. "How do I know it's all there?"

Damien held the light blue truth elixir bottle up for her to see. He tapped three drops onto his tongue—each drop equal to a minute of truth—and passed it to me. Carefully, I did the same. The last thing I needed was to accidentally dump the whole thing in my mouth and be forced to answer everything truthfully for a week. The sugary-tasting elixir absorbed right into my tongue.

"It's all there," Damien said. "A million soltans."

She reached for the bag.

"No, first you take this." Damien passed her the vial.

"You don't think I already took one of these?" she asked.

There was an itch in my throat courtesy of the elixir. "No."

"Smart girl." She plucked the vial from Damien's hand, draining it without care.

"Why only a million?" I asked like an idiot. She could have asked for far more.

The smile she gave me was predatory. "Because darling, I don't want to destroy you. You're my favorite thing to write about." She held out her hand. "I'm guessing you brought a memory elixir as well?"

Damien produced the gray vial.

Lifting it from his palm, she said, "Perfect. Shit is expensive. I can save the one I had for my next exploit."

"Of course, you do this regularly," I muttered.

Her upper lip curled in annoyance. "We aren't all as privileged as you, and while fun, investigating for the Alliance Access doesn't pay for this." She motioned to her home.

"I don't care. Give me what I came here for."

With a snap of her fingers, the manila envelope appeared in her open hand. I snatched it away, angling it so Damien couldn't see the contents. There it was, the photo and the now unfolded letter.

"Confirm there aren't any copies and that you've told no one," I demanded.

"There aren't, and I haven't, but before I forget," she tapped a long black nail against her temple. "I didn't expect what I read. If you want some advice, mortal to mortal, life's too short."

"You are the last person in Sorbis I want advice from. Take the—"

Damien stepped between us. "You stole something of mine. I need it back," he said, desperation scratching his voice.

Offering a pitying look, she shrugged and upturned the memory elixir. "That was gone an hour after I left your bed. An easy twenty-thousand soltans, even for as little as was left. Thousands of people in this city are clamoring for magic like that."

It was then that I noticed how Damien's fists were clenched at his sides, the veins looking like they would burst. He punched the door frame. "Fine, then give us every memory you've had since you laid eyes on me at Vermillion."

Rini snorted. "You'll be getting every memory after the sex." She clasped her hand to her chest. "You were the best lay I've ever had. That's sex I don't want to forget. Every memory you'll want is after."

There was the nausea again.

"I can't say the same," he said.

Pressing the bottle's rim to her temple, a thread-thin stream of gray shifting fluid began to refill it. Clutching the door frame for strength, she corked the vial, holding it out to me. I slipped it from her fingers and plunked the money bag in its place.

Rini stared at us anew. "Eden Alexander and Damien Valentine, both at my door. The fact that you two are standing here and this bag is in my hand must mean my plan worked better than expected."

Ready to leave, I asked, "What do you remember?"

Testing my patience, she tapped a long nail thoughtfully to her chin. "The sex, I guess, which was delicious, and then poof, I'm here looking at the two of you." Biting her lower lip, she threw bedroom eyes at Damien. "By the way, if you ever..."

Having heard enough, I put my back to them both, half running to the lake. Shuddering the last couple of hours off, I removed the photo, tucking it carefully into my back pant pocket. At the water's edge, I snapped my fingers desperately, feeling the slightest relief when a weak flame appeared at the tip of my shaking pointer finger.

It would do.

The corner of the crisp manila envelope met the small red flame, catching and spreading quickly. I watched it shrivel and blacken, the tightness in my chest easing as clumps of gray ash fell away.

"Money up in flames," Damien said, coming up beside me. "Was it so bad?"

The truth elixir tickled my throat, and whether he'd known I had a truth left in me or not, I hated him for asking. "Yes." I waited for the flames to lick at my fingers before letting what remained float away on a gust of wind, out toward the water. "Even if you were on the numb elixir, I can't believe you fucked her."

He shifted uncomfortably. "How did you know?"

"I've been looking into the eyes of various Valentines my entire life. I know when something is off, and your eyes had an unnatural sheen to them last night that they don't have today. Plus, there's only one elixir people would pay that much for a couple of drops of."

He watched me empty the memory into the lake, evaporating into the air before it even touched the water's surface.

A memory couldn't live outside of a mind.

With all my might, I threw the vial as far as I could into the lake. "You're better off without it." I looked up at him, eyes a golden green in the last light of the setting sun. "And I'd appreciate it if you'd give me your word that we'll never talk about this again."

He nodded once.

Great.

Before I could back out, I closed my eyes and wrapped my arms around his waist. "Back to the manor, please, and this better work as well as you claim."

CHAPTER SIX

16.SEVEN.4004

Carefully, I replaced the picture of Cole and me in the golden frame. The photo—taken not long after we started seeing each other—depicted a charmed couple I no longer recognized. Putting the frame back in position, I let out a deep sigh.

***

Lupine lay eerily still. The only sign of life was the very subtle rise and fall of her chest.

Rubbing my face, I collapsed onto the worn cushion of the sofa beside her bed. Hands clasped and head bowed, my words were a whisper. "I almost broke your heart today. If you knew what I'd done, what almost happened…"

Heat burned my eyes as the memory of the day she'd told me she wanted to nominate me for the Bidding came to me. How happy she'd been.

I scrubbed away the tears threatening to spill. "Don't worry, though. Everything is okay. I fixed it." Sucking in a shaky breath, I straightened. "Damien helped me. He—"

The clatter of metal snapped my attention to the doorway, halting my confession and sending my heart slamming into the wall of my ribs.

A metal tray floated in the doorway. The owner of the arms holding it hadn't completely crossed the threshold, meaning they hadn't heard me, but—what was this?

The next step brought forth a young man in a white pullover, straight black hair brushing his shoulders, tongue between his teeth, focused so hard on the tray one might think he was trying to levitate it with his mind.

I laughed my relief. "Q, what are you doing?"

"I thought you might be hungry, so I brought you some food—and you laugh, but carrying this thing is no joke." The youngest Valentine grinned at me, green eyes shining. "I was so close to getting this to you without dropping anything. It's a good thing you didn't need a fork." There was a scratch and a ting as he kicked it aside.

The words 'Thank you, but I'm not hungry' were on the tip of my tongue when my stomach let out a low, deep growl.

"I know that sound, and I know you." Sighing, Quincy set the platter on my lap and took the seat next to me. "You really need to stop forgetting to eat."

"I don't purposely not eat."

"I hear what you're saying, but it seems like you've been a victim of accidentally not eating daily." He tucked his long black hair behind his ears, putting the diamond studs he wore on full display. "I'm worried about you. All you've done for months is work and visit with my mother."

"You sound like everyone else." Grabbing the handles, I started to move the tray to the floor.

His hand came down hard on the lid, causing the metal to ring and vibrate in my lap. "If everyone is saying it, maybe there's something to it."

"How did you know I was in here?" I asked, wanting to change the subject.

He raised an eyebrow.

I rolled my eyes, conceding his point. "Okay, I'll give you that—but how did you know I was at the manor? I'm usually home by now."

He placed his other hand on my shoulder. "Because I saw you headed this way as I left dinner. I called out to you, but you were so lost in your own world that you didn't hear me. So I did what any concerned friend would do and turned around and went to the kitchen to grab you some food. Also, I knew you'd fight me, so I brought your favorite."

With a flourish, he lifted the lid. On the pristine white plate sat a mound of beef and pickled cabbage, oozing cheese and dripping mustard, stuffed between two slices of grilled rye bread. The smell made my mouth water.

"Your number one comfort food."

He was good. And he was watching me with the determined look of his I knew meant I wouldn't win this.

Obliging him, I picked up one of the halves and sank my teeth into the savory goodness. Okay, I had been lying to myself. I was hungry.

Quincy watched contentedly as I took another bite, having not entirely swallowed the first. In less than a minute, the sandwich half was gone, and my stomach yearned for more.

"Isn't that much better?" He slid his hand across my shoulder and started to pull me in for a hug, but stopped abruptly and leaned away, grimacing. "Was it onion day at work?'

Having forgotten about work, I lifted the neck of my shirt to my nose where the scent of onion and garlic had baked in. Impressive that Damien hadn't remarked on it. Maybe if I hadn't punched him in the chest.

"Never mind," Quincy said. "So, by now you've met Damien. What do you think of him? I haven't talked to him nearly as much as I'd like to, but from what little I have, he's every bit the badass Grayden claimed. You should have seen the crowd of people that swarmed the manor to see him yesterday and today, chanting 'Reincimmo.' They adore him."

Reincimmo, a master of the four aptitudes…quite the honorific. I took another bite, biding my time. Wondering what I could say that was true and wouldn't put a damper on Q's admiration for his long-absent brother. "He's fine enough."

He barked a laugh, nudging my elbow. "Hasn't impressed you then? Guess Cole didn't warn him how hard you are to win over. We're going out tonight for a boys' night type thing. You could come if you want? We'll go somewhere people can't talk. I could use my dancing buddy."

Even if I hadn't seen enough of Damien for the day, it was a horrible idea. Using the back of my hand to cover my mouth, I said, "Thank you for the invite, but I know you remember what happened last time. I can't handle a Cole meltdown right now." Especially not after the fiasco in the garden the other night… "And wouldn't my presence defeat a boys' night?"

Quincy's green eyes stared deep into mine, his voice firm as he said, "Far as I'm concerned, you're one of the boys. I know you could use a break. My mother is asleep, and Cole won't know—Grayden said something about him being up to his neck in dealing with some insurgent group in the farmlands. Oh, he's coming by the way, and I know you two don't get along, but I'll tell him to play nice."

I offered a smile. "I appreciate it, Q, but I can't go out tonight. I have work tomorrow, and I had a long day. I'd really just like to take a shower and relax tonight. Another time."

The light in his eyes dimmed as his lips parted, and I braced for the challenge, but he smiled instead. "I understand. But you'd better finish your sandwich and actually do it. Relax tonight, I mean."

My thoughts went to the vial of darkness elixir burning a hole in my pocket. A promise I could easily keep. "I will."

Standing, he kissed the top of my head. "Then I'll let you owe me. Goodnight, Eden."

A strange feeling gripped my chest, watching him leave. Like a warm darkness had enshrouded my heart.

My eyes fell to the last remaining bites of the sandwich in my hand. Returning the rest to the plate, I placed the heavy metal tray on the hallway table for the staff to collect on my way out.

CHAPTER SEVEN

22.SEVEN.4004

Word or not, after our encounter with Rini Rain, I decided it was best not to come around Lupine when Damien would be there—not until I'd had more time to think about trusting him—meaning it'd been nearly a week since I'd seen her, and the longest I'd ever gone without talking to her as well. It was with that absence at the forefront of my mind that I welcomed the end of my work week and the return to the manor.

I had a surprise for her. One so good I could ignore the two blatantly annoying shadows following me for the time being.

Entering her room, the greeting I had on my tongue died as I struggled to keep my smile. In my time away, her cheeks had hollowed, and a pallor had washed away the rich caramel color of her skin. The little amount of health she'd shown the night of the breki had been a fluke.

"Eden, darling, good morning," Lupine grinned. She reached a skeletal hand toward me, weakly waving me closer, the emerald of her Pledge Token glimmering in the firelight. Beckoning me for a hug I would never deny. "Where have you been?"

Smoothing a hand down my purple blouse, I pulled her gently to me, giving the faintest squeeze. Trying not to think about the bones I felt through her white nightgown. "I came by the manor a couple of times, but my days ran long last week, and by the time I got to you, Master Guardian Norris had given you your elixirs."

"Good morning, Eden," a now recognizable voice said.

Keeping my composure, I straightened and looked at him, lying on the couch as if he'd been settled there awhile.

On the couch, where I hadn't expected him to be this early in the day, blending into the darkness in his black attire.

"Good morning, Damien," I said, forcing a smile. "I didn't know you'd be visiting so early. If now is a bad time—"

"He'll be here all day," Lupine interjected. "You both are stubborn about leaving me alone, but I guess I should be grateful. It would be so incredibly boring otherwise. Join us, make yourself comfortable." She faced Damien, snapping her fingers hotly. "Sit up, son, make space."

"No, it's okay, I don't want to intrude. I can stand."

"No intrusion," Damien offered. Lifting his legs from where they dangled over the edge of the couch, he shifted into sitting and patted the space beside him. "Please."

Staring at the spot, I forced myself forward, wondering why this kept happening. To make matters worse, the space was still warm with the heat of him.

"How is Cole doing?" Lupine asked, twisting the thread of a blanket. "It's been some time since he's come to see me."

"Fine. He's gone to Charph with the king for the next several days." With that being all I wanted to say on the subject, I held up the yellowing, dog-eared copy of the Tales of Linolay I'd brought. One of only five copies in existence—each belonging to a member of the Misundre Five or their descendants. "I got the book you requested."

Lupine sucked in a breath, indigo eyes growing wide. "You found it?"

How shortly success lived. "No, I'm sorry. It's Rho's. You were right.

She did have her mother's copy. I promise I looked all over the manor—wherever I've seen books—but I couldn't find it."

Lupine waved me away. "It was a long shot. I haven't seen the book since Damien was little." She looked at him. "Speaking of which, do you remember when I would read you this?"

Damien leaned closer. "What is it?"

I presented him the cover.

His eyes widened a fraction. "The Tales of Linolay." He sat back, glancing toward the window. "I vaguely remember it."

"Your favorite was the tale of the Timekeeper and the Water Queen. You wanted so badly to be the Timekeeper. Why don't you start with that one, Eden?" Her gaze darted between us. "Is that okay, Damien? Eden usually reads to me. She has the loveliest reading voice."

Crossing his legs, he settled into the corner of the couch and closed his eyes. "Be my guest."

***

Master Guardian Norris came an hour early, interrupting me in the middle of a sentence.

Abruptly closing the book, I said goodnight to Lupine, giving her hand resting atop the blankets a gentle squeeze and letting her know I'd be back in the morning.

I woke up Damien in the process.

"Rest easy, Mother," Damien said somewhere behind me.

"I'll see you in the morning as well?"

"I'll be here."

I sighed. Perfect. Damien would be my reality until Lupine's pregnancy was over. I reminded myself to be happy she got to see the son she'd missed so much once more, possibly for the last time.

A sharp, knife-like pain sliced through my stomach, making my head spin. No. The pregnancy would be over soon, and it'd have a positive ending.

Quickly, I said a little prayer to the Immortal Idols for grace on Lupine's behalf and then laughed bitterly. I was wasting my breath. If the Immortal Idols were there, they either didn't hear me or didn't care if her state today was an indicator. How was it possible she was worse than she'd been?

I needed to walk. And I stopped a few paces from the door, remembering I couldn't.

"You okay?" Damien asked, snapping me to attention.

"Yeah," I said, reaching for the door.

"Do you mind if I join you?"

My hand froze on the brass knob. "You don't even know where I'm going."

"Anything is more interesting than Cole's apartment."

"That I find hard to believe, considering I put you to sleep most of the day."

"You should take it as a compliment. Not much does." He ran a hand through his hair. "And as backhanded as that sounded, I really did mean that as a compliment. Your voice is relaxing."

I nodded once. "It's okay, you don't have to explain."

"You didn't answer if I could join you?"

"Do I have any choice?"

Seemingly taken aback, he said, "You always have a choice."

Opening the door, I stepped into the hall, bringing the two Protectors across the way to attention.

Damien arched an eyebrow. "What is this?"

Not a choice. "My new shadows," I sighed. When there had been no immediate change following the events in the gardens, I'd thought Cole had forgotten, or maybe I'd escaped this fate, but no, he had simply been looking at candidates as the note he'd left informed me.

"I'm to have an escort at all times outside the king's and Cole's apartments."

I stared at the two men, fresh from the Academy, judging by how young and eager they looked. As I wasn't queen, those would be the only Protectors Master Guardian Saier would spare for this assignment.

"It's okay, gentlemen, I'll accompany her," Damien said.

They exchanged a look between themselves and narrowed their eyes at him. "We aren't supposed to let her walk around alone by order of Prince Cole."

"She won't be alone. She'll be with me."

One stepped forward. Several inches shorter than Damien, he looked comical puffing out his chest. "We're following orders, sir."

For Damien's part, he was enjoying the challenge. He stepped closer to the Protectors, lips parted slightly, looking like he was ready to lay into him.

"No need to be overzealous, gentlemen. You do realize who he is, don't you?" a voice sounded behind me—one of the Protectors guarding the door.

As Damien and the shadows turned to him and the other guard, I stepped to the side. The five of them entering a standoff.

The men's glares locked on one another, which meant no one was paying attention to me. Thank the Immortals for the dark halls, I thought, backing quietly into them.

Almost out of hearing range, I heard the Protector who'd spoken up say, "Prince Cole's Bidden is in safe hands. You're dismissed."

It was so tempting to scream back, *Yes, in my own safe, capable hands,* as I darted into a dark service stairwell, winding my way down to the staff quarters.

The dust in this part of the manor hung heavy in the air, itching my throat. Lupine told me once, long ago, that the staff quarters had been lively and at capacity. Hard to imagine now, looking into the dark rooms, empty for decades—the remaining staff now claiming the western quarters with windows facing the Ridge Woods.

Weaving through the halls, I turned the corner and stopped dead, my grip on the Tales of Linolay tightening. Up ahead, leaning against the wall, was Damien.

He smirked. "Hello again."

Silently cursing myself, I returned my attention to the hall, resuming my walk. "You know about the Hidden Halls." It was the only way he could have intercepted me.

"Of course I do." He fell into step beside me. "But even if I didn't, trying to evade someone of Charphan descent is useless, by the way. I could smell your path like you'd left me olfactive breadcrumbs. You want to grab dinner?"

"I'm not hungry."

"Really? You barely touched your lunch."

"I'm surprised you noticed what I did or didn't touch, considering how much you slept."

Damien spun on his heel to walk backward before me. "Apologies, sincerely, if that bothered you. If we aren't eating, what are we doing?"

I shifted my gaze toward the wall of the hall, decorated in swirling chains of Olinda Roses. "I'm going for a walk."

"Sounds lovely. I could use a walk."

Huffing, I shook my head. "You said I had a choice."

He pursed his lips. "That was before Protector Alon helped me get you away from your shadows, as you say. You're my responsibility now."

Determined not to react, I forced my face to remain impassive, clutching the book a little harder. There were going to be permanent indentations where my fingers were.

"What's wrong, Eden? Why are you avoiding me?"

"I'm not avoiding you. We spent the whole day together."

"Really?" Damien laughed. "Maybe you didn't avoid me today because my mother wouldn't let you, but I know you've been avoiding me because Protector Alon was on the door all last week as well, and I asked him to send you my way if you came by. Are you telling me he didn't relay my message?"

Annoyance pricked my skin. What in the fuck was this? How stupid could he be? My thoughts went to my two new shadows. Breathe. Breathe through it.

I stared at him coolly. "You do realize every exchange—everything the Protectors see—is relayed to Cole and your father."

"My absence hasn't made me ignorant of how things work here. Protector Alon owes me. A lot more than his secrecy. If he'd betrayed my trust, we would know by now."

"You don't think my being followed everywhere might be one of us knowing?"

"I'll give you—I'm sure, if Protector Alon had betrayed my trust, knowing Cole, it would have been fuel on the fire, but on a fire you had already started."

Breathe. "And today?"

"Protector Alon will handle them."

Damien stopped walking, clearly hoping I might as well. Instead, I sidestepped him without missing a beat.

"I gave you my word I wouldn't talk about that day," he exclaimed. Loud enough, it echoed.

For anyone on the floor to hear.

Immortals, he couldn't be serious. Spinning so fast my hair flew out, I grabbed his arm and dragged him into one of the vacant rooms, stopping inside the door.

Fuck composure.

"You promised me you would never talk about it, and now you scream it in the halls," I whisper-hissed.

"I didn't scream, and no one can hear us."

I folded my arms across my chest. "So you think."

"So I know. I can smell everything and everyone in the general vicinity. I was strategic in my choice of location to intercept you."

I narrowed my eyes. "You were prepping for this interrogation, lovely."

"I wouldn't call a simple question an interrogation."

"Why do you care if I am avoiding you?" I snapped.

Damien's eyes searched my face. "Because you mean a lot to my mother, and while I won't be here much longer, I don't want what little time we spend together marred by unnecessary tension, especially when that time will be spent with my mother, and it's clear she would like us to be cordial. Now, will you answer me?"

I glared at him, waiting for any sign of a lie. When one failed to appear, I exhaled my anger, dropping my gaze to the center of his chest. "You already know why."

"Does my word mean nothing to you?"

"It doesn't mean nothing, but I thought about it afterward, and I can't help but wonder why—if you weren't bent on telling someone— you don't drink a memory elixir?"

"I...hadn't considered it, but I didn't think it was necessary." Sucking in a breath, Damien ran a hand through his hair. "I could do that if it'd make you feel better around me, but if some issue arose regarding the situation in the future, I couldn't help you."

Biting my lip, I considered the possibilities. "Couldn't or wouldn't?"

"I guess I could." He stepped closer to me. Close enough I could smell his sandalwood and cedar scent. "That whole day would disappear for me, though, this moment too. I'd have to give you the last week to be safe. It'd be weird, and I'm not going to say I'd like doing it, but—I'm not going to share what happened with anyone."

"What issue might arise?"

Shaking his head, he said, "I don't know Eden, but there's always a possibility you or I overlooked something," he exhaled slowly, "Just tell me if that's what you want."

Cupping my chin, I nodded, needing a moment to process his words. Needing a moment to breathe.

We stood there, stock-still, letting the silence impregnate the foot-sized space between us. It was strange how, here, in the darkness and silence, time felt as though it had frozen.

Would it matter if he knew when, days from now, Lupine's health nightmare would be over and he would leave?

A strange feeling itching my chest, I put my back to him. "Okay."

"Okay?" Damien's voice cracked a little on the word.

I cast a glance at him over my shoulder. "Okay." If he was hoping for me to answer his unspoken question in any other way, his hope was sorely misplaced.

Sighing, I focused once more on the path I'd started. "I really need to walk. Are you okay with silence? When I walk, I like silence to think."

His shadow fell across my shoulder. "I'm fine with silence."

***

I pushed against the heavy wooden door, relishing the creak of the joints as it swung open, grateful for the release from its frame.

Freedom for both of us.

A cool summer breeze rushed up to greet me, sweeping around my neck and lifting my hair, carrying with it the scent of wisteria and water lilies floating atop the koi pond at the center of the gardens.

Taking the lead, I moved along the path, savoring the soft click of my steps on the stones, trailing my fingers idly atop the flowers, picking up speed as I drew closer to the path skirting the woods. We passed the Olinda Roses and the Eternal Tree, winding our way around until the gardens ended, giving way to a trail.

I jogged down the slight slope into the trees. Chest heaving excitedly, I looked back, coming to a stop.

Damien stood at the mouth of the path, staring beyond me to the trees ahead. While we'd been walking, he'd worked every button of his black wool coat into its corresponding slit, leaving only a sliver of the black sweater underneath exposed. A gust of wind cut down the path, shuffling the canopy of thick green leaves overhead, making the shadows they cast on us dance, and rustling his shaggy hair.

Bundled up, he looked…out of place. And a little ominous.

His green eyes flitted to mine. Bright against his deeply tanned skin. The only thing about him that said summer.

Smiling, I opened my mouth, ready to make a joke, but stopped, taking in his furrowed brow and the hard press of his lips.

"What? What is it?"

Narrowing his eyes, he continued to stare, jaw shifting to the side.

"I know I asked for silence, but my request was that you not feel compelled to fill silence with conversation, not that you don't speak at all."

Standing a little straighter, he cleared his throat. "This is where you go to walk alone?"

I took a steadying breath, recognizing the unsettled look in his eyes as they briefly flitted to me and back to the trail. "You're concerned."

My safety was going on the list of things I was getting tired of people preoccupying themselves with.

"I'm all for the freedom to do whatever you want, but this is an exception. There's an actual rule that you should never walk the river trail alone." Closing the distance between us, he lowered his voice. "You're aware thieves and traitors—who passionately hate my family, the Alliance Council, and anyone who associates with them—hide in the trees on the other side of the river, waiting to do any damage they can."

This was such an old topic. "No one worries about that anymore."

Damien inclined his head. "Who is no one? Because I haven't heard any mention of a change to the rule—a rule decreed while I was here, mind you. The manor's protection wards end here."

"I'm aware," I sighed.

"Surely someone has told you the story of the staff members who went for a swim and were murdered?"

I rubbed my hands over my arms. How many times would I have to hear this?

"You're cold." He tugged at his coat sleeve, forgetting he'd buttoned it.

Shaking my head, I took a step back. Not knowing what to say, I settled on, "You sound like your brother."

A muscle in his cheek twitched. "If you're saying that because of my brother's fear of someone getting to you in the manor's gardens, his fear is irrational. But as much as it pains me, if he's commented on this," he nodded toward the path, "he's right."

Right.

Shrugging a shoulder, I put my back to him. "I've walked it hundreds of times alone. Up until today, I've walked this path alone most days I'm here, and I'm fine. You're welcome to stay here if you'd like. No one needs to be the wiser. It usually takes me only half an hour to get to the river, so you can expect me back in about an hour.

Just in time for dinner."

His boots thumped the forest floor. "I'm not letting you walk alone."

"How magnanimous." Reaching up, I brushed a hand over a low branch, pulling a leaf away. Twirling it by its stem, I watched it dance, inhaling the moss and pine scents of the woods. "Then it's settled. You'll be walking it with me."

Listening to the birds chitter—the rustle of their wings fluttering amongst the canopy as they settled in for the evening—and the song of the crickets begin, we walked in contented silence, enjoying how it felt to be outside. At least I did. Damien grudgingly kept beside me. Judging by the way his fingers curled and relaxed at his waist, and he winced every time the slightest breeze blew through, miserable might have been a better word to describe him.

He raised the collar of his jacket and burrowed low as another cool gust came rushing down the path.

I couldn't help but laugh at him. He glared at me, a strand of black wavy hair fluttering into his eyes.

I jabbed my thumb over my shoulder. "When you tried to offer me your coat back there, that was real cute considering you never take it off for long and keep shirking from the wind like you're naked, and it's the middle of winter."

"That's what it feels like."

"You're a baby," I teased.

"That's not nice. I've spent the last twenty years in Misundre. I went from bright, blinding sunshine and the kind of heat that keeps your skin sticky with sweat no matter the time of day to this gloom."

Immortals, he didn't think it was sunny? We'd been having great weather. "Even winter?"

"It isn't this cold."

I nodded. "Well, I wasn't trying to be mean, but you're going to have a hard time come winter." My mistake was glaringly apparent once the words were out. "I know what I said about silence," I added quickly, "but there's something I'd like to ask…if you wouldn't mind."

The intensity of his gaze made my hands sweat. "That depends what you're going to ask."

Slowing my pace, I wiped my palms along the sides of my jeans. "Are you worried about her—Lupine?"

His eyes tightened. "There's no point worrying. There's nothing you can do that's not already being done."

An answer that wasn't an answer at all. "You aren't scared?"

"I don't get scared."

"Are you anything?" I snapped. Crossing my arms, I stormed ahead, stopping and turning when I realized how childish I was being. "I'm sorry, that wasn't fair to you. It's just—of all people, I thought you might be the one who cares as I do." I gestured in the direction of the manor, somewhere beyond the trees. "Quincy's in his own world. Cole visits her when he must, and all he says is that she'll be okay. Then there's Master Guardian Norris, who cares about her as much as she relates to the king." I flung my arms wide. "And your father he—"

I brought my fist to my mouth, cutting myself off from saying something traitorous as a hot, angry tear streaked down my cheek.

Damien came toward me, stopping a step away. He put a hesitant hand on my shoulder. "You can say whatever you want, Eden. I won't betray your confidence. Whatever you were about to say about him, I've said far worse. The only reason I never wished him dead is because of my mother."

I looked around on his behalf, triggering an uproarious laugh from him.

"That was so pure of you."

I shoved his chest. "I'm not pure."

Hand falling away, he smiled at me. "If you say so. You didn't ask me if I cared. That was the question you wanted an answer to."

Using the back of my hand, I wiped away the stray tear. "Do you?"

"I wouldn't be in a city I hate, that I swore I'd never step foot in again, if I didn't."

Swallowing, I let my attention drift to the haze of green and brown in the distance. "I'm sorry again. This time for being so emotional. I can't seem to stop worrying, or being scared."

Everything was so overwhelming.

"You don't have to explain, and you don't have to be sorry for caring about someone you love."

I met his eyes again, a somberness in them now. "Thank you for saying that."

Looking at him, I thought about what Lupine had asked of me the day she'd taken to bed. I hadn't told anyone. Damien was probably the only one I could tell. Leaning my back against a tree for support, I took another deep breath of the forest air. "You know she asked me to care for the child if something happens to her."

He kicked at a rock, eyes drifting back to where we came from. "From everything I've heard, I'm not surprised. Do you not want the responsibility?"

I shook my head. "That's not it at all. If something happens, there's no way I'd let anyone else take care of the baby. Certainly not your father. But I can't bring myself to think about if something happens. She wants this baby so much. It wouldn't be right if…"

Fresh tears needled my eyes, spilling onto my cheeks. I knew I couldn't bring myself to say the rest. Vibrant green filled my vision as Damien swooped up my face in his warm, rough hands. The sleeves of his jacket brushed along my chin as his thumbs scraped away tears.

"Don't do that," he whispered, voice distant. Pain lanced his eyes.

Deep-rooted pain—and I'd accidentally drawn it to the surface. "Don't get caught up in doom thinking. Ever, but especially if it's going to make you cry."

"Damien." His name—an attempt to bring him back—came out as a breath. I inhaled and tried again. "Damien."

His fingers stilled and fell away like a flower's petals. Clearing his throat, he stumbled back, running his tear-streaked fingers through his hair. "I...I'm sorry."

My hand went to the key necklace at my throat. "No, it's fine, but are you—"

"We should get back," he said abruptly. Turning on his heel, he started back the way we came.

His name hung at the tip of my tongue, waiting to drop. I swallowed it instead. The stiffness of his shoulders, the extra impact in his step. The brief flash of anger on his face.

It was all the result of someone who'd been seen and hadn't wanted to be.

CHAPTER EIGHT
27.SEVEN.4004

After our walk in the woods, Damien kept himself distracted and, aside from our time with Lupine, kept away from me. Every morning, as I sat down for breakfast, I glimpsed him disappearing into the guest room, reeking of cigarettes. After a few minutes, he'd emerge in fresh clothing, wavy hair wet, and leave. When I joined him on the couch in Lupine's room half an hour later, he'd settle in to sleep as I cracked my book.

Over dinner one evening, I learned from an excitable Q that the one night of brotherly fun had turned into an every-night occurrence.

His behavior hadn't escaped Lupine either, who I found glaring at her sleeping son routinely.

Such was the case today. I was on the last story of the Tales of Linolay, and he was fast asleep, snoring softly beside me, head cradled in the crook of the couch, dark lashes resting against his cheeks, looking at peace.

"I have a favor to ask of you," Lupine said.

I held my place in the story and looked up at her, finding her weary indigo eyes staring absently at the fire as she mindlessly brushed a hand back and forth over her stomach.

"I'm going to the Eternal Tree tonight to see the Olinda Roses bloom." She faced me. "I was wondering if you two might join me?"

A dry, throaty voice beat me to answering. "Of course." The couch cushion shifted beside me. "What time?"

I turned to face Damien, who met the angry question in my gaze with a raised eyebrow and then looked back at Lupine. My nails dug into my palm as I fought the urge to throw the book at him. "I don't think it's a good idea. Master Guardian Norris said you shouldn't move."

"Darling, he also said walks were fine," she smiled.

Short walks—to the bathroom, not the Eternal Tree on the other side of the manor.

"What about the Protectors? What about the Master Guardian?" If neither of them would stop to consider her health, surely the presence of Protectors or the elixir cocktail Master Guardian Norris gave her would put a damper on the idea.

Lupine waved away my questions like they were nothing. "I have them covered. Tell me you'll join us?"

Join us, because Damien had already said yes.

I stared at her, searching for something to convince her that the idea was terrible. The longer I looked, the harder it became. The hope of leaving her bed—one "yes" strong and one pending—had almost erased the shadows from her eyes.

And there was nothing more in the world I wanted than to make Lupine happy.

"I'll join you," I sighed. Like I had any other choice. Someone had to make sure Lupine was okay.

She clapped once. "Perfect. Now both of you scram. I need to save my energy for later. I'll see you both tonight at eleven forty-five."

Damien nodded and got to his feet, bolting for the door. Forgetting my place in the story, I shut the book and followed on his heels, counting five times that he dragged his fingers through his hair before we got to the door.

Clear of Lupine's room, I hooked his elbow and pulled him aside. "Can I talk to you for a second? We can't go through with this."

He looked to where my hand held him.

Worried someone might enter the hall and hear, I stepped closer, lowering my voice. "Why would you just leap at that idea? It isn't safe. Master Guardian Norris said short walks—a couple of steps here and there were fine. I know he wouldn't approve anything outside of this apartment."

I thought you cared. I didn't say the words, but he heard them nonetheless.

The corners of his mouth tightened. "I didn't agree because I agreed with it. If you had listened, she was inviting us—meaning she was doing it either way. I agreed because she'd be safer with one or both of us than on her own."

"We might have been able to talk her out of it."

"Have you ever talked my mother out of anything?"

My hold on him fell away. He had a point. "We need a backup plan in case something happens. You can't phase her back here."

"If something happens, I'll carry her back."

"Can you carry her?" I asked incredulously.

He laughed, stopping when I didn't join in with him. "Oh, you're serious." He frowned. "I could carry you both there and back without breaking a sweat."

"That won't be necessary," I mumbled. Hugging my arms to my chest, I started walking again, slowly accepting what we were going to do. "We should take the Hidden Halls to shave off distance."

It wouldn't shave off much, but the more we could reduce Lupine's physical exertion, the better. We passed through the sitting room to the hallway leading out.

"That's a good idea." He ran his fingers through his hair. "You know you shouldn't keep worrying. You've done—and do—everything you can."

I nodded, wishing it were as easy to do as it was for him to say. "You're one to talk. You keep running your fingers through your hair like that, you might pull it all out."

He stopped short of doing it again and lowered his hand. "Anxious habit. Not sleeping makes it worse."

Not moving made it worse for me, and wanting to see my shadows as little as possible, I'd denied myself walks. "And here I thought you were catching up on your sleep while I read."

"Napping isn't quite the same as a good night's rest." Humor glittered in his eyes. "It's funny to me how much it annoys you."

"It doesn't annoy me."

"You never fail to mention it."

"It's confounding," I snapped. "Maybe if you didn't spend the entire night partying, you might get one, but also, maybe you like destroying yourself." He stopped abruptly, and harsh as I knew I'd been, I kept going, ignoring his silence like I did the urge to apologize—itching the back of my throat like the truth elixir. The truth wasn't always nice, and something told me he needed to hear it. "Get some rest this afternoon. I'll need you focused and awake tonight."

***

Ignoring the fretful voice telling me how bad of an idea this was, I marched into Lupine's bedroom, smiling big. "Let's do this."

My readiness faltered at the scene before me.

Damien sat on the bed, staring somberly at the space between where his and his mother's hand lay. Lupine was busy fixing herself. Sitting up straighter and finger-combing her hair, the tears staining her cheeks shone in the firelight.

Immortals, what had I walked in on?

I considered questioning if I was late right as the mantel clock chimed three times quickly, marking forty-five minutes past the hour. Reaching for the necklace at my throat, I stupidly asked, "Is everything okay?"

Wiping the sleeves of her nightgown across her face, Lupine plastered on a smile. "It is. Let's go." Cradling her swollen belly, she inched toward the edge of the bed, kicking out her slipper-clad feet.

Damien and I both rushed to help.

Cautiously, we led her through the darkened halls, past the empty rooms. She smiled through it all, and I wondered how she always did it, if she ever got tired of it—smiling when certainly it couldn't make her happy to see what had become of her home. Smiling when she didn't want to.

Outside, the door was as unguarded as it had been when I'd entered, and conveniently, there was an entrance to the Hidden Halls across from the door where a portrait of the Immortal Valentine hung —head held high, straight black hair halfway down his chest, and green eyes looking down at all who passed by. Together, Damien and I led her through the portrait into the Hidden Halls. Narrow as they were, I took the lead, supporting her, Damien trailing.

We made it to the Olinda Roses without a second to spare, watching as collectively the silver-tipped petals of the buds opened toward the moon overhead, the collective sigh of their smoky fragrance flooding the air.

Gasping, Lupine clasped her chest. Her face, glowing with a faint sheen of sweat, contorted as she fought back her emotions. "I don't remember the last time I made it. I forgot how beautiful it was."

"Let's go to the bench at the end there," I said, glancing at Damien — looking like a rain cloud to his mother's sunshine. "Sitting there always makes me feel like I'm wading in a silver sea."

Guiding her to the bench, I helped Lupine sit and went back to Damien, who had stopped halfway down the path, his eyes resting on the white and silver blooms glittering in the light of the moon and stars.

Keeping my voice soft, I said, "You're being oddly silent and to yourself."

Damien looked down at me, jade green eyes staring long and hard. "Am I?" He eased into a smile that, despite having been looking at him in the eyes for the last minute, almost made me believe I'd imagined his foul mood.

I narrowed my eyes, debating the merits of pushing him. The wheeze behind me, coming from Lupine's direction, made my decision. This was not the time or place for fake smiles hiding foul moods. He needed to be clear-headed. I opened my mouth, but Lupine cut me off.

"Both of you come here," she croaked, smiling weakly from her place on the bench. "Eden, sit." Breathing hard, she patted the space beside her and turned her gaze to Damien. "You—do you remember when you were a little boy?"

Damien frowned, his eyes darting to me. "Now isn't the time for that."

Lupine considered her son. "There's never a wrong time to enjoy things that make you happy. Watching you search for the prettiest rose used to give me the greatest pleasure," she tapped the side of her foot against his leg, "and if I recall, you got pretty excited about it as well."

"I was five."

"And so much easier to deal with."

Lips pressed together, he inhaled slowly, nostrils flaring.

She waved at the sea of flowers. "Now go, find me the prettiest bloom, and stop sulking. Just because there's no history of a demi-immortal showing their age doesn't mean you should test it."

He rolled his eyes to the sky.

"Go, go," she exclaimed. "I want to enjoy a moment with Eden."

Grumbling, he stormed away.

Once Damien was out of earshot, she mumbled, "You'd think I'd asked him for his right arm and big toe."

I laughed, and she smiled at me.

Pushing against the bench, she sat up a little straighter. "I hope he hasn't been too much of a bother to you these last several days. I know you're used to more one-on-one time with me. I appreciate you sharing it with him."

Saying it like I had done her a favor. I shook my head. "I would do anything to make you happy."

The Olinda Roses glittering in her darkened indigo eyes made them look like a twilight sky. I stared at them, wanting to remember them like this.

She laid her thin, bony hand atop mine, her Pledge Token glowing eerily in the moonlight. "I know Eden. You have such a kind heart. You may not be my flesh and blood daughter, but you're everything I would have hoped for in one. I'm so proud of who you've grown into. I think you may be the best woman I've ever known."

Warmth sparked in my chest. What did I say to that? Thank you didn't seem right. She turned her attention back to the sea of silver, eyes finding Damien at a rose bush a couple of paces away.

A sense of awe washed over me.

It was one example of hundreds, but we were all three here, in the garden, despite obstacles that seemed impossible to overcome to me. Damien's return to Sorbis being the biggest one. Somehow removing six Protectors—the guards at both of our apartments and my shadows

—who would have stopped us. She'd taken care of Master Guardian Norris, too. All this was her doing, and she hadn't even left her bed.

"How did you do it? Tonight."

"Surprised a bedridden woman has some tricks up her sleeve?"

"No, just in awe of you. Your ability. Your strength. Your resilience. You say I'm the best woman you've ever known, but—"

"Eden." Her voice broke on my name. Looking at her, I noticed tears threatening to spill from her eyes. She cleared her throat. "Please, let an old woman have her beliefs."

Old. Always a strange notion from a demi who, just like their immortal predecessors, never physically aged past twenty-five. I nodded, refocusing on Damien, who had bent to pick a rose.

"It's time," she exhaled.

"Time for what?" I asked, turning back to her.

Lupine's shoulders sagged, her head bent so severely it rested on her chest. All my nerves switched on.

"Lupine?" I shook her gently. Heat wrapping like a hand around my throat. "Lupine?" No response. Was she starting to fall forward? Her words...*It's time.* "Damien!" I screamed. The promise of tears burned my eyes as I grabbed her, fighting to keep her upright, fingers fumbling to find a pulse. "Oh nononono, Lupine." I sobbed—loud enough for the whole kingdom to hear, yet everything was silent. "Damien! Damien!"

A black swathed arm wrapped around Lupine's shoulders, another sweeping under her legs.

"What happened?" Damien demanded. He lifted her to his chest and ran.

I was right behind him, trying to keep up, but he was too far ahead. "We were talking, and she dropped off," I exclaimed, doing my best to ignore the stinging in my eyes. "I think maybe the baby is coming.

Damien, is she going to be okay?"

Reaching the wooden back door, he yelled back, "Get Norris," and disappeared.

Passing through the door a moment later and into the Hidden Halls, I heard his voice come to me from somewhere to my left inside the maze, fading away. "Come on, stay with me…"

Against the will of my heart, I ran straight, cutting through thick cobwebs. The Master Guardian's apartment was at the heart of the west side of the manor on the second floor. I powered up the three flights of stairs, ignoring how hard my aching heart pounded the inside of my chest.

Huffing as I cleared the second-floor landing, I stumbled to the first room on the right, hammering on it with my fists as I screamed his name as loudly as I could.

The door swung open a couple of seconds later, and Master Guardian Norris's beady eyes glared up at me as he worked to secure the belt of a white robe around his waist. His thin lips curled into a snarl, exposing browning, chipped teeth. "How dare you disturb me, you infernal girl."

"It's Lupine," I blurted, gasping for air. "It's bad. She needs you."

His eyes widened and then narrowed, the red of his irises matching the fire blazing in them. "What have you done?" Turning his attention inside, he beckoned to someone I couldn't see.

All the while, his words hollowed me. *What have you done?*

My head light, I stumbled a step back.

"I'll grab the other Elders, Master Norris," came a delicate voice. The door widened, revealing a young Elder I'd seen attending Lupine on occasion, straightening her blue robes, head bowed. "You get ready."

"You remember the plan?" he asked.

"Yes, sir."

Master Guardian Norris slammed the door on us.

The Elder looked at me. "You should take a seat," she said. Taking me by the shoulders, she eased me against the empty expanse of wall and then wordlessly proceeded to knock on the next several doors down.

All of them opened within seconds of the knock. All of the Elders were awake and ready. All waiting for a moment like this. They filed past me in formation toward the main stairs. A blur of blue.

What had I done?

As the last Elder disappeared around the corner, the Master Guardian, now wearing his blue skills robe, emerged from his room, not sparing me a glance.

The sight of him jarred me from my spiral. That's right. Lupine. I needed to move.

I trailed behind him quietly, using the walls for support, not realizing I was in the king's apartment until I was in the hall leading to Lupine's room. Watching Master Guardian Norris closing the distance, I experienced a modicum of relief. Help was coming, Lupine would be okay…

He grabbed the collar of a figure dressed in black, staggering backward toward him. With surprising strength and swiftness, he yanked Damien aside. Slamming him into the wall, the Master Guardian held a long, yellowing nail to his throat. "You did this."

"You should be attending to my mother," Damien snarled.

His sneer deepened. "I wouldn't need to if you weren't a conniving, reckless shit. At least one good thing will come out of this mess. I've always wanted to put you away. I'm going to have you arrested for endangering the queen. You'll rot in the darkest hole—"

"It was me," I said, stepping closer, pulling the Master Guardian's ire to me. "She wanted to see the Olinda Roses bloom. Damien wasn't involved. He just happened upon us."

I barely registered the look on Damien's face, questioning my sanity.

Foaming at the mouth, Master Guardian Norris released his hold on Damien. Remembering me—remembering I'd woken him. "You—you stupid, stupid girl." He flew toward me, his hand coming down hard across my face. Hard enough my ears rang.

"What in the fuck do you think you're doing?" Damien roared.

"It's fine," I said firmly. Coolly. I kept my eyes downcast at the space between them. This wasn't the priority. This didn't merit attention.

Damien's hands clenched at his side.

"If she dies, her blood is on your hands," the Master Guardian snapped. His hand flexed, debating another blow.

Do it and get it over with, I thought. Whatever would make him fix his focus…

Blue robes whirling, he charged for the bedroom where he should have been five minutes ago.

I took a stumbling step back and then another, the stinging in my cheek subsiding as my body healed itself. And I wished it wouldn't. It felt good. It felt better than the warm darkness blanketing my heart.

CHAPTER NINE
28.SEVEN.4004

King Elias's office was the only room untouched in his and Lupine's apartment. The door to it had been closed and locked—with surprisingly only a key—and forgotten, like so many other things, by everyone but me. I'd picked the lock not long after he'd decided to start staying in Hotel Solta, and claimed the room as my hideaway.

Grabbing the first crystal decanter of whiskey I saw, I popped it open and chugged until I needed air, ignoring the burn as it went straight into my empty stomach. Reclining on the plush leather couch beneath the shaded window letting in a sliver of silver moonlight, I stared aimlessly at the mahogany ceiling, attempting to count the arduously carved concentric circles overlapping each other like raindrops pelting a puddle. Every time I lost count, I drank.

Drank and thought of anything other than what had happened. What might be happening in the next room.

"You move quick," came a voice.

Startled, I looked up from the bottle in my hands. Standing in the doorway was Damien, his eyes staring at the high ceiling where mine had been before, panning slowly down to me. "I didn't think anyone came in here of their own volition."

"They don't, not even the king. But that doesn't stop your father from keeping it stocked with the best whiskey in Sorbis, making it the perfect place to be. How did you find me?"

He tapped the side of his nose.

Oh yeah. That. Another drink. "Is she going to be okay?"

The corners of his eyes crinkled. "They're all in there now."

Hand shaking, I raised the bottle to my mouth once more. "You didn't answer the question."

"Because I don't know," he sighed, running a hand through his black waves, "but what happened was no fault of the night, and it certainly wasn't yours."

As nice as the words felt, nothing could undo the emptiness in my chest that Norris's words had created. Except maybe a drink.

"Do you mind if I join you?" Damien asked.

Blood beginning to warm, I shrugged and sat up, making room on the couch. "Take a seat, but you have a long way to go to catch up."

He eased the door closed. "How much could you have had in the few minutes we were separated?"

Holding the bottle up, I considered the question. "It was full." It was three-quarters full now. "I think you drinking double that seems fair."

His eyes grew wide. "You want me to drink half the bottle?"

"I've heard the stories of your drinking from Quincy. You can do it."

The cushion beside me sighed under his weight. "Can and should are two different things." He looked from me to the bottle.

Ignoring the implication, I drank. "Suit yourself."

Damien studied me carefully. Sighing, he snapped his fingers, a tall glass appearing in his hand. "Will this suffice?"

Passing him the bottle in acceptance, I sat back and watched him pour, filling the glass until it was brimming. "Before I drink this, is there a reason we're sitting in the cold and dark?"

I looked around, realizing he was right—no light charm had activated. "I hadn't noticed, but it wouldn't have mattered if I had. I'm not very good at charms." Taking the bottle back, I added, "High society women don't learn magic and all that."

"A stupid rule."

I shrugged, not wanting to think of the opportunities I'd never gotten to take.

"My mother says you can heal. That's impressive."

Unsure of what to think of them discussing me or why, of all things, that was what they'd discussed, I said, "The most I can really do is heal myself. When I try to heal others, I get lightheaded. Very useless."

"No. Untrained, not useless."

Pushing up his sleeves, he lifted his fingers. A solid snap and small balls of golden light began to play around the room's perimeter, and the air started to warm. One snap, and he'd executed both charms.

If that wasn't enough, there wasn't a beat between the charms and his drinking. He emptied the glass in three gulps. "That was almost as smooth as water," he sighed, refilling the glass—a normal amount this time. "Norris's ability to source good whiskey might be his only redeeming trait."

My heart faltered at the sound of his name, hating it and its owner so much, but more than that, the fear he triggered in me. I took a gulp, praying it'd steady my nerves. "A talent benefiting someone who can only be tolerated while inebriated."

Damien stopped mid-drink, the veins in his tan arms bulging. "Does Norris strike you often?"

I traced a finger along the rim of my glass. "When he thinks I've stepped out of line."

"Speaking of answers that aren't answers."

"The answer is subjective, and I'd rather not talk about that or him," I said, a little angrier than intended.

"Why did you take the fall?"

I shook my head. "Because I hate his threats. I hate his spite. I could hear it in his voice. He has a lot for you. I knew it wouldn't end well for me, but I couldn't stand to listen to it."

Damien's eyes glazed, locked on the glass in his hands.

Letting him process whatever it was that'd suddenly seized him, I looked up at the portrait of the Immortal Valentine on the far wall, hanging over a low bookshelf. He wore dark green robes, the Valentine insignia embroidered in gold, right over his heart, hand raised as if blessing those who looked upon him.

"Why are you snickering?" Damien asked.

I slapped a hand over my mouth. "I'm sorry. I didn't mean to interrupt your reflection."

"You didn't interrupt anything." The way he pulled his coat together, shifting his position to the edge of the couch, said otherwise. His green eyes met mine over the rim of his glass. "I'd like to know what was so funny."

I pointed to the portrait. "Just think it's funny how there are pictures of your ancestor everywhere, like he couldn't get enough of seeing renditions of himself."

A smile cracked his face. "While you aren't wrong, I think you're a little drunk."

"I am not."

His smile deepened, revealing the faintest dimple in his left cheek. "Whatever you say."

Feeling my face heat, I glanced toward the desk for a distraction. "You know, I've always wondered what's in the king's desk."

Damien drained his glass. "Nothing interesting."

"You've tried?"

"I've succeeded."

"How did you get through the wards?"

The corner of his mouth tugged up smugly. "It wasn't hard. There was no challenge to it."

"The Master Guardian of Charms wove those wards."

"My point exactly."

"Someone is high on themselves."

He scoffed, pulling back a little in feigned offense. "Because I think Rei is a terrible Master Guardian of Charms?"

"Because you think you're better than her."

"I know I'm better than her." He leaned forward. "We were in the same Academy class, both charms guardians, training to be Devotees. She has no sense of magic. Lucky for her, my ancestor was good at writing down everything he did, and she's a good student."

I stared down at my empty glass and the empty decanter. "Interesting."

"What?"

"You." And rather than let it fall silent again, or worse, hear his retort to my assessment of him, I scooted to the edge. "I'll get us more whiskey," I sighed. Launching to my feet, I buckled at the knee as my alcohol-saturated blood rushed to my head.

Damien—beside me in a flash—caught me at the waist, steadying me. "Be careful."

I glared at him. "You haven't had enough if you can still react that quickly."

Chuckling, he set his glass down. "Why don't we take a break from the whiskey for a moment, and I'll show you how easy it is to break one of the wards."

Extremely curious, I nodded, walking over to the king's desk, vaguely aware of Damien's hand hovering nearby in preparation for me to stumble again. I motioned to the center drawer.

Damien held his hands out before him as I'd seen Devotees do thousands of times.

"Wait, try the drawer. I have to make sure it isn't charmed to open for you."

He grabbed the brass handle, giving it a tug. The drawer didn't bother to rattle. "My father doesn't even want to see me. You think he would give me access?"

"I had to make sure."

"Of course." He lifted his hands again. This time, I wondered what they felt—what he felt. Running a hand over the smooth surface of the desk, I felt fortified, immovable magic, and when I reached for magic to challenge it, there was only chaos.

Eyes narrowed in concentration, he made a motion with his right hand, as if pushing something away and then pulling something down quickly.

He nodded at the drawer. "Okay."

"Okay?"

"It's open."

I snorted skeptically. "What was that, thirty seconds?"

"Not my best time, but I took a little longer to understand the ward. It's been a while, and I have no interest in rebuilding it, so I didn't completely remove it, simply unlocked the drawer."

I continued to stare, shaking my head.

He nodded once more. "The ward has a natural renewal aspect built into it, so it won't remain unlocked long."

I grabbed the handle and yanked, fully expecting nothing to happen. The contents rattled angrily as it slammed open.

My hands flew to my face. "You did it."

He looked down at me with a sly smile. "You really doubted me?"

"Master Guardian Rei wove those wards."

"Again, she's no savant."

"How did you do it?"

He shrugged. "I've been asked that all my life. It's like asking me how I breathe. Magic has always opened itself to me, and I've always been good at manipulating it."

Thinking of my own magic and my inability to use it, I frowned. "That must be nice." Reincimmo indeed.

He stiffened beside me. "Where did you hear that name?"

Shit, I'd said that aloud. But—had I said something wrong? Most people would love that title. I felt my blood heat. "I, uh," my thoughts jumped to Quincy, "the people in the farmlands, when they heard about your return, referred to you as such." Not a lie either. Since my chat with Q, I'd heard several people whispering amongst themselves about how Reincimmo had returned as I'd walked around.

Damien eased the drawer shut and put his back to me, grabbing another decanter of whiskey as he passed by the bar cart. Resettling himself on the couch, he welcomed himself to another drink.

I took a halting step toward him. "I'm sorry if—"

He looked up at me impassively. "It's fine, I—"

"In the king's office, plowing through his whiskey," came a husky voice. "Following your scents, that isn't what I expected to find you plowing, but I'm pleasantly surprised."

My nails dug into my palms as I turned to glare at Grayden Faldone, standing in the doorway, arms crossed, looking as morose as usual in his red Protector uniform.

Damien rolled his eyes. "What do you need, cousin?"

He pursed his lips. "I was sent to tell you the queen is dead."

A harsh barking sound escaped me. "As tasteless as ever. That was a horrible joke."

Grayden squared his shoulders, nostrils flaring. "I'm not laughing."

A sharp pain twisted in my chest, the world starting to spin.

Fighting against the sway, I looked between the two of them—Grayden with his stern red glare and Damien frozen in place.

"No, she isn't," I insisted.

Grayden ignored me in favor of Damien. "The king is on his way back from Charph as we speak. You both need to leave now. He wants everyone in the manor out."

He should never have been in Charph, I wanted to scream. Stumbling for the door, I said, "I want to see Lupine."

Grayden stepped to block me. "You're going home."

I jabbed my finger hard into the center of his chest, the words working themselves between my teeth like tough meat. "I'm not going anywhere until I see Lupine."

Nostrils flaring, Grayden's red eyes assessed me coolly. "You're drunk, Eden, and it's late. One of my generals will escort you home."

I relaxed my stance. "Fine."

He inclined his head, pleased by the easy concession. "Perfect, Protect—"

The moment he stepped aside, I bolted, making my way for the hall leading to Lupine's chambers. A group of blue-robed Elders clustered around the doorway looked alarmed as I rushed toward them. One second away from shoving through them, they parted.

"Lupine," I called. Because I wanted to scream her name. Tears streaked my face as I tried to force my legs to move faster.

"Eden," a voice behind me growled in response. Grayden.

No. Fuck. I couldn't let him catch me. Lupine couldn't die. Save her. I had to save her. I had to try. I made it one step inside her bedroom.

The smell of blood instantly soured my stomach, saturating the air so heavily I could taste it. Elders stood shoulder to shoulder around her bed, forming a blue wall, with Norris at the foot leading them in the Immortal's Invocation.

An Elder pulled away from the bed on the other side of the room, clutching one of the many blankets Lupine kept on her bed. Red droplets fell from it as she carried it to a bin.

A loud ringing superseded the harmony of the chant. Another elder came away with a blanket, the red on it coming out in a small stream. Red, everywhere. Dark red, bright red.

I lost my strength, stumbling back against something hard—certain I'd seen this before in a nightmare. The world tilted, every drop of whiskey making itself felt.

An arm swooped around my waist and under my knees, lifting me and pulling me back. "I've got you," came a soft voice at my ear. Damien.

"Damien…Lupine…"

"Sneaky," Grayden tsked.

My thoughts whirled around Grayden's words. *The queen is dead.* The smell of the room. The blood dripping from the blankets. The sanctimonious chant. The smile on Lupine's face an hour ago.

All of it took the air from my chest, plummeting me into darkness.

***

"Is she alright?" asked a high female voice.

"She passed out."

Jostled by a sharp rocking, I came to, peering up at a face of suntanned skin, green eyes, and night-black hair, surrounded by dark wooden rafters, the lights flickering along them like stars.

"Lupine," I whispered. We began to sink, the warmth at my upper back and under my knees slipping away, becoming a cool, worn leather couch and a satin pillow under my head. Had he been carrying me?

A white plush blanket brushed my chin. "Where are we?" I mumbled.

Rolling onto my side, I watched Damien sink into the tattered black armchair across from me.

He rested his elbows on his knees, dragging his hands down his face. "Vermillion."

"But it's so quiet."

He nodded. "We're in the apartment above the bar, which is charmed against sound. Mari's letting us crash."

"Why are we here?"

"You passed out, and we had to go. I tried to take you home, but I didn't know your building was warded, and I didn't think breaking the ward would be appreciated by the other residents."

An answer to my question, but not the answer I was looking for.

"That wasn't another nightmare," I said. My voice sounded distant.

Damien stayed silent, and I knew I didn't want him to say anything. I didn't want anyone to say anything. There was only one thing I wanted, and it wasn't going to happen.

That left only one option.

Rolling over, I let the hot tears stinging my eyes go.

CHAPTER TEN

28.SEVEN.4004

I didn't remember falling asleep, but when I awoke, it was to Grayden telling me Cole was requesting my return to the manor until further notice, having deemed it unsafe for me to be away while the city mourned the loss of their queen and the princess who hadn't managed one breath.

A little girl, Anemone. The little girl Lupine had always wanted. The little girl she'd wanted me to keep safe should something happen to her. Gone.

"What about Damien?" I asked, voice so hoarse and fragile I wondered if maybe I'd aged sixty years in those couple of hours.

He dropped his gaze, shaking his head. "I'm sorry, cousin, but neither your father nor brother said anything about you."

"But—"

"I'll be fine, Eden," Damien said.

And that was it.

Phasing with Grayden was worse than with Julien. One second, we were walking past the wards protecting Vermillion, the next, we were at the private entrance to the manor, and I was on my knees, retching every drop of the whiskey I'd drank, enduring Grayden's curses for ruining his boots.

***

Looking for a distraction from my tears and rage, I passed through the halls of the manor, headed toward the kitchen. The only sound to fill the void of silence was the strike of my shadows' boots behind me.

I was confused by the need for heightened security—the people had loved Lupine—until I learned from the staff that the king had decided Lupine and Anemone were to be buried in the Valentine Mausoleum in two days at ten in the morning; only family and the Alliance Council would be in attendance versus the customary royal mourning procession—thus denying the people their last chance to say goodbye to the queen who'd ruled them for half a century.

***

That evening, I worked up the courage to ask Elodie—temporarily serving me as a lady's maid—if she'd heard anything regarding why the manor had been cleared that night.

"It was the baby, miss," she whispered so low I wondered if I'd imagined it. "They didn't want anyone to see it."

It not *her*.

"There's whispers the Master Guardian had been performing dark magic on Her Highness. Praying to the Immortal Valentine to take the child in exchange for sparing the king of the Pledge Death. The princess had been dead within her for days. Someone who claimed they saw her said she was a gray, eyeless abomination."

The sharp, sour tang of bile stung the back of my throat. I'd known what to expect from staff gossip, but it didn't make the tale any less hard to hear.

Lupine's Pledge Token had gone missing as well, Elodie informed me. The emerald ring…irremovable since she had made the Eternal Pledge to King Elias…removed.

She was really gone.

CHAPTER ELEVEN

2.EIGHT.4004

Midnight before the funeral, exhausted from crying but unable to sleep, I wandered into the garden with a pair of shears, followed by my shadows. Usually, once sunrise came, the Olinda Roses closed and, if cut, lost their shine. But magic had been known to hear prayers even if the Immortal Idols didn't.

Fresh tears streaking my cheeks, I whispered to the three flowers I selected, asking them to continue their shine for the dead once morning came.

As the sun filtered through the cracks in the drapes the next morning, I rolled over to look at my dresser, expecting to see withered blooms, but the flowers shimmered.

***

A soft knock came at my door at eight. At my beckoning, Elodie walked in with orders to dress and escort me to the funeral. She helped me into a high-necked, long-sleeved black dress with a skirt that brushed my ankles, and plaited my hair into a single braid running the length of my back.

The procession, she informed me as we walked, would begin at the garden—away from the prying eyes of the crowd gathered at the gate—and weave its way through into the northern neck of the woods to where the mausoleum waited.

She left me at the top of the stairs, where the staff level led down to the rear foyer and event rooms. I descended, reminding myself to hold it together. Most of the gathered would be people I didn't want to see me cry. Not when they would use my tears to call me weak.

The wooden doors to the garden were wide open, letting the bright yellow sunlight illuminate the polished stone floor. A cool, perfect breeze carrying the scent of wisteria and grass rushed up to greet me.

The sky should have been dark gray, the clouds releasing a deluge of water on Sorbis. On me.

What have you done?

Standing on either side of the open doors, ignoring one another, were the four Master Guardians wearing robes in the respective colors of their aptitude. Norris blue for skills, Rei yellow for charms, and Gillian green for acuity. Saier—who hated the lack of functionality the robes offered—represented combat in the red Protector uniform, a distinguished gold cape flowing behind him.

Before the formal dining room doors on the right were Lord Stellan Faldone of Charph and his four sons—Grayden among them. All dressed in their red Faldone regalia. I followed Grayden's gaze across the room to the ballroom door where Oleander—Rho's mother and one of the founding members of the Misundre Five—fussed over my best friend, her youngest daughter. They stood with the other surviving founders, Ivy and Vervain, and the current members, Heath, Iris, Violet, Caladium, and Dahlia, as well as the founding members' other children. They were the only ones dressed in mourning colors.

In their varying groups, I couldn't help thinking how unallied the Alliance was.

Cole and the king stood at the center, looking like different versions of the same person. The only people missing were Quincy and Damien —if the king would allow him.

With his father was the only time I saw Cole shrink himself, rounding his shoulders and inclining his head while King Elias stood like a man who'd never had to bow to anyone, who'd never heard no. He kept his short black hair slicked back, and he wore the dark red suit jacket, white button-down, black pants combo that'd become as synonymous with him as Cole and his blue suit.

It'd been six months since I'd last seen him, and though I'd known better, I was surprised he looked much the same as he had then. As he had my whole life. As he had for almost a century now.

The only change—an amethyst stone the size of a grape, wrapped in gold, was missing from his left middle finger. The Pledge Token Lupine had given him. Its absence pronouncing what awaited him.

I'd crept in as quietly as a mouse, wanting to fall to the side and mourn unnoticed, but the drawn-out boom of my name dashed that hope.

"Eden, come here, won't you? Let me get a look at you." I looked toward the voice, meeting the green eyes I knew so well on his sons. The scowl he'd worn talking to Cole warped into a snake-like smile.

Walking toward him, I worked to keep my steps even. I could feel Cole watching me, but I didn't dare look at him, remembering the chastisement I'd received last time from the king about respect.

"What is this?" His eyes stayed on mine, but I knew he meant the roses.

"Good morning, King Elias. Olinda Roses, Lupine loved them."

"How quaint." He took my face in one of his cool hands, sending a shiver down my spine. My hold on the roses loosened as he ran his thumb along my jaw. "Tell me, is my son still allowing you to work at that orphanage?"

I managed a whisper. "I still help at Selene's House."

His green eyes narrowed, searching mine as if for an answer to a question he hadn't asked. "What a waste of your mortal life, giving the undesired a dream." His hold on my chin tightened, bones grinding against mine through our flesh. "Tell me you don't truly think that problem would be better left to resolve itself."

Blistering rage pooled in my stomach as I fought the urge to remind him they were his people and the only reason they had no family was because of him. Facts everyone in the room did their best to forget.

"It's not even noon, and you're parading ideas about the death of your people. How like you, father," Damien said, voice dripping with venom. The murmuring clusters to each side of us fell silent. "Why don't you let Eden go? She isn't the source of your problems. We all know who that is."

The corners of King Elias's mouth pulled down to his chin, nostrils flaring. He threw my face when he released me, fixing his attention over my shoulder.

"You watch your mouth, you miscreant bastard," he snarled.

Damien's sigh came from behind me. "How I know you wish I were a bastard—it's one of the few things we have in common."

"Who invited you?"

Cole stepped between his brother and father. "Damien, that's enough. I did, Father. It's our mother's funeral."

I only caught a glimpse of the self-renounced prince—looking like he hadn't slept or changed his clothes since I'd seen him last—as someone's fingers entwined with mine, tugging me away.

I thought it might be Q, that he might have finally arrived, but turning to face him, my gaze locked onto soft pink eyes.

"Hi there, my girl," Oleander smiled. Her bright pink curly hair, piled high on top of her head, wobbled on each step. "Why don't you come with me? Best not to stand too close where those three are involved."

"Thank you, Oleander," I said, finding my voice.

"Darling, I know I told you to call me Ole. Only strangers and people I don't like call me by my full name. You are neither."

I nodded, jumping slightly when the king roared for Damien to: "Get the fuck out before I have you arrested."

"I'm sorry we had to meet again under such sad circumstances. Maybe you'll tell me more about the vile Charphan boy my daughter is seeing?"

Glaring at Ole, Rho pulled me into a hug. "Mother, seriously?"

"Father, relax," Cole sighed. "Start the procession. Damien, you're drunk. Let's step aside."

A loud crash sounded from behind me, and this time I turned. Damien and Cole were gone, the doors to the dining room vibrating from the force they'd endured. Now it was just Quincy, who'd shown up some time while my back was turned, looking out of place beside his fuming father.

His wide green eyes settled on me, pleading for help.

"Let's get this over with," the king snarled. Turning on the heel of his boot, he stormed out into the bright, sunny day.

***

Creamy marble walls and crypts emblazoned with gold nameplates neatly arranged in a circular structure made up the mausoleum, where all the Valentines, except the Immortal one, had been buried. At the center were two catafalques bearing two white coffins.

Cole and Damien rejoined the group a minute after everyone had settled in—Cole joining his father at the center of the mausoleum while Damien joined Grayden along the far wall, partially obscured by a marble column.

The immediate family would speak first by order of age. Then, the Misundrans, because while Lupine was only blood-related to one, the

Misundre Five—old and new—were viewed as one as much as they were separate. Next, the Faldones and the Alliance Council, and afterward, anyone remaining, which usually meant the people of the city who wanted to pay their respects.

In this case, it meant me.

The king wasted no time, pulling his Pledge Token out of his pocket and tossing it atop Lupine's coffin. "Rest in peace, wife," he said, spitting the last word. Head held high, he looked at no one as he passed through the door and back out into the morning. Not a word for his daughter, Anemone.

The place was so quiet following his departure that I could hear my breath.

Clearing his throat, Cole stepped forward. "Thank you, Mother, for everything you gave for your family and your people. May you rest in peace." He had the decency to express the latter sentiment for his little sister, but he didn't wait for anyone else, trailing in his father's footsteps, with only the slightest nod at me.

Then it was Damien's turn.

Everyone watched as he untucked a thick letter from the interior pocket of his jacket and set it on her coffin.

"In this letter is everything I don't have the strength to say." He momentarily glanced around the room. "Don't get any ideas. I've charmed it to self-destruct should anyone try," he said, drawing forth a chuckle or two. Sighing, he bowed his head. "You were the light of the city. You were the best mother a boy could have had. The best queen a city could have dreamed of. I love you. May you rest in peace."

Pressing his lips to the white wood, he said goodbye and turned to the smaller coffin. "Little sister, I never met you. I never even saw you. Neither of those things makes me love you any less. My mother dreamed of you for so long. Quincy was supposed to be a girl." That got another little chuckle from the room. "Wherever we go in death, I know you're there with our mother. May you rest in peace."

Damien kissed it as well and resumed his place along the wall.

I watched numbly as the rest of the attendees took their turn. The rest of them moved quickly, most favoring a simple rest in peace for Lupine alone before leaving. The whole ceremony felt as cold as death itself. By the time they were done, the only people remaining were the three founding members of the Misundre Five, Heath, Rho, Grayden, Damien, Quincy, and me.

And it was my turn.

Despite telling myself I couldn't cry, a single tear slid down my cheek, determined not to be denied. "I don't know how to say goodbye to you. I don't know how to say anything. Just that I love you, and I'll see you again one day. Rest in peace, Lupine."

I set one of the three flowers I held at the center of Lupine's coffin and moved to the small coffin. "I—" my voice broke, another tear breaking loose. "You were so wanted and so loved. Rest in peace, Anemone."

The second flower I clutched found its new home at the center of her small coffin.

Finally, I made my way across the room to the crypt in the wall. The now dried-up wildflowers I'd placed in the vase to the side on my last visit were still there.

Behind me, someone sucked in a breath as I gave the last flower to Aevry Valentine. "Rest in peace, Aevry."

***

I sat on the bench beneath the Eternal Tree, staring out at the Olinda Roses, wishing to feel something but unsure if there was anything left. I couldn't believe it'd happened. I couldn't believe she was gone.

Grabbing the key necklace at my neck for strength, fresh tears threatened my eyes.

No, I couldn't cry. Not with an audience, even if it was Protector Olick who was so silent, I could forget he was there.

Temporary leave and demotion had been his punishment for disregarding orders that night two weeks ago.

How two weeks had felt like two years…

The sound of my name snapped me from my reverie. Damien stood at the end of the path, hands in his pockets, his long black coat buttoned up against the wind.

"You're still here," I said. "You disappeared after the funeral. I figured you'd left."

"My father only cares about my presence as much as he can see me, and he isn't here."

No, he wasn't. Neither he nor the Lord of Charph had been seen since the funeral. Seen at a pleasure house in the farmlands, I'd overheard Master Guardian Saier telling Cole at dinner before he left to do damage control.

"I meant left Sorbis."

"Thought I'd leave without so much as a goodbye to you?"

I offered a small smile. "I didn't know my reading meant so much to you."

He returned the smile but said nothing, looking from me to Olick standing off to my right. "Do you mind if I sit with you?" *Alone,* the unspoken word.

I looked at Olick. "Could you give us some privacy?"

Olick glanced at Damien and offered a curt nod. "I'll be at the edge of the garden if you need me."

Watching him go, it didn't feel right that he didn't curse my name, ruing the day I was born. To become a Protector was to endure years of training. Instead, when I'd tried to apologize, he'd clapped me on the shoulder and said it didn't feel like a demotion.

Closing the distance between us, Damien took the seat beside me. "I know I'm a baby, but it's actually freezing. Where is your jacket?"

As if to support his point, a cold breeze cut through my satin slip, licking up my spine, evoking a shiver. "I guess I didn't notice."

He started to undo the buttons of his jacket.

I put a hand on his shoulder. "That isn't necessary. I'll be fine."

"That's really not how I work." Shucking it, he passed it to me.

I held it up to my chin like a blanket. The jacket, warm with the heat of his body, smelled richly of sandalwood and cedar. Now exposed to the elements, he rubbed his palms together, drawing my attention to the mangled flesh on the back of his right hand, caked dark red.

My stomach twisted. "What happened to your hand?"

Startled by my notice of it, he covered it with his left, still intact, and bounced his leg, fighting the urge to touch his hair. "I, uh, punched a tree. Grief and rage are two sides of the same coin for me."

"It's small enough. It wouldn't take too much from me to heal you."

He shook his head. "I'll be fine. It looks worse than it is." Unable to hold back any longer, he ran his unscathed hand through his thick black hair. "As I'm sure you heard, as of this morning, my father is unofficially stepping down as king in every way but name, and Cole is to assume his responsibilities immediately."

An interesting development that Cole had failed to mention to me at any point today…I was too numb to be surprised, though.

He took a deep breath. "Cole has asked me to help support him as his second until Quincy reaches the Immortal Age, so I'll be extending my stay in Sorbis."

Quincy, being a couple of weeks older than me, meant Damien would be here for at least two more years. "As much as you dislike

Sorbis, that's quite the sacrifice."

He clicked his tongue. "Yeah, I'm still processing what I've agreed to —but hey, I wanted to ask you something. About earlier."

I looked at him, waiting for him to go on.

His eyes, sparkling in the light of the flowers, peered down at me. "Why did you put the flower on," his lip quivered, "my brother's tomb? You know it's...empty, don't you?"

Surprised by the question, it took me a second to answer. "I wanted to remember him. No one ever talks about him. No one even says his name. I know the mention of him is touchy, but all the silence around him makes me feel like no one wants to remember him. So much so, I didn't even know about him until I was maybe eleven, and we talked about Roan's War in my studies."

He dropped his gaze. "What do you know of him?"

"Not much, just that he died in the war."

He nodded once, and I thought that would be the end of it.

"Aevry," he started, stopping to take a breath as if saying his name had taken everything out of him. "His death was hard on the family. He was my best friend, my idol." The pain from the other day flashed in his eyes.

"Do you want to talk about it?" I offered.

He choked out a laugh. "No—thank you."

I'd expected as much. "I understand, but I wanted to put the offer out there."

"You're too pure for your own good."

Feeling a spark of anger—and it felt so nice—I said, "I'm not pure."

Staring at his feet, he smiled, but there was no happiness in it. "That isn't a bad thing, Eden."

We sat there in silence for a minute, listening to the insects chirping in the woods at our back. A heaviness filling the air. Two people who cared. Who'd lost the most important person in their lives.

Feeling the tears threatening once more, I stood and carefully placed his jacket back around him. "I'm going to try to go to sleep. If you ever want to talk, I'm here for you." And before I could change my mind, I bent and pressed a kiss to his forehead. "Have a good night, Damien."

I wouldn't sleep, but I would try.

I was halfway to Olick when he called my name again. I looked back at him, sitting on the bench, hands fisting his jacket. "Don't stop… remembering him, I mean."

Part II

CHAPTER TWELVE

10.EIGHT.4004

Checking my face one last time in the mirror by the door, I grabbed my basket and left. It was a bright, cloudless day in Sorbis, and the sun was out in full force—summer making its final stand.

Everyone I'd encountered on the way to the market that morning wore shorts or sleeveless flowing dresses, and anyone who could afford to would be outside enjoying the weather.

Hitting the last stair, I passed through my building's wards and tapped the signet ring. Appearing mid eyeroll, hands shoved deep into his dark green slacks, Julien bent his arm toward me.

"Good morning," I smiled. Hooking his elbow, I inched as close as I could to him, which in this case meant hugging his arm lightly to my side.

"What are you doing?" he sneered.

"You're going to phase me to the capital." As many times as I'd summoned him, never had he not known my intended destination—some built-in intuition of Runners.

"I'm not stupid. I know why I'm here. I mean your proximity to me. Don't think I haven't noticed your small adjustments. It's weird and unwanted."

Right when I was beginning to think he didn't hate me as much as I thought. "Being closer to you helps with my phasing-induced nausea."

"Sounds like a personal problem," he said, weaseling away. "Do it with someone else, mortal. Transporting you is enough."

Biting back the words I longed to say to him, I put as much distance between us as possible. The severe red sandstone facade of Protector Headquarters came into view a second later, shrouded in the shadow of the Capitol's golden-domed roof. Accompanying their appearance was crippling nausea, back in full force as if to say: *Miss me?*

Julien left almost instantly, and good riddance.

Clutching my stomach, I focused on breathing through the stinging waves. Breathing in the fragrance of the trees and fresh warm bread coming from Capital Bakery behind me. Listening to the rush of the River Sorbis and the children squealing in Alliance Park, their mother calling for them to settle down.

Smoothing my dress and tucking a strand of hair behind my ear, I started for the one and only entrance of the Capitol Building—installed across from Protector Headquarters for safety reasons, same as the manor.

There were only two recorded ways to kill an immortal. The first was by the hands of an immortal of equal or greater ability, as evidenced when the Immortal Valentine destroyed the Immortal Faldone. The second was through the Eternal Pledge, and considering that's how he went—and that he and the Immortal Faldone were the only immortals—why he had been so concerned with safety in his frequent haunts continually confounded me. But at least the Capitol was a fourth of the manor's size.

It was the first day of this month's Alliance Council session, and I didn't know where exactly they convened in the capital, but I knew Cole's office was in there, so that's where I'd start.

The Immortals were smiling down on me because, rounding the

corner of Protector Headquarters, I spotted him at the foot of the Capitol Building stairs wearing a crisp black suit.

On soft feet, I closed the distance between us, setting down the basket as I leapt up to cover his eyes.

"Guess who. Didn't think I'd catch you outside here," I whispered sweetly. "The black suit is a nice change. It flatters you."

"You know, I never thought I'd catch myself outside of here either," came an amused voice that wasn't Cole's.

Yelping, I dropped my hands, stumbling back—almost tripping over the picnic basket. A hand fell on my shoulder, steadying me.

"That was excessive," Damien said. His green eyes scanned my face, one corner of his mouth tugging up. "You came up behind me and put your hands over my eyes, and I didn't even flinch."

My whole body burned like it was on fire. "I thought you were Cole," I stammered, yanking out of his grip. "You're wearing a suit. You—you cut your hair and slicked it down—what is this?"

Cringing, he started to run his fingers through it, stopping himself short of messing up his pristine hair. "Horrid, isn't it? Grayden, of all people, said I needed to clean up my look before the Council convened." He ran his fingers down the lapel. "I'm glad you like the suit, though. I thought I cut a fine figure as well."

A fresh wave of heat tore through me. I'd all but hit on him. I glanced around, happy to see no one paid us any attention. "Where's Cole?"

Damien waved his hand at the Capitol Building. "The Council has adjourned for the day, and I haven't seen him leave, so I expect he's in his office. That's really not a question for me."

Frowning, I stared up at the towering building and its mirrored windows reflecting the city. The idea of wandering through it after thinking it'd been so easy was daunting.

"Do you know where that is?" Damien asked.

Collecting the basket, I dropped my gaze. "I've been a couple of times, but I've never found it without help. The place is a maze."

"I can show you."

"That's not—"

"It's no trouble," he said, bounding up the stairs. "I canceled my plans at Vermillion this evening, not knowing what to expect of the meeting. I've nothing else to do today. You coming?"

With no time to consider other options, I followed him.

Cresting the stairs, Damien held one of the large glass doors open for me. "You look nice, by the way. Would you like me to carry that for you?"

Inside the building was an atrium that extended up to the golden glass dome, where sunlight shone through, tinting the three floors below an amber hue.

Glancing back at him, I shook my head, waiting for him to retake the lead. "Thank you. Cole likes me in orange." Fingering the key necklace with my free hand, I added, "I hear we're neighbors."

I'd only been allowed to return to my apartment two days ago, but having received word from Grayden, Rho had stopped by after work to check in and then interrogate me regarding Damien, relentlessly asking me what I could hear, why he had moved into the penthouse, and what Cole thought.

As if I knew—I hadn't seen either Valentine since the day of the funeral.

Damien entered the stairwell off to the side of the entrance. "Yeah, the penthouse came up for sale, and I enjoy walking to Vermillion, so I couldn't resist. Quincy and Grayden informed me you're directly below me on the fifth floor. Hopefully, my moving in hasn't bothered you too much." He winked as we rounded the corner to the next flight of stairs. "What's in the basket?"

Hand sweating, I tightened my grip on the wicker handle. "It's not much—I'm not much of a chef, so I picked up a variety of sliced meats, cheeses, fruits, and a fresh loaf of bread at the market this morning. I hope he enjoys it, and I hope he hasn't eaten. He doesn't know I'm coming," I admitted.

"Sounds like a nice lunch and a nicer surprise. I'm sure he'll love it."

The space between us fell silent for a moment, the only sound the click of our shoes when the words came out. "Have you been okay?" I asked. "Have you cried as much as I have?"

Having reached the uppermost landing, he stopped stiff.

"I'm sorry. There's been no one I've wanted to talk to about her with. Many loved her, but no one loved her like you or I did, it would seem." I took a steadying breath as tears stung my eyes. "The ache in my chest never seems to go away. It's been such a lonesome feeling."

For all my efforts, one streaked down my cheek. I wiped it away.

"You don't ever have to apologize. You just caught me by surprise. No, I haven't cried. If I can be honest, the war and being a demi have desensitized me to tears and death. I do miss her, though. There's not a minute that goes by that I don't think about her. Even with my twenty-year absence, there's never been anyone else like my mother."

"And there won't be." I nodded, feeling silly for my emotions. "You can always be honest with me."

Surprising me, he cupped my chin in his hand, coaxing me to look at him. His green eyes held mine steady. "If that's true, then there are two things I want you to know. One, the ache never goes away, it simply becomes something you learn to live with, and two, you're never alone." Somewhere below, a door opened, and he turned away, releasing his hold. "Cole's office is through these doors and around the corner to the right."

Opening the windowless wooden door, loud laughter and a blast of cold hit me. Once it closed, the clop of the other footsteps in the stairwell disappeared. This level was charmed. Around the corner was the source of laughter—two Protectors who went stone-faced at my approach.

Damien, who'd seemed ready to walk past them, stopped abruptly, causing me to bump into him. "My brother's Bidden is here to see him. Would one of you kindly let him know?"

I stepped around to look at them.

The Protector on the left, a tall, thin man with straight red hair, spoke. "He's asked not to be disturbed."

The other Protector snickered, receiving a scathing look from his comrade and Damien.

"Go inform Prince Cole his Bidden is here," Damien commanded.

The bitter silence that followed the order allowed for the sound of the Protector's boots receding as he made his way down the dark hall, and the subsequent hard knock at Cole's office door. A crack of light broke the darkness, and a shadowy figure appeared in the doorway.

"Yes?" Cole hissed.

"Sorry, sir. Your Bidden is here to see you."

"Doll?" Cole exclaimed from down the hall, a weird edge to his voice. "What a pleasant surprise." He filled the entrance to the hall a moment later in his dark blue suit, his hair slicked to the side, a sleepy smile tugging at his lips. Cupping my chin in his hand, he pressed a kiss to my forehead. "To what do I owe this visit?"

The basket rocked as I lifted it for him to see. "I wanted to surprise you."

Green eyes gleaming, he leaned to kiss me again. "How thoughtful."

Damien shifted beside me, bringing Cole's attention to him. They stared at each other for only a second, but something silent passed between them, reminding me of their silent exchange that first night.

"Thank you for your help," I said, getting Damien's attention.

He gave a two-finger salute to the space between Cole and me, stepping back to the stairwell door. "It was no problem. Enjoy."

Cole stared after his brother, even after the door closed behind him.

"It's such a nice day," I said, pulling his focus to me. "I packed a blanket in here. I was thinking you could take a break, and we could have a picnic."

"As charming as it sounds, and as much as I would love to, there's work I need to do. Taking on my father's responsibilities has been anything but smooth. I'm sorry, doll, another time."

I knew that, given it was a surprise, it might not happen, but part of me couldn't help but feel let down. I knew the kingdom came first, but I hadn't seen him in days. Immortals, we hadn't spent time together since the evening before Damien's arrival.

Looking up into his sleepy green eyes, I forced a smile. "At least enjoy the lunch."

He touched a finger to my lower lip. "Of course—"

"Prince Cole," called Master Guardian Saier. "I have important news about the rebellion in Vivinmoor."

Cole pivoted to face him. Seeing me, the Master Guardian stopped.

"Lady Eden, apologies. I didn't mean to interrupt." Clutching a hand to his chest, he half bowed. "I'll come back later."

"No interruption. Eden was leaving." He pressed one more kiss to my forehead, pitching his voice low. "I'll send for you soon so we can have dinner, I promise."

Smiling, I nodded and watched the two head down the hall to the square of light marking Cole's office. Setting the basket where I stood, I headed for the stairs, needing to get as far from there as I could.

***

I summoned Julien, saying nothing as he phased me to the square and then promptly disappeared. Falling against the wall of my building, I stared up at the statue of Faldone and Valentine gripping each other's right forearms, gleaming in the painfully bright sunlight I'd found beautiful an hour ago.

Why had I bothered? I knew Alliance Council meeting days were Cole's busiest time, but it'd been almost a month. My fingers itched to write another note, but I couldn't trust that way of processing any longer.

Once the nausea subsided enough, I passed through the wards, stopping just shy of being trampled by Council Member Violet, blindly running down the stairs as she dug around inside her handbag.

My thoughts spiraled immediately. What was she doing here? How had she gotten past the wards on the building? How did she know where I lived? Had she broken into my apartment? That would be against Council Law, but as a member, it probably didn't matter. First Rini and now her. Why was this happening? If this continued, I would have to move.

"Oh," she exclaimed, looking up. She smiled tightly. "If it isn't Solta's Sweetheart. What brings you here?"

"I was about to ask you that," I said, returning her fake smile. "I live here."

Sneering, she lifted her chin. "Couldn't find anywhere else to go? Had to get your claws in all three of them, huh?"

I gave her a quizzical look, not in the mood for this or her. "What are you talking about?"

"Violet," a voice called.

Both of us turned to see Damien quickly descending the steps. He'd traded his suit for a black V-neck shirt, sweatpants, and slippers. "You almost forgot this." In his hand was a dark red bag.

Of course—Damien. I felt a mixture of relief and disgust, realizing what that meant. What was with him bringing home every woman who wanted to destroy me?

He stopped a step away, looking between us, noting my presence with a raised eyebrow.

I peered at Violet from the corner of my eye, trying her best to hide how she gritted her teeth behind a toothless smile.

"Thank you," she mumbled, taking the bag.

"I'll see you—"

But before he finished and I could run away, Violet darted through the wards, swiped the Valentine Bracelet—a prized, simple silver band afforded to those of the Alliance Council, which allowed her to phase —and disappeared. Leaving Damien and me to stand alone together.

"She tries that all the time," he exhaled. "Always tries to leave something behind so she has a reason to return." He looked down at me. "What did I interrupt?"

Side-stepping him, I started up the steps. "Absolutely nothing, and I hope you got all of it. I'd prefer I didn't see her around here again."

He jogged up beside me. "What do you have against her?"

"The source Rini Rain uses for all her negative articles about me? Violet."

"Do you have evidence of that?"

"Besides the fact all the articles sound like gossip she spouts about me at high society events? Or that the articles always come out after an Alliance Council meeting? Next week's issue, I guarantee there will be something salacious about me."

"Fair conclusion. I didn't expect you back so soon. Did something happen?"

I traced my finger up a grain in the wood of the railing, wondering how far I could follow it. "He was busy. Master Guardian Saier came to him regarding something in Vivinmoor. Lunch was a silly idea. A free moment is non-existent when the Council is meeting. I know that."

As if feeling like he needed to say something, he responded gently, "It wasn't silly."

Something twisted inside my chest, making me pause for a moment. Of everything that day, of all the emotions of the last hour, his pity was what'd found its way past the gate of my brain.

"I can't believe you slept with her," I said, wanting to change the subject.

He snorted. "A recurring sentiment you have for me, but I didn't. She wanted to see my apartment. We saw each other what—thirty minutes ago? You think I fuck that fast?"

My cheeks warmed. "I meant at all."

He cocked his head. "Do I detect a trace of judgment? I'm not the biggest fan of Cole, but I don't judge you for your relationship with him."

"Cole doesn't try to ruin your reputation every chance he gets."

"He might if I threatened him in any way."

I barked a laugh. "I don't threaten Violet. There's nothing I have or do that she can't get easily."

"As my brother's Bidden, I can confirm you do."

Stopping in front of my door, I looked up at him. "What are you talking about?"

After a long moment of staring at me, he ran his fingers through his hair. "You don't know? I won't tell you—"

Sighing, I clasped the knob, feeling the magic tingle in my hand as it recognized me and unlocked. If he wouldn't, I knew no one else would. "Thanks for letting me know about another secret I'm not privy to. I accepted long ago that there is a lot I don't know and will never know about this family."

I started to slam the door when something stopped it. A black bedroom slipper. That had to hurt.

"You didn't let me finish. Clearly, my brother didn't want you to know their history. I won't tell you out here," he nodded conspiratorially to the door across the way where an elderly couple lived, "but if I could come inside."

Narrowing my eyes, I asked, "And why would you tell me?"

"Because I thought you knew, and it isn't fair for you not to know," he sighed, "and maybe it's a reach, but I also think of you as a friend."

Kicking off my flats, I let go of the door, grabbing a box of matches from the entryway table. "Fine, shoes off and not a word on my mess."

Socks gliding pleasantly along the worn wooden floor, I headed for the kitchen, striking matches and lighting candles along the way. The door creaked shut a moment later, the sound of Damien's slippers thudding against the wall, officially marking his presence in my home.

"It's small," he wondered aloud.

"Compared to the penthouse, sure, but it's all I need. Would you like something to drink?"

"A glass of water would be nice. And you've got me there. The penthouse is massive, but I've taken on a Facto to help manage it. Where's this mess I'm not supposed to comment on?"

I glanced across the counter at him, making sure they hadn't disappeared. He stood in front of one of the end tables, carefully stacked high with books, reaching halfway up his chest. "Right in front of you. Cole says all my books are a mess."

"Looks artistic to me." He picked up the one on top, a dark blue tome. The first in a series of twenty books covering the history of the Kingdom of Solta and its cities, Charph, Sorbis, Vivinmoor, and

Misundre. "You like history?" His cringe as he asked told me what he thought about it.

"I like to read everything, but I haven't read that one yet."

He set it back on the stack, crossing into the living room. "Allow me to save you the trouble. It and its nineteen parts are a very dry read."

A snap of his fingers and the fireplace came to life. Quickly realizing what he'd done, he looked at me. "I hope that was alright. It's a little chilly."

Amazed and jealous at the ease with which he manipulated magic, I didn't even care when he lit the fireplace on one of the hottest days of the year. Suddenly self-conscious, I glanced at my matches, nodding wordlessly.

"Actually, while I'm at it…" he started, sweeping his arms through the air. "Do you mind if I make some improvements?"

"Like what?" I called back from inside my cupboard.

"Not to sound mean, but your wards are a nightmare. Anyone who can get past the wards of your building could come in and out of here."

"I thought you came in to tell me a secret."

"Not a secret, a story, and good thing because," he motioned around him, "this isn't good for general security, let alone secret sharing."

Curious to see what he'd do, I shrugged, setting two glasses on the counter. "Do what you need to as long as I'm not going to owe you anything for it."

"Your payment to me will be my peace of mind."

The space between us became silent as we worked, him back straight and eyes closed, drawing magic and weaving it in his mind. And me filling water glasses. How I wished the roles were reversed. I tiptoed, a cup in each hand, into the living room. As quietly as I could, I set his cup in front of him on the table and curled up on the couch across him with my own.

It wasn't until I settled back that I noticed him watching. Clutching my free hand to my chest, I tried to breathe, grateful I had somehow managed to keep the water from sloshing everywhere. "What. In. The. Fuck."

"That's what I'm wondering, what is all the delicacy about?" he laughed.

"You were focused, doing magic. I didn't want to interrupt you."

Brows pulling together, he shook his head. "Magic isn't that fragile, nor is my focus."

I traced my thumb along the decorative pattern of the glass. "If you say so, it always feels elusive to me. Every time I've tried, if I lose focus for the slightest moment, my charm collapses. That's neither here nor there, though. Tell me this story."

Considering me for a moment, he leaned back, sighing. "Alright, well, we've all known each other since we were children—my older brothers and I and her and her siblings. The woman you see today is much the same as she was then: high-maintenance, stubborn, very confident about what she wants, and not someone who handles 'no' well, though she at least tries to hide it now. Either way, she adored Cole, used to fawn at his feet, and could often be found forcing him to participate in pretend Pledge ceremonies, back when that was what this city still did. That only got worse as we all got older."

My stomach constricted. "Did they sleep together?"

"I don't know, probably," he hedged, taking a sip, "but I do know she wanted to be his Bidden. As you're aware, even if Cole wanted her, he would have had to get the Council's blessing first. Cole's twentieth birthday and his first Bidding, she offered herself, very sure it would happen, and everyone but her parents gave a no. It was a sight to behold. The rejection."

For the first time ever, I felt bad for Violet. "Did he love her?"

Damien snorted. "I don't think so. I'm sure, if anything, she was fun. I don't think she loved him either. But all of this was to say you got what she wanted."

I took a long drink. "Why do you sleep with her?"

"Slept," he corrected and shrugged. "The sex was easy and decent."

I frowned. "But from the sound of it, you're her consolation prize."

He snorted. "That's okay with me. I've lost nothing from that."

Awed, I leaned forward. "So that's why you don't just give her what she wants."

"You mean a binding token and a horde of green-eyed, black-haired, demi-immortal children bearing my namesake?" Meeting my eyes, he shook his head. "No, I don't give her that because I have no interest in giving anyone that. It's not my style."

"That's sad. Your mother wouldn't want that."

"My mother didn't want me to leave Sorbis either, and yet." Scooting to the edge of the couch, he set his glass down, getting to his feet. "That was the story—I should go. I have some damage control I need to do in my home."

My hand shot out with a mind of its own, latching onto his forearm. Eyebrow raised, he looked down at my white-knuckled hand.

"Will you tell me more?" I asked.

"There's nothing more to say."

Desperation stained my words. "I mean about your family."

Studying me through narrowed eyes, he said, "My natural inclination is to say no, but since you're information-starved, and you're to be queen, I'll say yes, but within reason." A shadow flashed across his face. "There are some things I cannot tell you, as I'm sure you're aware."

I nodded assuredly. "Tell me what you're comfortable with—I'll take what you can give me."

He gently pried my grip from his arm. "You don't have to sound so eager. When possible, I've always disagreed with my father's rule against sharing the past."

I stared at the spot where he'd been, remembering how Lupine used to tell me it was the only rule even she agreed with. Something Quincy had never been bothered by, but he probably wasn't part of the exclusion. "I've never understood it either."

There was shuffling as he worked on his slippers. "On a lighter note, your wards should be solid now, but if you experience any issues, let me know."

I looked to where he stood at the door, hand poised on the doorknob. "Thank you, Damien."

"Before I go..." Running his free hand through his hair, he took a deep breath, green eyes meeting mine in earnest. "I was wondering, would you like me to teach you magic?"

For once, it was my brain screaming 'yes,' but that only lasted as long as it took for the questions to come in. What would Cole think of that? He may have made him his acting second for the time being, but I knew it didn't mean Cole liked. Just like Damien didn't. A relationship of blood and respect. He didn't even like me hanging with Q. Not to mention the way his grip on me hardened defensively every time Damien came around.

I inhaled. I was getting away from myself. He'd asked me a question. Magic. Immortals, I wanted to say yes, so why couldn't I? "I..."

A raised hand stopped me. "It's alright. You don't have to answer me now. Something to think about." Then, as if he knew where my mind had gone... "It'd be our secret, of course."

CHAPTER THIRTEEN

15.EIGHT.4004

Dabbing my finger in a pot of cream-colored makeup, I erased the evidence of last night's poor sleep from under my gold eyes. I'd run out of darkness elixir the night before, and—as if my grieving during the day hadn't been enough—a dream of the night of Lupine's death came at me full force.

Slipping on my jeans and a sleeveless pink blouse, I tied my hair back in a low ponytail and headed out the door. At least I didn't feel as tired as I looked.

The heat of the morning hit me like a slap in the face, promising a sweltering day. Thirteen more days and the heat wave would be over, the weather shifting into cooler temperatures. I'd miss the warmth, but not the sweat collecting in areas I'd rather it didn't.

Entering the square, I expected to see a Runner or two in their black and green uniform, searching for early morning business, but it was only me and a lone figure on a bench.

Damien leaned forward, elbows on his knees, reeking of cigarettes. I thought he might be drunk, but when his head lifted to look up at the statue of his ancestors, his green eyes were clear. Never hot enough for him, he wore a heavy wool coat, a black turtleneck, and dark blue jeans.

An early morning breeze cutting through the streets—feeling

refreshing on my skin—made him shiver.

"Looking at you always makes me sweat," I said.

Startled, he looked right at me and smiled. "And your exposed arms and shoulders turn my blood into ice." He sat up straight. "You're up early."

Hearing the question in his voice, I said, "I couldn't get back to sleep, and I have extra work this morning, so I figured I'd get an early start. What's your excuse?"

His gaze fell to his clasped hands. "I never went to bed, and I couldn't sleep right now if I wanted to."

I stepped closer. "Something wrong?"

He shook his head. "I've kept myself so busy recently, and this morning, walking back from Vermillion, it was so quiet and everything…slowed, and there she was in my head."

I knew who she was and exactly what he meant. I'd idled away the last several days alone in my apartment, and they had been one never-ending window of time in which I'd been desperate to do anything but think about the hole in my heart Lupine's absence had caused. At least I'd finally stopped crying…for the most part.

"You're welcome to join me. Selene's House can always use volunteers. It probably won't be very exciting to you, but it'd be a good distraction." Offering him what I'd craved.

He looked up at me, considering, and then back to our building. "Isa will wonder where I am."

"Isa?"

"My Facto." He stood, brushing off his pants. "Alright, I'm in." Hands in his pockets, he started in the direction of the farmlands.

I jogged to catch up. "Do you want to go tell her? I can wait."

"I probably should," he sighed, "but I don't know, Eden. If I'd wanted to go home, I wouldn't have stopped and sat on that bench."

My heart twisted in my chest. "It's going to be okay, Damien, and if you ever need to talk, you know where I live."

He peered down at me. "How about you start distracting me?"

Heat stung my cheeks. "Volunteering is supposed to be the distraction, not me."

"Why can't it be both? Why don't you tell me why you work here?" He motioned down the road to where the taller buildings of the outer city were beginning to shift into the single-story buildings and trees of the farmlands. "If you'd only wanted to work, Cole could have easily put you in something like teaching in the inner city."

"That's a story."

He raised an eyebrow. "I have all the time in the world to listen."

I sighed, gathering my thoughts. "When people talk about Roan's War, it's always about the horrors and death, and it's important to talk about them—it's important nothing like that ever happens again—but there's hardly ever talk about the lasting damage, and if there is, it's in passing." I thought about the picture of my mother holding me as a baby on my nightstand and the father I knew nothing of. "Did you know the answer the Alliance Council gave in response to the orphan influx following the war was forbidding the Eternal Pledge and a minute expansion of the community budget? No effort to help children with trauma or help them get their footing when they've reached adulthood. Following the war, many of the older kids had children quickly and fell into bad situations, leaving their children behind as they had been. Some of them got lucky, were blessed with desirable abilities, and recognized by the Academy, but most, in addition to having no family or money, did not. Once they age out, they can't find work and wind up at the pleasure houses. The average life expectancy for them is twenty-three. People don't want to see their tax money go to these children or adults. They would rather see them gone. Which is really sad, and it could have been my life."

"Your abilities would have saved you from that life," Damien interjected. "Being a healer of any ability is quite impressive."

We passed the last building marking the outer city.

"Maybe," I agreed, "but I could have easily been magicless. Magic inheritance is becoming increasingly rare, and even when it occurs, many individuals are manifesting weaker traits. I could have easily been any one of the men or women who aged out and had to resort to a pleasure house for the whims of high society for survival. The only thing that kept me from that life was a chance connection and your mother's kindness."

Having laid it all out, I inhaled a fresh breath. "There's your answer."

"That was a really long-winded way of saying you see yourself in these children."

"I warned you." I nudged his side. "Tell me it would have meant anything to you, though, if I'd said it so simply."

"It wouldn't have. It's very endearing of you."

I dared a glance at him, trying to ascertain if he was being sarcastic, but his face was unreadable. I wanted to say something, but noticing where we were, I left it alone. "The first day of every other work week, Rho and I stop at shops around the community to see if there's anything unsellable but salvageable for the orphans. This is my first stop, but if you want to go on—"

Damien cut me off, his tall frame falling against the side of the building. "I'll wait."

Inhaling the smell of hot sugar, I dipped into the candy shop. The hardwood floors groaning under my feet alerted the man—dressed in a white apron and a white shirt—behind the counter to my presence. He straightened up so quickly from where he scribbled on a pad of paper that he came close to hitting the sign hanging over the counter.

Isaac beamed, pushing a stray strand of his flaxen hair to the side of his face. "Good morning, Eden. How can I help you today?"

"Hi, Isaac," I smiled. "I'm—"

Isaac's eyes moved beyond me and widened, his mouth falling open. I followed his gaze to the doorway, where Damien stood watching us curiously.

No longer a casual observer, Damien stepped up beside me, hand extended. "Damien Valentine."

Isaac's eyes grew a little wider. "Immortals. Dad," he screamed. "Dad, come quick."

Knowing how some of the people of the farmlands felt about the royal family—though I'd never suspected Isaac or his father were that way—I was one second away from suggesting leaving to Damien when Isaac took Damien's hand in both of his. "It's an honor. Thank you for everything you did. My father—he worked alongside you in the war. Dad!" He turned to yell again. "Please wait here—he'd love to see you."

Shifting on his feet, Damien smiled politely, his free hand fumbling for something in his pants pocket. "Absolutely. Maybe you can get me two slices of maple fudge while we wait for him." He nodded at me. "I can pay for hers as well."

"No—" I started, but got cut off by Issac's excitement.

"Here, you don't pay. Anything you want is on the house."

Whoa.

Emerging from the beaded curtain behind the counter was a middle-aged man I recognized as Isaac's father, gnarled hands clutching a wooden cane and hobbling a little worse than he had the last time I'd seen him.

The man brightened at the sight of Damien, taking his proffered hand and pulling him into a hug. "Immortals, I never thought I'd get to see you again. Do you remember me? You spearheaded my unit when Roan's army attacked the city's southern wall."

Running a hand through his hair, Damien smiled and nodded. "Of course, I remember you. Joseph, right?" I tried not to show my surprise that he knew his name when I didn't. "You were fucking crazy. I've never seen a non-mage charge at Assault Demons like you did."

Joseph laughed, clutching his stomach with one hand and patting his leg with the other. "That craziness is how I got this…"

Trying to be respectful, I tuned out the conversation, half watching Isaac fill the donation box, half watching the people on the street through the shop window.

A couple of minutes later, Isaac set two boxes on the counter—the one for me almost too big to carry.

"Thank you, Isaac."

He didn't hear me, eyes trained on his father and Damien, murmuring amongst themselves. I tapped Damien on the shoulder.

"I'm sorry to interrupt," I said. Looking between the two, it was hard to believe they'd fought together. Joseph was visually old enough to be Damien's father. Such was being a demi. "I'm fine if you want to stay here and talk, but I need to go if I want to make it to the orphanage in time."

A trace of panic momentarily entered his eyes. "No, I'm coming." He glanced back at Joseph. "It was nice to see you again. I'll come back soon to catch up more."

Joseph's milky gray eyes warmed. "I would love that. You're welcome here anytime."

Grabbing the box from the counter, I hauled it outside. Struggling under the weight, I barely made it to a bench out of sight of the bakery before I had to stop.

Damien came up beside me. "Do you need help?"

"No, it's just a little more than normal." A lot more. I lifted the lid and looked inside, stumbling back into a light pole. Almost collapsing in the street if it weren't for a solid hand steadying me.

"Everything okay?"

I stared at him in awe. "There's like a thousand pieces of candy."

"That's good news, isn't it?" He tucked the lid back in place and handed me his smaller box of fudge, picking up my box like it was nothing. "Where to next?"

***

"Shouldn't we be getting to the orphanage now?" Damien asked. Now carrying a bag of fruit and two bags of slightly used clothes in addition to the candy. I'd offered to help, but his ego refused to let me, and the former Devotee had actually broken a sweat. "The children don't need art."

We stood outside of Spectrum Sensations—a house turned into an art gallery with a room dedicated to every color.

I leapt up the single step to the door. "How untrue. Everyone needs art." As I opened the door for him, a tinkling bell announced our entrance. "We have a couple of minutes, and I wanted to show you something."

In the small foyer, there were three doorways, each covered by a black curtain, and a sign directing customers to begin their journey through the one on the left.

"You can leave all that there," I said, motioning to an unoccupied chair in the corner. "The owner knows me."

"They've all known you," he grumbled.

"And you as well." *Reincimmo.*

To that, he had no retort.

Pushing aside the black curtain, I stepped into the first room, the biggest and my favorite. Dedicated to green.

Green bowls, plates, cups, vases, and sculptures. Swirling and striped. Clear and opaque. Paintings in various styles depicting the Northern Forest or the Faldonian Mountains adorned the walls.

Damien's eyes scanned the rows of delicate glass creations.

"It's all handmade by the owner, Oona," I said, "or her late father, whom she took over for after he passed."

Motioning him along, I cut down an aisle and headed for the center of the room where a tree with a thick clay trunk and a rich canopy of tiny green glass leaves—gleaming like they were emeralds lit from within—sat.

"This is what I wanted to show you."

Damien reached out a hand toward it. "It's incredible."

"Don't touch it." Stopping his hand with mine, I pointed to the sign at its base. "I almost did the same thing the first time I came in, and Oona almost took my hand."

"Back again," a throaty voice laughed, "and with a guest, I see."

We both turned. Oona stood in the next doorway wearing a dark gray dress. The wrinkles fanning out from her eyes had tan lines from smiling in the sun. Looking between Damien and me, she smiled, making them disappear.

"Oona, this is—"

"Damien Valentine," she laughed, cutting me off. "I wasn't always a shut-in, my girl."

"It's lovely to meet you," Damien said, stepping forward to offer her his hand.

"The honor is mine, Reincimmo. Welcome to my gallery," she said, taking his hand in both of hers and shaking it. "I heard about your return with the rest of the city." She reached one gnarled hand up to pat his cheek. "Take after your mother, you do. I'm happy to see it. Your father's such an ugly man. In more ways than one. Don't need any more of his ilk running around. That brother of yours is more than enough." She glanced at me. "Nothing personal, my girl."

While I wasn't offended, I was surprised. Not many people would have the nerve to make such a comment regarding the king and his heir, even in the privacy of their own home. Let alone in the presence of a royal family member.

I wasn't the only one in shock either. Damien, who stared down at her speechless, burst out laughing. "I like you."

Immortals, both of them were treasonous.

"You know I had to show him this masterpiece," I said quickly, before this conversation could go further. I motioned toward the model of the Eternal Tree.

"Ah, yes." Tossing her graying braid over her shoulder, she stepped closer. "My father sculpted that. He was invited to your family's home once to do a portrait. Saw the tree from one of the windows and convinced himself he had to capture it. Drove himself half mad trying, particularly with the leaves. He claimed they moved as if each had a life of its own," she sighed. "He was never content with the result, though. Not sure what he expected, trying to recreate something the Immortal Valentine himself created."

"That's a shame. I think he captured it well," Damien said.

Oona patted his shoulder. "Thank you, son. It would have meant a great deal to him to hear you say that. How long are you two going to be looking around?"

Opening my mouth, a clock chimed somewhere in the home, cutting me off and announcing the end of our excursion.

Oona laughed knowingly as I reached for the bag at my side, shuffling around until I found four loose soltans.

She waved me away. "Girl, how many times have I told you I have no need for your money?"

Grabbing her flailing hand, I pressed them into her palm. "You might not need or want it, but I want to support what you do. I'll be back soon. Keep making beautiful things."

***

"Damien Valentine in Selene's House. At the coloring table with a bunch of five-year-olds. I never thought I would see it," Rho said. She held out my bag and Damien's box of fudge to me. "I also can't believe one appearance from him blew all our efforts out of the water."

I nodded my head, recalling how the community had flocked to him. "It was crazy, Rho. They loved him."

Matron Kate swept in to gather up the children. Knowing what came for them, they all jumped up, leaving Damien suddenly alone and surprised at the small table.

"It's time for a nap, you crazy animals," Matron Kate said. She snatched up one who hadn't managed a fast enough getaway and tickled his stomach, eliciting a giggle.

With a gentle tug, the ribbon tying my hair back came loose. I looked at Rho as she dropped it into my bag. "I'll clean up. You head out and take him with you. I can't stand to hear the older girls giggle over him any longer." Clasping my shoulder, she whispered in my ear. "Check your bag when you get home.

Grateful, I looked into her lilac eyes. "I'll pay you tomorrow."

Flipping her pink hair over her shoulder, she waved me away. "Just get those circles under control. You're worrying me."

Cutting through the lingering chaos, I made my way to where Damien sat, eyeing a crayon drawing one of the kids had created.

When I was close, he met my gaze, holding it up for me. A figure with a straight red line for a mouth and black squiggly hair jutting out in every direction from beneath a golden crown stared out at me from two green dot eyes. Gray clouds dotted the space over his head, several complete with blue raindrops and yellow lightning bolts.

"Is this what they think of me? Or is this Cole?" he asked, affronted.

Biting my lip, I fought a burst of laughter. "That's brilliant. What did you say to them?"

His expression fell flat. "Nothing. I complimented their coloring." He held up another image of a woman with dark brown hair, orange eyes, and pink cheeks, wearing a white apron and a pink blouse, similar to the one I was currently wearing. Red hearts surrounded the figure, a yellow sun hovering over her head. "They adore you."

I patted his head. "Don't take it too hard. I've known them since they were babies. I came to tell you it's the end of my day, and I'm heading home. Once again, you're welcome to stay if you like, but I didn't want you to think I'd abandoned you."

"No, I should be heading back. I've left Isa without word long enough." The wooden legs of the child-sized chair screeched along the tile floor as he pushed back. Snatching up the crayon drawings, he folded them neatly inside one another and nodded toward the door. "These should soften her anger."

***

"Thank you for letting me join you today," Damien said. "That was nice."

"Even the beginning?" I peeked at him from the corner of my eye. "Maybe it was my perception, but you seemed a little uncomfortable around all of the people who wanted to thank you and reminisce."

We stopped on my landing. The orange light of the sun filtered in through the stairwell window at my back, coming in at an angle, casting us half in shadow. His eyes shifted back the way we'd come.

"There's nothing happy for me in reminiscing over that time. I understand why they do, but..." He shook his head. "The thanking me gets to me as well. Would you believe me if I told you I don't think of myself as the hero they all do? I did my job. They all see me as a Prince of Solta fighting amongst the people. To me, I was anyone fighting for the kingdom's sovereignty."

Having not expected that answer, I was stunned silent, an ache creeping into my chest. I knew exactly where he was coming from—albeit on a much smaller scale—feeling uncomfortable whenever someone thanked me for my efforts at Selene's House.

Mistaking my silence, he smiled to himself, returning his gaze to me. "Sorry about that. You know there's something I've been waiting to say to you all day—the moment you stepped into the candy shop, that Isaac's desire exploded like a poorly woven charm," he laughed under his breath.

Leave it to Damien to go from heartfelt to joking in the span of a second. "What?"

"Come now, you can't tell me you didn't at least know he was interested in you. Cole would love to know about him."

I lobbed the back of my hand against his chest. "Don't you go spreading gossip."

"No need for violence. I was teasing." Feigning hurt, he tapped me on the nose. "Have a good night, Eden."

CHAPTER FOURTEEN

28.EIGHT.4004

"Eden!"

Curled up on the couch in Cole's office, lost in the pages of my book, I jumped out of my skin at the sudden exclamation of my name. Two seconds later, Quincy waltzed in wearing a white short-sleeved shirt and tan shorts. Using both hands, he moved his hair away from his face, the diamond studs in his ears glittering in the sunlight.

"Why did I know this is where I'd find you hiding?" he exclaimed. "Why aren't you ready?"

Fingering the next page, I raised an eyebrow.

Face falling flat, he swatted my knee. "Don't give me that look! It's jexie season. We almost missed it. Today is the last day. Now go get ready."

"You'll have to go without—"

He held up a finger, silencing me. "You have no excuse. All you're doing is reading. You denied me the night out, you won't deny me this. I'll call in my owe if I must. We've never missed jexie season."

We almost had…

I sat up. "What am I supposed to do about the Protectors waiting for me outside?"

He snorted, waving me away. "That's what you're worried about? I'll take care of them. You know the spiral staircase in the Hidden

Halls leading to the back exit?"

I rolled my eyes. "You know I do."

"Meet me at the bottom of those at eleven—that's in thirty minutes." Bouncing on his feet, he snatched my book away, backing for the door. "Go get ready."

"Fine, but I work tomorrow, so you have to take me home tonight."

He pointed a finger at me. "Deal." He held the book over his head. "You'll get this back when we're at the jexies."

***

Knowing Quincy's habits, I grumbled aloud to myself as I wound down the staircase. "Q, I swear you better be at the bottom of these stairs…"

Expecting no one, but not expecting anyone but Q, I halted on the last stair.

Damien leaned against the crumbling brick, arms crossed over his chest, looking up at me. He wore a short-sleeved black shirt and black swim trunks, a bag draped over his shoulder. Not seeing him dressed for winter was bizarre.

In only a cover-up and a dark purple two-piece swimsuit, I shuffled the towel I clutched to cover my chest and stomach. "Don't mind my asking, but what are you doing here?"

"Waiting for Quincy, same as you."

"Quincy didn't mention you were coming, or I would have worn something more…appropriate."

Damien rolled his eyes. "I'm not bothered. In Misundre, women don't wear clothes to swim. You'd be considered a prude there."

Grasping the towel a little tighter, I huffed a laugh, looking at my feet. "Even if that's true, we aren't in Misundre. Cole would be upset if he knew I was dressed like this." Around you, I silently added. He didn't even like it around Q.

"I doubt Quincy will tell him, and I know I won't. If he doesn't know, he can't get upset." He paused and added, "How are Cole and my father?"

Thinking I'd heard something, I glanced back up the stairs. "I don't know. I haven't really seen either of them. Since his return to the manor, your father has kept to his apartments in the northern wing of the house, and only a handful of people have been allowed to enter that area. Cole has been busy as acting king. I see him briefly at breakfast when I'm here, and he seems fine. You've probably seen him more than I."

"And how are you?"

I shrugged a shoulder, taking the last step. "I'm fine. Looking forward to going home today. Being here isn't the easiest."

Before I could ask him the same, a voice called, "Eden? Damien?"

"We're both here," I growled. "You're late."

Q rounded the corner, sans shirt in a pair of dark blue swimming trunks, triumphantly holding up a white wicker basket topped with a cream-colored blanket. "Because I was getting us food. Food is important, you know. Let's go."

Without slowing, he surged past me, out of the Hidden Halls, through the wooden backdoors, and into the light of day. The blanket flew off the top of the basket, catching and opening in the wind.

Groaning, I bent to collect it. "Quincy, slow down. You're leaving a trail."

"How about you move faster!" he called back. "We only have two hours before the illusion I wove wears off."

A step behind me, Damien stopped in his tracks, staring hard after his brother, gesturing to the manor. "You said we were going swimming."

That explained his agreement to this—he thought we were

swimming in the indoor pool.

Halfway to the tree line, Q leapt up into a spin, laughing. "Swimming in Five River. We're off to see the jexies."

Damien's mouth pressed into a hard line, looking like a stern dad.

Jogging to catch Q, I grinned back at him. "Didn't you say no one should walk the River Trail alone?"

A groan was my response as his footfall joined ours.

At the mouth of the path and the end of the manor's wards, Q pulled me to him, grinning wildly at his brother. "See you there."

I blinked, and we were standing in a small, shaded grassy section of the riverbank. The trees surrounding us on three sides kept the wind at bay, leaving the warm summer day to stand on its own. And it was nice. Sunlight filtered through the canopy of leaves overhead. The only sounds were the roar of the rapids up the way and the soft, rippling birdsong.

Abandoning the basket, Quincy ran nimbly across the rocks, making for where they abruptly converged with rushing dark blue water.

Out of nowhere, Damien appeared, watching as Q dove in, the splash sending the birds flapping and squawking from the trees.

Dropping my towel, I shook out the blanket and threw it up in the air, letting it fan out and come down. Smoothing it out, I set my bag and the basket at the foot.

"How is he always this excited?" Damien mumbled.

I made the mistake of looking at him as he hooked his fingers under the hem of his shirt and tugged up in one quick stroke. His chest, his arms, his abdomen—every inch of him was suntanned, carved muscle defined from decades of training and unfailing youth.

Fingering the key between my breasts, I looked away. In any direction but his.

Laughing, he stuffed his shirt into his bag and tossed it aside. "It's okay to look, Eden. I won't tell Cole."

I rolled my eyes and headed for the water.

Ahead, Quincy emerged, screaming for us to hurry in, grinning from ear to ear as he dove down into the water once more.

"Race you?" Damien challenged me, excitement creeping into his voice. Taking my silence as compliance, he leapt forward, traversing the rocks as adeptly as Q.

I watched him from my place on the shore, marveling at the way the muscles in his back danced and his clean dive into the water. Tossing my cover-up back to the blanket, I stepped into the shallow water, sank my feet into the soft sand between the rocks, and sat.

Resurfacing a moment later, he whipped his hair out of his face, clearing his eyes as he treaded water. "What are you doing?"

I ran a hand along one of the sleek black rocks nearby. "I can't swim."

"What?" he yelled, sending off any remaining birds.

"I can float. Kind of."

"You can't be serious. No one ever taught you?" He shot a look downstream to Q, who bobbed at the surface briefly and descended again.

I kicked the water half-heartedly. "Several have tried, but it's never stuck. My last teacher said my attempt had all the grace of a floundering cat." Closing my eyes, I held my face to the sky. "It would seem I was born to be land-bound."

"That's the mindset of someone who's had a bad teacher."

I smiled, the sun warming me. "What if I said you just decried the acting king of Solta?"

"My opinion wouldn't change, nor my words. If anything, you'd affirm them. My brother has never had patience, especially when it'd suit him."

Water sprayed me, snapping me from my reverie. I stared in horror as Damien plunked down in the grass beside me. "What are you doing?"

He cast a glance over his shoulder, back toward the blanket, waving to the woods around us and across the way. "After our walk in the woods, I'm surprised you even ask. I'm not going to leave you here alone. I can't believe Quincy does."

"I don't mind, I'll be fine."

"You know, I don't believe that you don't mind. Who enjoys being left out?"

I folded my arms over my chest. "You're not worried about Q."

"Why would I be when he clearly has an affinity for weaving charms strong enough to fool everyone in the manor for a couple of hours, and he can phase. He can handle himself."

A spark of rage heated my stomach. "You really like to assume I can't handle myself."

Leaning forward, he ran a hand over the water's surface, flashing a black sun tattoo on the inside of his wrist. The mark of proficiency Scholars received. "You struggle to perform the most basic charm, and to my knowledge, you have no combat training." He stopped, shaking his head. "Nothing's going to happen to you on my watch."

"Should I call you Protector Damien now?" I said curtly.

He exhaled his patience. "For future reference, my brother never intimidates me. He is my brother before he's royalty."

"The Alliance Council wouldn't agree."

"Another body of power that doesn't intimidate me."

I stared at the back of his stubborn head. "You're really not going to look at the jexies?"

"I've seen them."

"Suit yourself." Reclining into the soft bank of grass behind me, I closed my eyes, coaxing my thoughts to think of nothing once again, but charged by Damien's words, they clung to jexies.

Jexies, the colorful star-shaped creature found off the coast near Misundre, which once a year fought the streams of the river to come here for an unidentified reason. Every year since we were nine, Q and I had come here, and every year I'd watched from this rock, living secondhand on his stories once he'd grown tired of swimming.

"You're not wrong," I said, voice low. "I would like to see them, but I've come to accept there are a lot of things I'll never get to see or do."

Damien cleared his throat. "What does that mean?"

"I think it's clear what that means. There's no room for doing anything but what is expected of me if, at the end of my journey as Cole's Bidden, I say yes to being queen."

"If?"

I cracked my eyes to look at him. Wondering if I'd said too much. Damien wore a halo of sunlight around his head, wavy black hair dripping water down his face. His brow had hardened, mouth parted on the word.

I exhaled a breath. "You know what I meant."

"Guys, what are you doing?" Quincy called. "The jexies won't last forever, and there are purple ones this year."

"Did you know Eden couldn't swim?" Damien said. Sounding like the stern father he'd looked like earlier.

" I-uh yeah," Q said sheepishly.

"And you just leave her here while you explore?"

Sitting up, I glared at Damien and then out to Quincy, who offered me a silent apology. I slapped Damien's lower back lightly. "I told you it's fine."

He shook his head, eyes narrowed. *Liar.*

I raised my eyebrows in challenge. *So?*

"Why don't we all eat?" I suggested. "You hungry, Q?" Clapping my hands, I stood, dumping a load of water in Damien's lap as I pulled my feet out. "Oh," I pressed a hand to my chest, "how clumsy of me."

Damien flicked water after me, letting me know he knew it wasn't ungainliness.

Water splashing on each step, Q said, "I could eat."

Plopping down in the sliver of sunlight at the foot of the blanket, I smiled sweetly and handed Damien his towel. Wrapping it around his waist, he took a seat at the top in the shade and tossed Q his towel as he returned to land. Q did a quick wipe down of his hair and draped it across his shoulders, dropping beside his brother, still soaking wet.

"The jexies actually weren't that great," Q said conciliatorily. "The purple ones were neat, but nothing to write home about."

I gave him a reassuring smile. "I'm sorry to hear that."

Digging through the basket, Q passed out cloth-wrapped sandwiches, oranges, cookies, and canteens of water. I took one of each, taking two delicate bites of the oatmeal raisin cookie so Q couldn't accuse me of not eating, and set the rest aside, closing my eyes and reclining on the blanket, my sun-warmed hair fanning out around me.

With Quincy there, the conversation turned easy, Q carrying the load of it, telling me story after story about his time with a girl named Halle, whom he'd met on one of the many nights out he'd had with Damien and Grayden, and Damien listening in silence.

Nodding and responding as needed, I snuck glances at the water. Wondering if this was the year that, if I went to the edge and stuck my head under, I might be able to see them.

Shifting onto my side, I propped myself up on my elbow and looked at Q. "That's wonderful. She sounds like a great match for you."

A blush staining his olive-toned cheeks, Quincy swallowed and dropped his gaze. "I think so, too. I'm going to see her after this. I told her I'd meet her at one."

I shrank back. He couldn't be serious. "You realize we've been here at least an hour, and you were late. If it isn't already, it's almost one."

Dropping his cookie in the grass, he leapt to his feet. "What? I have to go. I'm going to be late."

"Quincy, wait—you agreed to take me home today."

"I can take you home," Damien offered.

Quincy snapped his finger and took one step back. "Thank you, brother. I owe you." And he disappeared, leaving me alone with Damien before I had a chance to protest.

Sighing, I sat up, tossing my untouched food and his half-eaten cookie into the basket. Usually, I let these moments go, but today I seethed.

"We don't have to go now," Damien said gently.

I fished a light blue dress from my bag and tugged it over my head. Untucking my hair, I said, "There's no point staying."

Damien leaned closer. "I can show you the jexies."

CHAPTER FIFTEEN

28.EIGHT.4004

Unclasping my key necklace, I set it atop my bag and met Damien on the rocks.

"Follow me," he said.

My stomach churning, I did. Immortals help me. I wanted to see the Jexies.

He took the rocks in much the same way he had before, but slower for me. Each step put the stones a little deeper and brought the water a touch higher up my body, depositing a drop of fear into my eager heart. *There's nothing to fear*, I reminded myself, breathing through the worry. Further out, the rocks turned jagged, the edges cutting into the soft skin of my feet, and as much as it hurt, the thrill kept me going. I was doing it—I was going to see the jexies.

"We're almost to the drop," he called back.

Nodding, I kept my eyes on my step, focusing on my breathing and not the coursing water ahead.

Damien walked right off the rocks, unfazed as he sank to the sandy ledge, the water rushing up to his chest.

My heart beat a little faster. I'd never gone further than this, never dared the ledge—a two-foot section of earth before a near-vertical drop. Two steps away and it'd either be swim, or sink—my head well under the water's cool surface before my feet found earth again.

Sitting on the last rock, I sucked in a sharp breath. The cold water rushed up to my breast, momentarily paralyzing me as it licked at my sun-warmed skin.

Humor glossed Damien's green eyes.

"What?" I growled.

He smiled smugly. "You look like I've felt every day since I arrived. Who's the baby now?"

I sent a splash of water his way, hitting him in the face.

Laughing, he wiped it away. "This is how you reward my taking you to see the jexies?"

I pushed off the rock onto my feet, the water hungrily lapping at my collarbone. The faint tug of the current pulled at me. "I'll determine how I reward you after seeing them."

He lowered himself before me, sending the water up to his neck. "This'll work best if you wrap your legs around my waist and your arms around my chest."

Heat bloomed along my skin. "You want me to do what?"

He tossed a glance over his shoulder and, seeing my trepidation, straightened up. "How did you think this was going to work?"

I pressed a hand to my stomach, hoping to quell the stirring. The thought of trying to learn to swim again had been enough. This was too much. "I thought with all your talk of having a bad teacher, you might teach me."

Angling his body to get a better look at me, he said, "I have no problem teaching you to swim, but that's not going to happen today."

"Is this some kind of ploy?"

Both hands shot up defensively, accidentally flicking water on me. "I was just trying to be kind. If you're uncomfortable, we'll go back and I'll take you home. We can start swimming lessons whenever you want. There's always next year to see the jexies."

I looked from him to the dark water and back. There wouldn't be a next year if I said yes to Cole.

I swallowed, hoping to drown the butterflies in my stomach. "I'm sorry." I reached for my key necklace, only to remember I'd taken it off. "Please get back into position." Sucking in a breath, I asked, "So, I'll be holding on to you while you swim?"

Damien lowered himself once more. "That was the idea."

Nodding, I let the breath go. Staring at his tan back under the surface of the blue water, I waded closer, noticing white, hair-thin scars running across his left shoulder.

My fingers so happened to slip right along the four streaks. I didn't spare a second to wonder what might have made them, as molding myself against his back, the number one priority became ignoring the heat of his muscled flesh pressing into my breast, stomach, and all the places our lower halves met. The scent of cool, crisp water, sandalwood, and cedar stirred around me.

"I feel like a child," I sighed.

Chuckling, he cocked his head, warm breath coasting over my hand as he said, "You weigh as much as one."

I bowed my head, his hair brushing my cheek. "I can't do your teasing right now, Damien."

"Relax, Eden. Breathe. Enjoy the ride. I'll be doing all the work, and don't mind me, but this," he started, peeling each hand gently from his shoulder and maneuvering it, palm flat, against his firm pectorals, "will be a lot better, and you can tap my chest if you get uneasy.

Already uneasy, I nodded my head against him.

"I'm going to leave the ledge and tread water. Are you ready?"

I nodded again.

The spring forward made my stomach drop. Where there had been ground—security, now there was Damien and a whole lot of nothing and water rushing over us. Reflexively, I wrapped my legs around Damien's waist, bringing us impossibly closer together. If he dropped me right now, I wasn't sure if I'd make it back.

That was all I could think as we started to sink. Cold water rushed up to my chin, moving faster than the sense of regret befalling me. I buried my face into his neck, contemplating an attempt for the rocks when the water settled around us.

The sinuous movement of his legs pushing the water held us steady. We were treading water. We were okay. It was okay.

"How are you feeling?" he asked.

"Fine," I squeaked, ignoring the pound of my heartbeat. We were so close together, he could probably feel it.

"Could you ease your grip a little, then? Your nails are sharp."

"Sorry," I whispered, flattening my hands. "I got…scared."

"That we'd drown?" His tone was half-teasing, half-affronted. "Would you really have come out here with me if you didn't think I could sustain us both?"

"No," I admitted. Realizing how ridiculous my fear had been.

"Then relax. I'm about to go under. Get ready to take a breath, and remember to tap my chest if you need to come back up."

Preparing, I squeezed him tighter. His chest dipped forward, his legs starting to kick. Sucking in a deep breath, I embraced the feel of the cold water—on my face, in my eyes, rushing into my hair—as we went under.

Below the surface, everything became calm, the birdsong in the valley above now a whisper.

Damien's arms made sweeping motions, parting the water, as his feet propelled us out and down, fighting the pressure trying to force us back up.

He stopped pulling us downward and patted my hand, motioning to something below.

We were only halfway there, but there they were, dancing around and stirring up sand, jexies in every shade of the rainbow. Glowing like suns the size of my palm.

When we were close enough to reach out and touch the floor, he did, but reaching toward the jexies. Three—a red, a green, and a blue—leapt for him. Brushing and skirting around his hand.

Holding tighter to him with my left hand, I reached to do as he had, but suddenly, we shot up, and it was all I could do to regain my hold on his chest. The water carried us up to the surface with little effort.

"What was that about?" I gasped. My lungs drank in the fresh air. "I wanted to touch one too."

Chest rising and falling quickly under my hands, he said, "You took too long, and I needed air."

"I thought demi-immortals were indefatigable."

He laughed breathlessly. "That would be the immortals, and I'm sure even they had limits. Give me a minute."

We floated there, pressed close to one another as the birds flew about overhead. With each breath he took, I became more aware of how solid his chest felt. The urge to run my hands along the other planes of his chest, I'd noted earlier, matched the awareness.

What was wrong with me?

I cleared my throat. "Are you finished yet?"

"Eden, you're relentless." A fact he sounded amused by. "Take a breath and remember to hold on tight."

I did, and as my chest finished inflated against his back, he dove. The second trip did nothing for my awareness. Moving faster than he had before, my mind shifted to wonder and admiration at how sinuously the muscles in his back and arms moved.

Reaching the bottom once more, my gratitude for the distraction of the jexies was unparalleled. I reached out my hand once more, and one of them, a purple jexie—floating amidst a flock of yellow—popped up, swimming toward me.

Testing me, it rubbed one of its slippery, soft appendages affectionately along my hand. A spark of light bloomed in my heart as it wrapped itself around my finger in an embrace, only letting go when Damien started his rise again, doing a little flourish as it leapt away, disappearing down the river.

We made the trip four more times, which is all my body would allow. I may not have been doing the swimming, but the diving was making my head spin. I made the most of each trip, holding my hand out to the jexies and watching them flock and dance around me, their squishy arms brushing along my skin.

Feeling nauseous, I tapped his chest as we surfaced. "That's enough."

He whipped his hair back out of his face, spraying me. "Are you sure?"

I nodded, fighting the urge to rest my chin on his shoulder. "Thank you for this. It was incredible."

Sweeping out his arms and kicking his feet gently, we closed in on the rocks. "It was my pleasure. Next year, once I'm done with you, you'll be able to swim to them yourself."

There was such a sense of pride in his words that I couldn't help but smile.

He hooked the ledge and shifted around, holding himself low so I could climb off. Going from buoyancy and the steady thrum of his feet to the unmoving ground—my swimsuit slogging—was strange and left me wobbly. A firm hand cupped my leg behind the knee.

Damien settled himself beside me. "Take it easy for a second. There's no rush, and as inexperienced as you are with water, it's best not to overdo it."

My gaze fell to the green eyes looking up at me, black hair dripping water onto his sharp, tanned cheekbones…

We looked away at the same time. I toward the far side of the river, he towards the water and the jexies somewhere below, his hand falling away from my leg.

"I never thanked you for what you did," I said, "that day you joined me at Selene's House—ever since we've received so many more donations, and more people want to be involved with the children. You accomplished what Rho and I have been trying to do for the better part of our time working there in one morning."

"I didn't do anything," he said, "but I am glad my presence helped you—helped the children."

I dared a glance at him, his eyes keeping steady on the water. "You know, I was thinking about the offer you made me, about teaching me magic." Taking a breath, I blurted the question before I could stop myself. "Would you still do it?"

"Of course," he said. No hesitation. "Just come up to my home any afternoon, whenever you want."

"Thank you." Dizziness subsiding, I took a step up onto the rocks. "I'm going to head back to our stuff, get dressed."

He nodded once, still looking away. "I'll be with you in a minute."

The walk back took half the time it had taken going out. Atop the rocks, a breeze blew, making my skin pebble. By the time I made it back to the blanket, my body was shaking violently. I ran the fluffy cotton towel over my face and secured it around my chest, shielding most of my body from the breeze while I pulled out my dress. Slipping it on, I dried my hair, taking in the silence.

When had it gone so silent?

The sound of a twig splitting snapped my attention to the trees. The crack too brisk for any animal one would find in this area. Checking over my shoulder, I spotted Damien still seated at the drop. His gaze on the tree line, he jumped to his feet.

There was a rush of leaves, another twig breaking—right at the uppermost edge of our blanket—and a flash of metal in the shade as a figure stepped forward.

My stomach twisted as I took a step back. Behind me, the water sloshed violently as Damien ran toward me.

"I wouldn't get any closer if I were you," a scratchy voice barked. The threat was directed at Damien, but the man didn't take his dilated, red-veined eyes off me. Eyes with silver sparks going off in them.

High on an aggression elixir. Lovely.

He took another step closer, entering the light. His water-laden, tattered clothes clung in strips to his deeply sunburned skin, mottled red and brown. Wet clumps of red hair hung from his head, emphasizing where he'd scratched patches away. The hand white-knuckling the knife shook.

He dragged his tongue along his dry, blistered lips. "Aren't you a pretty thing, ripe for picking. Why don't you come a little closer so I can have a taste?"

He leapt forward giddily, the smell of him—like he'd been marinating in his shit—riding on his self-made wind almost knocked me off my feet.

Another figure jumped forth from the tree line, making me stumble back once more. This man—all his hair and his clothes intact—was in better condition than his friend but had the same crazed look in his eyes. He brandished a blade toward Damien.

"Ah-ah." The man wagged the knife like a finger, gray eyes looking past me. "Take one step closer, and it won't end well for your girlfriend here. Scout, stop playing around and look through the bags."

The man—Scout—sneered at his partner, jabbing his knife at me as he sidestepped to our things. "I'll be back for you, baby girl. Don't move."

Meanwhile, the other man's hawkish eyes didn't leave Damien. "Looking a little shaggy, Prince Cole. With all the people's money, you can't afford a haircut?" He twisted the knife in his hands.

Damien didn't respond.

"I ain't good enough for your words, princey?"

Scout set the knife aside, turning Damien's bag upside down first and then mine, tearing through the mishmash of our things.

"What they got?"

"Not much, a necklace and a couple of elixirs," Scout grunted.

I instinctively reached for the key at my throat, coming away empty. No. That was the only thing I had from my mother.

"Let's see the necklace."

Scout held it up for his friend, the silver catching the light. "The girl'll probably fetch us a nice sum even after I'm done with her."

"What do you think it's made of?"

They were not taking my necklace. Without thinking, I made a grab for it.

Surprised, the man on my right spun. Arching back his arm, he released the blade. I prepared for impact, realizing it hadn't been meant for me as the water started to slosh again. Scout—slow to react —fumbled his blade. The key was right within reach…

A gust of wind caressed my back as an arm seized my waist, pulling me against a rigid body. Preparing to fight, I reared back my elbow. Stopping when I noticed the high, ivy-covered concrete walls surrounding me.

The courtyard of my apartment building.

Damien spun me around in his arms, green eyes furiously searching me. "Are you hurt?"

I shook my head, tears stinging my eyes. My hand still grasping at the space where the necklace had been.

His eyes came to rest on the spot. "I'll get your necklace." Without another word, Damien dropped his hold and vanished once more.

I stared at the spot where he'd stood, heart racing—thoughts switching between what Damien was doing and trying to understand what had happened.

Shaking, I got to my feet, pacing the courtyard of our apartment complex.

I'd gone swimming in the river. I'd seen jexies. Bandits had attacked me. Bandits had crossed the Five River. They were going to steal my necklace—I loved my necklace, but it wasn't worth Damien getting hurt. Damien. Was he okay? He'd be fine. He had to be fine. How had he phased us past the wards of our complex? And where was he?

Immortals, he'd better be okay.

A slosh followed a loud thump. Pivoting on my heel, I took in the sight of Damien, sodden, all our things in a bundle beside him in the grass. My key dangled from its chain in his fist.

Holding it out to me, a deep v formed between his green eyes. "Here."

Half snatching it from him, I brought it to my chest. "Damien, thank you—are you okay?"

He hawked a bitter laugh, collapsing onto a nearby bench. "Me? That drugged-up man came at you with a knife. Fuck," he exclaimed. Elbows resting on his knees, he buried the palms of his hands into his eyes. "That was reckless. If I had been a second later, something horrible could have happened."

"I'm fine, Damien. Stop. I heal, remember?" Then added as an afterthought. "Lupine always said I needed to live a little more."

Frown deepening, he looked up, confusion blanketing his eyes. "I don't think that's what my mother had in mind."

I shrugged, taking a seat beside him. Maybe, but now that he was back, and we were both fine, I felt on top of the world. "What happened after you went back?"

"I tossed them into the river and grabbed our stuff." He held up a finger. There was the stern father face again. "Don't you ever go walking out there again. Are you—"

"What is that?" A thin gash slicing up his forearm oozed a rivulet of blood.

He looked at it as if noticing it for the first time. "The one man threw his knife, and I deflected it."

My heart lodged itself in my throat. "You should let me heal you."

He started to say something, but my hand on his arm stopped him. The magic moved like light through me, flowing quickly from the center of my chest and into my hand. His lips parted in surprise as the light worked into him, stitching flesh back together.

"There, all better," I said proudly.

Wiping the blood on his damp shorts, he brushed a finger along the smooth skin where the cut had been, marveling. "Thank you—are you okay?" His eyes searched mine. "You seem okay, but I can't imagine why. Maybe you're in shock."

"I'm fine. We're both fine, so I'm fine," I smiled weakly. "A little sleepy, but healing does that. I'll be fine again in a minute."

I swayed forward, stopped by one hand on my shoulder and the other cupping my chin.

Worried green eyes stared down at me. Immortals, he was so close. "Is there anything I can do to help?"

Blood warming as I breathed in the scent of river water, sunlight, and cedar lingering on his skin, I shook my head. "The only thing that helps is time."

For a split second, his gaze softened—eyes dropping to my mouth—his lips parting on an inhale. My heart caught on a single word…

"Not this again," a voice said, dripping in cool rage.

I leapt to my feet, fighting the rush of blood to my head.

My gaze shifted from where Damien sat, now staring absently at the spot where I'd been, to the courtyard archway where Grayden stood in his dark red Protector uniform, arms folded across his chest.

Struggling to find my words, Damien answered him. "How did you get in here, Grayden?"

Grayden's narrowed eyes flicked to Damien. "I'm on your guest list, remember?"

"And why are you here?"

"I volunteered to come get you because of my access and your being my friend, and you better thank the Immortals it was me that found you."

"That didn't answer my question."

The Protector pursed his lips. "Your father has taken ill. Cole has called the Council and has sent me to retrieve you both." Grayden's red eyes returned to me, giving me a critical once-over. "You should go take a scalding hot shower with your strongest soap and change your clothes before we leave. You *reek* of your Bidden's little brother."

I glared at him.

"You have twenty minutes. Go," he snarled.

***

Shaking, I ran up the stairs to my apartment, my foot clipping the final step of the landing, knocking a dent into my shin and sending me to my hands and knees.

I barely noticed the pain.

Inside my bathroom, I cranked the shower's hot water to max, ripped off the dress and swimsuit, and jumped inside. The water pelted me like hot needles, and I accepted the burn, thinking about what Grayden had said—*you reek of your Bidden's little brother.* Grabbing the soap, I went to work with my loofah. I'd almost kissed Damien. Immortals. I'd nearly kissed Damien. I scrubbed harder. And fuck I'd wanted to kiss Damien. I scrubbed until every inch of my cream-colored skin was red and raw.

My Bidden's brother. The lover of my enemies. What in this life and the next had come over me?

But Immortals, I couldn't deny I felt good. I felt alive. And not in the mood to deal with Grayden.

Toweling off and brushing out my hair, I ran to my closet, selecting the first dress I laid my hand on. Forcing the long-sleeved dark purple dress down over my damp skin, I touched the key necklace—safely around my neck once more—asking the Immortals for patience and opened the door.

Grayden's voice hit me in the face before I could put a foot outside. "Go back in and try again."

Seems they misinterpreted my request as a test of my patience.

"I let your command slip earlier, but this isn't Charph. Don't think for a minute that you give me orders." Closing the door behind me, I looked to where his voice had come from. He leaned against my landing's window, his massive form blocking out the light from the street lanterns below. Only his closely cropped white-blond hair was visible. "I'm ready. Let's go." I stepped past him to the stairs. "Where's Damien?"

The leather of his uniform creaked as he moved. "You can follow my orders, or you can explain to Cole what you were doing with Damien."

I spun on him, coming inches from his face. Close enough that even in the weak lighting, I could see the red of his eyes and the annoyance that lived in them. I bet if I'd looked down, I would have found his hand extended, ready to grab me as well, which would have been a big mistake.

I stepped closer to him and crossed my arms, making him straighten away. "For someone who claims they have an unrivaled sense of smell, I'm surprised you can't smell the oat-scented soap I assaulted my skin with for the last ten minutes."

Grayden stared down his nose at me. "I can, but you still reek."

I glared back, refusing to budge. Not even the sound of the door shutting a floor up made either of us blink, but a muscle in Grayden's eye twitched.

Damien looked between us. "What happened to your sense of urgency? Let's go."

Grayden's scowl didn't falter, nor did he bat an eye at me, forcing the words through his teeth. "We have a problem. One of you still reeks."

Only me, so Damien apparently was perfect.

I looked to Damien—wearing his all-black suit and dress shoes, his wet hair combed to the side—and raised an eyebrow.

Lifting his nose in my direction, Damien inhaled purposefully and had the nerve to look discontented when he was done. His green eyes met mine, and the sight of them, despite the topic of conversation, threatened to reactivate the warmth that'd bloomed inside of me in the courtyard.

I frowned, shifting my eyes downward. "I did as much scrubbing as I could in the time I was given. Just short of scrubbing my skin off."

"At least as a healer, it would have returned quickly," Grayden grumbled.

I was going to punch him in the face.

"The only thing that'll remove my smell from you is time or a deodor charm," Damien said.

"Yes." Grayden snapped a finger. "Fuck, why didn't I think of that. Deodor charm her and let's go."

Damien shook his head. "If I mask her, I imagine that would be just as suspicious to Cole."

"Can you isolate your smell and deodor that?" Grayden whined.

Damien rolled his eyes. "Already working on it, though with all the talk of sourced magic dwindling at the last council meeting, I hate to waste it."

I opened my mouth, but Grayden said, "I'd rather waste the magic than deal with Cole's reaction to your commingled scents."

"Will both of you stop this stupid back and forth and just do it already?" I huffed.

"I need something unchangeable to affix the charm to," Damien said. "Do you mind if it's your necklace?"

I went so far as to hold it up for him, the metal of the key warming as the charm took root, changing my most prized possession into something new.

"Look at me," Damien compelled, his voice oddly soft.

My eyes flicked to his, the green of them intently studying my face.

He snapped his fingers, and the metal instantly cooled. "It's done."

Grayden leaned in close and sniffed at me. "Perfect, cousin. She smells as unpleasant as she always does."

Patience be damned, I shoved him away, making for the stairs. "*Immortals,* you're awful."

"You better get your shit together before we get to the manor," Grayden called after me. "You know what Master Guardian Norris will think of your attitude."

***

I cut my way across the manor grounds, leaving Grayden and Damien in my wake as much as my stride and nausea would allow. Gratefully, none of the manor staff were around to see me, the Protectors at the entrance to the apartment paid me no more mind than usual, and since I wasn't supposed to be there, there were no shadows to haunt me. The lights came on at my entrance, following me as I made my way to the sitting room.

Inside, the drapes were drawn, and the fireplace sat dark, giving the room a certain coldness. Fuck, I hated being back here. Pacing the width of the living room, I listened to Damien and Grayden whisper amongst themselves. And it only made me angrier. Everything made me angrier.

"What are you guys talking about?" I flung my hands wide. "Where's Cole? You were so urgent, Grayden, and yet no one is here."

"Meeting with the Master Guardians, but I've sent a Protector for him. He'll be here in a minute." He whispered some more and patted Damien on the face.

Damien swatted at him, but Grayden, expecting it, darted back laughing and left the room.

Boys.

The door latched shut, and then it was Damien and me.

"Eden, you need to relax," he implored.

Spinning on my heel, I moved right into him, knocking myself off balance. "Do not tell me to relax!" He caught my shoulders. Angry tears burning my eyes and lip quivering, I looked up at him. "I'm so angry. What's wrong with me?"

"Adrocin."

"What?"

"It's too much to explain now, but it's what happens when you mix adrenaline and magic, and it's what you're experiencing. You'll snap and draw unnecessary attention to us if you don't calm down." He lowered his voice. "Grayden is content to forget about what he saw, and he isn't going to say anything, but if we force his hand, he will. Think of something that brings you down."

"You want me to be sad?" I said, pulling away. "Even if that wasn't twisted, crying isn't going to help."

Damien pinched the bridge of his nose. "That's not what I meant. Think of something that doesn't make you feel…high. Something easy like—a horrible book you read or a food you dislike."

I stared at him flatly. "All of that makes me angrier."

He snapped his fingers. "Think about how I'm going to rot in the deepest cell of the Ground for murder if Norris hits you for an outburst. Consider how that'd make you feel."

It made me feel a mix of things, but guilt was the number one. It didn't matter, though, because it wasn't a real threat, and I waited for him to crack a smile that never came. "You wouldn't."

"I absolutely would. My hatred of the man is strong. I probably would have done it the first time I saw him hit you if you hadn't stopped me." He stepped closer. "I know exactly how I would have done it, too. With my hands around his throat."

A mix of horror, shock, and anger—no jealousy that he could say things so unabashedly—tumbled around in my stomach.

The front door opened, making me suck in a sharp breath. The patter of Damien's quick steps away was lost in the purposeful footfall headed toward us. He clasped his hands behind his back, looking credibly interested in a book about turtles resting on the coffee table.

Cole entered first, head held high, followed by the four Master Guardians. "It took you long enough, I—" His attention snapped to me, moving toward me in quick strides.

Cupping my chin in his hand, his green eyes evaluated me for what felt like an eon. Catching me by surprise, he pressed his nose to my hairline, inhaling.

Everything in me stopped.

"Your hair is wet," he moaned.

I brushed my fingers through a long, damp strand, considering what to say. "I was in the bath relaxing when Grayden arrived."

"Relaxing in the bath, huh?" Slipping his arm around my waist, he buried his smirk into my neck. "Is that all you were doing?"

The Master Guardians dropped their gaze.

This was unexpected. Which was good on some level, but— "Cole," I gasped as his lips sucked at my sensitive flesh. What was this? What had gotten into him?

Damien cleared his throat. "Brother, I know you didn't bring me here to watch you put the moves on Eden."

Cole's hold on me stiffened. "Why did we make that stupid verbal oath?" he groaned, nuzzling my neck. Prying himself away, he glanced toward Damien and started for the door. "Right, let's go."

"Wait," I said, grabbing his wrist. "Why did you send for me?"

Someone—I'd bet Grayden—sucked in a breath. Stopping abruptly, Cole looked down at my hand and then up at me, curiosity sparking in his eyes.

The metallic taste of worry tingled my tongue.

He nodded. "That's right. I almost forgot. In the interest of your safety, you will stay here at the manor until after the announcement of my father's illness is made."

"What?" I scoffed. Not anger, but not passivity either.

I caught Master Guardian Norris's lip curl into a snarl over Cole's shoulder, but my Bidden didn't bat an eye.

"Yes, doll, so get some rest. I need you at your very best." He twisted his wrist out of my hold and put his back to me once more. "Let's go, Damien. There's quite a bit of work to do."

The Master Guardians parted around him and followed.

Something inside me…fell and kept falling.

"Are you okay?" came a whisper of a voice.

Damien faced the door everyone left through, but his eyes were on me.

Absentminded, I started for the other door, the one that led deeper into the apartment. "I'm fine."

CHAPTER SIXTEEN

1.NINE.4004

A festival and ball—that's what I learned about in the morning. They'd decided the events would help quell any adverse reaction the people may have to their king's falling ill—a special one, open even to *commoners.*

I struggled not to roll my eyes at the announcement. It was always the *solution* the Council came up with. Never anything to actually help the people.

In the afternoon, a seamstress came bearing swathes of fabric, on orders from Cole to make me a gown for the event, and I spent the day at her mercy.

***

Having not known I'd be extending my time when Grayden came for me, I hadn't re-upped my darkness elixir. That night, I dreamed. I was at a ball, being spun around and around by a bony, white hand, the silver dress I wore blooming out around me, screeching laughter drowning out my voice as I begged it to stop.

All the while, the hand continued spinning.

By the time I gasped awake, my heart was a beat away from pounding through my ribcage, and my twisted sheets clung to my sweat-drenched skin.

Head still spinning, I ran to the bathroom to throw up.

A first.

CHAPTER SEVENTEEN

4.NINE.4004

Cole's apartment had to be the most boring place in the kingdom. However, as bad as boredom was, it was preferable to being watched constantly.

I spent most of my time in Cole's office, where being surrounded by books lent me peace.

Having read all the books I could reach on my own long ago and several times, I idled away my time staring at the ceiling.

The sky.

The door.

The bracelet Cole had made a display of giving me during one of the brief moments I'd seen him that morning.

Sometimes the window, wondering what it'd be like to jump and run.

CHAPTER EIGHTEEN

6.NINE.4004

In a fit of desperation, I scaled the bookshelves of Cole's office, shooting for the books on the top shelf. If I were going to take a risk, I might as well aim high.

Climbing bookshelves was blasphemy to my reader's heart, but Cole made a point of keeping any ladder out of the space—not liking the way they looked—and I wasn't about to ask for assistance, which would invite curiosity from others about my activities, leaving me with no choice if I wanted to get up there.

Flexing slightly, the wood groaned under my feet, but each shelf held as I made my ascent.

At the top, it was clear the books hadn't been touched in years, so thick was the dust layer coating them that I had to breathe through my mouth lest I sneeze and lose my grip. Releasing a hold, I started to grab one and stopped, my attention drawn to where a thin black book nestled itself in the void between the outfacing books and the back of the case. I reached over the books guarding it, careful not to disturb the thick layer of dust coating them.

Back on the floor, I used the sleeve of my sweater to wipe away the grime, revealing its peeling black cover and crinkled, browning pages. It most certainly hadn't been touched since it'd been put there.

The book cracked as I opened the cover, releasing a sour smell.

Written in perfect longhand at the heart of the book's golden end pages were the words: A Study of Demons by Aevry Valentine.

A piece of the forgotten brother. As much as it pained my heart, I couldn't fight the excitement of knowing anything about Aevry, and I'd never seen a book about demons—information reserved for those bearing the Scholar's Mark in the Records Repository of the Temple of the Masters.

Flipping to a random page, I landed on a theory of origin page written in meticulous script. There were sections where Aevry speculated on how Roan's military tactics incorporated demons. Detailed interviews with people who'd encountered them and survived—surprising since most people who'd encountered them in Roan's War and lived preferred to drink those memories away.

Aevry had sketched them as well. His drawings were as good as his handwriting. Dream Demons, Poison Demons, Feeder Demons…

The Feeder Demon stopped me mid-skim: the sketch of the tall, thin humanoid creature glared up at me from the crumbling page. Or it would have if the creature had eyes. Where eyes, a mouth, and nose would have been was a gaping maw filled with row after row of razor-sharp teeth. In place of fingers were long black claws, a note in the margin reporting they are sharp enough to cut through bone.

That their mouths widened like a snake's, and their teeth were sharp and hard enough to crush a human skull. That there were cases in which they had devoured the heads of their prey whole.

Something hit me, staring at the sketch. Sending the book clattering to the floor.

Aevry had been a Scholar. Had died in Roan's War. Researching demons.

You know it's…empty, don't you?

No…there was no way.

Covering my mouth, I barely made it to the bathroom, expelling the contents of my stomach as tears streamed down my cheeks. I tried to convince myself it was my imagination, but the darkness on Damien's face when he'd said those words—the way he struggled to say Aevry's name—overruled me.

I decided then never to reopen that book and didn't care if I ever saw anything about demons again.

Unfortunately, what I decided didn't matter.

Demons came to me in sleep, moving like whispers on the wind, the stinging burn of their poison dripping into my veins, their black claws ripping at my flesh, and teeth shredding me into oblivion.

CHAPTER NINETEEN

10.NINE.4004

I sat at the dining room table, staring blankly at the breakfast before me—a plate with two over-easy eggs, strips of perfectly cooked bacon, and a freshly baked roll, a bowl of fresh fruit coated in honey and mint leaves, and a pot of steeping hot black tea. People all over the city would be grateful to be greeted by such a breakfast every morning.

So why didn't I feel that way?

Maybe it was because I couldn't leave the apartment by myself. Fucking shadows.

Maybe it was boredom.

Maybe it was Aevry's book…

Maybe it was because I hadn't slept, and I was never going to sleep again.

The answer, I decided, staring absently at my glass of water, was it was all getting to me. This place was getting to me, and the only thought meandering through my mind was how I wanted to go home.

Tilting the teapot, I watched as the steaming, dark brown liquid filled the pearly white teacup.

Usually, I took my tea black, but today I plunked two sugar cubes into the dark brown liquid, hoping it might give me life.

"Good morning, doll."

Dropping the teaspoon with a clatter, I sat up straight.

Cole walked toward me, working rose-shaped diamond cufflinks through the white buttonhole peeking out from the sleeve of his dark blue suit jacket. He glanced from me to my breakfast and casually plucked the flaky roll from my plate. "I didn't expect you to be awake at this time."

I held my hand out to the seat across from me. "I thought we could have breakfast together."

"I'd love to, but the Alliance Council session begins today."

"Please, it's just breakfast," I begged. "Five minutes?"

Cole leaned his hip against the table, lightly running his free hand down my hair. He wrapped a single dark brown strand once around his pointer finger. And again. "Apologies, doll, things have been crazy, but you must understand, making the transition from my father to me as seamless as I can for the kingdom has been more difficult than I imagined."

I stared at my tea. "Were the festival and ball not well received?"

"No, they were. The city has been abuzz with preparations for a new era. One of the items on my agenda today is to work out the event semantics with the Alliance Council. It's the number of little things as well as big things that keep being brought to my attention. Nothing you should worry about, but I'll be staying at my office for this session, working from sunup until exhaustion takes me, so you won't be seeing much of me."

I already didn't. "If everything is fine, and you won't be here, can I go home? Can I resume my role at Selene's House?"

His finger released the strand of hair, the muscles in his jaw tightening. "I like to think of the manor as your home."

"I didn't mean it like that. I simply miss my things—"

"We should talk about you moving your things here. It's time you started making the adjustment."

My stomach twisted. Not this, not now, not yet.

"I don't have time to get into that now." Sighing, he shifted back onto his feet. "I understand you've been cooped up here, so today you may take Julien and go to your apartment or shopping or whatever it is women spend their time doing," he slipped what I now recognized as a money pocket from his pants and sat it on the table, "but I'd prefer your presence here until after the ball. Following that, I guess it doesn't matter if you return to your job."

I kept my composure as my heart screamed its joy. "Of course, thank you, Cole."

Pleased, Cole leaned down to press his lips to my forehead. "We're going to make a grand entrance together, you and I. I want the city to get its first look at what the future looks like."

Fighting the way my skin chilled, I beamed at him. I wouldn't let talks of the future ruin the relief I felt, though. For now, I was going home.

***

The book clutched to my chest, I paced the landing of the penthouse, going back and forth with myself on whether to knock or leave the book for Damien to find. Turning toward the stairs, my decision made itself.

Damien stood frozen between the last step and the landing, dressed in a black suit, his black hair combed to one side. That was right. He was now part of the Alliance Council. He hadn't even been home.

My skin burned. I was caught. So caught. "Hello," I blurted.

Grinning, he hopped up onto the landing, hands sinking into his black dress pants. "Hi." He inclined his head toward the door. "Couldn't bring yourself to knock?"

I dropped my gaze, unable to stand the amusement in his eyes. "I did, and you weren't home, so I was waiting a couple of minutes to see if you'd return."

His green eyes glowed a little brighter. "That'd have been a good lie if I didn't know Isa was home. If you'd knocked, she most certainly would have let you wait inside."

Isa. His Factotum. My dignity sank into the pit of my stomach.

"Come now, don't look so aggrieved," he said. "What brings you up here?"

Remembering the book I clutched like a lifeline to my chest, I held it out to him. "I found something and wanted to give it to you."

"What is this?"

I nodded at it. "Open the cover."

Making a show of playing along, he accepted it and did as instructed. I knew he'd found it the moment the humor vanished from his face.

He pointedly blinked twice and shook his head. "Where did you find this?"

"Behind some books on the top shelf in Cole's office."

Shutting the book, he returned his attention to me. "That's Aevry's office, not Cole's. Cole's never read a book in his life. They used to share that apartment as customary for the heir and spare. When I saw what he'd done to the place, I assumed he'd gone through and got rid of everything of my brother's, and was quite surprised he hadn't touched that room." A pause. "Did you read it?"

A flicker of anxiety stirred in my stomach. "Why?"

"Was wondering if it's why you look…haggard."

I glared at him. "How do you get off being kind one moment and a complete ass the next?"

He grinned. "Anything to spark a little bit of life in you. Is giving me this all you needed?"

Biting my lip, I took a deep breath. "I came to learn magic."

Damien straightened in surprise. "Now isn't the best time. I had a long morning with the Alliance Council, and I told Mari I'd help her at Vermillion this—"

Heat stinging my cheeks, I started for the stairs. "Of course you're busy. I'm sorry. It was a silly idea."

His hand shot out, grabbing my elbow. "We could go over the basics for an hour if you'd find that interesting? I wish I could give you more time today, I do, but I have to be at Vermillion at six."

I nodded once, then again rapidly, excitement tingling in my chest. "That works. Anytime you can afford me."

Damien opened the door into darkness. A privacy ward. "None of that. An hour is nothing. When I made the offer, I was expecting whole afternoons, which is what you should expect next time."

Hesitantly, I put one foot into the void, pushing through the privacy ward pressing against me and coming to a stop on the other side of the door, eyes going wide at what it hid.

Before me was a vast, open floor plan, encompassing the living room to the right and the dining room to the left, the air rich with the scents of herbs, roast, and potatoes. Orbs of light rained down from the two-story-high ceiling in a slow, steady stream, setting the place aglow and making the tan walls flecked with gold glitter.

"Superfluous, I know. I'm not sure what to make of it still," he said as if reading my mind.

Two huge black leather couches, covered in white pillows and throws, squared off the living room and the white marble fireplace, which was currently ablaze.

My eyes continued their journey to the ten-person dining room table, a gray runner dividing it. At the center was a black vase containing white calla lilies and two white pillar candles. In the wall just beyond was a small cutout through which the kitchen could be seen with four bar stools underneath.

"For someone who doesn't know how to feel about it, your furniture does a good job of complementing it." I stepped toward the dining room table, running the tips of my fingers along the top of one of the high-backed, black lacquered dining room chairs.

"All Isa's doing. I simply paid the bill."

"For some reason, I doubt she chose the theme of black, white, and every shade in between."

"I may have given some guidance. I've never been a fan of color."

"Yet you named your elixiry Vermillion," I countered.

He shrugged a single shoulder. "It was supposed to be ironic."

I nodded slowly, eyes going to the winding metal staircase I'd somehow missed on my first sweep of the space, located at the corner where the living room and dining room met. It led up to a small balcony and what I assumed was the master suite. "I know. It isn't exactly subtle."

"You would think," he mused, "but no one else has ever commented on it. I believe they all think it's in homage to my Faldone heritage."

"It's still warm outside, you know," I said, nodding to the blazing fireplace.

He waved a hand at the door, sending it shut. "To you. I'm still acclimating."

At the sound of the slam, a woman with a silver bob popped her head out of a room at the far end of the hall. "You're home. Dinner is —" Spotting me, she covered her mouth, shooting Damien a glare. "You have a guest. You didn't tell me to expect company. I didn't make enough for three."

Damien shook his head. "Relax, she isn't here for dinner."

I smiled at her, offering a little wave. "Hi Isa, I'm Eden. It's lovely to meet you."

The Facto burned red, flapping the copy of the Alliance Access she held. "Damien, that's no way to treat a guest. Especially not a lady."

"No, he's right, it's fine." I turned the sweetness up a notch, hoping it'd assure her. "I won't be here long."

Unconvinced, Isa's eyes narrowed at Damien.

"We'll be in the suite if you need us," Damien said in finality before dashing up the stairs.

"I have no interest in seeing your bedroom," I hissed after him.

"My bedroom is the first door on the right," he sighed. "Now come. Need I remind you I have an hour?"

Metal stairs rattling under my feet, I jogged to catch up to him.

At the top, I barely registered the massive bed filling the giant room or the rummaging coming from the closet, favoring the panorama window. One giant pane of glass and one story higher than all the surrounding buildings, it provided a view for miles—to the edge of the farmlands where the city met the forest and the land turned into a sea of green.

I pressed my hands to the glass, my breath fogging it. Wiping it away, I looked to Damien, who stood a couple of feet away—now absent his suit jacket and the book—holding two black mats. "This view is incredible. Why don't you use this room?"

He gestured around to the mostly empty space. "It's too big for one person, and I have almost the same view from my bedroom below."

I turned and, catching unexpected movement, yelped. "What is that about?"

Fighting a laugh, Damien's eyes met mine in the reflection of the wall-sized mirror. "Nice, isn't it? Another interesting facet of this place. I think the previous owners had a kink." One of the mats snapped as it unfurled. "Come, let's focus. You know there are two types of magic: that which is innate, like my phasing and your healing, and that which is sourced and is coursing through everything around us?"

I rolled my eyes. "I'm not that out of touch. Elders versus Devotees."

Unrolling the second mat, he took a seat at the center, holding up a finger. "There isn't a rivalry, but yes, Elders and Devotees is a way to look at it." He held his hand out toward the space across from him. "Since we're working on charms, we'll be focusing on the latter." When I didn't immediately sit, he asked, "Is something wrong?"

Rubbing at my upper arm, I stared blankly at the mat. "What is this?"

"In all your books, you never read about meditating to connect to magic?"

"I've read about it, tried it, and it did nothing."

He patted the center of the mat insistently, pulling my attention to him, green eyes firm. "Then you did it wrong."

Holding his gaze, I collapsed cross-legged on the mat.

"Close your eyes." He instructed me, watching until I did. "Now tell me, how does magic feel to you?"

Taking a sharp breath, I let it out as a sigh. "It feels chaotic, and at the same time, it's immovable like stone and solid like earth. It feels like everything, like it's everywhere."

"That's because magic *is* everywhere. Sourced magic, the magic we pull from in charms, is rooted in the four elements—really, earth, since fire is exhausted, and the others have never been formally cultivated. The city was built by an immortal made of magic, and he imbued a lot of himself in his creations—that's the immovability—"

I cracked an eye. "What does it feel like to you?"

"Malleable warmth because I've honed my connection to it. If you'd waited, I was about to tell you that." He was serious as he said, "I thought you wanted me to teach you?"

Shutting my eye once more, I bowed my head. "I do. I'm sorry, it's just that I know how to feel for magic. My issue is that I can't lock on to sourced magic for long enough to do anything."

"That's why we meditate, to build our connection. You don't reach for it blindly. It's like a muscle you build. Straighten up, take a deep breath, and let it out slowly. Try to reach for the earth, focused solely on it."

Hands rubbing my knees, I took a breath, sifting through the chaos.

"Stop fidgeting. You'd get a cane on your wrists at the Academy for that."

Frowning, I locked them down. We sat there in silence as Damien's eyes bored holes into me. Breathing in through my nose and out slowly through my mouth, my shoulders relaxed, my body appreciating the rhythm.

"Have you found the connection?"

"Yes."

"How does it feel?"

"Like…heaviness. It reminds me why I never reach for earth."

He huffed a laugh. "If you aren't reaching for earth, that's part of your problem. Don't fight the feeling, and don't lose your focus. Let it in. The more you give yourself over, the stronger your connection." Adding, "What magic do you reach for?"

"Air." I touched the necklace at my throat. "Earth feels so starved. I swear it feels like it wants to pull from me instead of me pulling from it."

"You can feel that?" He sounded surprised.

I opened my eyes, finding his. The green irises of his eyes drank in the golden light of the late afternoon sun filtering in through the window. "Can't every magus? Everyone's always talking about it."

"Yes and no," he said. "Every magus has the ability, but the chatter happens because word gets around. Most aren't attuned enough to notice it."

"I guess all my attempts weren't useless," I smiled. "You made me wonder something—why aren't demis at least partially made of magic like an immortal?"

"I'm flattered you think I would know the answer to that, but that was a question the Immortal Valentine couldn't even answer. I would argue that our ability to stay young forever is our partiality."

"You demis got the lamest part of being an immortal."

He raised an eyebrow. "You think never aging and the potential to live forever is lame?"

"Compared to the raw ability to create and being magic itself? Yes." I tapped my chin. "You can smell me—would you teach me that magic as well?"

"That can't be taught."

"Why not?"

Damien rolled his eyes. "When did this become question hour? You're supposed to be focusing."

"I did focus—I was focusing—but then I started thinking, and there's so much I want to know, and you're the first person to answer my questions."

"You aren't going to get the answers to all your questions in our remaining time. There's plenty of time for this later."

I stuck out my lower lip, the excitement boiling inside me reduced to a simmer.

"I'll answer your question on two conditions." Sighing, he glanced around, looking for something, settling on the signet ring on his pinky finger. Twisting it off, he set it in the space between us. "You summon this to you, and you answer a question of my choosing first."

I looked from the concentric circles at the center to him. "If I can't?"

"Then you'll spend the rest of this hour focusing and working on your connection to earth. This isn't hard. The bigger the order, the more you must listen to the magic, the more you have to weave. Something small like summoning this ring, all you need is a touch of magic and intent."

"And what about the question?"

"Whatever I want to ask."

Narrowing my eyes, I considered him and what he might possibly want to ask me. Deciding there wasn't anything to know, I said, "Fine."

He reclined against the bed. "Perfect."

I shifted my focus to the ring. Sitting straight up, shoulders back and head high, I closed my eyes. My breathing took a moment, but I went to the earth once more—or it came to me—and this time, I let it in. The magic felt like cold mud in my veins, dragging along. Not like the light when I healed. Or the warm rush of air when I did pull from it successfully. I fought the urge to shiver as it crept along, settling in like a weary traveler.

"We don't have—"

I held up a finger, silencing him—he might not need quiet, but I did—then shifting my middle finger to meet my thumb, I snapped.

The metal ring warmed the palm of my hand, sending a wave of success blazing through me. My connection to the earth had left in an instant, but I'd done it.

Lips pursed, Damien plucked the ring from my hand, slipping it back onto his pinky. "You can sense the magic in the earth disappearing, and you did that on the first try. Has your ignorance been an act?"

I grinned at him. "No, but your advice was good. Much as I hate to admit it. Now, what's your question?"

"I want to know more about your nightmares."

I shrank away. "That's what you want to ask about?"

"That is what I asked." Holding my gaze, he pressed his thumb into his lower lip. "I assume they're why you look like you haven't slept since the last time I saw you."

The mat squeaked as I shifted. "I guess they aren't nightmares—not always. They're dreams that feel too real. Vivid in color. Sharp in sound. Full of emotion. They feel like life. I've had them as long as I can remember, but they've gotten worse with age."

He tilted his chin. "That's adorable. You're a dream-walker."

I stared at him blankly.

"You live your dreams."

"I may never have gone to the Academy, but I'm not stupid. I've never heard of a dream-walker."

"That's because it's not a useful ability to have. It's unverifiable as well. There's a whole bunch of useless skills that have been recorded over the years."

Finally, I started to nod, my eyes falling on the space between us. "You're making fun of me."

"I'm not. I'm telling the truth. How often do you have them?"

I yawned, feeling suddenly sleepy. "That's a second question."

His eyes twinkled. "My question was to know more about your nightmares. I'm simply streamlining what I want to know for the sake of time."

Thinking of my bed two floors below—my mind longing for the peace it'd been denied—I shrugged a shoulder. "Almost every night without a darkness elixir.

The look on Damien's face became one of horror. "That's not real sleep. How are you even getting that?"

Realizing what I'd volunteered, I snapped to, my hand going to the key around my neck. "It's better than no sleep."

"That's arguable, but you still didn't answer my question."

I needed to leave. "And I'm not going to." Immortals, what had I done? Frustrated, I stood. "Forget the question. Thank you for today."

Damien leapt in front of me, using his body to block me as I tried to sidestep him.

"Damien!"

"A panatat merged with my body," he blurted. "You asked me if I could teach you the magic behind my ability to smell, and I told you I couldn't. That's why."

What. "A panatat…one of the big predatory cats of the Faldonian Mountains…merged with you." I could feel my eyes grow wide as I said the words slowly, questioning each one.

He ran a hand through his hair. "Come on, surely you've read about the Charphan practice of merging with an animal."

"Charph, its history, and its practices tend to make me irate, so I avoid it, but I do recall reading something."

He nodded. "Every male citizen of Charph has gone through the process. It's a rite of passage for all thirteen-year-olds to merge with an animal of their choice and inherit their characteristics. I was given the option due to Faldone being an ancestor."

"And you went through it…and now you're part cat?"

"I…" He looked to the ceiling. He was really struggling with this. "I've never thought of it like that. I guess so? But I never fully got in touch with it. Not like my cousins Luno and Aiden did."

The mention of Lord Faldone's oldest sons made me shiver. "They give me the creeps, at least now I know why."

"They are good at that. I have to get ready, but," his eyes softened. "I'll see you tomorrow?"

Liking the sound of that, I nodded, "That sounds great." Stepping around him, I made it to the door before I stopped and looked back at him, rolling up the mats. "What do I smell like?"

He composed himself quickly, but I saw alarm briefly register in his eyes. "We agreed on one question."

Fair. "But I don't reek, do I?"

He laughed, turning away. "No, Eden, you don't."

An hour later, clutching Julien's arm—the darkness elixir carefully tucked away—I remembered I wouldn't see him tomorrow.

CHAPTER TWENTY

14.NINE.4004

The festival had started at noon, but we were to make our entrance at one-thirty. We all stood in the Capitol facing the doors, protected from the bustle of the crowd by the building's many wards, and between it being my first walk and not knowing how many people awaited, I wanted to eat my fist.

The Misundre Five were to lead the procession, followed by Lord Stellan of Charph and his brooding, shadowy heir, Lord Luno. Next came heirs, but as Cole had no children, Q wasn't officially his second, and Damien was only acting second, it was decided they'd both walk. They stood several paces before Cole and me now—Damien in a black suit, Q in a tan suit. Both looking far more at ease with the pomp and circumstance.

The Master Guardians took up the rear, with Master Guardian Saier and Master Guardian Rei immediately behind us and Master Guardian Norris and Master Guardian Gillian behind them.

Cole lifted our joined hands to his lips, pressing a kiss against my knuckles. "No need to be nervous, doll."

I looked up at him.

For today's events, he'd traded his dark blue suit for Alliance regalia —a green and red brocade suit jacket, gold buttons running from the bottom of his throat to his navel, where it parted to reveal a sliver of the black shirt underneath, tucked into black slacks. Pinned on each side of his collar was the Valentine Insignia, and the final touch, resting atop his pristine black hair, was a crown molded to look like interwoven branches.

The sight of the twisted crown reminded me of its sparkling counterpart now pinned into my curls—a gift Cole had given me that morning for the express purpose of this event—and the knots in my stomach. Letting go of the key resting at the center of my breastbone, I ran a hand down the tulle skirt of my light green dress.

I wasn't nervous, I was terrified. Of what this meant.

Processions had always been for the Alliance Council and the royal family. I'd always watched from somewhere safe in the crowd.

Right as I opened my mouth to lie and tell him I was fine, the sound of shouting people stole my words, pulling my attention to the door and the quickly moving parade. My heart was beating so fast I thought I might pass out.

The crowd's shouts amplified as Damien and Q disappeared into the gray light of the day. When we stepped out, half pulled by Cole, the cheering became a deafening roar, my mouth going dry.

The air had been cold and the sky threatening rain when I'd arrived earlier that morning to get ready. White tents had started to pop up, but for the most part, it could have been any other day in the capital. Now, the sky had remained overcast, but the air was warm with the bodies of thousands of excited people, and white tents were everywhere I looked.

"Lady Eden! Prince Damien! Lady Eden!"

"Prince Cole!"

"Prince Damien! Prince Damien!"

"Prince Cole!"

What started as simple excitement quickly became a tug of war between the people over the two princes, with my name interspersed.

Damien looked how I felt. He smiled sheepishly and waved, but kept his head down and to the side as if trying to make himself invisible. His desire to hide only encouraged them as his name came more frantically.

I smiled at people and waved, trying to tune out the division in the crowd. Trying not to stumble—thank the Immortals they'd let me wear flats. The people ate it up, whooping and clapping as we walked past. Some people cried, expressing their sympathies for the loss of the queen. Some shouted their love for me. There were compliments about how lovely I looked. What a perfect lady I was. That I gave them hope. And while all of it came from a good place, it was overwhelming.

Cole kept his head high, but what his smile didn't betray, his hand did. Every time someone called his brother's name, Cole's grip on my hand got a little tighter, nails digging into my knuckles. By the time we completed the parade loop—a whole lifetime later—entering the main ballroom of Hotel Solta, I thought my hand might have broken several times and healed incorrectly.

Our hands still entwined, Cole stepped toward Damien, like he was going to say something, but not seeing him—and knowing him, not even caring if he had—Damien slipped away, running his fingers through his hair.

Grumbling to himself, Cole tugged me along again, half yanking me into a space off the main room where several seats had been arranged in a semi-circle, the Council close behind.

He stopped before a small sofa at the center of the arrangement and fell into the seat, nodding to the seat beside him. "You're with me, doll."

Zapped of energy, I took my spot with all the grace I could muster. It wasn't what I'd expected, but the isolation would be nice.

Once everyone was seated, Cole snapped his fingers, summoning waitstaff who rushed toward us, carrying glasses of sparkling wine on golden trays.

As I prepared to refuse one, the intent of the space became apparent. Protectors took their place on either side of the door and on either side of Cole and me.

Outside the ballroom door were the beginnings of a line.

***

As darkness seized the sky, the festival transitioned into the ball, and the hours of public greeting ended. Most of the Council cleared out when Cole waved them away. Only Master Guardian Norris and Lord Stellan remained behind, heads bowed and exchanging whispers in the corner. It was only then that Damien stumbled into the room, a glass glued to his mouth, and took his seat—the seat that'd been empty all day—to the right of Cole.

The acting king shifted his arm around me, pulling me near, his fingers fighting for purchase in the tight fabric at my waist.

"The city adores the celebrations. Well done, brother," Damien exclaimed, a slight slur to his words.

A waiter came through, swapping my empty glass for one fresh with bubbly golden liquid. I took a grateful sip. It'd been the only thing that'd made the day and my growing list of people to try and help endurable.

"I see you've spent your day getting drunk," Cole remarked.

Hadn't we all? Cole had drunk triple what I had. How he wasn't on the floor was beyond me.

Damien raised his glass. "How else does one survive these things? Excellent bar, by the way."

Cole nodded, gulping down a glass of red wine that a staff member nearby quickly replaced.

195

Wanting to be anywhere but on display any longer, I took my chance. "Cole, would you mind if I called it a night? It's been a long day, and I'm exhausted. I need to get home. I have work in the morning."

Languid green eyes met mine. "Work," Cole chuckled sourly. Taking a sip, his gaze shifted to the key at my neck. His cold, condensation-laced fingers brushed it, moving along the tops of my breasts. "I'm so glad that isn't something I'm going to have to worry about much longer. I should have canceled your work tomorrow. You should be coming back to the manor tonight."

I didn't say anything, afraid he might do just that.

Sighing, he waved me away as he had everyone else. "That's fine. Julien, take my Bidden to her apartment."

It didn't escape me that his sudden concession happened as Violet entered the room.

The Valentine's personal Runner, chatting up a Protector by the door—smiling for the first time ever—turned and frowned at me.

"Let Julien have fun. I can do it," Damien said. He emptied his glass and got to his feet, setting the glass on the floor by the leg of his chair.

Cole turned sharply to face his brother, the nails of his hands still at my waist, scraping against the fabric of my dress.

Damien didn't so much as blink. "It's a simple offer, as I'm done here as well, and we're virtually going to the same place. Julien has lived hundreds of years at the beck and call of our family. Give him a night off."

His voice stone cold, Cole glanced back at Violet. "Fine. Take her, don't be seen."

***

We cut through the kitchens, passing staff carrying food-laden trays to the party. My stomach ached looking at them. Appetizers had made

196

the rounds throughout the day, and I'd waved them all away. Even if my dress hadn't been a second skin in places, there was no way I could eat while being the spectacle of the city.

Exiting through a service door, we broke out into the night, right into the rain the sky had promised earlier. It descended on the capital, beading up on my skin and dusting my dress. I raised my face to the sky, embracing how delicious the cold water felt after being in that stuffy room. How the lush pitter-patter calmed my worn spirit after hours of smiling.

Thank the Immortals for rain.

Damien had his jacket half off when I stepped deeper into it. "Eden, you shouldn't—"

I met his gaze, the green of his eyes bright with drink. "I'm going home, and it's just rain. I'll survive."

Thanks to the weather, no one was outside. No one saw us as we stepped into the middle of the empty sidewalk, clear of the anti-phase wards around the capital, or when I got close to him.

In a moment, the warm light of the colonnade lining the River Sorbis —blurry through the drizzle—and the cacophony of the party were replaced with the cool lights illuminating the apartment's courtyard and the brutal assault of a downpour.

Damien slipped his hand into mine, warm against the cold rain, and tugged me toward the stairs. In the two seconds we'd been exposed, my dress had become a sponge, drinking in the water thrown at it.

"That was insane," he laughed, chest heaving. Fat drops of water fell from the ends of his black hair. "I'm sorry—you're soaked."

I nodded at his drenched jacket. "Nothing your jacket couldn't have protected me from."

The corner of his mouth tugged up, causing my stomach to flutter.

Remembering his hand in mine, I pulled away, tucking a soaked strand of hair behind my ear. "Thanks for bringing me home." Lifting the sodden skirt of my dress, I started up the stairs. "I'm going to change." I cast a glance over my shoulder to where he stood, watching me. "Do you want to make us a drink?"

Eyebrows raised, he said, "I thought you had work in the morning?"

"I do, but that doesn't mean I'm ready for bed." I couldn't sleep right now if I tried. Exhausted and drunk as I was, I couldn't stop thinking. And I didn't want to be alone. "I wanted to leave. If you don't want to, that's fine."

Damien cleared his throat. "I could go for a nightcap."

"Great, see you in five minutes."

He called after me. "I'll leave the door cracked for you."

Throwing the tiara onto my bed, I quickly undid the buttons going down the side of my dress and peeled off the sopping wet mess, tugging on some soft black lounge pants and a creamy white sweater. Climbing the stairs between our homes, my thoughts started to demand what I was doing. A question I had no answer for.

The door was cracked as promised, and I let myself in, pushing right through his blackout ward. Draped over the chair at the head of the table was Damien's suit jacket, dripping water onto the hardwood. His shiny black dress shoes lay skewed about as if he'd removed them in a rush.

I found him in the kitchen, dressed in black sweats and a black V-neck. He looked up as I entered, wet hair combed back out of his face. On the counter sat a crystal glass of whiskey beside a jar of honey and a lemon with a portion of its peel cut away. He dropped the peel into the glass. "I should have asked for ten minutes. I felt like I was scrambling. I hope you like it."

My blood, heavy from glass after glass of sparkling wine, warmed anew at the sweet-tasting burn. Nodding to the cabinet door behind him, I asked. "Do you have anything to eat?"

Damien laughed, and there it was again, a tingle in my stomach. "Isa would be insulted. Let me get her—"

"Don't you dare. It's late. You are not bothering her for me. I thought maybe you'd have something ready, like leftovers."

He shook his head. "Isa doesn't believe in those. She's a staunch believer in fresh food and making the right amount."

"Always?"

He shrugged. "I assume so. She doesn't throw anything away, and there's never anything left. She really won't mind—"

I grabbed the loaf of bread on the counter, ripping it into chunks. "No. Pass me some butter, jam—anything—a spoon, and a knife."

"She'd kill me if she knew you were about to eat this morning's bread. That's for the ducks tomorrow on her walk through the park."

"It's for me now."

He set the requested items and a plate between us, curiously watching as I prepared. "There was so much food at the party. Didn't you eat?"

I scraped a glob of butter over the soft center of each chunk of bread and dropped a spoonful of jam on top. "You saw my dress, right?" I jabbed the spoon at the door, thinking of it in a wet heap on my bedroom floor. "I wasn't going to fit in that dress if I ate anything, and when was I supposed to find the time? All I've had today is...fifteen glasses of sparkling wine." Was that right?

He blinked. "I forgot about the ridiculous things women do here to accomplish a look."

Be glad you have the freedom to forget. But I wasn't drunk enough to say that. "I'm sorry, by the way."

"For what?"

"I told you I was coming back after our training session, but Cole wanted me at the manor. I remembered too late."

He waved me away. "No hard feelings here...I'll be here all day tomorrow if you want to come by."

"I'd like that." I grabbed the plate and my drink and moved to the couch, closer to the fire, which was finally appropriate. The smooth black leather cushion let out a soft puff under me. Taking a bite, I savored the creamy, salty goodness of the butter, along with the contrasting sweetness of the blackberry jam.

Collapsing on the couch perpendicular to me, he crossed his legs. "The table wasn't good enough for you?"

Swallowing, I lifted the ends of my hair, dripping water. "Do you want me to catch a cold?"

"You wouldn't heal from that?"

I shrugged. "I don't know. I guess so. I don't remember ever being sick unless it was from alcohol."

A drop of water from his hair slid down his face. "That sounds like a yes to me."

"You could catch a cold."

He twisted the glass resting on his knee. "You could heal me."

"Not if you make me sit in the kitchen where it's uncomfortable. I've had enough of that for the day."

He cocked his head. "You did fidget quite a bit."

I laughed through a mouthful of food. "I love that you're going to talk like you witnessed anything other than the bar."

"I know that ballroom better than most of the staff. Little boys aren't in love with high society events, you know. Lots of vantages and hiding places. I saw what I needed to."

"Maybe you would have known how uncomfortable it was if you had stayed."

"My presence wouldn't have done anyone any good."

"Because the people love you more than Cole?" Fuck. Immortals help me, I'd said it.

Choking on his drink, he held up a finger. "Don't ever say that to my brother."

Flexing my right hand, I could only think it didn't matter. "Did you like being a Devotee?"

His eyes narrowed. "Are we playing question for a question again?"

"Sure," I said, mouth full of bread.

"Short answer is I did until I didn't." Fiddling with his glass, he laughed, but there was no humor in it. "Long answer, well, I'm not drunk enough for that."

Swapping the plate out for my drink, I angled it toward him. "I'm sorry."

His eyebrows knitted in confusion. "What are you apologizing for now?"

"That you had the experience of something you enjoyed become something painful."

He touched the tip of his tongue to his front teeth.

Finishing my drink, I asked, "What did you want to ask me?"

"You've been asked enough today. I'll save my question for a later date." He snapped his fingers, and a bottle of whiskey appeared in his hands. "Another?"

CHAPTER TWENTY-ONE

16.NINE.4004

I was walking home from work when I saw her. Panting at the foot of the stairs, stooped Isa, several tan cotton bags in each hand.

"Isa," I called. "Wait right there, I'm coming to help."

She looked up and, when she spotted me, smiled.

"Hello again, Eden, right?"

"Yup." I reached for the bags in both her hands. "Please let me carry these for you."

"You're a dear. Between a variety of gourds for fall and a sale on meat, I got a little carried away at the market today. I was beginning to think I'd have to drag everything up the stairs. Thank you so much."

As the weight shifted to me, I almost fell forward. A little carried away was an understatement. How she'd managed this far with them was beyond me.

"No, thank you. You've reminded me I need to run to the market myself." Searching through the cold cabinet that morning had yielded armfuls of spoiled food forgotten during my time at the manor. Only condiments remained.

Passing through the building's wards, I wondered if I could do this; my arms and calves were already on fire by the first landing.

"Did you just get off work?" Isa asked.

"Yeah," I said. "I work at Selene's House, just ten minutes away from here."

"Damien mentioned you work there. He brought me the sweetest drawings from his visit with you the other day. I must say they captured him well."

I wheezed a laugh, remembering the depiction of Damien. "The kids had a lot of fun with him. Not everyone gets a portrait."

"He had such a lovely time. You know, I've known him since he was little, and I've never seen him in such a good mood as he was that day."

Not knowing what to say to that, I was grateful when Isa jogged up the last flight of stairs to get the door.

By the time I hit the sixth-floor landing, a sheen of sweat laced my brow.

Warm brown eyes gleaming and silver bob bouncing, she looked back over her shoulder at me. "Thank you again for your help. It was so darling of you."

The door opened to Isa's touch, and I stumbled after her, setting the bags on the table, on the floor—whatever flat surface I could manage.

Damien, sitting on the couch in sweats and a tee—journal and pen in hand—leapt to his feet. "Did you buy the whole market again?" Frowning, he looked from me to Isa and settled on me. "How did you come into this?"

Wiping my face, I glared up at him. "I was returning from work and saw Isa struggling with groceries. It's pretty crappy that you expect her to haul all your groceries up five flights of stairs. Why didn't you go with her or give her a grocery-sized money bag or something?"

"One, she doesn't like it when I accompany her, and two," plucking the bag off the table, he nodded toward the door, "a bag like you described is right there, and it never moves. She claims magic changes the taste of food."

"That's because it does," Isa trilled.

Damien rolled his eyes. "You missed training yesterday. What's your excuse this time?"

The frustration I felt gave way to shame. "I know, I'm sorry. No excuse, but little sleep and dealing with the worst hangover I've ever had left me barely wanting to live. Work was enough, and when I came home, I had nothing to give anyone or anything. I honestly figured you wouldn't be in any shape either." We'd spent the rest of that night on our respective couches in his living room, quietly passing the bottle back and forth until it was empty. I shifted my mouth to the side. "Might you forgive me once more?"

Damien opened his mouth as Isa shoved herself between us. Taking my hands in her own, she looked up at me. "What would you like to eat for dinner?"

Surely she'd meant to ask Damien that? "Oh, nothing—"

Damien furtively cut his hand at his neck.

"—too special. I'm not picky."

Isa clapped her hands together. "Perfect. I'll make you my famous meat pie then. You will love it. Everyone loves it."

"I'm sure I will," I said, "but only if it's all right with Damien?" I dared a glance at him.

He nodded as Isa spun back towards the kitchen, calling over her shoulder, "What he wants doesn't matter. You'll stay and eat. Dinner will be ready in a couple of hours. Make yourself at home, my darling."

Damien put his back to me as well, starting up the stairs to the penthouse. Not knowing what to do, I stared absently at the cracked door he'd said was his.

The clang on the stairs stopped. "You better come up before I change my mind," Damien called down.

And I ran up after him.

The black mats we'd used the other day were set parallel to one another before the panorama window, Damien standing between them. In his hand was a small black box, which he proffered to me. "This is for you."

Curious, I lifted the lid, looking down at twenty blue-green vials. "What are they?"

"A special concoction I made that will actually help you sleep at night. I started working on it after your confession. Half a vial a night should do it."

He'd made me an elixir.

Overwhelmed, I looked at him. "That's very kind and thoughtful of you. Thank you."

"It's nothing. Also, I wasn't hungover. I made an elixir to nullify the negative side effects of liquor and elixirs. It didn't occur to me to make you one, and for that, I'm sorry."

"It's fine. I shouldn't have drunk so much, but I guess I was having fun."

"You guess?"

I shrugged.

Collapsing cross-legged onto his mat, Damien nodded at mine. "Take your seat. Time to focus."

Placing the box gingerly to the side, I did. "Will you teach me how to make elixirs?"

He raised an eyebrow. "Already imagining making your own?"

I shifted my mouth sheepishly.

"Eventually, but first you need to master your connection with magic. Now focus. We're going to practice weaving strike charms."

***

"Again," Damien commanded from his seat on the corner of the suite's bed.

Glowering at him in the reflection, I huffed a breath, sending a strand of brown hair that'd escaped my ribbon fluttering. Squaring my shoulders, I inhaled through my nose and held out my hands for the fiftieth time. My flowing white blouse fluttered as magic charged the air. Holding my golden-eyed gaze, I let earth in. That, at least, had grown easier, though no more pleasant.

"Remember, your thoughts guide the magic. Have a clear intent. If your connection—"

Magic blasted the mirror, cracking it into two, startling us both.

Clapping my hand to my mouth, I stumbled a step back. "I'm so sorry. This is impossible. I'm never going to get it. I'll buy you a new mirror." Though it'd take me a while to afford it. "Thank you for—"

"Stop being a quitter, Eden. You aren't focusing."

Kicking the baseboard, I raised a finger to him. "If you say that one more time, I swear on the Immortals—"

Waving his hand, the crack erased, smoothing my reflection.

I gaped in awe, my failure and annoyance momentarily forgotten. "How did you…I'll never be able to do that."

He snapped a finger. "None of that. I started perfecting my charms at twelve. That was almost forty years ago."

Turning, I stepped toward him. "Don't try to play humble now. It didn't take you forty years to master this." Rubbing my hands against my face, I sighed. The twenty-fourth year of life is when most citizens of Sorbis went through the Academy, which meant… "It took you no more than thirteen. *Reincimmo.*"

Leaping from the corner of the bed, he removed the space between us, filling the air around me with the scent of sandalwood and cedar.

"And I was formally trained," he said. Carefully, he pried my hands away from my face. "Whereas you have never had someone teach you anything until, well, me." He smiled thoughtfully. "Taking the sad and untrained under my wing, I am awesome, aren't I?"

I shoved his chest, but couldn't stop my smile. "You're awful."

Clasping my shoulders, he turned me to face the mirror once more. "Awfully generous. Now I have an idea that I think will help, but as I'm tired of my help and kindness being seen as a ploy, you'll have to give me your word: you'll spare me those comments."

I arched an eyebrow, to which his hard-pressed lips said *You're going to have to go with it*. "Okay, I give you my word."

Damien pressed himself flush against my back, making my whole body go stiff as a board.

"Okay, come on. I know what I said—"

"Then you know not to say anymore," he said softly. "Tell me your word means something to you? I'm only trying to guide you. Relax, Eden."

Glaring at him in the mirror, I eased my shoulders and relaxed against him.

"Now, follow my breathing."

Taking a deep breath, his chest pressed into my back. I watched mine rise and fall in the mirror, my body truly relaxing after several breaths.

"Leave out the magic and follow my instructions. Are you ready?"

I nodded.

"Bring your arms up."

Ignoring how dumb I felt after so many failures, I brought my arms shoulder height, palms facing toward the mirror, fingers slightly curled.

Damien's hands overlaid mine, molding himself to my shape, his fingers overwhelming mine by an entire digit.

Tucking his thumbs into my palms, he whispered, "Move with me."

It was the dip of one finger and the tap of another. A swoop of the hand and the curl of the other. Over and over again. A dance. Sometimes, my swoop would lag, or I would tap the wrong finger, but slowly, the dance gained traction.

"That's it. Now, open yourself to magic."

Cycling through the movements once more, a faint ball of pale green light the size of a pea appeared in my hands. Together, Damien and I continued the dance, going until the pea expanded to the size of an apple.

Slowly, Damien removed himself from around me and took a step back. "There it is."

Entranced, I looked at the ball of energy we'd created, twisting and gleaming in my hands. My chest rose and fell excitedly. Magic rippled off me in hot waves. "We did it."

"You did it, Eden."

My eyes—looking like liquid ore in the bright light—found his in the reflection.

The last light of the sun burnished his black hair and set his olive skin aglow, but the light in his jade-green eyes came from within.

"Dinner's ready," Isa called.

CHAPTER TWENTY-TWO
1.TEN.4004

Sighing dramatically, Rho set this week's donations on the rickety kitchen table across from me. Quite the haul based on the multiple thuds hitting the counter.

"I almost dislike Damien more for making me carry all of these bags," she grumbled. "If I wanted a workout, I'd go for a run with Grayden."

Laughing, I ripped the green crown off a strawberry. "It's a good problem to have."

"Which is why I'll let it go." Her bright purple shoes squeaked on the tile floor. "I was in the Shadow Market District yesterday to get some ecstasy elixirs when I remembered something." She slipped two vials into the back pocket of my jeans. "Though I'm not sure if you need it—you haven't been looking half-dead recently—I picked up some anyway."

The elixir Damien had made me was working so well, I'd half-forgotten I had nightmares. I slept well, and when I dreamed, it was how I imagined dreams were supposed to be.

Looking up from my de-crowning to give her the finger, I stopped slack-jawed. "What are you wearing?"

Rho wore a lime green turtle-neck sweater, her long magenta hair contrasting sharply with the color.

I dropped the strawberry I held and rushed over to her. "Even when you were acclimating to Sorbian weather, you never wore sleeves. What happened?"

She looked up at the skylight. "Grayden was awful."

I took a deep, calming breath. The only thing that kept my mind from jumping to the worst conclusion and threatening to go and stab the Charphan with the paring knife I'd been using was knowing, with every fiber of my being, that Grayden would never hurt Rho. It still didn't explain the sleeves, though.

Wiping my red-stained hands on a towel, I folded my arms across my chest. "That's the understatement of the century."

"He can be very sweet."

I poked my finger at my open mouth, sticking out my tongue.

Rho rolled her eyes. "Really, Eden." She smiled. "He isn't all bad. He has his moments."

Caring less about his moments, I asked again, "What happened?"

"He saw me talking to my neighbor and snapped." She grimaced. "He thought we were flirting."

"The cute neighbor?"

She nodded.

"Were you?"

She shrugged. "It was innocent, but even if it weren't, Grayden and I had never talked about being exclusively together again after our last break. I thought we were only having fun. Anyway, Grayden punched him in the face. When I finally managed to get him away and inside my apartment, he launched into his usual tirade about how I needed to stop working here. How he wanted to provide for me, that he could provide for me. We spent a lot of time bickering." She flicked the worn wooden table, leaning in conspiratorially. "Immortals Eden, he asked me to bind myself to him. He mentioned children."

"He's Charphan, of course, that's what he wants." When she didn't volunteer anymore, I asked, "And what did you say?"

Her violet eyes met mine, telling me with a look that I wouldn't like the answer. "I told him I'd think about it."

"No."

"We've been together for five years, and I'm not getting any younger. I want to settle down and have kids. He'd be a great father."

My eyes grew so wide I thought they might pop out. Children. With Grayden. "You're a demi. Age isn't a problem for you."

"Old in spirit. He makes me happy."

Grabbing her chin, I tilted her head to the light, getting a better look at her eyes.

"What are you doing?" she asked.

"Looking for signs that he's slipped you some kind of elixir."

She swatted my hand away.

I shook my head, not knowing where to begin. "You know how I feel about Charphan men. Women are subordinate to them from birth, first to their fathers, then to their partners. As a Misundran, I don't even know how you've been with him for so long, let alone how you're contemplating this."

"I know," she groaned. "We're supposed to meet tonight, and I'm going to give him an answer. Tell me you'll support me if I do say yes?"

I gave my friend a tight squeeze. "That goes without saying, but you still didn't answer about the sleeves."

She glanced down at the bright green sweater as if surprised to see it as well. Tapping a white nail against her chin, she grinned mischievously.

I gagged for real this time.

"There may have been a lot of sex as well, and he may have been very eager," she sighed dreamily. "It was phenomenal, but I may have a dozen or so love bites, and this is the only thing I had."

Returning my attention to the strawberries, I retched a little harder, earning a soft slap on the back.

"What does Forrest have us doing today?" she asked.

I motioned my knife towards the massive bowl of strawberries I had been working on and the small piles of pumpkins and butternut squash waiting to be prepared. "He wants the strawberries quartered, the pumpkins and the squash cut in half for roasting."

Grabbing an apron off the hook, she said, "Speaking of bond proposals, are you ready for Cole's birthday party?"

Of course, she asked that right as I went to slice. My stomach performed a flip. "There's nothing I need to do. A seamstress took my measurements the last time I was there, and a dress is being made for me. Everything else—"

She held up a hand, stopping me short. "I'm not letting you play dumb today. You know what I want to know about."

The one thing I actively avoided thinking about. "While it'll have been one year since the Bidding, Cole has been very busy taking over for his father. We haven't discussed anything."

I could feel her staring at me, the pregnant silence between us held a question she hadn't brought herself to ask. And if Rho couldn't flat-out ask it, it was a question I wouldn't want to answer.

"Will you be there?" I asked.

She plucked a piece of strawberry chunk from the pile and popped it into her mouth. "Sadly, if mother is there, I'm there."

"Oleander will be there?" The former Misundre Five members visiting for a birthday wasn't unheard of, but it wasn't common.

She nodded, dropping her gaze. "In light of Lupine's death, some of the Misundre Five—current and former—are unhappy with the

Alliance Council. She thinks it's important we show support." She took a breath, and I knew immediately it wasn't to say more about the tension. "Are you going to—"

Forrest, who rarely left his side of the kitchen, burst through the swinging doors, white apron splattered in red stains. "Ladies, today is not the day for gossip," he said, looking at Rho. He grabbed a huge knife and started slicing into the squash. "I needed these done thirty minutes ago. Get to work."

Saved.

CHAPTER TWENTY-THREE

2.TEN.4004

Per Damien's instructions, I got up at first light to come over and assist with the elixir we were making before heading to my shift at Selene's House. It was him I expected at the door when I knocked, a little past six, but it was Isa who answered, dressed in a long-sleeved yellow dress and white apron.

Bright-eyed, she stepped aside. "Good morning, dear. Come in, come in. Perfect timing. Breakfast is almost ready."

Having had dinner with Damien and Isa every night I came up, it made sense that she thought I was here for food. "Good morning, Isa. I'm actually only here because Damien asked me to stop by before work to help with something, but maybe I misunderstood him."

I expected to see him on the couch or at the table—some remark about my being late at the ready—but there was no sign of him.

"I know why you're here, dear. Last night, Damien informed me you'd be here early and asked me to let you in should he be unavailable. I just thought you might enjoy some breakfast." She shook her head and pulled me close. Nose scrunched, she lowered her voice to a scandalous whisper. "He went out with that Grayden last night. Only came home an hour ago, reeking and grumpy."

As if on cue, the door to Damien's room flew open.

"Isa," a scratchy voice called. He emerged a second later, the hard planes of his chiseled chest on full display, moving the eye down to where his hand kept the towel taut below his navel. It was the second time I'd seen him shirtless, and just like the first, heat bloomed under my skin.

"Where is my—" As if sensing the audience at the door, his gaze shifted toward us, locking in on me. Running a hand through his dripping wet hair, he straightened, making the muscles work. "What are you doing here?"

Patting my arm, Isa abandoned her post by me, making her way toward the safety of the kitchen with her head down.

"You told me to come over early, remember?"

He looked down. "Right…I did." He pointed towards the stairs. "Go set up the mats. They're in the closet. I'll be up in a moment."

I dared a look at the kitchen where Isa pretended to make rolls, looking as skeptical as I felt.

The exchange didn't escape Damien. "Chat time is over, Eden." He disappeared back into his room, slamming the door behind him.

I was unfurling the second mat before the window when he came storming in, clad in a black sweater and dark gray sweatpants. "You were five minutes late."

So much for escaping a comment. "Does it matter? You weren't ready. You didn't even remember."

Sighing, he collapsed onto the mat cross-legged. "You already know what the answer to that question is."

"Isa said you went out with Grayden last night. Have fun?"

He brought his hands, one nestled in the other, into the center of his lap. "It was fine. Let's start to focus."

I mirrored his position. "Where did you go?"

Frustrated green eyes met mine. "Is this an inquisition?"

"Nope, just thought you might tell me about your boys' night."

"Tell you what? That I got drunk and took a girl home? Bedded her and left before she woke up—why would you want to hear that?"

Unfazed by his abrasiveness, I held his gaze. "Rho and Q tell me about their love interests."

The muscles in his shoulders stiffened. "I'd hardly call a woman I'm never going to see again, if I can help it, a love interest."

"Doesn't it get old?"

His eyebrows pulled together. "Having sex?"

"Having casual sex. Never committing to anyone. Seems like the constant turnover and lack of loyalty would get boring."

"I find it quite thrilling, and it's never failed me. You really don't think having sex with the same person is boring? Not to mention, there's nothing to say that because you're *committed*, there's loyalty."

I dropped my gaze, looking at the city below. "That's not how a relationship is supposed to be."

"That's how so many of them are, though." He smacked the front of my mat, bringing me back to center. "Focus. You know what's not going to help you learn magic? All these questions or staring out the window."

So snippy. I leaned forward. "What did you do the last twenty years of your life?"

Slack-jawed, he rubbed his hands along his face. "For Immortal's sake—I'm too tired for this."

"You told me you'd tell me your family's secrets and stories," I pushed. "It's been a minute since you've done that."

"My family's—the ones I can share. Not my life story."

"What's the difference? We're friends, right? Seems strange to hang around you all the time and not know you better."

Shaking his head, he fell back against the bed. "Are you telling me you don't want to train today?"

"As complicated as you claim crafting elixirs to be, it's not like you're in any condition to train me anyway." Motioning to the mats.

The error dawning on him, he snapped his fingers, a glass of water appearing in his hand. "You've got me," he grumbled. "I'll answer your question, but you know the drill. You have to go first. I want to know about your life."

An easy enough agreement. "There isn't anything to know. I haven't done much."

"Humor me."

Cupping my chin in my hand, I stopped to consider what anyone would want to know. "You know both my parents died as a result of Roan's War. Your mother took me in as her ward. I moved out of Valentine Manor into my parents' apartment at the age of sixteen. The same year, I started working at Selene's House, and that brings me here."

"Why did you choose Selene's House?"

"I told you—"

"You told me why you chose the cause, not why you chose that particular orphanage."

I held up my hands. Wasn't it obvious? "This building is where my parents lived. That orphanage would have been where I was sent had it not been for your mother."

He considered my answer over a sip of water. "Is that how you and Rho met?"

Taken aback by his shift in interest, it took me a second to answer. "No, when she moved to Sorbis, she hung out around Lupine a lot. We bonded over our mutual love of going against what is expected of us," I smiled. "She started working at Selene's House after I mentioned it. I love everything about her, but her taste in men. The sooner her relationship with Grayden ends, the better. No offense."

"That's never going to happen," he snorted. "They're mates."

"What are you talking about?"

"Someone hasn't been doing their reading." He drained the glass. "Your friend and my cousin are mates. At least she is his. Mating culture is only a part of the Charphan lifestyle. Anyone with a drop of Charphan blood has the instinct to have a mate. The more that's in your blood, the stronger it is."

I crossed my arms. "She's never mentioned anything about that."

"Grayden was determined he wouldn't find a mate—that he didn't want one—so he's trying to fight it, but it's hard to deny something that primal. The fact that their relationship isn't stable, I doubt he's told her." He laughed dryly. "It's honestly the greatest irony that it'd be a Misundran woman. The complete opposite of Charph."

"Lovely."

Damien considered me. "Why do you dislike him?"

"Besides the fact that he referred to me exclusively as Bottom Feeder until the Bidding to Cole?"

Sucking in a breath, Damien clicked his tongue. "That's a fair reason."

"I think the better question is, why don't you?" I continued. "Would you be so fond of him if you weren't related?"

"Yes, Grayden is one of the most loyal people I've ever known."

"Don't you mean the most domineering and controlling?"

"Most of your verdict is limited to how you see him with and through Rho. I won't defend that behavior, but I won't condemn him for it, either. Rhododendron isn't faultless, and he's struggling. I've heard the rejection of a mate drives one crazy."

"Does that explain you?" I teased.

He smiled to himself. "We aren't talking about me quite yet. You have so many thoughts about everyone else's relationships—what about yours? You conveniently left that out of your summary."

I held myself a little tighter. How had this become about me? "I'm your brother's Bidden. There's nothing to know."

"There's been no one else?"

Shaking my head, I exhaled, "Why don't you ask what you really want to know?"

His green eyes grew wide. "What is it that you think I want to know?"

Biting the inside of my cheek, I stared at him and his unwavering fake innocence. "You want to know how many men I've been with. You probably want to know if one of them is Q. I guess I shouldn't be surprised you want to know. Everyone in the city wants to know those things. They're the only things somehow no one knows." I took a deep breath. "If I answer that, you have to answer something you don't share with people when it's your turn."

He shrugged. "That's fine, but to make you feel more at ease, there's been zero women I've been interested in for more than sex—there's your answer about a mate. The number of women I've been with, I doubt you really want to know."

Tucking a strand of hair behind my ear, I nodded. "I don't. Q and I haven't slept together, but I've never let people believe otherwise, and neither has he, out of courtesy to me, because who I have or haven't been with isn't the public's business. When it comes to love interests, I've had two, both very quiet." Having confessed in a single breath, I sucked in another. "One started right before I turned sixteen and lasted about three years. And then another when I was twenty-one, just before Cole, that lasted less than a year."

He twirled the glass in his hand. "Why did they end?"

My gaze coasted along the high white ceilings of the suite. "The one didn't like the secrecy around our relationship, but didn't like the idea of the attention either. It's crazy to think about now because I was convinced I'd have his baby." I laughed at myself. "The other one I ended when Lupine told me she wanted to nominate me for Cole's Bidding." Bringing my knees to my chest, I leaned against them. "I think that's enough about me."

Having slouched, he sat up, putting the glass aside. "Alright. Usually, the only way I traverse the past is with a drink. Lucky for you, I'm tired, and that's equivalent. You want to know what I've been doing for the last twenty years? I surfed. I hiked. Went swimming. Fished in the harbor. Camped in the forest for extended periods."

I raised an eyebrow.

"You don't believe me."

"That you went from the hero philanderer prince of Solta to loner nature boy?"

Humor glittered in his eyes. "I guess you really wouldn't believe, then, that one of those camping trips lasted five years?"

I kicked his foot. "Don't play with me. I didn't play with you."

He held up his hands defensively. "I'm not playing at all. I am a man of many facets. The idea when I left was I'd leave everything behind I associated with life here."

"Why?"

He dropped every finger on his hands but the index on his right hand. That, he pointed at me. "If I answer that, that's your personal question."

I nodded my acceptance.

A shadow crossed his face, his brow furrowing. "I…had a hard time the first couple of years after the war. I couldn't sleep. I was anxious. I drank and smoked a lot. The only reason I ate food was because my Uncle Heath would make me."

My heart twisted in my chest. "Why didn't you make yourself an elixir?"

"Magic was a part of my old life," he inhaled. "Anyway, when I finally got over that, I knew I wanted to spend some time alone. It started as a day trip here and there, then it became a couple of days away, then weeks, and months, and finally, I committed to it. The woods north of Misundre go on for forever, I swear. I told myself I'd walk for as long as I could and make my home where I collapsed, and I did. The only reason I came back is a promise to my uncle that I would after five years."

"Was your hair down to your waist with a bushy beard to match?" As curious about the answer as I was determined to make him smile.

He huffed a laugh. "No, I took basic things like a knife with me. I'm sure I looked awful, but I have a certain grooming standard I like to maintain."

"Why didn't you go back?"

He peered at me from the corner of his eye. "Wishing I had?"

I nudged his foot with mine. "You know, I'm glad you're here. Who else would I be annoying right now if you had?"

"Some other tired fool, I'm sure." But he grinned while he said the words, a playful glint in his eyes. "To answer your question, I arrived at my uncle's place and took a hot shower. Afterward, the people I cared about bombarded me with food, and I realized I'd missed it. Company. Food accessibility—catching your own food sucks. Sex."

And just like that, a touching moment was ruined. I fake retched. "With Violet."

"There you go, making assumptions. I said that I missed sex. Nothing happened with her until years later." Rolling his eyes, he got to his feet. "I think that's enough of your non-magic-related questions. I'm going to get some rest now. I don't even have the energy to make it downstairs, so looks like I'm going to use this room for once. I'll see you at dinner."

Getting to my feet, I looked up at him. "You want me to come back later?"

He nodded. "I should be fine then."

I padded toward the door. "I'll be here."

"And Eden?"

I turned to look at him. Big mistake as he had his shirt half tugged up over his head, giving me a view of the smooth expanse of his back. Couldn't he have waited a moment longer?

"The only person I took home last night was Grayden. He showed up at my door not long after you left, wasted on elixirs and alcohol. I took him home and stayed with him. I'd never seen him so worked up. Apparently, he proposed to Rho, and she was to give him her response yesterday evening, to which she told him no and that she needed to take a break. He also claimed it was your fault, that you put all these ideas in her head because you don't like him. I spent the night listening to him denigrate you, among other things."

He sighed, tossing the shirt aside. Averting my eyes away, I caught him watching me in the reflection, a mischievous smile on his face.

"Anyway, I spent most of the night reminding him of rational things and facts like that their relationship issues are not your fault, you're Rho's best friend, he hates violence against women, and ultimately, you're Cole's Bidden."

Unsure how I felt about my presence as Cole's Bidden being the ultimate reason Grayden shouldn't revert to violence, I nodded. "Did he tell you he assaulted a guy?"

"Several times, though in his mind, he was protecting his mate."

I shot him a look.

"I said I don't condone his behavior, simply relaying his perception."

Standing a little straighter, I said, "I did express my lack of approval for him when she asked me my thoughts. I'm sorry I caused you a problem."

Shrugging, he flashed me a smile. "It's no matter. Even if it were on you, you were being a supportive friend. Grayden should be grateful Rho has that, even if it makes him angry."

I drummed my fingers against the doorframe. "Why did you let me believe differently—about your evening?"

The comforter of the bed whooshed back, Damien slipping in. "I think the better question is, why do you still make assumptions about me? You can give me an answer to that another time, though. I'm going to bed."

Snapping his fingers, the glass of the panorama window darkened, and he collapsed onto the pillow.

CHAPTER TWENTY-FOUR

7.TEN.4004

I finished packing my overnight bag and paced the door, working to hype myself up to summon Julien and go back to Valentine Manor.

Waiting for me, on the other side of the door, was the question I'd been given a year to answer. A year since the Bidding. Cole and I hadn't discussed it, but I knew it would be soon.

Which is why, on the other side of the door, I didn't fully register what I was doing until after I'd knocked, so lightly I wondered if they'd heard.

Hugging my arms to my chest, I looked to the stairwell window, letting my eyes come to rest on the faces of the Immortals Faldone and Valentine, looking amicably at one another. A gust of wind caught my hair, tossing the brown strands everywhere.

This had been nice. This opportunity. This friendship.

"I figured you'd be at the manor by now," a voice said, breaking my daze. Damien stood in the doorway, his chest rising and falling a little breathlessly. "You coming in? Or should I leave it cracked? You know how I feel about losing my beloved heat."

I smiled up at him. "Hi, Damien."

His eyes narrowed a fraction. Throat bobbing as he swallowed, he nodded his greeting and stepped aside.

Kicking my flats off by the door, I called, "Good evening, Isa."

Her head popped up in the kitchen window a second later. "Hi, darling! Are you hungry? I can make you some food."

"Oh no, I'm not hungry, and I can't stay long, but thank you." I turned to Damien. "But you can make me a drink."

"I can… Meet you upstairs?"

Nodding, I wandered up to the suite, taking a seat on the cold hardwood floor before the panorama window, drinking in the view of the city under a moonlit sky. Snapping my fingers, I brought forth a bottle of wine I'd seen in one of Damien's cabinets. Another snap, and the cork appeared in my hand.

Smiling to myself, I drank several long gulps and rested the bottle on my knee. As the wine moved down my throat and into my stomach, it oiled the knots there, easing them apart.

"Did I hear things correctly? I thought you asked me to make you a drink?"

"You were taking too long. Your efforts aren't for naught, though. I'll need that one as well. This is almost empty." I reached up to take the drink he proffered me—purple and smelling of honey and lavender.

Sitting beside me, he inclined his head toward the bottle. "Is that from my collection?"

"It is." I grinned sheepishly. "I saw it looking abandoned when you opened the cabinets the other day."

He placed his drink at his feet and plucked the bottle from me, twisting it around to inspect it in the silvery light. "You opened one of the good ones. I snuck this from the manor's cellar before my father's return home. Believe it or not, this is one from the days of my immortal ancestor." He pressed the mouth of the bottle to his lips. "Tastes like it, too."

"I guess I won't be getting points for my taste tonight then."

He smiled to himself. "No, but you've gotten better at summoning, and for that I'm proud."

Needing to do something with my hands, I felt for the key necklace at my throat. "Is it okay if I didn't come up to train tonight? I just wanted to talk."

Damien opened his mouth, but I waved him away. "None of that. I know the Academy wouldn't have allowed me to skip training."

Something shifted in his eyes, his attention a little too focused. "As you wish…Is everything okay?" he asked.

I needed another drink. "Why wouldn't it be?"

"I guess I've never seen you brood."

Huffing a laugh, I worked the bottle from his hand. "Only men brood. I'm daydreaming."

"About?"

"What could have been." I hiccuped. "What I could have been. If I'd done this or done that. If I'd said yes instead of no and vice versa." Raising the bottle, I washed the taste of the words away like a nasty elixir.

Leaning forward, Damien picked up his drink. "I used to do that a lot, but I always came away with a deeper sense of regret than I did going in."

An easy warmth moved like a breeze through my body. Lazily, I scanned the buildings across the way. "Why?"

"Because the only thing worse than the struggles in life you survive is knowing that there were options and you didn't have to endure the things you did."

Shifting to face him once more, I asked, "What's your biggest regret?"

He spewed his drink. "I'll answer that if you will."

I made my eyes wide and sad, sticking out my lower lip a touch.

Snapping for a napkin he rubbed across his face, Damien waved his finger. "That shit doesn't work on me. The longer you do it, the more convinced I am that all of the elixirs and alcohol in the kingdom wouldn't make me give you an answer."

I stayed strong. Hearing what he said, but sure I could crack him.

He sighed. "How about I trade you my last regret for a question?"

"Deal."

"I regret not coming back to Sorbis sooner."

"Why?"

"Because I missed a lot." He tapped a finger testily against the glass. "Now, what's really bothering you?"

Heat needled the back of my neck. I couldn't tell him the truth, so I told him the next best thing. Which wasn't *not* bothering me. "I think Cole's sleeping with Violet." Saying what I'd been speculating for nearly a month now was equally liberating and suffocating.

His mouth turned down slightly. "What makes you think that?"

"Just a feeling I get, and since you told me about their history, I've noticed the way he and Violet are around one another. She looks at him like—"

"Like she's power hungry?"

Wagging my finger, I set the empty wine bottle down and grabbed my drink. "I know you think that because she slept with you, but if she wanted only power, she could've tried for Quincy as well. He wouldn't say yes, but she could try. Violet stares at Cole longingly, and after what you told me about their history together, I wouldn't be surprised if there was still something there. I think she went after you because she wanted to make him jealous."

He pursed his lips. "I feel like that was somehow the greatest insult to my sexual prowess I've ever received."

Rolling my eyes, I shoved his chest. "I'm probably crazy."

The sound of rustling as he twisted toward me broke the silence that followed. Damien sucked in a breath, the humor gone from his eyes. "If you weren't…would you want me to tell you?"

I didn't get too far down the spiral of hurt that he'd known something and not shared it before remembering, even if he had, it wouldn't have done any good. I was Cole's council-appointed Bidden. There was interest and lust there, not love. I'd expected this. Not before we were bound, but when I'd grown old, or at least not for the first ten years. Twenty-three years around Lupine had taught me enough of what to expect from being bound to the King of Solta. It was why her decision to nominate me almost a year ago had surprised me.

But Lupine had never done anything but the best by me.

And if Damien had told me, would I even have believed him?

Having zoned out on Damien's chin, I met his eyes. Green eyes—begging for forgiveness—searched my face, a hand frozen in his hair. His mouth opened and closed as he began to speak, then changed his mind.

Finally, I looked down at the drink he'd made. "No, I wouldn't."

The shift in the air between us was palpable. Amicable warmth to cold stillness. I wanted to know what he was thinking—what he thought of me—and I didn't. His clenched hand around the glass said enough.

"Will you be at Cole's birthday party?" I whispered. Testing the water.

His words were forced. "I have no choice."

I tried again. "It's strange that it will be at the manor and not Hotel Solta."

"Yeah."

I nodded once, accepting what I'd done. "You're upset with me."

Damien finished his drink and snapped for another bottle, letting silence fill the space between us.

Fair enough. *I'd come to say goodbye to this anyway.*

Tears pricked my eyes. "I'll leave." Thinking he might say something, I stood slowly. When he didn't so much as bat an eye, I knew I'd been naïve to hope. "I'll be at the manor for the next couple of days," *maybe forever,* "preparing for the party. Will you let Isa know for me?"

Damien didn't move. "Why don't you tell her yourself?"

"She always has a disappointed look on her face when I mention Cole," I admitted, fighting the urge to hug him, "and I hate letting people I care about down."

One person tonight was enough.

Padding softly across the floor to the door, I knew I couldn't leave things how they were. I'd say goodbye to this, but hopefully not goodbye to him. "I'll see you at the party, Damien," I said and left.

CHAPTER TWENTY-FIVE

9.TEN.4004

This evening's bespoke gown glowed sunset orange, with a satin corseted bodice and a delicate tulle skirt. Elodie, who'd dressed me, had pulled the laces so tight, I had to sit perfectly erect in the armchair in the living room to keep the pressure off my lungs and back.

Every time the door opened, the soundproof charm broke, and the perfect silence gave way to boisterous music and high-society chatter. Some of it was about how cute the Protectors guarding the door were, but most of it was derogatory comments about my lack of attendance. *Wonder what she could be wearing tonight that's taking her so long to get ready? If I looked as plain as she did, I'd probably be getting prepared well into the party, too...Sorbis's Sweetheart is too good to hang out with us. She'd probably rather hang out with her beloved orphans...And as always,* my favorite: *She's such a freak I can't believe she's who the Council chose.*

There had been many variations of the latter comment. In fact, as Elodie bid me goodnight and took her leave, I heard it once more: *she doesn't deserve to be queen.*

I'd give them all one thing: I was much later than usual.

An hour late entrance was normal. That was how the royal family—and I by association—did it, but this? I allowed myself a glance at the mantle clock, five minutes past seven. The party had been in swing for two hours, and Cole had yet to get me for our entrance—a suggestion he'd insisted on that morning.

Something had to be going on.

I brought the book nestled in my hands—still on the same page as when I'd opened it—up in a last-ditch effort to read it, but all I saw were odd black shapes on a cream page, not letters making up words.

The door cracked once more, sending a fresh wave of anxiety over me. What would I hear now?

"Have you ladies nothing better to do than congregate outside my apartment?" a voice teased.

Cole.

"Your Highness," a group of women cooed in unison. "Happy birthday."

"We knew everyone would be on you," a familiar voice purred. Violet. "We wanted to beat them to you." Her *we* sounded more like an *I*.

"You're too thoughtful," Cole chuckled, "but you should all go enjoy yourselves. I'll see you all at the celebration."

The creak of the door shutting followed his words, along with the sharp strike of his dress shoes against the hardwood floor. Setting the book aside, I ran my sweaty hands down the skirt of my dress, putting on my best smile.

He appeared in the doorway a moment later wearing his green and red Alliance regalia. "Doll, I apologize for keeping you waiting. The boys wanted to have a drink to celebrate, and they kept me longer than expected." The signet ring on his pinky glinted in the light as he extended his hand to me.

I rose to take it.

His free arm encircled my waist, sweeping me up against him. Dragging his nose lightly along my cheek, he kissed my jaw. "You look gorgeous."

"Thank you, you look very handsome yourself," I said, ignoring the roiling in my stomach. "Happy birthday."

"A very happy birthday indeed. Are you ready?" He steered me smoothly toward the door, holding it open to the chaos, encouraging me out.

A group of women huddled together—no doubt the ones I'd heard—looked up at our exit, all staring after me, speechless. At the center of them was Violet, who gave me a once-over and sneered.

The Protectors flanking the door started to follow, but one head shake from Cole stopped them. His hand slid along my lower back, coaxing me on as we headed away from them.

I looked up at him, expecting his attention to be forward, but his cool green eyes watched me unreservedly. What was going on? "I thought the party was in the Magnolia Ballroom?" Which was on the northwestern side of the manor.

Cole smiled down at me. "It is, but I need a break and thought it might be nice to have a moment alone together before we enter."

Fighting the burning in my lungs, I returned his smile.

Side by side, he led me through the halls and down a set of stairs, the party and its chatter growing fainter with each step.

We were halfway there when muscle memory overtook Cole's lead. How had it taken me so long to realize where we were going? This was the way anyone would take from the eastern side of the manor to the gardens. Excitement warmed my stomach, putting a vigor in my step he registered with a half-smile. Having had no interest in being watched by my shadows, I hadn't visited them or the Olinda Roses since the night of Lupine's funeral.

We passed by drunk party goers who'd stumbled away from the celebration, and paid us no mind on our way out the back door, and on the other side—greeted by the pinkish orange light of sunset, the rustling of the leaves of the trees, soft chirp of crickets, and faintest sound of music from further up the way—I could breathe. The cool air of the fall evening felt lush in my lungs.

Cole let go of my hand, letting me wander through the garden but staying a couple of steps behind, the stone path clicking under our shoes. At this time of the day, the roses were a sea of black flower buds waiting for their hour. It occurred to me I'd never visited the Olinda Roses before midnight, and something about being here now felt unnatural.

Lightly, I brushed my fingers along the tip of a delicate bud, imagining its silver-tipped bloom. Twisting to look at him, I started to say *we should come out here later this evening,* but only made it as far as we should, stopped by the sight of the sapphire and diamond ring Cole clutched between his thumb and forefinger.

Dread bubbled in my stomach.

I stared at it, wondering if this was one of my nightmares. Waiting for the moment I'd wake up.

Cole's lips parted, flashing his perfect white teeth. The poised smile I saw him use when he addressed the people. "Eden Alexander, will you be queen to me and my people?"

My heart lodged in my throat. I was supposed to have more time. "What?" It was the first anniversary, and I knew we'd be talking about it soon, but it wasn't supposed to happen tonight.

The corner of his lips twitched. "Be my queen, Eden."

I fought to control the sudden shaking in my hands, forgetting it could translate to my voice. "We haven't talked about this. We were supposed to talk about this."

His eyebrows knitted together. "We've talked about it dozens of times."

"You told me we'd talk about it before you asked. That we'd discuss if it made sense—if we worked."

Cole's smile faltered. "What are you saying?"

I'd spent the last several days, last several months, last year thinking. *I haven't been happy. I don't think it makes sense. I tried. This isn't the life for me. I thought I could. For Lupine, I would have done anything.*

But Lupine was gone, and I—I was still here, and if this was it, I couldn't do it.

Shaking my head, I backed away, unsure of what else to do. Heat stabbed at my eyes. "I'm sorry, I can't." I'd said it. Immortals, I'd said it. Aloud. To him.

The hand holding the ring dropped away, his eyes narrowing to slits. "What do you mean you can't?"

Fire rushed through my body, forcing me to take another stumbling step back. "I can't be queen, I can't, I'm sorry."

Cole froze, eyes unmoving, mouth neutral, and jaw hard. Even his chest stopped its rise and fall.

Not knowing what else to do, I turned on my heel right as a tear fell onto my cheek. Followed by another. And another. One for every step. I feebly scrubbed them away with the back of my hand.

"Eden, wait…" I thought I heard him say over my clacking heels, a hint of desperation in his voice.

My heart leapt in my chest. I could fix it—

Don't you turn back, don't you dare turn back. Run.

I stopped for half a heartbeat to rip off my shoes and did what the voice said.

CHAPTER TWENTY-SIX

9.TEN.4004

My feet and the bottom of my dress damp from running through the grass—wet from the afternoon rainstorm—I burst through the wards. Hands shaking, I reached for the signet ring on my finger, my hand finding flesh instead of metal.

No. Fuck.

I could picture where it rested on the dresser in my bedroom. Back in the manor.

Not like Julien would come for me anyway. Cole had to know. He had to know I couldn't go anywhere. That's why he hadn't pursued me. I was trapped.

No, I wasn't trapped because I refused to be.

Trying to breathe, I went through my options. No one at the party would help me—everyone was here for Cole, everyone served him— what would they want with me? I had no friends or allies at this party. No, I had some—or I'd had. Quincy and Rho. Damien. But with Lupine gone and my connection to Cole broken, would I be anything to them now?

And either way, all those roads led back to the manor. I wouldn't— couldn't go back.

Something inside me shattered into a million tiny shards and fell, creating a million little cuts. I wiped away the fresh tears blurring my vision.

It'd take me days to walk home, and in this dress—I slammed my fists into the tulle—fuck.

"Eden?"

A brush at my exposed shoulder made my lungs seize. I'd forgotten to check behind me. Jerking away faster than a lightning strike, I turned sharply on my heel, my orange shoes clattering to the ground.

I looked at the figure—the twilight to their back, surrounded by trees so dark they looked black—catching a glimpse of green eyes and a black suit. It couldn't be…

"Damien?" I stuttered.

"Yeah."

Something shot out toward me, the movement sending me another step back.

Damien held up his hands. "Hey, it's okay. What's wrong?" Stepping closer, he came into focus, motioning slowly back toward the path. "Why don't we go back to the manor and talk?"

My heart slammed into my ribs. "Don't take me back."

"Take you back where?"

"To Cole," I croaked.

Damien's eyes widened a fraction. "What happened?"

I shook my head. I'd ruined everything. I'd let everyone down. Everyone who'd praised my name in the street, who'd told me I gave them hope for the kingdom, who thought I would be the perfect queen, and told me I'd changed their life—that I'd saved them.

Lupine.

It was crippling.

My breath started coming out in rapid bursts. "What have I done?" Trying to breathe, I braced my hand over my heart and the key necklace hovering there, collapsing to my knees in the dirt. Sobs wracked my body. "Please, don't take me back. I just want to go home."

Hot tears dripped from my chin, soaking into the bodice of my dress.

Damien fell to his knees before me, pulling my broken, shaking body tight against him like a splint. "Hey, I'll take you home, but breathe for me, please?"

Unable to hold my head up any longer, I laid it on his shoulder, tears soaking the collar of his suit. I tried to breathe slower, but the breaths came in spurts.

A gentle hand coasted down my hair. "Breathe, Eden, I have you."

Shutting out the thoughts, I closed my eyes and tried. Inhaling slowly against my body's will and coughing so hard I expected a lung to come out. Little by little, my system accepted air again. Accepted breathing and the smell of sandalwood and cedar soothing me.

All the while, the stroke on my hair continued—the beating of the heart beneath my ear as calming as the sensation.

The stroking stopped, and the world went quiet. The warm, firm hold around me became something soft and cool. I opened my eyes. Lying down. I was lying down, and there was a view of the farmlands before me, reaching as far as the eye could see.

"I'm in the suite," I rasped. My tear-weary eyes scanned the room. How had I gotten here? Was there still a chance this was all a nightmare?

"You are. Would you like to stay?" Damien asked. I looked at him standing a step away. "The suite is yours."

I shouldn't, but I didn't want to be alone. "I can't intrude."

"It's no intrusion." He ran his hand once more down my hair. "But let me get you something more comfortable to wear. I'll be right back."

I listened to him leave, his hard footsteps threatening to bring down the staircase, and then I listened to my heartbeat, so tired from hammering, it beat the minimum it needed to keep me alive.

Numb, I sat up and found a girl looking back at me in the mirror. A broken girl. The bottom of her gown, dirty and sodden, now several shades darker. Her long, dark brown hair, once perfectly coiffed, hung in loose waves, black streaks of eyeliner and mascara running down from her bloodshot eyes.

I moved closer to the reflection to confirm, yes, the gold shine my irises once held was gone like the life in me, cooled to a steely brass.

Sitting before the mirror, I snapped my fingers. No image in my head, only a desire. A decanter of whiskey appeared in my hands—the golden-brown liquid dancing in its glass cage.

I wanted to die. The thought made my stomach twist. No, I didn't— that wasn't it. I wanted to be forgotten, even to myself, indefinitely.

Cold crystal to my lips, I drank and drank until my body, starved of air, forced my hand.

I marked the things I'd left at the manor. Things I'd never see again because I'd never go back, and I never wanted to see Cole again. Thankfully, not much. My necklace. I touched the key resting on my breastbone, grateful for my insistence I wear it.

The sound of Damien's steps rattling the stairs jarred me. He came through the door a moment later, a neatly folded pile of black clothes in hand.

His eyes went from mine to the bottle. "You're drinking."

I stared down the mouth of the bottle, smiling. "Can't get anything past you." I upturned the bottle and gulped, draining it in one go.

He set the clothes beside me. "Isa is making you food."

I shook my head. "I'm not hungry."

"Would you like to go for a walk?"

A dark laugh escaping me, I wagged my finger at him. "Always making jokes."

He reached to take the empty bottle from me, and I let him.

"Is there anything I can do?" he asked.

"You can grab me another bottle. I'd like to drink myself into nothingness."

Damien considered me warily but conceded a nod, disappearing into the suite's bathroom.

Returning my attention to my reflection, something flickered at my ears. I unhooked the citrine earrings—Cole's most recent gift and the perfect bauble for a doll—and threw them away as hard as I could, landing somewhere in the room in a clatter. Triggered by the reminder of him, everything had to go. I reached behind my back to undo the laces, desperately searching for the ties and failing. What if the dress was part of me now?

Clawing at the satin bodice, something like rage consumed me. This dress. I hated orange, and I hated this dress. A cry of frustration escaped me, pain lancing my ribs as my futile attempts pulled the laces tighter.

Damien fell to his knees beside me, his green eyes meeting mine in the reflection, concern furrowing his brow, a small bottle of something black and sparkly in his hands. "What's wrong?"

I buried my fists into the skirt of my gown. "These stupid laces, these stupid infernal gowns."

"Would you like help?"

I nodded so fast everything blurred. He passed me the bottle.

One by one, Damien loosened and undid the laces, his cool fingers brushing my hot skin. I took a drink of the shimmering black elixir—tasting like grape—to stifle a whimper as one vise-like lace tightened a hair more and released.

When he was done, he stared in horror at my back. "How…"

Glancing over my shoulder, I took in the sight of the white panels of skin and red lines the corset had impressed on me.

Setting the bottle aside, I slipped the shirt on over the dress and stood, feeling a hundred pounds lighter as it fell away, and the shirt unfolded to my mid-thigh.

"Thank you," I said, pulling on the pants. Too long for me, but the cuffs kept me from walking on the leg's hem. I picked up the bottle. "This isn't whiskey."

Damien stood, throat bobbing. "It isn't. It's a special elixir I made years ago. I don't touch it any longer, but I always keep it on hand." His next words were a breath. "I call it Oblivion."

My eyes widened in appreciation for the name as I helped myself to it.

He watched me, arms crossed. "Do you want to tell me what happened?"

"Cole asked me to be queen," I whispered, wincing. "But you already know that. When I saw you earlier, I thought he'd sent you after me. I don't know how you were there, but you knew, didn't you?"

"I did…Cole told us before the party started. You didn't say yes."

I flinched. *Us.* "I didn't."

Damien swallowed. "Why didn't you?"

Tucking a strand of hair behind my ears, I exhaled, preparing to tell the truth because it was over now. I had nothing left to lose.

"Because I couldn't say yes. I couldn't do it anymore. Because I was scared. Scared of being a living doll for Cole to parade around. Scared of being a glorified bed warmer. Scared to have children live that kind of life, with all the expectations. I saw how it wore on Lupine. I was afraid to love Cole. You shouldn't be afraid to love someone."

I paced the length of the room. "That's all I've thought for the last year. It's all I thought over and over when he pulled out the ring. And it was so loud. *You shouldn't be afraid to love someone.* I knew before. I knew before tonight. I realized it so clearly this past summer, and I tried to write away the feelings in that stupid note. I care for Cole, but I don't love him, and I'm not in love with him. The other night, in this room, I lied to myself." I hugged my arms. "I thought I had more time to turn the lie into a truth. I wanted to love him—I tried so hard, but I can't, and I don't. I don't want to be queen. I never wanted to do it." Abruptly, I stopped pacing and looked down, shoulders shaking. "I've lost everything tonight."

Damien moved to me. Taking my face in his hands, he wiped away the tears I didn't know had sprung as they fell. "What is it you think you've lost?"

I looked up at him. "Everything, Damien. All the people I've ever thought of as family, all my friends—they're loyal to him first. I only had any of it because of Lupine and Cole. Worst of all, I let Lupine down. This was what she wanted. Lupine, on Cole's sixtieth birthday, when she nominated me, was overjoyed. I never understood why she wanted it for me, but there's nothing I wouldn't have done for her."

Damien stopped—his thumbs, his breathing. "My mother didn't want you to be with Cole. She didn't want you to be queen."

"What?" The word caught in my throat. "What are you talking about?"

He nodded urgently. "It's true, she didn't. My father threatened to have you killed if she didn't nominate you for the Bidding. She did it to protect you."

My forehead tightened. "Then why wouldn't she tell me that?"

"It was my father's doing. He tricked her into making a blood oath. She couldn't tell you. She couldn't tell anyone in Sorbis."

Breaking free from his hands, I stepped back, the oblivion elixir thudding against the hardwood. "Then how do you know about this?"

"There was a loophole in the bargain. My father never expected her to speak with anyone outside of Sorbis alone. She told me about it the night we went to see the Olinda Roses—right before you arrived. She asked me to tell you the truth."

Fire licked through me. "Then why didn't you?"

He reached for me. "I—I didn't know how. I didn't think it was my place to—"

I slapped his hand away. "To what? Be honest with me?" I snapped. "I've been sitting with the shame of letting her and everyone else in this city down for months."

Unable to think—unable to look at him any longer, I stormed for the door.

The stairs shrieked as I descended them, Damien close behind me. "Eden, please wait—I'm sorry. I didn't know you felt the way you did, and I was so caught up trying to uphold my Absolution Oath to be your friend, to protect you."

The final admission felt like a knife dragged across my throat.

A final request made by the dying in the hopes of redemption.

I spun around so quickly he stumbled back. Sneering, I charged toward him, incredulity seeping from every pore. "You made an Absolution Oath to be my friend? To protect me?" Laughing sardonically, I stepped back, throwing my hands up. Everything suddenly making sense. "That's what all of this has been about. Why you didn't go back to Misundre—the training."

A v formed between his brows, his eyes pleading. He started to take a step toward me, but one look stopped him dead. "No—she asked me to look after you, but," he stumbled, "Eden, please, I—"

But I didn't want to hear anymore. Now or ever again. "It's a good thing the only thing you lose in breaking an Absolution Oath is your honor." I smiled bitterly, letting everything hit me. The whiskey and oblivion elixir were working—I felt everything, but I didn't care. "I can't believe I ever thought we were friends. I must be the saddest woman in all of Solta." I met Damien's eyes one last time—deadened, looking like the wind had been knocked from him. "Do us both a favor and go back to Misundre. I won't be coming back up here, and I never want to see you again."

Slamming the door, I didn't look back.

Part III

CHAPTER TWENTY-SEVEN

15.TEN.4004

Tucking my hair into a dark red knit hat, I steeled myself to go outside.

The Alliance Access broke the news of the dissolution of my Bidding to Cole the day after his birthday, and Union Square flooded daily with people booing or cheering my decision—all of them hungry for answers I'd never give, so I'd avoided leaving my apartment.

My stomach let out a low, deep growl as if I needed reminding that time had come to an end.

Not knowing if or when I'd be back to my apartment, I'd eaten or tossed my perishable food before I'd left for the manor, lest it be forgotten and left to rot—a smell I never wanted to encounter again. That'd left me a bag of dried beans, two packs of crackers, a jar of mustard, and blueberry jam.

All of it was gone after the first three days, and the last two, I'd been surviving on water.

Last night, the hunger pains kicking in, I'd tossed back half of a vial of dream elixir and decided to attempt the market first thing in the morning. If I timed it right and moved fast, people would be gathering by the time I came back, and I could miss most of the unwanted attention.

Stepping into the chilly fall morning, the blinding orange light of the sun made it impossible to look left. Good, I didn't want to see the steps leading up to the next level. Not knowing how serious he'd been about his position as second to Cole, Damien could still be up there, and I wanted to forget his existence.

Damien the Traitor. Who I thought was a friend—someone I could trust. Who I'd shared things with that no one knew. Who'd withheld the truth from me. The thought of his name made my stomach turn and my chest ache. I had barely processed what he'd told me about Lupine—where did I start when it came to the man himself?

At the foot of the stairs, I spotted only two people in the square. A woman enjoying an early morning walk unbothered, and a man by the statue with his back to me.

I dared a glance in the direction I took to get to Selene's House, the sky in that part of the city a quickly fading brilliant indigo and deep blue. It was the first day of my work week, and while I could have used the distraction, I knew the matrons and the children didn't need the negative attention I'd bring. I couldn't face it if Rho stopped talking to me either. The only reason we'd connected was because of my ties to the Valentines. I was enemy number one to them and the Alliance Council now, and the daughter of a Misundre Five leader— even a former one—couldn't risk being seen with me.

"Eden! Eden Alexander!" a deep voice shouted. Loud enough for it to wake up anyone in a half-mile radius. The echo of it rang in my ears.

My stomach dropped. It was the man by the statue, waving a notebook at me.

I started moving again in the opposite direction as expeditiously as possible. It didn't matter. Shoes striking the stone, he was beside me in a second, shoving his notepad in front of my face and rattling off a dozen versions of the same question: *What happened?*

Putting my head down, I charged ahead, turning down a street. The old brick building of the market came into view, nestled in the bend up ahead.

"Please, leave me alone," I sighed.

Ignoring my plea, he skipped in front of me. A tactic I dodged adeptly, picking up my speed. I just needed to get to the market, I reminded myself. Out here in the open, I was an easy target. Inside, he wouldn't be able to follow—reporters being forbidden from harassing people in private establishments, which every place of business in Sorbis was considered.

Almost there…

"Eden—don't worry, I'll wait for you right here!" the reporter screamed after me.

Great.

Passing through the doorway, an amalgamation of food smells and silence welcomed me. Thank you, sound charms. This early in the morning, the market was refreshingly empty of people, and all the stands were brimming. I followed the smell of fresh fruits and vegetables, lured by my nutrient-starved stomach.

Finding the produce, I plucked an apricot from the wooden crate and held it to my nose, the fresh, sweet scent making my mouth water.

A second from throwing five into my bag, the stall-keeper said, "The Runners delivered those from Misundre this morning."

Forcing a smile, I replaced them in the crate. Fuck Misundre. Fuck you, Damien.

Tossing several apples, tomatoes, a head of broccoli, a bunch of carrots, an onion, and a bundle of grapes into my bag, I counted out the proper amount of soltans and presented it to him.

He held a hand up, stopping me. "Everything's already covered."

"What do—"

"Good morning, doll."

The sound of his voice and that fucking nickname sent a shiver down my spine.

"I bought out the market for the day, so take your pick. Whatever you like."

Pinching the inside of my left wrist, I slowly turned from the stall-keeper to face him. Cole stood a step behind me, looking as put together as ever, hands buried in the pockets of his dark blue suit.

Run, that voice in my head said, my heart seizing. The bag in my hand slipped in my sweaty grip.

He cocked his head to the side, a hard, teeth-baring smile curling his lips. "Do you mind if I join you? I want to talk, since you're so keen about doing so."

Run.

I need groceries. I can't run.

The fruit and the vegetables are enough to get you through a couple of days.

I already ran once, and if I want anything to resolve itself, I have to endure this.

Swallowing the bile creeping up my throat, I sidestepped him and pivoted for the cheese stand, now empty of its keeper. No witnesses. "If what you say is true. The market is yours. I'm your guest. You can do whatever you please."

He fell into step beside me. "I bought it out for you."

Did that mean I could ask him to leave? "That wasn't necessary. I'll pay you back." Another thing to figure out.

"Nonsense, it's a gift. I figured I could donate what you don't take to shelters and orphanages. I thought you might like that."

I stopped in front of a white and purple crumbling cheese.

"I tried to come to you, at your apartment," he continued, "but you revoked my access through your building's wards. Grayden's have also been revoked, so I've had to resort to passing letters through your building attendant. Has he not been delivering them?"

"I received them." Slipped under my door after I'd refused to open it. All five remained intact and untouched on the floor.

"And?"

I met his eyes, and for a moment, I saw Damien when he'd told me Lupine had offered me away and felt remorseful. That he'd been guilted into staying in Sorbis to be my friend. How could the green eyes of the Valentines be so different and so much the same?

"How did you know I was here?"

He fingered a log of soft cheese. "I instructed the Protectors I have watching your home to inform me when you leave. Which took... longer than expected."

I dropped the hard cheese I'd been looking at. It rolled around on the floor, stopping at his shoe. "You're having me watched?"

Grabbing another chunk, he dropped it into my bag, sighing. "Yes, doll. Come now, you can't possibly think I let you continue to live out here and work at that orphanage completely unprotected."

I would have been sick if there were any food in my stomach. "What do you want, Cole?"

He considered me. "Have you thought about it?"

"Thought about what?"

Annoyance flashed across his eyes. "Saying yes to the blood bond. Being my queen. I understand I asked you without discussing it, as we agreed, but you've now had time to think about it. I don't want to play games."

My grip on the bag tightened. "I'm not playing games. I told you I couldn't do it. The only thought I've had since then is that I'm glad I said no."

He grabbed my elbow, digging hard into the joint. "You don't know what you're saying."

Anger burning away fear, I stepped closer. "I actually do. I don't want to be queen."

Shadows blanketed his gaze. "Is there someone else?"

The question was a cold bucket of water. How could he even ask that? I twisted against him. "Don't be absurd."

His grip on me intensified, making my knees weaken. "Is it my brother?"

I shook my head. "Quincy and I have never—"

"I meant Damien," he snapped.

A laugh cracked my throat—shocking us both—as the heat of rage torched my skin. "You can't be serious."

He leaned closer, lowering his voice. "It isn't unreasonable to suspect. I know his ways. You spent a lot of time together with him and my mother. He moved into the penthouse above your apartment —and I know he accompanied you to Selene's House a few months ago. You've been seen frequently in this market over the past month with his Facto. He leapt to take you away—"

I watched the evolution of my reaction in the green of his steely eyes, from incredulity to horror. He pressed his lips together and straightened, nostrils flaring.

"Don't look at me like that," he snarled.

I ripped away, ignoring the pain flashing through my arm as it hung limp. "Do you even hear yourself?"

Smoothing his jacket, he turned, grinding the heel of his shoe in the dirt. "Fine. So what, you need time? You need space. I can give you that." He threw a glance over his shoulder. His eyes narrowed, the corners of his lips making a hard downturn. "We aren't done, Eden. You'll come around."

"Cole, I don't need—"

He was gone. I blinked, and he wasn't there.

When someone phased abruptly, I couldn't help but question if they'd ever been there or if I was crazy. The empty market and the fading ache at my elbow assured me I wasn't.

Feeling freshly hollowed, I stared at the place he'd been for a minute, trying to make sense of his words and the sense of dread they stirred in my stomach.

No longer hungry, I skipped the other stalls except for one, the last one on the way out. Wine and elixirs. It wasn't the smartest thing to fill the rest of my bag with, but I was past the point of caring. I just wanted a break.

It also wasn't the smartest thing to uncork one and drink half before leaving either, but I did, and stepped back outside, the flash of a camera startling me. Having gotten word from their friend, there were now twenty reporters waiting for me. They screamed my name, shoving their paper pads before me as I pushed through them.

Their racket was a whisper in my ears, Cole's words ringing loudly.

We aren't done, Eden.

CHAPTER TWENTY-EIGHT

22.TEN.4004

I stared at the assortment of wigs Rho had brought over—apple red, blush pink, starlight silver. All the options she'd thought might work for me but hadn't made the cut.

"I can't thank you enough for this," I said.

"Thank me?" she scoffed. "This is what friends do for each other. I don't need your gratitude. If you want to give me anything, give me another apology for thinking so lowly of me, for making me worry sick about you."

Escorted by my old, weary building attendant, Rho had shown up at my building yesterday morning demanding an explanation—a cake, a dozen cheeses, and several bottles of wine in tow.

Over drinks and junk food, I'd told her about everything—everything but Damien—and apologized a million times. As far as I was concerned, there would never be enough apologies for not trusting in our friendship.

"I'm sorry. Eternally sorry. I know I'm terrible…I didn't think anyone would want to be associated with me once the news broke."

She grunted. "Just never forget, whether my mother wants me to or not, I would never choose Cole over you. He might be the next king, but I've always found him disgusting. I spent the last year wondering how you tolerated him, and now I know. He's so much like his father, and the King is despicable."

"I wish you'd told me you felt that way."

"My feelings didn't matter as long as you were happy."

Staring blankly at the space between us, I shook my head. "I wasn't happy. I was afraid to let people down."

Lovingly, she ran her nails through my hair. "You can't worry about letting people down, my darling. You have to live for yourself, especially as a mortal."

"You sound like Rini Rain," I sighed, recalling that dreadful night.

Her stroking stopped, her mouth curling into a sneer. "You've talked to Rini Rain about this?"

"Not because I wanted to. Damien took her back to the manor when he was staying in Cole's apartment. She found a note I wrote while she was there. She blackmailed me. It's a long story, but Damien helped me get it back—and he didn't know what it said," I added quickly, "and we wiped her memories, but not before she bestowed her advice that life was too short to feel the way I did."

Rho pursed her lips, her lilac eyes glaring down at me. "You forgot to mention that," and, sighing for the thousandth time, said, "I wish you'd told me."

Shame filled my chest. "I'm forever sorry."

Inhaling through her nose, she placed a hand on my shoulder. "Believe it or not, after the initial shock, I looked at it from your perspective. We haven't spent much time together outside of work this past year, but you're my best friend, Eden Alexander, and I will always be on your side first, not the King or the Alliance Council." She picked up a compact. "Now for the final touches."

Using a cream-colored brush, she dabbed blush across the apples of my cheeks. Examining me closely, she fixed a mistake with her finger and leaned back, considering me. "Annnnd I'm done. You're the most beautiful mortal I've ever seen—okay, most beautiful woman I've ever seen, and I hate you."

Throwing my arms around her neck, I pulled her to me. "I don't deserve you. Thank you for doing this for me."

"You never need to thank me for giving you the freedom you deserve. It's ironic that it's gotten worse now that you've ended it with Cole."

I stiffened at the reminder.

"Relax, it'll eventually pass. They'll find something else to care about."

When I'm dead…

She fluffed the ends of the chin-length wig she'd affixed to my scalp. "This blue hair looks good on you. It really brings out your gold eyes. I love your dark brown hair, but now I'm thinking you should go to a modifier to make a change."

"I'll think about it."

"You only say that because you haven't seen yourself." Grinning, she motioned with two fingers for me to get up and spin.

Following instructions, I stared at my reflection. Silvery-blue eyeshadow shimmered atop my black-lined eyelids. The soft pink on my cheeks caught the light from every angle, pulling the eye upward. Everything she'd done had been to draw attention to my eyes, and it'd all added up to make them look like pools of the purest honey.

"I feel like the short hair says I'm beautiful and fearless. And in that dress, you won't have a problem finding someone to take you home." Referring to the black body-hugging dress she'd loaned me, complete with paper-thin straps, a plunging neckline, and a short hem that would send Cole into shock.

I'd never worn anything so bold—makeup or clothing—in my life. I didn't even recognize myself, which is precisely what I wanted.

"I'm not trying to take someone home. I just want a night of freedom."

"Mmm, well, a girl can hope for her sexless friend. You know, I was thinking about what your name should be for the evening, with your eyes and this wig. I think it should be Daisy."

Head tilted, I met her gaze in the reflection. "I thought only descendants of the Misundre Five were named after plants and flowers?"

"Pah, you might as well be. You're my chosen sister and were the ward of one," she grinned. "Now go, the sun has set. Maximize your freedom."

Passing me my shoes, she pushed me toward the door, but she didn't need to. I didn't fight back. Every part of me needed this, and I was done shying away.

Standing outside my door, I took a deep, settling breath, slipped the simple black flats on, and listened to the chaos coming up from the square. The chatter of a group of friends—clearly drunk. *We love you, Eden!* Followed quickly by another voice screaming *Fuck Prince Cole,* and then the whole group shushing their friend. I welcomed the raucousness even though their words made me feel odd. Rho had said I'd caused a serious rift among the people, but I hadn't actually believed it. I was no one.

I looked back at her, her eyes a deep purple in the darkness. "Don't forget—"

She waved me away. "I'll leave in an hour to throw off the hounds. I'm such a good friend."

Too afraid to, I hadn't left my home since Cole had cornered me in the market. This wouldn't even be happening now if Rho hadn't come to beat down my door yesterday. And her presence gave me hope that Q might still want me in his life.

Unable to help myself, I wrapped my arms around her, pulling her in for another hug. "Thank you again."

"Stop thanking me. Just have a good time and be safe!"

Rho shut the door in my face, removing my urge to linger. Nodding to no one, I padded down the stairs.

Scanning the square, I took in everything from the friends—still there—clustered together and looking up at the window on the fifth floor, cackling to themselves, to the woman rolling her eyes at the group as she tried to enjoy a night stroll, to the couple pressed against the statue at the center of the square making out, and finally to the reporter for the Alliance Access watching the group and the window as well.

Only the reporter noticed me as I exited the stairwell, and he turned away. He'd been there when I'd come down to get Rho, and having not seen Rho leave, for him, it was safe to assume his target was still whiling away five floors up.

Immortals, it felt good to be invisible.

It only took fifteen minutes to get where I was going. The glowing blood-red sign set against the backdrop of the black brick calling to everyone who needed an escape like moths to a flame.

Stopping by the door, I questioned my decision to do this for the first time. Though Vermillion had just opened for the evening, the line outside stretched halfway down the street. It wasn't my first choice, but being out of practice, something familiar and close made sense.

And I knew the traitor put in his hours in the morning, so I wouldn't have to worry about him.

Committed, I managed a step when a hand clasped my shoulder.

It was one of the bouncers, eyes not bothering to hide how he drank me in. He unhooked the rope separating everyone from the entrance. "You can go in."

CHAPTER TWENTY-NINE

22.TEN.4004

Two and a half hours later, I sat in a booth in the corner, four shots of whiskey and two glasses of happiness elixir deep.

Vermillion wasn't anything like I'd remembered it being.

Firstly, there was no dancing, which is the only reason I had wanted to go out. The smoky air, irritating my eyes and throat, was so thick that it became part of Vermillion's aesthetic, adding a hazy quality to the black lacquer tables, black leather booths, and people idling about.

The lights were low and placed just so along the deep, velvety, red walls and ceiling that—even without the smoke—seeing anything more than a couple of feet away was difficult. Music pulsed the air, but charged by heavy drums and guitar, it wasn't the kind you danced to, and it was so loud everyone half screamed to be heard.

Everything strategically tailored to make everyone get a little closer.

And then there was the black hole to the back, where a wisp of light helped people find their way to either the exit, the bathroom, or one of the curtained booths couples flocked to for a more private experience if they couldn't control themselves long enough to get home.

My seat offered the perfect view of the darkened doorway, and I had seen more than a dozen couples enter and emerge, looking contentedly roughed up.

This is what Damien liked. This was the real Damien. Not the man

I'd gotten to know. It shouldn't have surprised me, as that man had been putting on a show to be my friend.

Staring into my glass of golden happiness elixir, I felt anything but. Sure, there was a false sense of light surrounding me, and it was nice to be out in the world, but underneath it all, the thought that this might have been a bad idea took root.

"Are you enjoying your drink?" the mistake I'd made thirty minutes ago asked.

Twirling my glass by the stem, I raised my eyes to look at him. Prian, he'd said his name was. Watching everyone around me have the best time of their lives had been the catalyst for this. That, and he was the only person, besides a waiter, to have approached me since I sat down.

Dark gray eyes set into his square face stared at me besotted, his curly blond hair jutting out in every direction like I imagined it would first thing in the morning. Most of our conversation consisted of me showing a mixture of emotions at the right time while he complained about his boss and job.

His intermission to ask me something must have meant I missed one of my cues.

"I am, thank you." I took a placating sip of the drink he'd brought me. "I'm just still reeling from what your boss said," I offered, recalling enough of what he'd ranted about to hopefully reignite his fury and take his attention off me.

Prian took the bait and ran. Launching into another tirade. My ears immediately regretted the tactic.

The more I listened, the more uneasy my stomach felt. How did I tell him *I'm sorry, I'm not interested,* after saying yes when he asked if he could join me? I sipped my drink, wishing it were any elixir to provide courage.

And then an idea hit me.

Standing abruptly, I said. "I need to go to the ladies' room. Would you give me a minute?" Time to think of something to say. And if all else failed, the separation would embolden me to leave.

Startled, Prian stared, nodding as I slid out of the booth.

His sweaty hand covered mine atop the table. "Don't be too long," he huffed shyly. "I'll be lonely without you."

Smiling, I slowly slipped mine from under his. "Of course not."

Working my way through the crowd, hand clasped to my stomach like it might control the roiling, I passed into the back hall. In the darkness, the music was louder, but not even it could compete with the scream of pleasure one woman offered from behind one of the curtains.

I wondered how many times Damien had taken a woman behind the curtain of one and shook it off. Why was I thinking about that?

Stumbling into the bathroom, I locked the door, activating the lights, and stared at myself in the mirror. My golden eyes were glossy from whiskey and happiness elixirs, the edges of objects starting to soften. What was I doing? Disguised, drunk, and alone at an elixiry.

Turning the faucet on, I ran shaking hands under the cold tap and dabbed them lightly to my face, neck, and breasts, trying to cool down. I repeated the process several times, only stopping when the door handle jiggled.

"That's enough," a woman whined. "I have to pee."

Deciding to leave—the bathroom and Vermillion—I unlocked the door. The woman rushed past me, her hand at the waistband of her pants, before I was out. I made it one stumbling step toward the exit when a hand caught me by the shoulder, pulling me back into one of the curtained alcoves.

I staggered as I spun, the ends of my blue hair slicing the air.

Another hand stabilized me at the waist.

Green eyes stared down at me like I'd manifested them.

"Damien," I said. His name a soft breath.

Reading something in my face, the harshness in his eyes eased. "I'm —"

The lightness in my chest whooshed away like a blown-out candle. Damien. Damien the Traitor. Damien, who wasn't supposed to be here.

Shoving free of his grip, I stepped away. "You scared me." The 's' in 'scared' slurring. Immortals, I was drunk. "Where did you come from? Did you follow me?" I shivered, remembering Cole had me watched.

Damien's jaw tightened, brows knitting together. "I own this elixiry and work here. It isn't beyond the realm of expectation that I might be here."

I folded my arms over my chest. "You work in the mornings."

"What do you think you're doing here? You should go home," he continued, like I hadn't spoken, motioning toward my face. "You have one of the most recognizable faces in Sorbis, and the whole city is looking for you—someone will notice you."

Scoffing, I hugged myself a little tighter. "So far, no one aside from you has noticed."

"The wig and make-up are only going to get you so far. If any Protectors from Charph wander in here, you're done. If anyone deduces who you are, it's going to lead to trouble. You need to leave before someone sees you. It isn't safe, and I don't have the energy to spend the night making sure you're okay."

I stared at him incredulously. Did he really think he was in a position to patronize me?

Stepping forward, scowling so hard I could feel the skin of my forehead bunch, I jabbed my finger into my chest. "I didn't ask for you to make sure I'm okay. I *never* asked you to make sure I'm okay. I don't need your protection. Fuck off, Damien."

Sharp on my heel, I turned away, leaving him standing there, mouth gaping. Marching back into the main room—ignoring the uneasiness of the movement—toward Prian, which hadn't been the plan, but in the moment, I wanted to be anywhere but where Damien was. And I didn't want to give him the satisfaction of thinking I was leaving because of him.

Prian straightened up at the sight of me, eyes going wide.

As the room tilted, I clutched the edge of the table for support. "I'm sorry. Thank you for the drink. I had a nice time, but I'm not feeling well, so I'm going to head home."

"Let me see you home—" he started to get up.

I raised a weak hand, meeting his gray eyes and smiling. "That isn't necessary, but thank you. I just didn't want you to think I'd abandoned you." Which is very much what I'd been planning to do.

Prian's eyes fell to my half-finished drink, looking sad, and nodded. I didn't wait to see if he had anything more to say.

Leave, I needed to leave.

Head down, I wove my way through the crowd once more, focusing everything I had on my movements, repeating the words *one more step* like a mantra. Each step felt heavier and made the spinning top my brain was riding on go a little faster.

I made it as far as the second nook in the back—a man moaning behind the curtain—before I had to stop to get my breath. My skin was on fire. What was wrong with me?

An arm snaked around my waist, pulling me hard against a sweaty, fleshy body.

Prian's voice came hot and breathy at my ear, his thumb grinding ardently into my hip. "Let me help you, Daisy. I insist."

CHAPTER THIRTY

23.TEN.4004

I awoke to my head throbbing like it and my heart had swapped places, a sour taste on my tongue. Thank the Immortals, I didn't have anywhere to be.

I lay in bed, my room nearly dark except for the cracks of light cutting through the drapes, providing just enough light to make out the rough shapes of things. Digging my elbows into the mattress, I forced myself to sit up, leaning against the headboard for support. As if the nausea and headache weren't enough, my lungs seized.

Covering me were black blankets and black silk sheets. Too fancy. Not my bed.

In place of the black dress I'd been wearing was an oversized black shirt, which wasn't mine either.

What had happened? What had I done? If my clothes were gone, then... Hands shaking, I touched my hair, bringing forth long, dark brown waves.

No.

A harder hit of panic came over me as I moved my hand to my neck, finding a warm metal key—a slight relief in this waking nightmare.

I was in someone else's bed. Someone I'd done Immortals knew what with. Someone who knew my identity. Who was probably selling the story of whatever happened last night to the Alliance Access that very minute.

I groaned my dread, the vibrations of which did nothing for my headache. Exhaling, I rubbed the heel of my hand against my forehead as if I could knead out the pulsing ache, trying to recall what had happened. All I remembered was a blond man with gray eyes—what was his name?—buying me a drink.

"Glad to see you survived," a voice said.

With the same slow energy I'd used to sit up, I lifted my head a fraction in the direction of the voice. A figure stood in the doorway, backlit by sharp white light.

Moving closer to me, a tan hand came into view, holding a glass of something golden. "Here, drink this. It'll help with your symptoms."

That voice.

"Damien? Where am I?" I demanded, feeling as confused as I was relieved.

"My bedroom."

Accepting the glass, I took a cautious sip, instant regret washing over me as the sour elixir rolled across my tongue, stinging the back of my throat—a fresher version of the taste plaguing my mouth.

"What is that?" I coughed.

"It's an elixir I made to help you. I gave you a milder version of it last night because I didn't have this put together, but something told me you'd need the full-blown version this morning, and based on the look of you, I was correct."

Unable to lift my head further, I glared at his crossed arms. "Why do I need help at all? Why am I here? What happened?"

"What do you remember?"

Cringing through another gulp, I shook my head. "I was in a booth at Vermillion, drinking with this guy. I remember you trying to boss me around." The elixir working quickly, I moved my glare to his face, taking in his frown. "Prian—that was his name."

Damien's body went rigid as a board. "Lovely, I have a name to hate."

I rolled my eyes. "What happened, Damien? Why am I here?"

"Prian," he sneered, rage flashing across his eyes, "slipped you one of the most vicious elixirs I've ever seen someone use. I found you with him in the alley outside Vermillion, with his hands climbing up your dress while you hallucinated. I took care of him and brought you here. Isa changed your clothes and helped me get you in bed."

And just like that, I felt sick again.

"What do you think you were doing last night?" he demanded.

Frustrated by his condescending question, I snapped. "Trying to live my life."

"You shouldn't have gone out alone."

"I was trying to lay low. Rho is the only friend I have left, and if I'd gone out with her, it would have been clear who I was. I wanted to dance and have fun without being hounded. I can't even go to the market right now without a reporter from the Alliance Access breathing down my neck, badgering me to know what happened."

He stared at me for a long moment, lips pressed together in a firm line. "Rho isn't the only friend you have. You should have come to me."

I snorted. "Our friendship and my times of coming to you are through Damien. You made sure of that."

"I said it that night, and I'll say it again. I'm sorry I didn't tell you, but it didn't exactly feel like it was my place—"

I tilted the glass up, chugging until it was empty, and threw back the blankets. "It wasn't your place to tell me what to do last night, and it didn't stop you." Remembering more as the elixir took effect. "I guess this one time I can say I'm grateful for that, so thank you, and thank you for the elixir. I'll be going now."

An arm cut in front of me, stopping me at the edge of the bed. "You're right, but last night—and it's no excuse—I was only concerned about your well-being." I looked up into his green eyes, shadowed with remorse. "I shouldn't have to pay for my mother's wrongs. I may not have shared her true wishes with you, but I've done everything in my power to be a good friend to you. And yes, my time with you may have started as a favor to my mother, but that's not all it was to me. Does my transparency count for nothing?"

Taking a long breath through my nose, I reluctantly admitted, "It doesn't count for nothing, but it still doesn't change the fact—"

"If I'd known how you felt—that she was why you stayed with him —I would have told you without hesitation. In my defense, you suspected every kindness was a ploy. How was I supposed to be blindly forthcoming—would you have believed me?" He leaned closer to me, close enough I could feel the heat of his body. "Eden, let me make it up to you. Please."

Cocking my head, I raised an eyebrow. "And how would you do that?"

His lips parted, clearly not expecting to answer right then. I pushed against his arm, the muscles tightening once more as he blurted, "You want to dance and have fun without being noticed—what if I helped you? Provided you a better disguise, accompanied you—also in disguise."

Skepticism growing worse, I crossed my arms. "How are you going to do that?"

Pressing the tips of his fingers to the center of his chest, he said, "I know elixirs that would work better than that cheap disguise."

"I'm going to tell Rho you said that." Realizing, as much as I meant the comment, she'd lose her shit if she found out what had almost happened.

And because sense didn't always win with me and fuck—being here, looking at him, remembering how I'd felt when I'd seen him last night—I'd missed him, I said, "You get one chance."

His face brightened. "Give me until the end of this week. I need to get the ingredients, and it'll take some time to brew. Oh, and you'll need to think of a name for your alter ego. "

I considered those adamant green eyes, twinkling with a touch of hope, and moved his hand away. The shirt I wore shifted off my shoulders as I stood and made my way to the door. "If it's going to take you that long, I'll give you two. I intend to return to work next week."

That was another gift Rho had given me: the assurance that I wouldn't be an issue for Selene's house. That the matrons, Forrest, and children were worried about me and missed me as much as I missed them. I couldn't hide forever either; I knew that for them, I could face the hounding.

"I would like to make one request," Damien called after me.

Stopping in the doorway, I tossed an uneasy glance over my shoulder. "You aren't exactly in a position to make requests."

"It isn't for me, at least not directly," he said, eyes softening. "Will you come back tonight? For your dinner visits, I mean. Isa hasn't been pleased with me since I took away her confidante."

A light of happiness exploded in my heart for the second time in two days. "I didn't know she missed me. I figured," I figured a lot, but mostly, "she would have visited, and that when she didn't…"

"She believed when you were upset with me, you didn't want to see her by association." He held up a hand, palm out, placatingly. "I learned before she left for the market this morning, in case you were wondering."

I shook a finger at him. "Don't make light of trust and honesty." And then quickly, "I would love that, though. I've missed seeing her as well."

A genial smile tugged at the corner of his lips. "I would never, just proving myself every chance I get." He stepped toward me. "I'll charm the door for you so you can just start letting yourself in."

I stared at Damien for a long moment, looking away when a strange warmth started to stir in my chest. "Okay."

CHAPTER THIRTY-ONE

7.ELEVEN.4004

Damien made good on his word.

I was sitting at the dinner table—as I had every evening since his apology, almost like things were back to normal—staring at my third glass of whiskey, considering my ask, when he tapped me on the shoulder, nodding toward the stairs to the suite.

"You ready?"

Believing he didn't own any clothes that weren't black, the sight of him in a light blue button-down tucked into dark blue jeans was jarring.

Finishing the whiskey in a gulp, I got to my feet, smoothing the skirt of my dress.

"Wait," Isa screamed from the kitchen. She came running in, the smell of freshly baked chocolate cookies trailing her.

Wiping the back of her wet, soapy hands against her apron, she wove her soft, damp fingers between mine. "If he does something this time, don't you let it come between us." She narrowed her brown eyes at Damien, a single finger raised. "You better behave, Damien Valentine."

From the corner of my eye, Damien's mouth gaped.

Immortals, I adored this woman. I pulled her into a hug. "Isa, the next time Damien pisses me off, which is bound to happen, you're welcome any time in my home. Don't worry."

Damien's feet hit the metal stairs. "Good to know how you both really feel."

Isa and I exchanged a grin.

Jogging after him, I caught up to him halfway across the expanse of the suite. "Are you going to tell me how we're doing this?"

"So impatient."

Opening the door, the light charm of the bathroom activated as he stepped inside, and I stopped dead. All the times I'd been in the suite, but I'd never bothered with the bathroom…

Dark red walls, splattered in gold, filled my vision. The white marble counter cluttered with jars of herbs, liquids, and vials of elixirs had four sinks and a huge mirror. A tub the size of a small pool hid behind the vanity, and beside it, a room-sized shower with shower heads spaced every couple of feet. The floor, a mosaic of mirror pieces, had me shortening my stance. All the fixtures and the toilet were gold. Like that would ever be needed. Like any of this would ever be needed.

The suite had definitely served a unique purpose.

He watched me in the mirror, suppressing a grin. "Your imagination having fun?" He selected a small glass from the counter, leaving behind a circular reddish-brown stain, and passed it to me. "Drink this. It'll allow me to manipulate your appearance."

Thick, grainy, and beet red, the mixture smelled like iron and petrichor. I gagged hard. "What's in this?"

"I don't think you want to know."

"You just sealed my determination to know," I said. "You see, after our talk, I went through my copy of *The History of Elixirs and Their Applications* and found nothing about an elixir that allows you to change form."

"That's because this elixir isn't in that book."

I drummed my nails against the glass. "The only elixirs not in that book are those using blood magic." Answering my own question, my stomach turned. "Your blood is in this."

Pursing his lips, he leaned his hip against the counter. "I said you didn't want to know."

"The Alliance Council forbids blood magic."

"Putting aside the fact that I am currently a member of the Council, I know the law well, and it's only forbidden if you're taking it from the practitioner. I'm giving it to you of my own volition. I'm sure they wouldn't like this conspiracy, but I don't think anyone ever stopped to think about someone giving away their magic, since no one likes to share."

For some stupid reason, I took another whiff. "I can't drink this."

"You will if you want to go out unseen and do what you want unbothered. I understand that it isn't appealing, but it's our only option."

"Make-up and a wig…"

"I can manipulate your smell with that which is key to staying undercover. There's not one Charphan Protector—of which there are many roaming all over the city, thanks to recent insurgent activity—that doesn't know your or my scent."

"Why don't you just cloak me?"

"For the same reason I want to change your scent. Your lack of smell will catch their attention just as easily. Cloaking a scent is the number one thing the insurgents are doing to hide their activity."

"I haven't heard anything about any insurgents or insurgent activity."

"And you wouldn't. The Alliance Council is working hard to smother it. Look, now is not the time for that. What are we doing,

Eden?"

Making a mental note to ask him more about that later, I gripped the counter and took a deep breath, searching for courage. I'd done a lot of stupid and disgusting things in my short mortal life, but none so stupid or disgusting as blood magic. "A glass of water, please."

Damien snapped his fingers, a glass appearing in his hands. He filled it with water from the sink and passed it to me.

"This better be better," I groaned, choking it back and quickly chasing it. Eyes watering, I held the back of my hand to my mouth, fighting the urge to throw up as it moved like mud down my throat.

Damien watched my displeasure play out with some amusement. "That bad?"

Something hit my nose hard. "What is that smell?"

He raised an eyebrow. "What does it smell like?"

Cringing, I pointedly sniffed the air. "Like everything," where to even begin, "but mostly cedar, jasmine, leather, sandalwood, lavender —a lot of lavender." Catching a whiff as I waved my hands, I held my arm to my nose, dragging it from wrist to elbow. Lavender. "This is what you're smelling all the time?"

Damien pinched his chin. "Interesting. It would seem the elixir has worked better than expected. I don't know how it's affecting you exactly, but when you're bombarded by scents all the time, they don't stand out as much."

I barely heard him, distracted by the weight permeating every part of my being. Not only could I smell everything, my connection to earth magic was solid—the chaos I knew still lurked, but buried deep —curled at the forefront of my mind, at the edge of my fingertips, whispering for release. And Immortals, it felt good.

Grinning, I met his gaze. "This is what magic feels like for you. This is wild. Could I phase?"

Mischief clouded his eyes. "Someone is quickly learning why blood magic was made illegal. Probably if I'd given you more, but it'd take up all the magic in your system trying. Tonight, you can either try phasing or we can go out."

"Next time, then."

Damien cocked his head. "Next time?"

Every inch of my skin burned with shame. "Or not. I'm sorry, I wasn't trying to—I promise I wasn't—"

His laugh cut me short. "Relax, Eden. I have blood to spare. We can try phasing whenever. Do you know what's more illegal than blood magic?" As he spoke, the vibrant green of his irises became the yellow of the sun at high noon, and his black hair lightened to a brilliant bronze.

I stared, mouth agape. His clothes making sense. Being Charphan, I decided, was a whole other level of magic.

"So let's not get caught." Grinning, he grabbed my hand and tugged me into the bedroom, stopping us in front of the mirror wall. I stared at the reflection of myself in a flowing mauve dress with lace sleeves and a hem that hit my knees. "If you thought that was impressive, wait until you see yourself. What would you like your alter ego to look like?"

"I've always wondered what I'd look like with blue eyes and pink hair like—"

The magic tingled in my cheeks and along my scalp. I watched my hair lighten into a lotus pink, the gold of my eyes melting into sky blue. A smattering of freckles dusted my cheeks.

I ran my fingers along them. "How did you know?"

"I didn't. This kind of magic is inherent. It knows what you want. I just guided it where it needed to go. Now, think about what you want to smell like." I took a deep breath, noting his new leather and patchouli scent.

On my next inhale, I smelled a rich fruity sweetness.

He raised a curious eyebrow. "Raspberries and vanilla?"

"I thought it fit the look."

"Does the name you picked fit the look?"

I inhaled. "Nedeah."

The corners of his mouth twitched. "Where did that come from?"

"It's a pseudo-anagram of my name," I admitted sheepishly, fingering a strand of pink hair.

"Cute. You can call me Finn."

Everything for him had been too quick—the look, the name. He'd done this before. "And yours?"

Impishness twinkled in his yellow eyes. "Another time."

Having forgotten his hand in mine, it surprised me when he jerked me toward the center of the room. "This part I've been excited about. I made a little change to the building's anti-phasing wards. I should now be able to phase us in and out of the suite."

Moving close to him, I took a deep breath, the smell of leather and raspberries so strong I could taste it. A second later, a cool breeze cut through my dress, instantly reminding me I'd forgotten my jacket at the dining room table along with my key necklace.

"Why are we here?" I asked. My eyes drifted around him to Rini's house—lights on—and my stomach soured.

Damien, hands clasping my shoulders, rotated me toward the market, his voice a whisper on the breeze coming off Soltan Lake. "If she's here, she won't know it's you."

He pointed toward the market. A section of it had been cleared out, string lights winding their way around the wooden beams and up into the structure's open rafter roof. Where stalls had stood, there was now a makeshift dance floor packed with sweaty dancers. At wooden tables surrounding it, people clapped and bobbed their heads to the band's bright, melodic, twangy music. There was even a small bar on the far side of the place serving liquor and elixirs.

He nudged me forward gently. "You said the art district was your favorite, and you hadn't been for a while, so I figured this was a good, simple place to take you."

"I didn't even know they did this." Lured by the music, I started to walk toward the glow, enjoying how it all eased me.

"It isn't a place you're likely to find many members of high society."

As we walked, Damien shifted, shielding me from the wind gusting off the water. "Aevry and I came here once. He left an hour in. I figured maybe he'd gone home with someone, but I found him at sunrise on that bench," he nodded to a rickety wooden bench further down the promenade, right off the water, "reading a book because he couldn't stop thinking about it. It's where he'd been since he'd left."

I looked up at him and clutched my free hand to my chest, momentarily forgetting his yellow eyes and brown hair.

Damien laughed under his breath. "Don't forget what I look like once we're there."

I nodded. "I'm sorry. What book was it?"

Running his free hand through his hair, he took a steadying breath. "The Esoteric Codex."

"I've never heard of it."

"There was only one copy. It was an obscure little book gifted to him by the Savior Selene. It was handwritten, full of manic tales someone had dreamed up about the Kingdom of Solta's history." Trailing off, he waved it away. "It wasn't a real book, but Aevry was into that kind of thing."

I knew from the sudden distance in his words not to ask more.

Sidling up to the bar, Damien ordered drinks. Two glasses and a bottle of whiskey in tow, we searched the area for a table, pouncing on one as a couple left, second row from the band and the dance floor. I looked from the dancers to him as he plunked down onto one of the high stools.

"What are you doing?" I asked.

He shrugged. "I'm here to watch."

Stomach twisting, I glanced at the dance floor. "If this is going to work, you have to dance with me."

Damien shook his head. "I don't dance. You can find a dance partner out there."

My eyes widened a fraction. Damien Valentine couldn't dance—finally, something he couldn't do.

Anxiety needled my stomach. "No one will dance with me if I'm dancing by myself."

He gave me a once-over across his glass. "For some reason, I don't believe that."

"Please," I whispered. "Look, a lot of people can't dance, but the floor is crowded. I doubt—"

Swirling the whiskey, he said, "I didn't say I can't dance. I said I don't."

I continued, pretending not to hear him. "I could teach you. There's nothing to it."

He leaned forward, elbows on the table. "That's not what I said."

"Can't, don't..." It all meant the same. Shrugging, I looked up shamelessly through my lashes. "You said you were going to make it up to me."

Jaw shifting, his yellow eyes stared at me flatly. I had him. How many times had Damien Valentine been bested? I gave him my sweetest smile.

He drained the glass, holding up a single finger. "One dance—the next one—then you're on your own."

Going for the bottle once more, he was stopped short by the song ending. Some dancers made their way from the sultry, sweat-soaked air of the wooden slat dance floor, desperate for another elixir or a glass of water. Many stayed; those without partners paired up with other newly free solo dancers.

The way Damien grimaced made me want to laugh. He looked like a five-year-old who'd been told no to dessert. Not wanting to be late to the song, though, I kept myself in check, holding out my hand to him. Biting the inside of his cheek, he accepted it, reluctantly leading me onto the dance floor.

In an empty spot, we stared at each other under hundreds of sparkling lights, his bronze hair gleaming. My excitement fell when I noticed a sheen on his brow and an uneasiness in his eyes. He was really uncomfortable doing this.

The band started, and we stood there.

"I'm sorry," I said. "I guilted you out here, and I shouldn't have done that. I know what it's like to be forced to do things I don't feel comfortable with."

With a splendid flourish, Damien tugged me toward him, his free hand sliding into place along my exposed lower back, causing my heart to attempt an exit through my chest. I'd thought we couldn't get any closer than when he phased us. I was wrong. So wrong. Every part of my chest and abdomen was flush against his—our bodies fitting together like puzzle pieces—his fingers twining with mine, my right leg between both of his.

Putting me right where I could feel a more intimate part of him.

"For the final time, I can dance. I don't dance."

My free hand on his shoulder, I looked up at him as he led me through the mix of dancers, moving his feet to the rhythm.

He smiled at my surprise. "You'd think one of these days you'd believe me, and while that tactic was sly for you, I understand you're anxious." Interest twinkled in his yellow eyes. "Did you think you'd forced my hand?"

"You certainly looked like I had."

"I don't know what I looked like, but I can tell you I was simply processing doing something I vowed I'd never do again."

He turned me, but instead of a twirl, he pulled my back tight against him to sway. The feel of his hot, hard body pressed to me made every inch of my body tingle.

"Your cheeks are so red," he laughed. "You recall you asked for this?"

Unable to find my voice, I said nothing. Immortals, I could barely breathe.

"I like that I make you blush," he whispered, almost as an afterthought, making me burn hotter. He turned me once again, bringing us back to our starting position.

"Question for a question?" I asked.

Eyes searching my face, he nodded.

The song's tempo increased. "You're clearly as good at this as everything else—" he grinned big at that "—so why don't you dance?"

"The hundreds of hours my mother forced me to do it when I was fourteen and would have rather done anything else. What's worse is that it was only me. My father insisted his heir and spare wouldn't be busied by such nonsense."

Lifting his arm, he sent me into a twirl.

On the return, I noticed he seemed to be holding his breath. "What is the necklace you wear?"

Surprised—especially after the event with the jexies—I hadn't mentioned it somehow before that moment, I said, "My mother left me an empty apartment, a small sum of money, a photo of me as a baby, and that necklace. Its presence grounds me. It reminds me who I am when the noise of life is too loud."

Spinning me, Damien drew my back to his chest once more. His hand coasted to my abdomen, the palm of his hand centering over my belly button. His breath moved across my hot skin, making my flesh pebble. Relaxing, I lay my head against his chest, raising my eyes to the lights.

The scent of mint and honey bloomed and coalesced around me, creating a deliciously comforting aroma.

His fingers curled into my abdomen, bunching up the midsection of my dress.

As the song reached its crescendo, I shimmied slightly and faced him, his hand gliding smoothly to my lower back. Yellow eyes as bright and clear as the sun on a cloudless day stared down at me as we swayed chest to chest once more.

Feeling light and free, I couldn't help my stupid grin. To my surprise, he returned my smile, the truth of his happiness in the coyness at the corner of his mouth.

Our movements started to slow, but my heart continued to beat faster.

Not thinking, I ran my hand along his shoulder, letting it come to rest on the back of his neck. As the song came to an end, he bent slightly, drawing a little closer. Close enough, I could smell the mint on his hot breath.

It was brief, the drop of his gaze to my lips. Just like the moment after the jexies. Except this time, Cole wasn't there in my mind holding me back.

Throat bobbing, he stumbled a step back, shattering the moment. He ran his fingers through his hair. "You should have a number of contenders to dance with now."

I stared after him, watching him make his way swiftly back to our table, not sure what'd just happened but knowing my stomach ached like it'd taken a blow.

Sweat slickening my neck, I lifted my hair and fanned. I only had a second to consider what his reaction was about as a shy voice interrupted my thoughts. "May I have the next dance?"

CHAPTER THIRTY-TWO

8.ELEVEN.4004

I smelled it on every inhale—sandalwood and cedar.

Lying on my stomach, I slid against the cool silk sheets, relishing where they touched the exposed skin of my feet and thighs.

"Sleep well?"

The voice startled me into an upright position. Beside me on the left lay Damien, one arm folded casually behind his head.

I slapped one hand over my mouth and the other over my erratic heart. "What happened? Did we…"

Trailing off, I tried desperately to recall how I wound up here, but all I could remember was being drunk and happy. Dancing a lot. And coming back to the suite.

"Nothing happened, Eden," he sighed. "You were drunk when we got back. You wanted to eat the cookies Isa made. I gave you a nullify elixir and went to shower. When I came out, you were passed out on my bed with that." He nodded to the nightstand where, sure enough, a plate of cookies sat, several with single bites missing.

Processing this, I glared at him. "You couldn't sleep somewhere else?"

"You fell asleep on my bed, and think I should find another place to sleep?"

"You did the other night."

"There's a difference between when you need my help and I let you have my bed, and you pass out drunk on it." He sat up, causing the blanket to fall below his navel, bringing his tan, chiseled chest to my attention.

"Are you naked?" Gasping, I turned away, blood flooding my cheeks.

"Why are you acting like this is the first time you've seen me shirtless?"

He threw back the bedding and slid out of the bed. He may not have been naked, but the sight of his snug briefs made my whole body burn like he was.

"I've never done that…slept in a man's bed that I haven't…"

"Slept with? And I've never let a woman I have or haven't slept with sleep in my bed. A first for both of us." He disappeared into his closet, reemerging a moment later in a black sweater, black slacks, and a black suit jacket.

"You can stay there if you like, but I have to go. I have to meet with His Highness." The name he'd taken to calling Cole. He grinned, eyes going to my waist. "Don't let Isa find you rubbing one out on the sheets, though."

I pressed my lips into a hard line. "You're disgusting. That's not what I was doing."

"That sure wasn't what it looked like." His eyes dropped to where the skirt of my dress sat hiked around my hips. "Nice underwear."

Grabbing a pillow, I lobbed it at his head. He snatched it from the air with ease, the corners of his lips turning up. "Was this supposed to hurt me?"

Hopping out of the bed, I tugged the hem back down over my thighs, making for the door. I yanked it open to Isa's fist, poised to knock, a paper bag in her free hand.

"Oh, I'm sorry," Isa said. Face flushing, her gaze flickered to my shoulder and then up past me, where Damien stood, close enough that I was sure if I took a deep breath, my back would brush against him. A dark red blush stained her tan cheeks. "I didn't mean to interrupt you guys, but Damien, I knew you were going to be on the move today, and I wanted to make sure you had something for lunch. I can make you breakfast, Eden."

An arm reached around me, plucking it from her hand. "No interruption. Thank you, Isa. Don't worry about Eden, she's leaving."

Isa looked to me for confirmation.

"That's very kind of you, but he's right. I'm going to put in extra time at Selene's House." Something I could do now without having to abide by Cole's restrictions.

Holding up a finger, she ran to the kitchen. "Then wait there. Take a muffin at least."

Damien's body shook behind me, confirming his proximity as the fabric of his suit jacket brushed my spine. I peered up at him to make sure he was okay, only to find his seizing was due to the laughter he fought.

I elbowed him lightly. "What's so funny?"

He shook his head, mouthing, *Outside.*

Isa came back then, a huge smile on her face as she passed me a basket containing half a dozen muffins and sent us on our way.

As the door clicked shut behind us, Damien took one look at me and burst into laughter, eyes gleaming playfully. "I do believe Isa thinks we slept together. Like had sex slept together. I've never seen her turn that red."

My skin heated several degrees. "That isn't funny. Why would she think that?"

"Besides the obvious?" Smile faltering, he flicked off the shoulder of my mauve dress. "That reaction was priceless."

I pulled it back into place. "Why didn't you tell her?"

He feigned consideration, shrugging. "I was enjoying myself too much."

Inclining my head to the door, I said, "Clear the air, please. I can't have her think I'd stoop so low."

Jaw dropping, he started to laugh once more. "I'd like to think that'd meant you aimed high."

I folded my arms over my chest and waited.

Sighing, he opened the door and poked his head in, calling into the dark, "We didn't have sex, Isa."

I rolled my eyes, halting his closing of the door with a firm hand at the center of the white wood. "I'm serious."

Damien's smile returned, clearly enjoying my annoyance. "She heard me. She can hear me now. The privacy ward is one-way, like the suite. She can hear outside. We can't hear in."

I blinked, taking this news in. I hadn't even known the suite was charmed.

Lifting my hand away, he shut the door, catching the tail end of my stupor. "You didn't know that, did you?"

"No, but now I want you to show me."

Damien draped his arm around my shoulder, pulling me into his sandalwood-scented embrace and steering me toward the stairs. "Oh, Eden, so distrustful. Later, or I'll be late."

Releasing me a step before my landing, I started for my door, going over to-dos. A sudden thought had me turning, expecting to see him at least two steps into the next section of stairs, but he stood where I'd left him, staring after me.

A little ache gripped my chest. "Damien?"

Snapping to, his green eyes flicked to mine. "Yes?"

"Don't forget you promised me a night out tomorrow."

He raised one suspicious eyebrow. "Was not being able to remember last night an act?"

Half inside my home, I shrugged one shoulder and tossed him a grin. "No, I still don't remember the cookies or wandering into your bedroom, but I'll let you know if I do."

Huffing, he put his back to me, muttering something about selective memory under his breath.

CHAPTER THIRTY-THREE

20.ELEVEN.4004

Ever since the dance and the morning after, something had changed. Something the spreading, weird little ache was refusing to let me hide from any longer—a truth I'd been denying: I liked Damien as a friend and more, and I wanted him. In a way that I'd never wanted Cole.

A stupid-on-so-many-levels crush because, putting aside my status as his brother's former Bidden and that Cole had me watched, Damien didn't date—which meant if I fed the urge, it'd only be physical, maybe for only one night.

And maybe I was kidding myself, but it seemed like something had changed for Damien, too.

Every night, despite his apparent reluctance to go out, he always said yes. And then, every night, at whatever table he settled into, he'd drink and glower. When he manipulated my features, he'd carefully brush his hand down my hair.

Then there was the way his eyes shifted every time I referred to him as a friend.

Or how his hand lingered on my waist when he phased us— moments I marked in heartbeats because mine pounded so hard it could have been a third presence.

Or maybe I was losing it and reading too much into everything.

It doesn't matter, he doesn't date, the voice of reason said.

None of that mattered to my heart, though. It would take whatever it could get, and it wanted him.

"Can I see you tomorrow for lunch?" Zadre asked.

I looked from the mass of moving bodies dancing to the man sitting beside me. Blue-green eyes stared back at me from the deeply tanned face of someone who spent from sunup to sundown outside. He wore his straight brown hair in a ponytail at the nape of his neck and an easy smile, and smelled like freshly cut grass.

Zadre had seized my hand the moment my feet touched the dance floor, and two dances later, nobody would come close to me. The sudden reluctance from previously willing eyes told me one thing: I had attracted someone in the area with clout.

Cutting my losses, I'd walked to the bar, hoping to lose him. Instead, he'd followed, sliding onto the stool beside me, which conveniently became free at his approach—a lot of influence then—and asking me so many questions it was starting to get hard keeping track of the necessary web of lies.

Several times I'd debated the hand gesture Damien and I had discussed for if I were in an uncomfortable situation, but while I was, it wasn't the kind I'd been in with Prian. And for all his muscles and magic, I wasn't sure how Damien would fare against someone like Zadre, who could have easily competed with Grayden in size.

Smiling to myself, I stood. "That's sweet of you, but I have work tomorrow. Speaking of which, I should head out. I need to get some rest."

It was early, but this had gone on long enough.

Zadre grabbed my wrist. "Early dinner tomorrow night, then? Here? I like you a lot. I want to see you again."

The moment triggered memories of Prian, which, for better or worse, had found their way back to me. Working to ignore the unease tingling at the back of my neck, I stared into his blue-green, lovestruck eyes, a scent like wet hay rolling like fog off him, and gently touched his shoulder. "I'll be here."

His whole body sagged in relief—his hand going limp on my wrist—and before he could consider other questions, I disappeared through the crowd, making my way to Damien.

I found him—the brunette version of him—guzzling whiskey straight from the bottle.

Leaning in so he could hear me over the music, I asked, "Why are you drinking like you're trying to forget?" A flicker of light hit us, and I shrank away, not wanting to be spotted by Zadre should he suddenly decide tomorrow wasn't soon enough.

Damien's eyes met mine—a strange pain glossing the yellow—looking like he wanted to say something to me.

Snatching my jacket off the empty seat across him, I nodded toward the door. "Let's go quickly, please."

Finishing the bottle, he slipped on his jacket and stood. "I was worried I would have to pry him off you."

Despite my sweating and the sweater dress, I shivered. "I thought you were going to have to as well. Did you notice how no one approached me after he set his eyes on me? He was too much. Let's get out of here before he decides my promise to see him again tomorrow is too long of a wait."

He retracted, eyes hardening. "Do you always make promises and touch guys you consider too much?"

Stepping out into the night, I shrugged. "Only if necessary. Sometimes, you have to give more than you want to give them to escape."

A muscle ticked in his jaw, and I hoped he wasn't thinking about Prian. "I call that being too nice. I could have stepped in. You know the hand signal."

I smiled gratefully, diving down the nearest street out of sight of the elixiry. "It wasn't like that. Plus, after almost a year of your brother, it was good to get an idea of what men are like now, which is basically the same as they were."

"Not all men are like that," he said defensively, adding quickly when he realized I hadn't provided a definition, "What about him was too much?"

I didn't stop walking as I fumbled to find the sleeves of my jacket. "He was attractive and sweet, but he kept saying how nice a wife I'd be before the end of the first dance and asking me about children at the end of the second."

"Isn't that what you want?"

Jacket secured, I looped my hand under my hair, untucking it. Not knowing what to say, I settled on, "I don't know what I want anymore."

Damien absorbed what I said, a distant look in his yellow eyes. "Where to next?"

Grabbing his elbow, I tugged him into a shadowy side street. "I was thinking home. That was enough adventure for me tonight."

His shoulders visibly relaxed.

I stepped up to him, wrapping my arms around his waist and pressing my face to his chest, the warmth of him seeping through his sweater, the smell of leather enriching every inhale. He braced his hand on my hip.

The cool evening breeze gave way to the dry heat rising from the downstairs fireplace.

Standing before the view of the city, his fingers grazed my hair, guiding the magic to release its hold on my appearance. In the window's reflection, I watched it unravel from the root of my hair down, bringing forth dark brown waves. The scents of lavender and jasmine blossomed around me, as did sandalwood and cedar.

I looked up at him, happy to see his black hair again. "You want to come back to my place? I'm not tired at all, and Isa deserves a night off from my antics."

The white light of the moon set his green eyes aglow. "You're going to make me a drink for once?"

Breaking our closeness—fifteen beats his hand had lingered—I grinned, motioning him to follow. With soft footsteps, we moved through the silence of the penthouse, Damien trailing two steps behind. As one door eased shut, another eased open.

"Whiskey?" I asked. Kicking off my shoes, I hung my jacket on a hook behind the front door and disappeared into the darkness.

"Sounds perfect." Snapping his fingers, soft, warm lights began to rotate around the perimeter of my home, and the fireplace came to life, fighting back the cold fall evening seeping inside.

Back to him, I pretended to be focused on his drink while my ears stayed hyper-aware of the sound each of his movements made. The gentle thud of each of his boots as he sat them down. The sweet creak of the wooden floors under his weight as he came closer. The soft drag of his fingers running along my walls.

The lack of noise hit just as hard. The absence of our banter. My almost non-existent breath.

The possibilities regarding what the next sound might be played out in my thoughts. The soft rustle of my hair as he touched it once more? Him sighing at my ear?

The last sound I expected was the click of the door to my left, followed by a long whine as it yawned open, the dancing lights rushing to accommodate the new space.

My bedroom.

"What are you doing?" I called after him, trying to control the mortification seeping into my voice. "Don't go in there."

"Whoa," he laughed.

Quickly, I rushed through my most recent memory of what it looked like. Old bookshelves along the walls, sagging under the weight of the books. Not too bad. My unmade queen-sized bed sandwiched between the two bedroom windows, covered in a dozen decorative pillows. Getting worse. The piles of dirty laundry haunting the floor…

A soft oomph followed by the groan of my bed frame was more than I could take. Grabbing both glasses, I ran—as fast as the sloshing drinks would allow—into the space, assessing the damage.

There was one more pile of clothing than I'd remembered, displaying outfits from our various nights out and a bra. My stomach shriveled. On the bedside table farthest from me, where the picture of my mother and me sat, was an old glass of water and one of Isa's muffins, half-eaten.

Damien lay at the center of my bed on his stomach, eyes closed, looking content.

Taking a steadying breath, I asked, "What are you doing?"

Rolling onto his side, he pulled one of my many pillows under his elbow. "Returning the favor. Maybe I'll drunkenly pass out and see where you decide to sleep." His eyebrows jumped pointedly. "You have a lot of pillows," he added, digging out another from amidst the mess of the blanket. "What is this one?"

Just when I thought it couldn't get worse.

I could have died right there, incinerated from the inside out, I burned so hot. I shifted my lips, trying to find a plausible enough lie. The precision with which he'd located it—clearly, he could smell exactly what *this one* was. Was there even a point to lying?

Yes, I decided.

"I like to sleep with a pillow between my legs." And it was kind of the truth. "I can't believe you came in here. My room is a mess. Come out and please pretend you never saw this."

"I'm fine where I am," he said.

Shaking my head, I pushed back a stack of books on the nightstand closest to me and set my water there before crawling onto the bed beside him, mirroring his side position. My hair flowed down around my shoulders, pooling on my purple cotton sheets.

"Do you even need this?" I held his glass up. "Seems like you're doing fine without it."

Plucking it from my hands, he swirled the glass, smelling it. "Is this the stuff I gave you?"

"It is. I didn't think you'd settle for anything else."

He tipped the glass. "You've learned."

I shoved his chest playfully, watching him closely as he relaxed once more, resting the glass in the space on the sheets between us.

My heart set to racing. Alone with Damien on my bed. Should have picked a different night to take a break from whiskey and elixirs. Especially since he watched me with a quiet intensity that made me aware of every breath I took.

"You must get tired of watching me. You do it every night," I said, emboldened. "Say something."

He took a sip of the drink. "No wonder you were drooling on my pillows. Yours are lacking."

"Your self-restraint is admirable."

He raised an eyebrow. "What is it exactly you think I'm restraining myself from?"

I smiled to myself. "Speaking your mind. I sometimes feel like nothing stays a secret after I've drunk whiskey or an elixir. I'm sure you've noticed during our recent escapades."

"Did you think you'd get me into your bed, and I'd confess my thoughts?"

"You're the one who came in here," I laughed, tucking a strand of hair behind my ear. After a moment, I added, "I'm glad your mother forced you to be my friend."

He winced—there it was—shoulders stiffening. "My mother didn't make me do anything. What she did was show me someone who needed help and knew I wouldn't be able to say no."

"Then I guess I'm happy you couldn't say no."

"You're happy I'm easily manipulated?"

"Easily manipulated isn't how I'd describe you at all."

He snorted, taking another drink. "How would you describe me then?"

I searched his face, taking the question seriously. "I'm sure my perspective is skewed since your decision benefited me, but I'd describe you as someone with morals—at least a sense of them. Something high society and the Alliance Council is severely lacking."

Nostrils flaring, his gaze shifted to my hips.

My dress lifted slightly as I curled my legs higher. I'd upset him. Not enough to make him leave, but enough to shut him down.

"What did I say?" I asked softly. "Tell me what's on your mind. Your silence is killing me."

Green eyes peered up at me. "You want to know what I'm thinking —how about a question for a question?"

"What do you want to ask?"

"Why do you like dancing so much?" The question came out on a low growl.

I grinned. His frustration cute. "It's freeing to share your body with someone else while dancing. It's being intimate without the obligation or commitment—something you can appreciate—and there's no follow-through. I've never been casually intimate with someone. I've never had the courage," I sighed. "But dancing, I guess I push that."

He tapped a finger to the lip of his glass. "You say that like a lack of casual sex is a bad thing. Commitment has never been my thing, but I don't fault anyone for wanting more."

Despite my lustful desire, the reminder of his stance twisted my naïve little heart.

I shrugged a shoulder. "It's not just commitment. It's wanting to know someone. It always felt like a weakness. Especially now. Rho thinks I need to lose myself with someone." My face heated at the admission. "That it'll help me move past everything with Cole."

Jaw shifting, the corners of his mouth turned down, his eyebrows locking together.

"Enough about that, though. You owe me an answer."

"I'm thinking about..." Rotating to reach back, he set his glass beside the picture and returned to tap me on the nose. The impish grin on his face as I swatted at him made me wish I'd gone for a full assault. "How you have work tomorrow, and I should go."

I sat up. "Was that a joke?"

His lips stretched until his grin was ear to ear, shaking his head. "It's been another fun night."

"Damien—it's like you want me to kick you out."

Scooting to the edge of the bed, he hopped to his feet, triumphantly saying, "You can't kick me out if I'm leaving."

"Damien Elias Valentine," I screeched. I grabbed for the first thing my hand could get a hold of and lobbed it at him.

"That's my nam—" He turned around in time to catch it.

Lucky for him, it was a pillow.

Unlucky for me, it was *the* pillow.

He looked at it and laughed, tossing it up like a coin. "What is with you and throwing pillows at me? It isn't very nice. In fact, it's going to cost you."

Jumping to my feet, I launched toward him, arms flailing. Trying in vain to reclaim the stupid thing, but he held it high above his head.

"Fine, then go, get out," I demanded, cheeks burning. Hands on his chest, I pushed him to the door, not even caring that he let me.

"My shoes—"

Yanking open the door, I let loose an exasperated sigh. "Held hostage until you surrender my pillow. Now get out."

"Goodnight," he crooned as the door slammed in his face.

CHAPTER THIRTY-FOUR

21.ELEVEN.4004

The front door to the penthouse swung open at my touch. My shoes were half off as I charged through the wards, kicking them to the side. Damien Valentine—standing at the table wearing a crisp white button-up and slim-fitted black slacks, filling wine glasses—didn't know what was coming for him.

Through the cutout in the wall to the kitchen, I spotted Isa hunched over at the counter, putting the final touches on dinner. Something buttery and tomato-rich, from the smell of it.

Ignoring the growl of my stomach, I stormed toward him on the pads of my feet, not stopping until I was right up on him. "I want my pillow back." Heat stirring in my abdomen for the millionth time that day, remembering him in my room, lying on my bed as I'd tried to feel him out.

What he now possessed.

Giving in to the smile he fought, he peered at me over the glass he was filling. "My day was fine, thanks for asking. How was yours?"

He held the glass out to me. I took one glance at it and shook my head.

"It would have been fine if I'd slept okay, but someone took my leg pillow."

"That's why you can't sleep now, is it?" Setting it aside, he settled into the seat at the head of the table and, cupping his chin in his hand, considered me thoughtfully. "You have a hundred decorating your bed. I'm surprised you didn't simply use…a different one."

"That's the only one small and thick enough to fit comfortably between my legs."

He bit the tip of his pointer finger. "You like small and thick things between your legs, huh?"

Every inch of my skin burned. "You're disgusting. That's not what I meant—just—ugh—please?"

"After you made me walk back up here in my socks? Not a chance. Speaking of…" He glanced at my hands, clenched into fists at my sides. "Where are my boots?"

"Enough of this bickering," Isa sighed. We both turned to look at her, mittened hands carrying a deep glass baking dish filled with layers of noodles, cheese, and tomatoey meat sauce, still simmering at the bottom. "It's time to eat."

***

I'd never been the kind of woman who saw a guy they wanted and went for it, but tonight that was going to change…whenever I'd consumed enough whiskey to unlock my remaining courage, having used up all I'd managed so far to put on the cherry red dress I wore.

Straps made of pin-sized red crystal held up the tight stretch of fabric covering my breasts. Below that, the views continued. The back and most of the sides of the dress were sheer panels, and a strip of red just thick enough to cover my belly button connected the top to the skirt, which came threateningly high when I did anything but stand.

The dress was a remnant from the options Rho had brought over for me the night she'd helped me get ready. Rho had called it a fuck me dress and said if I wore it, I wasn't going home alone. With remarks like that, it seemed my best choice for what I had planned. And with the looks I'd been getting from men and women, it was safe to say she wasn't wrong.

Watching Damien from our table, ordering drinks at the bar—bronze hair shimmering in the low lights, his shirt clinging tight to the muscles in his chest—I divided my thoughts between wondering for the millionth time what he was thinking and coming to terms with what I was trying to do.

I huffed a laugh. The fact that I wasn't a virgin was a miracle.

"What's so funny?" Damien grumbled.

I looked up from my hands as two glasses—one of whiskey and one of water—slid across the table. Dropping onto the stool across from me, his eyes scanned the crowd. Lifting the brimming glass of whiskey he clutched to his lips, he drained half of it, all the while looking grumpier than he did after a day of dealing with Cole's mood following a spontaneous summons.

Butterflies beating their wings against my stomach, I took a sip of my whiskey. "Just a thought I had. Is everything okay?"

Damien smiled wryly, fisting a handful of the nuts sitting at the center of the table. "I'm fine. Go dance, Eden."

Dancing, that was my window. I glanced down at my dress—everything still looked good—and then back to him. "Will you dance with me?"

"You don't need me to dance with you. Any man or woman in this room would be happy to, we've proven that."

Or maybe he wasn't interested.

I swallowed the fear swelling my throat, but my voice betrayed my insecurity. "Dance with me, please."

His chest swelled, and for a moment, it seemed like he'd say yes... "I can't. Not tonight."

Opening my mouth, I prepared to beg him, but something about the slouch in his shoulders told me to let it go. I studied him carefully, not knowing what to do. I thought about suggesting we go home. An idea that would lead to questions I didn't want to answer.

Slipping on my coat, I stood. This had been a mistake. I was a girl with a stupid, nonsensical crush on an entirely uninterested boy. I couldn't go home, but I couldn't stay here. "Let's go somewhere else."

He spared me a glance, yellow eyes glazed and brow furrowed. "We only just got here—nothing interests you?"

Tucking a strand of pink hair behind my ear, I threw back the whiskey and took a sip of my water, nodding toward the door. "Can't say it does. Let's go to the next place."

We'd go around until it was safe to say the night had been a wash, and I could go to bed, forgetting this miserable attempt.

Downing his drink, he grabbed his coat. "Lead the way."

And I did, up until the door where he overtook me—hands shoved into his pockets and collar upturned against the cold wind rushing to welcome us—as if he couldn't get away fast enough. Feet pounding the cobblestones, Damien put space between us in a few strides.

What was with his mood?

"There's a place I like a few streets away," he grumbled.

He didn't bother to glance back to see if I followed. I waited until he was almost out of view before giving up hope he might.

Pulling my coat tight around me, I jogged to catch up, stopping myself as I started to call out his name. As if sensing the desire, he turned around, shoulders sagging in clear annoyance. I swore I saw him roll his eyes.

I was a quarter of the way to him when someone caught my wrist, jerking me to a halt. Immortals, why did people feel compelled to grab me?

"Nedeah?" a voice asked. "Is that you?"

It took me a moment to remember that was my fake name.

The man who owned the voice stepped from the shadow of a dark alley, blue-green eyes—pupils dilated and whites bloodshot—staring down at me. An aggression elixir. How did this guy know me?

A black knit cap covered his hair except for the brown ponytail bound at the base of his neck. "I waited for you. For hours. I waited until I couldn't wait any longer."

Oh, fuck.

I forced a smile. "Zadre." How was this happening?

"Mm, boss, she smells like candy," purred a voice from the shadows.

"Can we help you?" Having almost reached the next street, Damien's voice startled me.

"Who is this?" Zadre asked. He nodded to Damien, whose shadow fell over my shoulder.

"Some high society boy, from the looks of him," spat another voice from the shadows.

Zadre's grip on my wrist reached bone-breaking strength. "You chose this guy over me?"

I ground my teeth together, refusing to bow for him.

"Let her go, or you're going to have a big problem on your hands," Damien growled.

"I don't take orders from your sort," Zadre sneered.

A black-clad figure stepped forward on Zadre's left, popping their knuckles. "Let's teach this high-society pretty boy a lesson about absconding with our women."

Before I could blink, a fist shot past my head, landing at the center of Zadre's face with a sharp crack, stunning him enough that his hold on me dropped, another slipping into its place, wrenching me away.

The metallic scent of blood assaulted my nose.

"Run," Damien hissed.

An unnecessary command, as we both shot down the street at full speed, Zadre and his friends close on our heels.

"Why don't we phase away?" I asked, barely keeping up.

"Because I can't—"

"Maybe if you hadn't guzzled a whole glass of whiskey," I hissed.

He shot me a look over his shoulder. "And we wouldn't be in this situation if you had simply told him you weren't interested."

Damien tugged me down a street, then another. My legs and feet were on fire, attempting to keep up with him, but it didn't matter how much I tried, the ache was morphing into a simmering numbness.

He must have sensed my desire to slow down because he said. "Just a little further."

They weren't far behind, and they were gaining on us.

I looked up at him. "What are we—" But I stopped myself, noticing two things at once: we were back where we'd started the night—an alley separating a butcher from a cheese shop, shrouded in shadow— and Damien's glossy brown hair was as black as the darkness he pulled me into.

The force and warmth of his body pushing me into the brick wall took my breath away. He tapped a finger to his lips. "Hold very still. I'm going to cloak us."

Why was his disguise gone? Why wasn't he phasing us away? I nodded, forehead brushing his chest. I was so close. Footfall and angry voices growing nearer, my heartbeat so hard he had to feel it. Our pursuers had to hear it.

"We were right behind them. Where did they go?" asked one.

"I think they went this way," said the one standing at the mouth of the alley.

Damien's chest inflated.

"I've lost their scent," came another. "There's no trace of them."

"How can a Charphan lose a scent on an empty street?"

Magic. I'd thought we were running mindlessly, but he was choosing his route, backtracking, and wiping us away. I touched the ends of my hair with my free hand—the one still clutched in Damien's, hot and sweat-slick. Brown again. How much magic had it cost? He must have been exhausted.

"All I smell is you fuckers. Would it kill you to bathe?"

"It doesn't matter," Zadre snarled. I caught a glimpse of him around Damien's shoulder, holding the bridge of his nose, blood running into his teeth. "Let him have her. We have a mission to accomplish before daybreak."

Hungry for blood, they grumbled, steps falling away.

Damien and I stayed that way, unspeaking, for another minute. "I think we're good," he whispered—his breath light against my hair.

Neither of us moved. "How did you know he was Charphan?"

"Because I was paying attention. The one said you smelled like candy—what did you call that man?"

I rolled my eyes, wondering why it mattered. "Zadre."

"Zadre Trite?"

Yanking back the inch I could to look at him, I asked, "You know him?"

Damien's eyes—green once more—met mine. "I know of him. Learned about him at the last Council meeting. He's part of the insurgency plaguing the Alliance Council right now, him and his horde. They're stirring up as much trouble as they can, calling for a separation of governance for parts of the outer city and farmlands. The last thing we needed were Charphan Protectors, who are trying to track the group's movements to pick up our scents around areas of their activity. I've disguised us well, but we aren't infallible."

"Thank you." Remembering what I'd assumed, I said, "I'm sorry for what I said about the whiskey. That was wrong of me."

I thought he might take a step back then since the threat was gone. Instead, his thumb made circles on the wrist he'd never let go of, sending tingling sensations up my arm. "It's fine. It didn't help. I was a little slower weaving than I like to be."

I should say something…

His lips softened at the corners. "It just occurred to me—what you said the other day—of course no one was going to approach you after he set his sights on you. I'm sure everyone in there knew who he was. Not only did you attract a member of the resistance, but you also attracted one of the leaders. You know how to choose them."

I slapped his chest.

"That wasn't very nice," he laughed softly. "You make promises to the men you think are too much and strike the ones who save you. How do you behave for the men you like?"

I stared at him, my heart still hammering the inside of my chest, though for a different reason.

It's now or never. It's now or never.

"We should—"

Swallowing my fear, I stepped onto my tiptoes, cutting him off with a featherlight kiss on his soft lips. "Would you like to find out?"

His eyes were suddenly clear. The rise and fall of his chest coming to an abrupt stop. "Eden."

"Damien." His name barely made it out of my mouth as my throat started to close. Immortals, what had I done? My head spun so fast I was sure I would be a mess on the ground if not for his body holding me up. Every second felt like a life lived. "I'm sor—"

"Don't. Don't apologize." His other hand settled on the curve of my waist. "Can we try that again?"

Unable to speak, I nodded.

Shyly, as if prodding the line I'd crossed, he brushed his lips against mine—the gentle touch tickling me—before settling into me. Damien's kiss was light and sweet, tasting faintly of the mint I'd smelled on his breath the other night. His lips moved confidently, meeting each move of my mouth without hesitation—his ability to read me stirred something hot, low in my stomach.

"Is this okay? Do you want me to stop?" he breathed.

A little delirious, I stared at his mouth, glistening with our kiss, wanting to taste him again. "No, I don't. I just hope I'm okay."

"Yes," he laughed. "Eden, yes."

Half-hearing him, I took his face in my hands and pulled him closer. "Kiss me, please."

Damien was more than happy to oblige, pressing his mouth to mine, a new hunger to the movement. His tongue brushed along my lower lip, asking for permission, and I opened to him like a well-worn book. With nothing separating us, his hot tongue slipped inside, exploring my mouth greedily. I inhaled deeply through my nose, dragging my tongue along his teeth, the taste of him driving my need, and I never wanted to stop.

Running my hands up into his hair, I ground against him, begging to be closer.

Reading me again, he tightened his hold around my waist. My coat catching on the rough exterior, he lifted me, legs around his hips, and pinned me in place. I barely registered the absence of my skirt around my hips, my attention going to the feel of him against my now exposed inner thigh.

My heart fluttered. I hadn't stopped to think about that, but there it was. Big enough to be a third leg and hard as the wall he had me pinned against. Immortals.

I kissed his cheeks, his jaw—every exposed inch of him—as he slid his free hand up the side of my thigh, pulling a moan from me as his fingers brushed the band of my underwear. Damien let out a low growl as I writhed against him.

His fingers coasted along the fabric, going up along my hip and down my ass. A fresh wave of heat washed through my core. It felt so good. Every touch. My whole body was alight. Singing for him. A chorus of yes.

Damien bowed his head, lips sinking into the flesh of my neck where he licked, kissed, and sucked. I worked my hand between us, fumbling with his belt, slipping the button of his jeans from its hole.

I would let him have me there.

No, not here. I wasn't that savage. Even if this was all I got, it couldn't be in some alley in the farmlands. I broke away from him.

Fiery green eyes stared down at me.

"Take me home. I want to lose myself with you," I breathed.

Rough stone became the cold glass of the suite's panorama window. The shadowy alley into the moonlit king-size bed.

Desperation, a delirious rush.

Hand still locked in his hair, he pulled away to look at me and asked gently, "Are you sure you want to do this?"

Nodding feverishly, I returned the question. "Yes. Do you?" Despite the hard length of him between my legs, I needed to hear him say it. Immortals, how I'd wanted to hear him say it.

"You have no idea." Lips latching onto my neck, he sucked hard.

A heady moan broke my voice.

Stumbling back to the bed, I ran my fingers over his shoulders, freeing him from his coat. A soft sigh escaped as we hit the mattress, Damien on top of me.

My fingers were fumbling with the buttons on his shirt when he abruptly pulled away.

"No, no, I'm sorry, I can't do this," he exclaimed. He moved swiftly to the opposite side of the bed.

Shocked by the suddenness, I sat up. "Did I do something wrong?"

Hands shaking, he redid the buttons I'd managed. "You want someone to lose yourself with. I don't want to be that person."

I moved onto my knees, reaching for him, not caring that my dress was around my waist. "Damien, I don't want to lose myself with just anyone. I want to lose myself with you."

He dodged my hand. "That's not what I want. I don't want you to *lose* yourself with me. This is a mistake. I'm sorry."

Those words.

Stricken, my heart sank into my stomach, taking my voice with it. "No, I'm sorry," I managed softly. "These last couple of weeks together —I thought you might want me too."

"Eden, that's the problem. I do want you—I like you—too much. Enough that I don't want to be your one-night plaything to help you forget Cole." He anxiously finger-combed his hair back from his face over and over. "Fuck, as much as I've thought about this, I can't believe I'm saying that."

Despair soaked every breath of air. "That's not what I meant when I said I wanted that."

"What did you mean?" he asked skeptically. His eyes met mine, burning feverishly.

I stared at him, mouth agape, as I tried to think. "I don't know. I do want to forget Cole, but I don't think of you like that. I like you too. I —"

This was too much. A hot tear fell onto my cheek.

Damien's eyes grew wide at the shimmering drop. "Eden, no."

"I'm sorry," I croaked. Needing support, I scooted back to the headboard of the bed.

One tear was all it took for others to come.

"Please, don't," he begged softly. The heat of his body greeted me as he pulled me into him. "I can't stand to see you cry. It makes me physically sick."

Taking my face in his hands, he ran his thumbs across my cheekbones, sweeping the tears away as fast as they came.

"I'm sorry," I whispered, peeling his hands gently away from my face. "I feel so stupid. I messed up. I told you my history. I know nothing of casual sex. All I knew was that you didn't do relationships, and I wasn't sure if I was ready for another relationship anyway, but I like you, so I figured I'd meet you on your level." I took a deep, shaky breath, trying to relax. "And I do want to move on from Cole, but that wasn't a driver, it was just a facet. I'm sorry."

His eyes searched mine. "Stop apologizing like everything is your fault. I could have told you how I felt, but I was scared—as casual sex isn't your strength, sharing my feelings isn't mine. And with everything that's happened the last several months, my feelings felt selfish." He huffed a bitter laugh. "I've spent every second since I came up here and found you in this dress dreading tonight because if watching you these last couple of weeks has taught me anything, it's that nothing burns my blood more than seeing anyone else touch you how I want to." He let out a conflicted sigh. "I hope you won't mind when I say that I don't want to be with you while you're still healing from Cole. I don't want to be a rebound."

"I don't want you to be a rebound either." Swallowing the lump in my throat, I smoothed the dress down as much as I could. "Should we just pretend like this didn't happen then?"

Confusion blanketed his eyes, his grip on my hands tightening. "I— is that what you want?"

It would have been best to lie, salvage the line I'd slashed—who knew how long it'd take me to get over the trauma of Cole? But my heart shriveled like a grape in the heat of the sun at the thought. "No, but I don't know when Cole won't be a factor, and it doesn't seem right to toy with something that has an indefinite start."

Damien's grip on my hands relaxed. "That's it. That's why you asked that. I didn't mean get together as in being with you. I meant it as in having sex with you. I don't want our first time together to be clouded by my brother. I meant...I would like to take it slow with you."

My heart warmed. "You want to be in a relationship?"

He smiled. "Don't sound so surprised, but yes, if you'd like that. If you'd want me."

My thoughts went back to a moment ago, the way we'd burned together, our bodies understanding each other, the scent of him beckoning me closer, feeding the yearning. "No sex is going to be rough, but I would like that. To have you, to be yours."

"You're telling me," he laughed. "I can smell your sweet honey scented desire now—everywhere—and it makes me feel mad."

The blush heating my body seemed to intensify it. Groaning, he broke away, rubbing his hands along his face as he fell back onto a pillow. "I can't believe I suggested abstinence."

I lay down beside him, propped up on my elbow, fighting the urge to touch him. "I have something that will douse your desire."

He joined me on his elbow. "The only thing that would douse this is if you've had a sudden change of heart about being my girlfriend, and as the first, that would just be cruel."

Ignoring the giddy feeling in my stomach at the use of the word girlfriend, I touched the tip of my pointer finger to his lower lip. "What do we do about your brother?"

The one question asking a thousand.

Lifting a stray strand of hair, he twirled it lazily around his finger before tucking it behind my ear. "The only thing we can do. We take it one day at a time."

Not an answer, but he was right. It was the only answer we had. Hand slipping inside my jacket, he hooked my waist, resting the palm of his hand on the small of my back, and sliding me closer.

Pushing his black hair out of his face, I stared into those bright green eyes. "Damien," I whispered.

"Eden," he breathed.

We brushed lips and came together, the line between us so easily gone. The kiss started sweetly, savoring each other, and deepened into a tangle of tongues and teeth. His hand sliding down my hips to my exposed thigh.

I hooked my leg over his waist, needing to be closer to him.

"Eden." This time, my name was a word of caution as he broke away.

"Should I go?" I asked, shifting my lips to the side. If we were going to take it slow, I knew I should, but I didn't want to.

His nostrils flared as he inhaled.

Not ready for another rejection, I said, "It's okay, I know, slow, I know—"

Damien's grip on my waist tightened, the hot, sweet taste of his kiss cutting me off. "I would like you to stay."

CHAPTER THIRTY-FIVE
4.TWELVE.4004

Not a night apart since our confessions to one another, we had fallen into a routine, and I knew the meaning of the lazy circles he made around my belly button well. Wanting to stay in the magic of the moment a little longer, I worked to keep my breathing shallow.

It was nice. This. All of this.

The long talks we had on the couch or in his bed, sharing thoughts, secrets, and dreams. Moments when I'd look up from playing a game with Isa to find him watching me from the couch when he was supposed to be writing in his journal. The way he squeezed me closer, arm snug around my waist, before sleep took him, his gentle breath against my neck.

Or teaching me magic when either of our attention spans would allow for it. And it was hard when all I thought about as he guided me was how nice his warm, hard body felt against me, that he smelled like sun-warmed sandalwood and cedar, and tasted like freshly picked mint. How I wanted to taste his skin and other parts of him.

Groaning, I shimmied my shoulders slightly and rolled over, sliding my feet along the satin sheets, inhaling the scent of him everywhere like an addict. I looked right into the cool green pools of his eyes, shining in the cracks of light coming through the drapes, sleep-tussled hair jutting out in every direction.

"Good morning," I whispered.

He dragged a finger slowly along my cheekbone, sliding a stray strand of dark brown hair behind my ear. "Good morning."

I scooted closer to him under the blankets, close enough to share breath, to feel the delicious warmth of his body radiating through his sleeping shirt and mine, which also happened to be his. Close enough, he could feel the tips of my breasts through the thin material—something I knew drove him crazy.

"What are you thinking about?" he asked.

Nuzzling our noses, I said, "That I've never slept as well as I do with you."

"That's funny. I barely sleep at all for fear I'll wake to find you gone, and this was a dream."

Brushing his lips across mine, I grabbed the back of his neck and sank into our kiss, the hot taste of his mouth greeting me. His hand ran down my back, triggering a moan he savored in his mouth. Draping one leg around his waist, I pressed closer, relishing the hard length of him. So close. We were so close. In so many ways. A single hot breath whooshed from him.

This is how it was every morning until…

"No," Damien said, breaking the kiss. The word surprised me every time one of us said it—mostly him—because we were both aching for it.

But Cole still lingered. Not in the mornings but in the evenings, when we talked and I realized how deep the insecurities I'd developed with him ran. Insecurities aching like tight muscles that Damien kneaded every night.

Sighing, I rolled onto my back, hands folded safely atop my stomach. "It's your turn." For the metaphorical bucket of ice water we took turns dumping on the flames that caught between us.

Propping himself up on his elbow, he sucked in a breath through his mouth. "That's easy to say when you aren't breathing in the smell of my desire. I've got nothing."

No thought or news to spare either of us the torment.

"A story." I ran my fingers up into his thick, black, wavy hair, sweeping it away from his face. "A beautiful story, one I've never heard."

"That's going to be impossible. You've read everything of interest."

I dragged a finger lazily down the bridge of his nose. "Tell me a story about Misundre? They've always been reluctant to share their history."

His eyes searched my face, making me wonder if he was thinking of a story or something else. "Do you know the story of how Misundre became a city?"

Opening my mouth, I started to say yes, realizing, "I've never thought about it, but no, I don't. I know they had no Immortal Idol."

Hooking an arm around my waist, he pulled me closer once more, making my shirt lift. "I don't know about that. Just because we don't know of one doesn't mean there wasn't one at some point in time. A lot of history was lost when the Misundrans fled Magea."

Interest piqued, I sat up a little. "Magea?"

He traced a finger along the section of exposed stomach, my skin pebbling at the sensual, lazy touch. "A series of beautiful islands somewhere in the White Sea. Where the Misundrans came from. A place described to me as thick and lush with green, white sand beaches, purple and gold sunsets, ripe fruits picked right off the trees, fresh fish, gentle breezes, and hot weather year-round."

"It sounds like you described Misundre."

Eyes gleaming playfully, he dipped a finger into my belly button. "You're supposed to be listening. I'm telling you how it was told to me. It does sound the same, though the sand in Misundre is more of a golden brown."

"If it was so beautiful, why were they fleeing?"

He arched an eyebrow. "This is how it's going to be the entire time I tell this story, isn't it?"

I smiled, widening my eyes in a plea.

That finger dipped once more. "A story for tomorrow, now shall I continue?"

I stuck out my lower lip but nodded.

"After several days—fighting through the whirlpools off the coast, the wind and rain lashing their boats—they washed up on a beach guarded by two waterfalls and surrounded by mountains covered in thick green trees."

I sat up fully. "The Postern Waterfalls and Linolay Beach."

"You know it?"

"Only its description, that it's beautiful and sacred to the Misundrans."

"It is. More beautiful than you can imagine." His eyes dropped to my lips, and something told me we weren't talking about the same thing.

My excitement got the better of me. "You've been?"

His smile reached his eyes. "Many times, would you like me to take you?"

"What? Yes—seriously? A thousand times, yes."

Leaping on me, Damien took me back down to the bed, his legs to either side of my waist as he lowered himself. "So adorably pure," he mumbled, burrowing his face in the curve of my neck.

"Not pure," I grumbled, slapping his chest lightly. "Does Magea still exist?"

"You're dipping into tomorrow's story, but I'd say no. Disaster hit the islands, which is why they left."

"No one's ever tried?"

"People have tried, crazy people if I'm being honest, because no one in their right mind would attempt to sail that way. The currents immediately off the coast quickly push you back, so you need strong magic to push against them and eventually break free. After that, there's maneuvering around the whirlpools, which can easily swallow the fishing boats Misundrans use."

He sucked gently at my neck, making my back arch. I wound my fingers into his thick, smooth hair, wanting to do the same to him. As nice a distraction as it had been, the story hadn't helped.

Scenting me, he groaned and pried himself away, sighing the words that always cooled me off. "You're going to be late for work."

CHAPTER THIRTY-SIX

14.TWELVE.4004

"Eden?"

Eyes widening, I looked to Isa, who was already running toward me, a plated breakfast muffin in hand, mouthing *go, go*.

Taking it from her, I mouthed *thank you*, almost forgetting the white-wrapped package on the counter.

In my absence, Damien had opened the drapes, letting the blinding white light of the winter morning wash over everything. He had one tan hand woven into his hair, propping him up. The other, he ran over my wrinkled side of the bed, frowning.

"What is that look?" I teased.

Twisting to see me, the sadness faded away.

Using my hip, I eased the door closed. "I leave for a minute, and you look at the spot where I was lying like a lost puppy."

Laughing, he ran a hand through his messy black hair. "That's…a bit like how I felt." He nodded at the plate. "What is this?"

"I had to get up before you, or I wouldn't have been able to surprise you." The neck of my bed shirt shifted back onto my shoulders as I held up the muffin and package, grinning. "Happy birthday, Damien."

He looked from me to the muffin—wax from the silver candle at its center, beginning to drip—and back to me. "Did Isa tell you?"

"No, believe it or not, your mother celebrated the day every year with cake. And I remember all days with cake quite fondly." I sat on the edge of the bed. "I am curious why you didn't mention it?"

Shrugging, he sat up. "I didn't intentionally not tell you. I haven't celebrated it in years, and I've had other things on my mind." He raised his eyebrows suggestively.

Holding out the plate to him, I said, "Well, we're celebrating this year. Now, blow out the candle."

Accepting it, he knocked the flame out with a puff of breath and set it on the nightstand. He turned to grab me, but expecting the move, I shoved the gift into his hands.

"I wish I could say it was something exciting, but it was the only thing I could think of getting you. It's hard to get something for a man who can buy anything he likes."

He considered it. "If I open it now, will you come back to bed?"

I nodded, motioning for him to go on. He peeled away the tissue paper, revealing a black leather-bound journal with gilded gold pages.

"I love it. I can always use a new journal."

With Protector-level skill, he set the journal next to the muffin, simultaneously sweeping me onto my back, knocking the wind from me.

"Didn't trust me to comply?" I asked.

"I didn't want to risk it," he mumbled. Green eyes twinkling, he crawled on top of me. "There are most definitely things I like that I can't buy."

My heart quickened in my chest. "You're right. You can't buy me, but I'm already yours."

"And hearing that is the best gift." He proceeded to place erratic kisses on my chin, my cheeks, the tip of my nose, and my temples.

Laughing, I squirmed underneath him, bringing one very responsive part of his body to attention. A low, pained groan escaped his lips as he contained himself. He was getting too good at that.

Breathless, I looked up at him, wishing—as I ran my finger up the bridge of his straight nose—for birthday's sake, he'd let loose on me. "What do you write in them? Your journals?"

"Everything, anything. The events of the day, my feelings."

"Would you ever let me read one?" My finger continued its journey along his slightly arched eyebrow.

"I'll think about it." He brushed his nose along my ear. "Want to read all the dirty fantasies I've had about you?"

My cheeks tingled. "Are those in there?"

"I did say everything and anything."

I wound my fingers up into his hair, my next words a whisper. "Maybe I'll let you try one for your birthday."

Stifling a groan, he ran his rough hands up my shirt, along the flesh of my waist. My breath caught at the sensation, my body warming. Damien stopped at the bottom of my breast, tracing his thumb along the swell. This was the furthest we'd gone. Even above my clothes, he'd kept things tame. Shivering at the touch, I dipped my back, trying to get him to go higher, but his hand stayed firm. His self-restraint was better than mine, and I hated it so much.

Realizing I'd closed my eyes, I opened them, staring right into a sea of jade green.

Looking smug with himself, he ran his tongue over his top front teeth. "I know which one I'd like to try."

Everything inside me burned white-hot.

Continuing the stroke, he lowered himself to suck lightly at the flesh where my neck and shoulder met. "But you'll have to wait and see when I return."

Throwing the covers off himself, he jumped from the bed and slipped toward the closet.

I grabbed the pillow he'd been lying on and threw it hard and fast at him, garnering a laugh as it nailed his lower back.

Feeling crazy, I flopped back against the bed. "That was cruel." Groaning, I kicked my feet and threw my head into the pillow. "Fuck, I hate the Alliance Council."

***

Sitting in a fitted black dress before the fireplace in Damien's room, I stared at the cake and the bottle of wine waiting on the accent table.

Not nearly the prettiest cake I'd ever seen nor the nicest wine, but following Isa's instructions, I'd made the cake myself—surprisingly, she'd let me into the kitchen—and she'd diligently overseen the process, so I had high hopes it'd taste fine, and the wine—with the certainty of Cole still having me watched and followed—it seemed the least conspicuous option at the market for a woman who rarely had company.

A little after nine, a gentle hand clasped my shoulder, startling me. Isa stood in her nightgown, her short silver hair hanging delicately around her face. "I'm going to bed. Wish Damien another happy birthday for me when you see him."

I twisted in the chair to face her more completely. "You don't want to stay up with me? I'm sure he'll be home soon."

Her rich reddish-brown eyes drank in the warmth of the fire. "He better be, but no, whatever time is left of the day should be for you two."

At half past ten, I put down the book I was trying to read and poured two glasses of wine, draining one of the glasses in a couple of gulps. Clearly, something had come up. I could only hope he was all right.

The bedroom door clicked shut behind me, startling me.

As if the thought had conjured him, Damien stood before the door, his black suit jacket draped over his shoulder and an ardor in his eyes that heated the space between my legs.

I leapt to my feet. "You're home."

Damien crossed the distance between us quickly, swooping me up against him and burying his cold face in my neck, breathing me in. He reeked of whiskey, smoke, and fruity perfume, but happy to see him, I didn't even care.

"Immortals," he groaned, "it's so good to see you. To hold you and soak in the heat of you. To smell you." He ran his hand up along my neck, fingers weaving into my hair, making my breath catch. "Eden, I'm so sorry. I thought today would never end. Grayden and Cole ambushed me after the Council adjourned. I tried to get back sooner, but it was one elixir after another, and—all I wanted to do was be here with you." He laughed at himself. "Look what you've done to me. I'm a blubbering fool."

"I'm glad to see you too, and I'm sorry to hear you didn't enjoy your birthday." I touched my fingers to his jaw, guiding his attention to the table. "Do you have a glass of wine left in you?"

"For you, I'd do anything, including drink cheap market wine." Gaze returning to me, his mouth tugged up at the corner. "That cake doesn't look like Isa's handiwork."

"That's because I made it." I swiped my finger through the icing for him to taste…

He raised an eyebrow. "Should I be worried then?"

…and smeared it along his nose instead. He scoffed, jaw going slack, an impish glimmer flashing in his eyes. I squealed as his hold around me tightened, and he nuzzled his nose against my cheek, smearing the icing.

And then licking it off.

"Hmm, and here I thought you couldn't get any sweeter," he said.

"You did a good job on the frosting."

"I'll let you get away with that since it's your birthday," I groaned.

He wiped both of our faces with his sleeve. "What else can I get away with?"

Renewed awareness of how close we were, my eyes dropped to his lips, my skin flushing hot. "Whatever you want."

Letting out a low growl, he whispered, "I'm glad you said that because I have an idea. Something I couldn't stop thinking about doing with you all day, even more so after all my running around." In one smooth motion, he lifted me into his arms. "A bath."

Clinging to him for dear life, I asked incredulously, "A bath—that's what you've been thinking about doing with me all day?"

The lights of the bathroom flicked on, illuminating the sizable bathroom. Looking at the sage green walls, the white porcelain tub, and simple silver fixtures, it was hard to believe this was in the same apartment as the suite bathroom upstairs. Damien sat me on the chair right inside the room and turned on the faucet, bringing forth a torrent of hot water.

A snap of the fingers and a milky bottle appeared in his hand.

Emptying the contents under the steaming stream, he said, "Yes, a bath. I'd like to wash the stench off me while enjoying you." He held the empty vial up. "I actually made this for you the other day."

Inching to the edge of the chair for a better view, I noticed a faint sheen to the water. "What is it?"

"A transdermal elixir for the bath. It's a special concoction I developed. There are a number of things in it, but the relaxer is the key element."

"Are you trying to tell me I need to relax?"

Capping the empty bottle, he threw a smile over his shoulder. "I wouldn't dream of it."

Undoing the buttons of his shirt, he tugged it off, laying it all out there. The sight of his broad shoulders and his muscled back made the room a little warmer. His skin, a soft sand color after months without seeing the sun, made the faint scars on his left shoulder nearly invisible. Scars he'd quietly told me one night were the result of an Assault Demon during the war. I wanted to touch him, to touch them, and soothe him…

He didn't even bat an eye as he reached for the snap on his pants, shrugging them down, exposing even more of his muscled physique. Thumb tucked into the band of his briefs, they dipped slightly, and it was at that exact moment my brain took the opportunity to remind me I hadn't seen him naked—nor him me—sending my heart into a tizzy.

It was a good thing I was sitting down. "Damien…"

Snapping from his casual undressing, he looked at me—eyes a little clearer—taking in my anxious face. "I'm sorry, I'm so inconsiderate. You need me to unzip you." He reached for me.

Getting to my feet, I motioned to the water. Why did the air feel so heavy? "I don't know if I can do this." I hadn't imagined it like this—a slow reveal in bright lights. A single glass of wine for courage. "What if you don't like my body?"

"That's what you're worried about?" he laughed, taking my hands in his. "I don't need to see you naked to know that nothing about your body is disappointing." He paused. "I've seen you in a swimsuit."

My cheeks tingled. I'd forgotten about that. Hugging myself, I took a breath. "A lot has changed since the summer. I've gone up a dress size."

He gave me a slow, heated appraisal. "I'm not sure what you're talking about, but I want you to be comfortable, so would this help?" Raising two fingers, he lowered them, bringing the lights down too.

"It doesn't hurt."

"We don't have to do this if you don't want—"

I shook my head vehemently. "No, I do—I'm sorry." Embarrassed, I rubbed my face and walked to the counter. "I'm just in my head." I stopped myself there, hoping I hadn't ruined the night.

This was all Cole's fault, every flaw he'd subtly pointed out. *His raised eyebrow when I reached for bread or dessert at dinner. A firm, warning squeeze, measuring the fleshy portion of my thigh or the soft part of my stomach under the table. The sigh barely suppressed when he glanced at my updated measurements left behind by the royal seamstress.*

Damien stepped up behind me, the heat of his body easing me. "What if I distracted you by telling you about my day? There's something I was going to wait to share, but I think it might help."

"I thought it was terrible?"

"There was one redeemable moment."

I nodded my head, willing to try anything.

Tenderly, he lifted my hair, moving it over my shoulder. "After working our way through every elixiry in the inner city," he planted a kiss at the nape of my neck, "I thought it might end then, but someone wanted to go to the farmlands."

I bristled, knowing who he referred to and where this story went.

His voice was a whisper in my ear. "I promise you'll like how the story ends."

The zipper at my back slowly worked its way down. He sighed, a hot breath against the exposed skin. "His Highness insisted that for my birthday, I pick a girl to take into a room in the back, his treat," he said, anger tinting his words, "and there was a girl who'd aged out recently."

I gripped the counter for support, thinking of all the men and women who suffered at the hands of those in high society.

Hitting the end of the zipper, he dragged a finger lazily up my exposed spine. "I gave her my money pocket—about five thousand soltans—in exchange for her pretending to leave with me so I could come back to you."

My heart swelled at his words. That was close to half a year's salary for most. "What?"

I watched the faint outline of his head nodding in the steamed-up mirror. His hands ran over my shoulders, pushing the thick straps off and sending the dress into a pile on the floor, leaving me in my underwear. "It wasn't a lot, but I hope she uses it to better her life."

Clearing the mirror, I met his gaze in the reflection. "Damien, that was very generous of you."

His arm snaked around my exposed waist, his hand pressing tight into the soft flesh of my abdomen, pulling me against his bare chest.

A sigh caressed my shoulder.

"What's wrong?"

"Nothing, only thinking how grateful I am that you never had to live that life. Gratitude to my mother for saving you from that."

The ribbon holding my bra on came loose. I sucked in a breath. His eyes didn't leave mine as he removed the delicate lace.

Inching up across my stomach, every nerve in my body lit up as his rough hands moved along the bottom of my breast, his calloused thumbs brushing my nipples. I sagged against him.

"You're so beautiful," he whispered. "You're the most beautiful woman I've ever seen. I don't know how anyone could even look at you and dream of saying anything but. And I wish I could take away the horrible things people have said that make you feel shy. I want to know every part of your body, Eden. I want to hear every moan you make. So selfishly, I want you to be mine."

Closing my eyes, I gave myself over to him, enjoying the feel of him hard against my ass as he touched me. "Don't stop," I whispered.

My underwear were tugged free from my hips, as were his. This was it, and all I could think was he could have me in any way he wanted.

Leaning down, he pressed his lips to my neck, dragging his tongue gently along the vein there. "We need to get in the bath."

He snapped his fingers, shutting the water off.

I ground against him. "No."

He sucked in a sharp breath, his hold of my breast tightening. "Naughty, naughty," he tsked, swooping me up into his arms.

"Why do you keep doing that?"

"Because it's so easy to do."

I glared up at him, receiving an innocent smile in return.

The elixir started working the moment it hit my skin. A warm calm, like the kind experienced when cocooned in bed early in the morning, settled over me. Little by little, we disappeared into the shimmering milky water, still steaming, but surprisingly, the perfect temperature.

Damien settled me in his lap, the more intimate part of him bobbing between my legs. So very close. Stretching out his arms along the rim, he reclined, eyes gauging me. "Would you like to lie back with me?"

There was something I wanted quite a bit more, but since it was sure to evolve from this bath, I could wait a little longer.

Pointedly rubbing my ass along the length of him, I rested my head in the crook of his arm, so I could look at him. The tips of my breasts came to the surface of the milky water, which seemed to make his cock harder.

"How does the water feel?" he swallowed.

"Perfect." Below the water, I reached between my legs, taking him in my hand, so thick I couldn't even wrap my fingers around him. *Take me*, my body ached.

"No," he whispered, carefully pulling my hand away.

My heart caught in my chest. "Don't you want me?"

He raised an eyebrow. "You can clearly tell I do."

"Then why? I thought this was just foreplay."

He ran his free hand across the surface of the milky water. "Are we rushed? Besides, it's my birthday. You said I could have anything I want."

"What do you want?"

"To savor you," he whispered. I caught a glimpse of his proficiency tattoo as his hand glided along my stomach, dipping beneath the water. "To hear you moan my name."

The tips of his fingers brushed delicately along the bundle of nerves at my apex, triggering a gasp and making me shiver despite the heat of the bath.

His eyes became languid green pools. "Do you like that?"

"Yes…but this is what you want?" I asked breathlessly.

He nodded. "And I was getting here, but someone has no patience."

"Patience is for immortals and demis."

"I guess I shouldn't wait to do this, then?" A finger prodded gently at my entrance.

I nodded, electricity shooting through my body as one long, thick finger pushed inside.

"Fuck," he groaned. "You're so smooth, tight, and warm," his forehead pressed to my shoulder, "and wet."

"We are in the bath," I gasped.

He huffed a laugh, working me with his palm as his finger dipped in and out in aching slowness. He teased a second finger at my entrance, and greedily, I lifted my hips in acceptance, wanting as much of him as he'd give.

Damien's lips brushed along my ear. "I want to taste you, Eden. I want your thighs around my head and your fingers in my hair, moaning my name as I feast on you."

The lower half of my body clenched around his two fingers, working me slowly, much to his pleasure.

"I'm going to fuck you slow like this when I take you. Savoring your hot, wet tightness around my cock. Immortals, Eden," he breathed, his hair tickling my cheek. "I want to finish inside of you. Would you let me?"

Heat surged up my stomach, painting my chest red. "Yes."

Moaning, he kissed my neck while his palm continued its slow circular movements against my core, those fingers of his moving in and out a little faster.

"That's it," he whispered. "Enjoy me."

"Damien," I moaned. Desperate for more, I worked myself harder against his hand, against him still hard between my legs.

My fingers locked in the hair at the base of his neck, pulling his head against mine. A mischievous grin cracked his face. Needing to taste him, I angled my head, pressing my mouth hard to his.

We moved fervently together, my back against his chest, his hand working me, my ass moving along the engorged length of him. Our tongues slid along one another, probing deeper like ecstasy was at the back of the other's throat if we could just reach it.

Water sloshed out of the tub as we both moved quicker—weeks of kissing, touching, coming close and denying ourselves, feeding the moment.

I arched back, my head falling against his shoulder as pleasure undulated through my body, burning endlessly. Moaning so loud, if he hadn't charmed the apartment, someone in the square would have heard. Damien's grip on my waist tightened as a pulsing heat rushed between my legs.

"Eden." My name was a low rumble in my ear.

A sharp cry escaped me as something sharp pierced the soft, taught flesh of my neck, turning everything black for a second before sweetness took its place.

Two bright red streaks of blood streamed down my right breast.

Whoa.

I touched my shoulder, feeling two small circular punctures already healing.

"Fuck," Damien panted. The ecstasy fading too soon from his words. "Eden, I'm so sorry. That's…never happened before."

I looked up at him, an explosion of red quickly receding into horrified green eyes.

"Your eyes," I exclaimed. My gaze fell to his mouth where he lightly tapped his tongue against the tip of his canines, which had almost doubled in length. Staining his lips were drops of blood. "Your teeth—Damien…"

I turned on his lap to look at him full on. His eyes were mostly green again, but cracks of red splintered them.

He ran a sopping wet hand through his hair, slicking it back. "I've only heard about that happening."

"You changed."

He nodded, dropping his gaze. "It just happened. I think it was the smell of you—it was everywhere, and fuck, when you came—apparently, it spoke to something deeper inside me…" Cupping a handful of water, he washed away the two streaks of blood from my chest, his hand shaking. "I'm so sorry. I didn't mean to hurt you."

I tapped his chin, coaxing him to look at me. "Stop apologizing. I'm fine. If I'm being honest, it strangely felt…good. But, I thought you told me you couldn't change form?"

Damien's thumb swept over my nipple, making it pebble and sending a fresh wave of pleasure through my core. "I can't, not completely. I only ever managed to take on characteristics of a panatat, like random patches of fur, a couple of claws...the fangs are very much new."

I ran my hands up his chest and over his shoulders, my fingers meeting behind his neck. "When you said you were going to eat me..."

"Not what I meant. Biting is a mating practice," he admitted sheepishly. "Male panatats bite their partner so others know to stay away. The one I merged with is probably crippled by the quickness with which you healed."

"So, you've marked me for mating."

He shook his head, green eyes wild. "And you ruined the bath."

I smiled proudly, remembering he'd come as well.

"That wasn't the plan all along?" I shifted my hips along him—still hard—hoping we could ruin it further.

A sliver of red cracked his green irises. "Insatiable little thing."

Yes. "I want to give you whatever you want."

Holding my gaze, he leaned to kiss me. "I have what I want."

CHAPTER THIRTY-SEVEN

1.ONE.4005

"Isa, I'm here," I called into the home.

The smell of warm spices and buttered bread rushed to greet me on the other side of the wards. I slipped off my scarf, hat, and coat, placing them all neatly on hooks by the door, shivering my appreciation for the home's heat—it'd finally gotten cold enough to justify Damien's continual use of the fireplace.

A sharp gasp, followed by a plate shattering, pulled my attention to the kitchen.

Isa ran toward me, brown eyes beading with tears. "Your hair." She took my face into her gnarled hands.

With the whole city focused on celebrating Union Day and the new year, nearly every street empty, I'd had no problem escaping into the salon I'd passed thousands of times on my way to and from Selene's House.

I'd been confident in my decision. Until now. Running my fingers over the ends—resting on my collarbone—I said. "You hate it."

High society women of Sorbis never cut their hair, believing it a sign of status—short hair was reserved for women who worked. While I'd never thought of myself as such, as a representative of both Lupine and Cole, I'd been expected to conform.

Not anymore.

She wiped away the moisture in her eyes. "Don't be silly. I loved your long hair, but I think this is more you. You shocked me, that's all." She swatted my arm. "You should have told me before doing something like that. My heart doesn't have many shocks left in it."

"It wasn't something I planned, just something I felt I needed to do."

Putting her back to me, she motioned for me to follow. "I have a mess to attend. Tell me, how were the children?"

"Very excited for the light show tonight, as usual. They loved your cookies—I think you may have started a competition with the candy shop. I was asked at least a dozen times before I left if you might make them again."

Knowing exactly how my presence in the kitchen would be received, I climbed onto one of the bar stools at the counter, taking in the scene. The plate had broken cleanly into three large pieces, with only a handful of splinters.

"I'm happy to make cookies for the children anytime." Glee radiated from her words despite the grim look on her face as she reached for the broom.

Thinking about how the plate had looked and what I wanted it to look like, I let the magic in—still not smooth or pleasant but coming to me faster—and snapped my fingers. The shards of the plate disappeared from the floor, reappearing whole in my hand.

Pride swelled my chest.

Taking the plate from me, she held it up to the light for a brief inspection and put it away. "You're going to give Damien a run for his money."

I smiled. "I'll never be that good."

Huffing her disagreement, she set a ball of dough and a rolling pin on the counter.

"Before I get started with this, you forgot this this morning," Isa said, placing a milky white vial on the counter between us. "You both did."

My contraceptive elixir. To be taken every seven days, and something I hadn't failed to take since I'd started eight years ago. I uncorked it, and right as I emptied it into my mouth…

"I'd hoped it was intentional." Isa slammed the rolling pin into the dough. "Was hoping I was going to get a baby to take care of."

I almost spit it out. What choice timing she had to mention her hope… "It's not even been two months," I swallowed.

She glanced up at me from the dough she rolled. "I've known couples who have bonded and are almost two months pregnant in the same period."

"Did they all just get out of toxic relationships with the acting king of Solta?" Self-consciously, I touched my stomach. Immortals, pregnant. With Damien's baby. I hadn't thought about it before, but I was now, and it surprised me how my body seemed to warm at the thought.

Immortals, thinking about a baby, and we hadn't even had sex. "Damien doesn't even want kids."

"But you do. You love children." She waved the rolling pin at me. "You're telling me you don't want one of your own?"

I shifted on the stool. What I wanted didn't matter. It wasn't something I'd push him on. "We're supposed to be having girl time. How about we stop talking about a baby for at least another month, and I help you with what you're making?"

"Fine." Isa set a spoon and a bowl of cream cheese, butter, and sugar on the counter. She really was upset if she was letting me help. "You can mix this until smooth."

I pushed up the sleeves of my sweater. "What are you making?"

"Almost forgot," she mumbled to herself. She shuffled through the cold cabinet until she found what she was looking for.

My stomach instantly turned at the sight of a huge bottle of breki. She filled two small glasses I hadn't noticed with the dark purple drink.

Setting down one by my hand, I watched her throw her own back. "It is a tradition in Charph to celebrate Union Day with curried goat and rice, cinnamon rolls, and breki. Lots of breki."

My jaw went slack, eyes ready to pop out of my head. Isa, who never mentioned Charph, who despised her birth city—spitting at the mention—was making their traditional meal?

"Don't give me that look," she said without even a glance up. She dragged a butter-soaked pastry brush along the rolled-out dough, offering her work a sympathetic smile as she sprinkled brown sugar on top and began rolling it into a spiral. "I may have no loyalty to my city of origin, but Union Day is one of my favorites. More wholesome than other holidays."

The salty licorice taste coated my tongue as I tossed it in and forced myself to swallow.

I was still surviving the awful flavor when she placed the cut-up rolls in the oven to bake.

Plucking the bowl away and refilling my glass, she said, "You know he'd give you anything you want."

Not this still. "Isa."

Downing her second dose, she waved me away. "I know, I know, but I had to say my piece. He loves you."

There she went again, making me nearly spit out an elixir. My heart gave a stupid little flutter. "What did you say?"

Her glass hit the counter, and she refilled it. "Oh, don't act like you don't know that."

"Did he say that?" I asked. We clinked glasses.

"He hasn't, but he doesn't have to. Look at everything he's done since his return to Sorbis. It's all been for you." She jabbed the spoon at me. "The biggest gesture of all being that he stayed in Sorbis for you. No man acts the way Damien does for a woman unless he loves her."

Realizing Isa had completely neglected critical context to arrive at her answer, I returned to the glass of breki. No point ruining what she probably thought of as a real-life version of one of her romance books.

Maybe it was the several glasses of breki on a nearly empty stomach manipulating my perception of time, but the cinnamon rolls were ready after a minute, and the sweet smell of hot sugar and cinnamon mingling was ecstasy. I watched her like a feral dog as she smeared the icing onto the tops, thinking how unfair it was that dessert had to be eaten last.

Reading my mind, Isa slid a cinnamon roll and another glass of breki across to me. "Spare yourself your lust. Tonight, we dine without order."

I chased the breki with a bite, the soft, warm dough melting in my mouth. "These are dangerous."

Sinking her teeth into her own, she said, "Wait until you try the stew. It was my grandmother's recipe."

Feeling elated, I devoured the roll and several more rounds of breki unthinkingly. Isa slipped another roll on my plate, setting a shiny black piece of paper beside it. "Stew will be ready shortly. I'd like to hear this if you can."

I stared in awe at the sheet of preserved music.

She stabbed her fork toward it. "That's one of my proudest possessions. It was the first thing I bought after I left Charph. I've never played it."

Enough glasses of breki in, I met her red-brown eyes, blurting, "Why did you come out of retirement for Damien?"

A question I'd been dying to know since Damien had explained more about Factotums and Isa's former household—the Faldones under Lord Stellan's deceased wife, Lady Alicesa. I couldn't imagine wanting to be associated with a custom of being bound to serve someone in any capacity, even if that wasn't anything like the bond she and Damien had made to one another.

Though she seemed surprised, she shrugged. "I enjoy being a Facto —I enjoy being part of a family and being a caretaker—I never wanted to say goodbye to that. And despite what I'm sure you've heard, working for Lady Alicesa was a blessing compared to many other households. When she died, and I was freed from my bond, I always imagined I'd do it again if it felt right. When Damien came to me, to be honest, all I could think of was the sweet little boy I used to watch read while his parents and brothers went to dinner with the Lord in the state dining room. I was aware of his time during the war and his departure. I don't know why, but it felt like this was right." She smiled, the wrinkles around her eyes crinkling. "And look at me now on this Union Day, supporting the two best people Solta's ever known."

Tears pricked my eyes.

Clapping her hands, she wagged her finger at me. "None of that, the music, if you will."

Staring at the sheet, I let the magic flow in and snapped. We both listened to the silence in anticipation. The smile on her face as a dramatically grand piece of piano music filled the penthouse was the kind I felt honored to be on the receiving end of.

Abandoning her station, she picked up her cinnamon roll and swayed to the music.

***

The music stopped, and my eyes opened from one dream into another.

Glittering green eyes stared down at me from a tan face—awash in moonlight—hovering a breath away. His wavy black hair, slicked down and to the side, shimmered like gossamer.

We were in the suite, at the center of the massive bed, panels of silver light painting the ceiling. I, under the blanket, completely removed of my clothes, and he propped on his elbow atop the blanket in a thick black sweater, his body conforming to the outline of mine. The lingering smell of Isa's curry and cinnamon rolls rose from the kitchen, but the scents of sandalwood, cedar, and mint were quickly enveloping me.

All the scents I'd come to know as his.

Groaning, I rolled onto my back, the silk sheets of the bed brushing against my nipples.

Surely, this was a dream. Everything looked so surreal. I felt so good, as if my body were weightless. And this, being here with Damien, felt like home.

Working a hand loose from the blankets, my pale skin glowed as I touched his cheek.

"Are you real?" I croaked, voice dry from disuse and too much breki.

The corner of his mouth ticked up as my fingers brushed the delicate skin under his eyes, moving across his temple and into his thick hair. I pulled my fingers outward, bringing the hair to stick out like it did in the morning. Like it did after we'd fooled around.

"That's better," I sighed.

He laughed, a soft gust of breath caressing my face. "I was about to kiss you awake."

"I can pretend to sleep."

"Another time." He proffered me a tall glass of nullify elixir. "Drink this for me."

Clutching the sheet to my chest, I sat up, fighting the swimming in my head and the sudden wave of nausea flowing through me. Ignoring the sour taste, I drank every last golden drop.

"I would ask how much breki you two drank, but I saw the empty bottles." He let out a low whistle.

Barely keeping my head up, I looked at him from the corner of my eye. "Would you believe me if I told you most of it was Isa?"

"It's always the quiet ones."

"Is she okay?"

"She's fine. Was reading one of her romance stories in her armchair, looking high off her ass. I'm not sure she completely registered my presence until I tried to offer her a nullify elixir." Chuckling, he set the empty glass on one of the bedside tables. "Would you believe she snapped at me and told me nullify elixirs are for the weak?"

As the swirling fog in my brain cleared, I dared a laugh.

"It seems like you and Isa had quite the evening," he continued. "Was there a reason every blanket in the house was on the floor amidst the dining room table chairs?"

I nodded slowly, remembering what he referred to as a bunch of other memories came back. "We were going to build a blanket fort, but then we decided to do a puzzle."

"I saw that on the table—and the flour disaster in the kitchen I cleaned up?"

"That was me, trying to make muffins," I cringed. Noting to myself to never attempt to measure flour using magic again. One slip of my hand and white had covered every surface within three feet of the flour jar. "That's why I came up here, to get the nullify elixir. I knew

I'd overdone it, and I knew there was no cleaning up as gone as I was."

"And instead, you removed all your clothes and got in bed."

"I...I just remember being hot—" Shaking my head, I ran my free hand through my hair, the sensation making me remember something else. "I cut my hair."

"I noticed."

Pressure seizing my chest, I looked down at him. "Do you like it?"

As if sensing my insecurity, he tugged at the arm I held clutched to the sheet and my chest, coaxing me to lay back with him. "I do. Long or short hair—you're beautiful." He slipped his free hand into my hair, running through and down my neck. "I'll have fun with this. Much faster to run my fingers through. Still long enough to fist when I fuck you."

A tingling sensation ran from where his hand rested at the nape of my neck down to the tips of my toes. "Is that how it's going to be?"

We were so close that I could see my gold eyes reflected in his as they searched mine.

"I'm going to have you every way you'll let me." His nostrils flared, eyes widening a fraction, telling me he'd scented the effect his words had on me. "Ask me about my day," he groaned desperately, pressing his forehead to mine.

I traced my finger lightly along his jaw. "How was your day?"

"Egregiously boring. Cole was in his usual foul mood," he sighed. "I know I've said it in jest in the past, but I really think something is wrong with him. He spent most of his day not speaking to anyone and sneering at those who tried to approach him.

"What are Grayden and Q's thoughts on his behavior?"

"As a Protector, and more specifically Saier's second in command, Grayden has to keep those thoughts to himself, and I haven't seen

Quincy since Cole's birthday."

I sat up abruptly once more, hair shifting over my shoulders. That was going to be something to get used to. This whole time, I'd assumed everything had been normal, and he'd been ignoring my letters. "What?"

He nodded. "I hadn't mentioned it because I didn't think it was anything, but today was different. Cole told me Quincy had asked to spend the day with his girlfriend, and he'd allowed it."

The Union Day Parade was supposed to be a show of support for the king, and as a second point, he would have been included. A knife-sharp pain ached my stomach. "There have never been exceptions."

"Hey, I didn't tell you to worry you. I told you because I knew you'd want to know." Wrapping his arm around my exposed waist, he pulled me on top of him, reversing our sides on the blanket. Gratefully—between the home's warm air, my anger at Cole, and Damien's heat—I didn't freeze. "I intend to look into it. Don't spend another second thinking about it."

"You know that's not how it works for me."

He cupped my face in his hands and planted a kiss on my mouth.

I turned from him. "That isn't going to work."

"Really?" One shift of his hip, and he had me on my back, his arms on either side of my head, knees by my thighs. He rained kisses on my cheeks, my nose and jaw, and my throat.

And for the life of me, I couldn't help but giggle.

"Immortals, that sound." Shifting the blanket aside, he exposed my chest to him, kissing his way further down. "I think it might be my second favorite sound in the world."

"What's your favorite?" His tongue grazing my breast, I barely managed the words.

Wrapping his soft lips around my hard nipple, he dragged his teeth lightly across the sensitive skin, making my whole body burn.

Fisting my hand in his hair, I sucked in a sharp breath. "Damien."

I couldn't help my laugh or the warm flutter in my chest when he grinned up at me, answering my question.

But as good a job he'd done scattering my thoughts, my mind wouldn't let it go that easily.

"Just—promise me you'll check on Q?"

Sighing at his perceived failure, he looked up at me, already calculating what to do differently next time, and nodded.

CHAPTER THIRTY-EIGHT

12.ONE.4005

I stood at the stove, stirring the pot, watching the celery, carrots, parsley, noodles, and chicken chunks swirl around in the simmering broth like dancers. One more minute and it would be done. Chicken soup would pale compared to anything Isa dreamed up, but it would do the trick on such a frigid day.

The door to the penthouse clicked open, and feet pounded the wooden floor quickly.

"Welcome home," I called from the kitchen.

The only response I received was sudden silence.

Wiping my steam-dampened hands along the white apron, I peeped through the serving window to make sure I hadn't imagined it. Standing by the foot of the spiral metal staircase was Damien, the heel of his hand pressed into the space between his eyes. His other hand was clenched into a fist at his side, his arms shaking. The rise and fall of his chest faltered as he struggled to breathe.

Watching him, I found my lungs in my throat. "Damien—what's wrong?"

Fist shifting to the center of his chest, he barely managed to say, "I can't," pivoting on his heel and slamming the door to his bedroom.

The message clear: *I need to be alone.*

Anxiety buzzed around in my stomach like an aggravated wasp's nest as I stared at the door, wondering if I should heed the message and determining I'd give him a moment.

Isa needed my attention first.

I took a quick peek into her room. With purple curtains, a red armchair, and a sky-blue bed frame, dresser, and vanity, it was a pleasantly stark contrast to the rest of the home. She lay curled up at the center of her queen-sized bed under her sunshine yellow duvet, sleeping soundly. When I'd come home and found her on the couch complaining of stomach pain, I'd run to the suite's bathroom to look through Damien's elixirs only to remember I had no understanding of his organizing system, and at her insistence I stay instead of heading to an elixiry, I'd given her the only elixir I knew of to help the discomfort: a quarter dose of sleep. Something to hold her over long enough until Damien made it home.

Wandering back to the kitchen, I paused at the window—offering a perfect view of the closed door—my head and heart going back and forth on what to do about Damien.

Plucking a white bowl from the cabinet, I filled it, realizing which part of me had won the debate as I set it and a spoon on a wooden tray.

Balancing the tray on one hand, I eased the bedroom door open, slipping inside. I'd had a dozen ideas for what to expect on the other side, but closing the door behind me, unearthly quiet and darkness hadn't been one of them.

The drapes had been closed, the light charm killed, and no fire warmed the room. Shifting the tray to both hands, I clutched it a little tighter, ready to whisper his name into the void, but a rush of water followed by a sharp gasp yanked my attention toward the bathroom and a sliver of golden light.

I tapped lightly on the cracked door, and despite the voice in me screaming to give him space, when he didn't answer, I pushed my way inside.

Keeping my head down and my back angled away from him, I noted the pile of hastily discarded clothes as I set the tray on the sink counter.

"I'm sorry," Damien said, barely audible.

My hands froze on the tray. "For what?"

"I shouldn't have slammed the door. It wasn't fair to you."

I turned to look at him, forever silencing the voice that'd screamed to give him space.

He sat in the tub—shimmering milky water up to his neck—black hair dripping water down his face. Looking small for a man who easily filled the bath.

A shell of the man I knew.

My heart in my throat, I said, "You needed space. I can understand and respect that. Though I must say, it took everything I had not to run in after you…May I come closer?"

He scoffed in surprise. "Eden, of course."

Even if he'd said no, I wasn't sure I would have held back.

I knelt by the bath. Resting my arms along the rim, I lay my cheek on my hands and assessed him. "Will you tell me what's upset you?"

Hollowed-out green eyes peered into mine, debating. A slight pain ached my chest that he didn't immediately want to tell me, but for all Damien had shared, I knew there were things I had yet to learn, and he would tell me in his own time.

He dragged a wet hand down his face. "The problem with the rebellion in the farmlands has gotten worse. Cole decided that from here on, executions would be used to make a point to insurgents. It was something that he wanted the Council to pass. He decided out of nowhere that they'd start today, and…it got to me. Particularly, this boy, who couldn't have been more than fourteen…they had beaten him so badly one of his eyes had swollen shut." He swallowed hard, eyebrows pulling together. "He told me his father had shared tales with him about Aevry and me. That we were his heroes." His eyes shifted to a milky swirl in the water. "Cole executed fifty-three traitors today. Several of them were children. Most of them were *traitors* because the Alliance Council had failed them."

Listening to him, my heart had slowed. I held out a hand to him. "Sounding like a traitor yourself."

Weaving his wet fingers through mine, the relax elixir in his water tingling my fingers, he dared a glance at me. "Are you going to turn me in?" Sounding almost like he wished I would.

I pressed my lips to his shiny knuckles. "No. Not even if I disagreed with you. Which I don't."

Traitors together.

"I wish there was something I could do," he sighed.

Knowing where this was headed, I said the words I knew were the cause of his turmoil. "Many would say you could. You're a member of the Alliance Council, a Prince of Solta."

"If only they knew how useless those titles really are. They wouldn't stop Cole from branding me a traitor and doing away with me."

"I know." The words I always wished someone had said to me in these moments. Peace to ease the heart. The gift of understanding.

The grip on my hand eased, and his shoulders relaxed as if a weight had been removed. The hope I'd helped him lasted a moment, the shadows descending on him once more.

Shivering, he dropped my hand, pulling away from me. "I hate that you know. You should never have been exposed to any of this."

The last thing he should be thinking about.

I stood. Arms locked behind my back, I undid the apron's knot and removed it, tossing it onto the chair by the door. Only because Isa would have my head if I did what I was about to do to her apron.

The rest of my clothes, I couldn't have cared less about. There was only one thing at that moment that mattered to me, and it was helping Damien. Helping him like he'd helped me so many times.

On the tips of my toes, I climbed the step of the tub, setting a foot down on either side of his hips and sinking into the water, seating myself on his lap. The pink cloth of my shirt ballooned before me, taking on a glossy sheen as it soaked up water and collapsed to the outline of my body as I shifted closer to him.

Taking his face in my hands, I lifted him to look at me. Reluctantly, he met my gaze, like he was ashamed of what I might see, but all I saw was him, and all I felt was light. Bright and warm and golden like the sun after a storm, and I wanted to shower it on him.

I planted gentle kisses across his left cheekbone, traversing the bridge of his nose to do the same to the right. Each kiss seemed to soften him. Thumbs kneading his temples, I wove my fingers in and out of his wet hair. "Damien, come back to me," I whispered.

Winding his arm around my waist, he pulled me tight to him. His other hand slipped into my hair as he buried his face into my neck, inhaling. Breathing me like I was air. Clinging to me like I was life.

I ran my hand over every part of him I could touch—swirling patterns on his skin, kneading muscles. Anything to remind him I was here. I was his.

We stayed like that until the water went cold.

"Eden." My name was a contented sigh on his lips. He lifted his head to look at me, the glow I recognized as his growing in those green eyes. Tucking a strand of hair behind my ear, he asked, "Does Isa know you took her apron?"

My laughter obliterated the shadows on his face. "No." I shifted my mouth to one side. I hated telling him so soon, but deeming it better to tell him now, I said, "She's been in bed since she came back from the market complaining of stomach issues. I gave her a bit of my sleep elixir to ease her until you came home."

His hand stilled, his body going stiff. "What? Is she okay?"

"Relax, I've got it under control. I checked on her before I came in here. She was still asleep. After this, you're going to teach me your elixir system, though, so next time, I can help her instantly, should it ever happen again." I nodded to the bowl on the counter, no longer steaming—but nothing a quick finger snap wouldn't change—and tapped him lightly on the nose. "I'm taking care of you two today."

A soft smile warmed his face. "We're lucky to have you."

My heart grew to fill my whole body. "I'm glad you say that because I feel the same about you and Isa. Speaking of which, I should change and check on her. She should be awake now. Meet you upstairs?"

Nodding, he released his hold of me. "I'll be out in a minute."

I rose to my feet, sending down a waterfall. Outside the tub, I undid the drawstring at my waist, and my waterlogged bottoms fell straight to the floor.

"Are those for me?"

Having forgotten the red lacy underwear, I tossed the pants into the sink and met his lustful gaze in the mirror, grinning. "There you are."

I was at the door when he called my name.

"Eden, I—" he croaked.

Hand braced on the door, I glanced back at him.

"I think you should take the shirt off here, too," he said, eyebrows raised in a flirty challenge. "So you don't make a mess."

Laughing, I did just that. His view lasted as long as it took the shirt to go from my hands to the tub, landing perfectly at the center of his face in a wet smack.

CHAPTER THIRTY-NINE

22.ONE.4005

I was under attack. First, the enemy disrupted a perfectly peaceful morning by flopping on the bed. Then they assaulted my face and neck with kisses.

"Damien." His name a moan and a curse.

"Go put on the warmest clothes you own and meet me in the suite," he whispered.

"It's so early and so cold outside." Groaning, I reached for him. "Come back to bed."

He jerked away. "It's the first snow of Sorbis. There's something I want to do with you."

Rolling onto my back, I propped myself up on my elbows, considering him. "There's something you want to do with me that involves snow and me putting my heaviest clothes on first thing in the morning?"

"Correct."

"Are you sure you aren't confused? That you don't want my clothes to come off?"

"As much as I would love that, it won't do for what I have in mind." Hopping off the bed, he tossed me the clothes I'd worn up here—draped over the footboard—on his way into his closet. "Let's go. Time is of the essence."

Grumbling, I crawled out from under the blissfully warm blankets, an idea forming in my head. I tugged my sleeping shorts—a pair of his black briefs—down, right in plain view. Back to him, I didn't see his face, but the chaotic shuffling in the closet came to a curious halt…and resumed. Letting me know there was nothing in the kingdom killing this idea.

When I was done dressing, I looked at him. He faced away from me, working on a pair of thick black jeans.

I palmed the shirt—warm with heat and surely smelling of me. "Hey, Damien?"

He turned right as it covered his face, groaning my name.

"Be back in a sec." If I was going to suffer, he could too.

At the dining room table sat Isa, a hot cup of chocolate—based on the rich, mouthwatering smell coming from the kitchen—in one hand and the newest issue of the Alliance Access in the other.

I jabbed my thumb over my shoulder. "Do you know what this is about?"

She tsked, shaking her head. "Immortals know with Damien. You wouldn't find me going out in this weather if my life depended on it."

Outside in the stairwell, the cold bit hard. The fat flakes of snow that'd been descending on Sorbis, painting the city white since early yesterday, had brought down the temperature with them.

And my apartment, having been empty of me for a couple of days, was somehow even worse. Teeth chattering, I did as he requested. The warmest things I owned were a heavy brown wool coat, a large purple scarf and matching hat, bright red sweatpants, and black knee-high boots. *Let the chaos of my outfit be another declaration in favor of staying home,* I thought, slipping on my key necklace and scurrying back up the steps to the penthouse.

Damien stood before the panorama window, looking out at the

white-roofed buildings and the white-dusted trees of the forest beyond, clad in a black knit hat, a heavy fur coat, and combat boots. Leaned against his hip was a wooden sled.

"What is that?" I asked.

He pivoted on his heel to face me, beaming. For someone who hated the cold, he was certainly excited, and Immortals, if it wasn't contagious. "You've never seen a sled?"

Coming closer, I dragged a finger along the polished blond wood, hooking the rope and giving a gentle tug. "I guess I meant, why do you have it?"

"I'm taking you sledding."

I looked up wide-eyed. The words making my heart dance in my chest. "What? Really?"

"You've never been sledding," he said, taken aback by the revelation.

I smiled to myself. "As little as I've been allowed to do, I'm surprised you're surprised. Quincy and I asked Lupine to buy us one once, and all she said was that sledding was dangerous, and if we ever attempted it, she'd find an orphanage to drop us both in."

He grinned guiltily. "You have Aevry and me to thank for that. When we were twelve and eleven, we tried to perform a flip on one down a hill. I broke my arm, and Aevry cracked his head. I had to phase him home. He was in a coma for a couple of days. It scared my mother pretty bad."

My jaw slackened. "You say that so lightly."

"It's a happy memory in hindsight. His first words when he woke were that he knew what we needed to adjust to succeed."

"I'm shocked that with that kind of story in your history, you want to take me sledding." The moment the words were out, I realized how dumb I was to speak.

He arched a knowing eyebrow. "It's only dangerous if you try to pull a crazy stunt like we did. We won't be doing anything like that." He nodded at my clothes. "The only thing I'm worried about is what you're wearing."

"What's wrong with it?" I asked, expecting a comment about how ridiculous I appeared.

"Nothing if you're going on a walk around the city," he said.

Foiled again.

I frowned. "That's as warm as I've ever needed to be."

Pulling off his gloves, he proffered them to me. "Put these on. It'll make me feel better."

The gloves swallowed my hands, but being wool-lined and Damien-warmed, they felt good on my chilled fingers.

"For the rest, looks like you'll just have to stay close to me so you don't freeze."

Stepping up to him, I pressed my body flush to his. "That sounds nice."

The blessed warmth and four walls that offered us protection gave way to crisp mountain air, ankle-deep snow, and cold that cut straight to the bone.

As I burrowed into his thick black sweater, thinking it was too cold for life, Damien inhaled deeply, like he enjoyed how it hurt to breathe.

A gust of wind swept over us, making my body shiver violently. "Where are we?"

"In the Faldonian Mountains, three days' walk northwest of the manor. We're actually about halfway to Charph. Aevry and I used to come out here to camp in the summer."

Slowly acclimating, I dared a peek.

We stood on the gentle slope of a mountain heavily blanketed in snow. Pine trees speckling the mountainside dripped crystalline icicles. Below and off to the right was a snaking river, glossy and dusted white, splitting the mountains and separating us from a small herd of deer.

I exhaled, my hot breath a cloud of white, my eyes following the slope of the opposite mountain up to the wispy white clouds and the hydrangea blue sky. "This is incredible."

His cold finger shocked the skin of my cheek as he brushed some hair out of my face. "Yes, it is."

I looked up at him, finding my reflection in somber green eyes. "Hey, what's on your mind?"

"Just remembering something Aevry said the last time we came here. I wish you could have met him. He would have adored you. You would have loved him."

The way he said the last sentence made me think he didn't mean it as a friend.

Taking his freezing-cold hand in mine, I brought it to my lips. "I would have loved to have met him, and I know I would have loved him as you did. I'm sure we would have been fast friends."

His grip tightened on me. "Eden, I..."

"None of that. Come back to me, Damien. I'm here with you." I grinned at him. "You're going to take me sledding." Breaking away, I tossed the sled into the snow and sat down in front, bringing my knees up to my chest. It was starting to slide when Damien grabbed it.

"Whoa, definitely don't sit on it without the pull rope in hand. That's how you steer." He settled himself behind me, plunging the heel of his boots in the snow.

He reached around me, grabbing for the rope.

"You pull left to go left and right to go right. To stop or slow down, put your hands or feet out to the side."

Anticipation destroying me, I nodded, laying my head against his chest, content to let him drive. "Got it. Left to go right, and vice versa. Let go of the rope and kick out wildly to slow down."

Laughing and shaking his head, he kissed my cheek. "Alright, then, smartass. Hold on tight." He kicked us forward, and squealing, I clutched his thighs.

The thrill of what we were doing hit me as the wind did—sharp, quick, and free.

The course Damien had plotted was a gradual slope, weaving through five trees and then finally a steeper, nearly treeless slope that leveled out at the bottom, just before the river. Every time we veered toward a tree, my grip on him tightened ever so slightly in preparation for impact, only for him to pull the rope at the last second and skirt around, making me gasp and laugh. Plummeting down the final slope felt like how I imagined flying to be.

"I like this. Again."

And we did it again. And again. Basking in the rush and always at the end wanting to know it once more.

After a dozen trips down, he reset us at the top of the hill—both of us breathing hard—and passed the pull rope to me. "Why don't you try?"

Accepting the corded rope, I jumped onto the sled.

Damien's laugh echoed through the valley. "Remember to go left—"

"Pull left, I got it." I shifted back, rubbing my ass against him in the process. "Reconsidering how you want to spend our morning?" I teased, pointedly repeating the motion against the now firm seat of his crotch.

He kicked us forward, snapping me to attention as we plummeted down.

"That was not funny, Damien," I screamed, my heart in my throat as the wind sliced around us. My focus turned razor sharp, hands sweating as we approached the first tree. I pulled right—a little prematurely, but better safe than sorry—and we skated around.

And I felt good.

I glanced back at him, smiling. "I did it."

He grinned, nodding ahead. "There's another."

I did it over and over until we crested the wide-open drop. Sliding to a perfect stop at the bottom, I stared at him breathlessly. "Again."

He kissed my temple. "As many times as you want."

He phased us to the top, and this time, when it came to kicking us off, he motioned for me to do it.

I pushed the limits, cutting closer to the trees and basking in the thrill of clearing them with seconds to spare. Damien's hand always tightened on me in preparation, but he never needed to move.

By the time we hit the final drop, his hand had relaxed on my hips.

It was two seconds into the rush of our descent that a baby deer loped out from behind a tree, right into our path. Damien shifted behind me, hand reaching for the rope, but it was too late. I tugged the rope sharply to my chest, dodging the deer—by some miracle—and sending us into a spin.

"Damien," I shrieked.

His hold on me vanished as he tried in vain to grab at the earth, flinging up mud and slushy snow instead. We were at the steepest part of the incline and turning wildly. Both of his feet came down beside me, dragging briefly, and then gone. He was gone. Whirling wind rushed at my back now, and without his added weight, the sled spun faster.

Through the dizzying blur, I caught a black figure rolling dangerously down the hill, the force that'd propelled us continuing to push him on. As it occurred to me to try and slow myself down, something hard slammed into my side, and there was no longer any earth to dig into.

CHAPTER FORTY

22.ONE.4005

One second, I was flying across the land on the sled, Damien steadfast at my back, relishing the rush of the cool mountain air on my face, the thrill in my chest, the heat between our bodies. His hands on my hips.

The next I was alone.

The abrupt halt of the sled's momentum against the rocks transferred to me, sending me flying through the air, aimed for the thick ice covering the river. No—an illusion. At least at the point where I landed. The finger-thick sheet of ice shattered under the force of my weight. I barely managed a breath as the freezing water rushed up to claim me, the current catching me and dragging me along.

Desperate to get back to the hole I'd made, knowing my best chances were there, I clawed at the ice, feeling for a hold, forgetting I had gloves. Sodden and ill-fitting, they dragged uselessly across the smooth, waterworn ice.

I tried beating against it, the sound of my attempts muffled by the rush of water, but if I was making any impact, I was moving too quickly to reap the reward.

Think, Eden.

Damien would get to me if he were okay. Immortals, was he okay? I'd only managed a fraction of a glance at him, right as his body rolled to a stop. What if he were hurt and he needed me?

I beat against the ice again. Fuck. I wanted to scream—I wanted to cry. But neither would do anything for me.

Magic hummed at the tips of my fingers, ready to bc woven. That was the last thing I had, and it only mattered as much as I could do it right. I stopped fighting the current, stopped thinking about the last of my breath fading away, and focused on pulling the magic in, moving the invisible threads as he'd shown me. Releasing it, I was almost sure I'd done it right. The explosion loud enough to hear through the rush of water.

And the shockwave of it was brilliant, blasting me sideways into the detritus along the river's banks, knocking out the little air remaining in me.

And I inhaled. Not air.

Ice-cold water burned my lungs. Not only because it didn't belong, but it burned the way cold attacks heat, leeching like death.

This was it.

A loud crash broke through the rush of the water.

Something tightened around my waist. Death, pulling me into it.

In an instant, my darkening suspension in the freezing water became falling through the air onto a warm hardwood floor.

Breaking from the arm lingering around my waist, I rolled onto my hands and knees and coughed up all the water I'd sucked in desperately, replacing it with air.

Air, *air*. Warm, delicious air. I'd never take it for granted again.

I barely registered the fingers brushing along my cheek, gathering my hair, and holding it back as I hacked.

"That's good. Get it out."

Damien. *Damien.*

Had I not been fighting the violent shaking of my body as it tried to warm up or the rattling in my lungs as I coughed up the last of the water, I would have hugged him. He was okay. Immortals, he was okay, and I was okay. He'd saved me. I was alive. Breathless and soaked to the bone in impossibly cold water, but I was alive, and he was okay. I lifted my head to look at him, green eyes wild with a mixture of fear and relief.

Releasing my hair, he scooped up my face in his shaking hands, thoroughly inspecting me. "Are you hurt?" His chest rising and falling so quickly, I thought he might pass out. "It carried you away so fast. I've never moved so quickly—"

"I'm fine." In fact, thanks to my ability to heal, I didn't feel any different than I normally did. Looking at his dripping black hair, absent of his hat, I realized my own was gone, swept away by the river. He froze at my touch as I reached to push it back out of his face. "Are you hurt?"

Tearing away, he dropped his hands to my coat buttons, fingers fumbling. "You're shaking. We need to get you out of these clothes and warmed up."

I laid my hand over his, stilling him. "Damien, I've got it. You're shaking as well. Worry about yourself. Let's get warm together."

Nodding absently, he shifted to his feet, shucking the water-swollen fur jacket. It landed with a thud in a pool of sunlight. "I'll...go get you some dry clothes."

And before I could say any more, he was gone, hands running through his hair. He must be in shock. Maybe I should be in shock, but gratitude was the only thing I could feel. Gratitude that we were both safe.

I wandered into the suite's bathroom, leaving puddles in my wake.

The gloves and boots came off first, exposing reddened, pruny flesh. Buttonholes waterlogged, my coat took some effort, but it eventually came off, thudding onto the mirrored floor and leaving me feeling weightless. The rest of my clothes came off in quick succession, and I relished their absence—the dry, warm air licking at my naked pebbled skin.

Reaching for one of the decorative towels, I caught my reflection in the mirror. Watched drops of water dripping endlessly from the wild mess of tangled hair, streaking my breast and back. Took in the stark whiteness of my soaked skin, the vibrant tinge of red in my cheeks. Finger-combing my hair triggered a rainstorm that drenched the floor.

"Eden?" Damien called—a trace of panic in his voice.

I clutched the towel tighter. "In here."

He was still in his sopping wet clothes when he entered the bathroom, a stack of dry clothes tucked between his hands. "Why don't you get dressed in the bedroom?"

Nodding, I took the clothes. Just out of view, I tugged on the sweater quickly, grateful for the excess it provided me to burrow into. If I weren't so desperately shaking for warmth, I would have abandoned the sweatpants. Pulling the string at the waist as tight as I could left them barely clinging to my hips, not to mention they were half a leg too long. I was rolling them up when I happened to glance back at Damien, now standing in only his briefs, curiously inspecting the side of his chest in the mirror.

A nasty red and black bruise assaulted the left side of his body.

"What is that?" I demanded. Abandoning my rolling, I entered the bathroom, the other pant leg slogging through a puddle of cold river water.

Putting his arm down, his eyes flicked to mine in the mirror. The stupor he was in momentarily gave way to reluctance. "It's nothing."

"That's not nothing," I said. "Show me."

He didn't move.

"Show me, Damien Elias Valentine, or I swear—"

"My full name isn't necessary," he muttered, moving his arm aside.

I brushed my fingers lightly across the damaged skin, triggering a flinch. "Did that hurt?"

He forced a smile. "No, your hands are very cold."

Liar. "What happened?"

He shifted his jaw. "I think I broke a rib in the tumble."

I swallowed the vomit crawling up my throat. "Let me help." I tried to grab him, but he took a step back.

"I'll be fine. You should lie down."

"Are you serious?" I glared at him.

"I'll be fine."

"Hold still."

"Eden, you've been through enou—"

I folded my arms over my chest. "Only death will stop me from helping you."

He winced but didn't move when I reached for him again. My hands pressed hard into his chest. The energy moving from my body into his erased the pooling blood in a matter of seconds. He rested his hand loosely on my waist, waiting for the negative consequences, but I felt strong and proud when I stepped back.

Dour green eyes stared down at me, his mouth hard.

"What's wrong?" I asked

"Nothing."

"Stop with this. Don't play with me, and don't lie."

He ran his hand down the lower half of his face. "I'm sorry. We shouldn't have done that. I shouldn't have taken you to do that. It was reckless. The woods with the thieves, the rebels chasing us—all these situations I put you in where bad things almost happened. You almost died today. Immortals know how close you came." His grip on my waist tightened. "I almost watched you die. I get why my mother and brother never wanted you to do anything. It won't happen again—these things won't happen again. I need to protect you."

Angry, incredulous tears stung my eyes. Not him, not this.

"Don't reduce my life down to my mortality," I snapped. "That isn't fair to me. You're ageless, not indestructible. You were at risk as much as I was. Lupine may not have asked me to look after you, but that doesn't mean I don't get to, and you know what? I would never let my desire to protect you lead me to tell you that you won't be doing things again. Not to mention, when Lupine asked you to look after me, I doubt she meant to smother me with safety. She wanted me to live my life. I'm going to die one day, Damien, and you need to accept that. And that day may have almost been today, but at least it would have happened living." My heart ached. Shaking my head, I twisted on my heel, breaking from his hold. "I'm not going to do this with you."

Damien had said he never moved faster in his life, but as quick as he grabbed my wrist when I put my back to him, I'd beg to differ.

"Don't." The word a desperate plea. "Eden, don't walk away from me." He pressed his chest to my back, burying his face in my wet hair. "You know you've been doing that since the night we met, and you take something from me every time you do." He let loose a sigh. "Why is it so easy for you to walk away from me?" His following words were so soft, I almost didn't hear them. "You never walked away from him."

"No." I turned in his hold to look up at him. "But I ran away from him. For forever, because in his eyes, I was nothing but an opinionless, freedomless, fragile doll to display. And it isn't easy. It takes something from me as well, but no matter how much I love you, I have no intention of letting that be my life again."

The air between us stilled, a dreamy glow dissipating the somber sheen blanketing his green eyes, like the sun breaking apart a fog.

"You love me?"

The heat of anger became a blazing rush of reticent embarrassment as I realized what I'd admitted. That was not supposed to happen. I'd dabbled with the idea I might several times—especially after Isa's comment on Union Day—while watching him sleep or lying against him as he journaled. Still, I hadn't consciously come to a conclusion.

Until then, it'd seem. Of all the times.

I loved him. And I'd told him as much.

I dropped my gaze, my stomach catching in my throat. "Now isn't the time for that."

He tucked his forefinger under my chin.

"When it happened today, when I knew the sled and you would hit the bank. The first thing I thought was that I couldn't watch you get hurt—healer or not. Seeing you get hurt, I'm not sure how I would have handled it, and knowing I'd been the cause behind it, it's all I could think about. It ruled me. But then you skipped straight past getting hurt to almost dying. And that scared me so much more. When I heard the ice crack and saw you go through…"

He took a steadying breath. "Today was something I wasn't ready for. It was a reminder that our time together is limited, and the last thing I want to do is limit it more. I'm sorry for my rash reaction. It wasn't fair to you, and I can't promise you my reaction will be any different if something like that happens again. I can promise you that I will try to do better, because I don't want you to ever feel the way my brother made you feel. I don't want you to feel suffocated. With that said, though, I ask you to be patient with me because I'm not perfect, Eden. And like some twisted joke, my love for you undoes me in ways I hate, as much as it makes me feel alive."

My heart gave an uncalled-for skip. I rolled my eyes. "You don't have to say it just because I did."

He squeezed me tighter. "I didn't. I've been trying to say it. I wanted to say it the other day after the Alliance Council meeting. I wanted to say it today, but I just wasn't brave enough. Just as I wasn't brave enough to tell you how I felt, I was so adamant I'd never feel it, let alone say it." His thumb traced my lower lip. "I love you, Eden." Exhaling the words like a breath of air.

We stared at each other, letting his admission settle. Letting everything we'd both said settle.

"I love you, Damien," I said. The words feeling light on my tongue.

I'm not sure if it was Damien or I who moved first. Only that one moment, we were staring at each other, a growing sense of desperation between us, and the next, our lips were locked together in an uncontrolled fervor. Desperate to get closer to him, I wrapped my arms around his neck, successfully pulling him off balance. My back slammed into the bathroom wall, rattling the vials on the counter.

We broke apart laughing, our eyes meeting again.

I became acutely aware of my sweatpants around my ankles and the hard length of him rubbing my abdomen through his river-soaked underwear.

Take me.

Our mouths found each other once more, like they were pulled to one another.

Hands cupping my bare ass, he lifted me—my sweatpants falling away—and carried me to the bed, his briefs off before we hit the mattress, thanks to my deft hands. He slipped the sweater over my head, his body replacing my clothes as a source of warmth.

The only thing left between us was my key necklace, which he unhooked with one hand and set aside as he sucked at my neck, working his way down to my breasts, to my stomach. Kissing and sucking every last inch of my body, breathing me in. My hands kneaded his back, tugging at his hair, bringing him up to kiss me. I had no time for games and no interest in foreplay—the last couple of months, mostly denying ourselves, had been nothing but. I wanted him badly.

No needed him. So intensely, I couldn't bring myself to say anything for fear of hearing the words not today. Words that would break me in two.

Take me.

Shifting his weight to one side, the head of his throbbing, thick cock slipped along the slick folds between my legs. Seeing him shiny with my desire for him made my whole body burn.

"Tell me you want this," he whispered, fisting the sheet by my head. Red splintered the green of his eyes.

I slicked a stray piece of black hair away from his face, angling my hips up so the head of him aligned with my entrance.

"Yes—yes," I breathed.

Grabbing his face, I pulled him down, wanting to taste him, wanting to feel him everywhere. Our mouths devoured one another's, tongues tasting, sucking, exploring. The only place there wasn't restraint in that last second before we gave each other everything.

He bit at my lower lip, and I inhaled him, my fingers running through his hair and down his neck, settling on his shoulder blades.

I was his. In this way and all ways, I belonged to him.

A sharp, delicious pain surged between my legs, causing my back to arch as Damien pressed himself into me. My sex opening and wrapping around him, he let out a low moan in my mouth.

Stilling, he broke our kiss to look down at me, concern bracketing delirious red and green eyes. "Did I hurt you?"

My mind screaming its desire for more, I hadn't even noticed how my fingers dug deep into his back, or the way my breath had caught in my lungs.

"No, just adjusting," I whispered, moving my hips to take him deeper. On the tail of another split second of pain was a wave of bliss.

Nails ripping down the sheet, he let out a low growl, pinning me in place. He pressed his forehead to mine, his breathing labored. "I'll go slow."

Little by little, he sank, my body easing around him as he stretched and filled everything I had to give. Sensations of pleasure hitting harder the deeper he went. The biggest when we came flush together —ecstasy flashing through me like light.

Grinning, he planted a series of kisses along my jaw. "You fit me perfectly."

My body melted under him as he slipped out slowly and worked himself back in, letting me adjust to the feel of him.

"You feel so good, and the smell of you..." The red splinters in his eyes became solid cracks.

"Are you going to bite me again?" I moaned.

Catching him off guard, his steady rhythm faltered, betraying the hard and fast way he wanted to have me.

Yes, please, my body groaned.

"Would you like that?" The pleasant surprise in his voice let me know how much he wanted it.

"Yes," I whispered. I ran my fingers over the scars on his shoulder, draping my legs around him to meet each thrust deeper. It wasn't enough. More, I wanted more. "Damien—"

"I know what you want, fuck, I can smell it, but I—"

Aching and uninterested, I locked my legs around his waist. In one fluid motion, I flipped him onto his back, settling so deep on him I could feel him at the end of me. He made to prop himself up, but I pushed him back down with a firm hand to the chest.

"You've had enough play, and I want it my way."

"Play?" Damien flashed a perfect grin, taking my hips in his hands, continuing to move me along him. The gentle motion and depth of him combined in the most perfect way, hitting all the right places. "I'll let you have your moment."

I eased up the length of him. "You'll let me?"

His eyes rolled back into his head, his words a breathy moan. "I did tell you the first time I had you, I was going to take my time."

Falling to my hands—one on either side of his head, so I was parallel with him—the tips of my breast brushed his sweat-laced chest, the red of his eyes erasing the green.

One of his hands slipped away from my hip to cup my breast, thumb teasing the nipple. "This does offer a lovely view."

I moved my hips in quick, long strokes along the length of him—my own pleasure building.

His free hand left my waist, fingers weaving up into my hair, pulling it away from my face. The tips of his elongating fangs appeared in the darkness of his slightly parted mouth. "If you keep riding me like that, you're going to make me come."

"Inside of me like you promised?" I breathed.

That earned me a throaty, claiming growl. He rocked his hips hard into me, simultaneously hitting the bundle of nerves at my apex and a very receptive point inside me on each sweep.

Holding back. Fuck—even with me on top, he'd been holding back. I wasn't going to last much longer—months of flirting, teasing, and fooling around guiding every nerve inside of me to one destination.

My body was desperate for him, savoring the way his hand fisted in my hair, how he pinched my nipple gently. The soft pant of his breath, smelling richly of mint, neither of us slowing.

I cried out as the delicious heat building low inside of me undulated in waves, wracking my entire body. I didn't—no, couldn't stop—feeling lighter on each movement.

Eyes burning red, Damien bucked harder into me, encouraging just that. I could feel him trying to hold out—to last longer—but one sharp inhale of the air, and my desire had his cock twitching between my legs, the warmth of his seed flooding me. Snarling softly, he sank his teeth deep into my neck and sucked hard. Another rush of pleasure crashed through me, and I gave myself over to him, waiting for him to release me before I collapsed beside him.

I lay there on my side, breathing hard, a strange absence where he'd been softened by the warmth of him seeping out between my legs. Sweat slicked my back, my neck, the space between my breasts, and everything inside of me felt warm…euphoric.

Damien, who'd been gazing contentedly at me, slid a rough hand over my waist to my backside, grabbing my ass. "I'll have my moment now."

Lifting my head, I raised an eyebrow at him, taking in his very red eyes. "Again?"

Sweat decorating his brow and blood his lower lip, he sat up, nudging his still hard cock against my leg. "Surely you didn't think that was it?"

"Why else would you be worried about finishing then?" My pointer finger ran lazily along the underside of his length, shining and wet.

"Because it was the only way to redeem my promise of taking you slow."

"You've made a lot of promises," I mused.

Damien ran his tongue over his fangs. "Yes, and you have no idea how ready I am to make good on them. Do you remember the promise I made you—that when we finally fucked, I was going to spend the whole day between your legs?"

"We'll see about that."

"Yes, you will." Leaning in, he took my exposed breast into his mouth, dragging the tip of one fang over my nipple, making my body shudder anew. He flicked his tongue lazily back and forth.

"In case you were thinking about it again, there will be no switching this time. I'm in charge. Do you hear me?" The cool command in his voice made my entire body flush in preparation. He kissed his way up, stopping when we came face to face. "Get on your knees," he commanded.

"That took you long enough," I moaned.

A look of pure impishness took hold of his face. "Face the wall. Grab the headboard."

When I didn't immediately move, he gave my ass an encouraging spank.

Doing as he said, I wondered what was coming for me as I climbed onto the firm pillow, and knowing whatever it was, I wouldn't say no. He could have me.

The bed shifted behind me as he got on his knees. Using his legs, he spread mine wider. His right hand snaked around my body, clasping my left breast and pulling me into a near vertical position, lifting me slightly. His teeth nipped my ear. "You can suck my cock another day." The tip of him bumped my entrance, teasing me. "Do you trust me?"

My heart pounded in my chest. "You know I do."

"Then you should trust when I say, by the time I'm done, you aren't going to be able to walk." His other hand slipped between my legs, busying itself with the receptive bundle of nerves at my apex.

Slowly, he entered me again.

I'd thought I'd known every inch of him, but this position made the other pale in comparison. I could feel the ridge at the head of his cock and every smooth detail of him massaging me open.

Mischief dripped from his voice. "Since you made me break my promise, and I know how voracious you are, I'm going to go slow until you beg me for it."

Moaning pleasurably, I rested my head on his chest. "That's evil."

Damien sucked gently at my neck, drawing a gasp from me as he pumped away unhurriedly, working himself against my ass. The heel of his hand grinding its circles on the bundle of nerves he loved to tease.

It dawned on me then, as I thought to run my fingers through his hair, that this position had been chosen for control. There would be no lifting my hips or teasing him with my breasts. The only parts of him I could touch would be the hands, teasing and securing me to him, and to lift one hand off the headboard would be to risk losing my balance. While I had been okay with any position, I hadn't stopped to consider ceding all control.

"You like that?" And I knew he was asking if I was comfortable.

I nodded. The way his hard muscles worked on me and into me—how could I not be?

He slid the hand on my breast up my neck, cupping my jaw in his hand. His thumb pushed my head in the direction of the mirror wall.

The sight of our glistening, flushed, naked bodies pressed to one another, almost no space to spare—his body moving into mine, his hands all over me—knowing we were joined—it all turned my blood into liquid fire.

He held my gaze in the reflection as he pressed his lips to my ear.

"I want you to watch me as I fuck you." The words came out as a low growl. "I want you to watch me touch you, knowing from here on, your body is the only one I ever want to know. That I love you. That you've ruined me, and I love you even more for that."

The space between my legs slicked. More, I needed more. I need it all.

"Fuck, I love how wet you are for me. And you smell…so fucking good."

Emboldened, I removed a hand from the headboard and ran it along the section of his forearm, clutching my chin. "Faster."

Grinning, he clicked his tongue, his voice hot like crackling oil. "Slow as I can go. I could fuck you like this forever, and I would like that very much."

"Immortals, Damien, if you don't fuck me—"

"I'm the only one making demands right now."

Rocking my head from side to side, I moaned. "Damien, please. I love you. I'd let you do whatever you wanted with me—whenever you want—but right now, please."

That earned me two quick, unrestrained, core-splitting thrusts.

"Don't say those words lightly," he growled, more animal than man. He dragged the tips of his fangs—nearly an inch long—down the shell of my ear. "Because I want you, Eden, and I'll take everything you offer me."

I shook my head, my desperation growing painful. "I don't. I want you to have me in every way, but right now, I need you to fuck me. Please."

"Eden…fuck," he moaned. Slamming himself into me, the bed shook, and my remaining hold on the headboard had it banging into the wall—chips of paint falling away—his hand working the spot at my apex hard.

"Damien," I moaned, finding my release again—his name more like a scream. The pleasure rippling through me made my whole body slacken; his hold of me the only thing keeping me up.

Sinking his teeth into my neck, he emptied himself once more, throbbing so hard it stretched me a little further, his moan vibrating my neck.

"I was trying to hold out longer," he panted, shaking his head against me, "but the smell of you and you saying things like that…I'm going to have to work on that."

"Practice makes perfect," I sighed.

"Does that mean you're ready to do it again?" He wiggled his hips, reminding me of his presence inside.

My body hummed at the thought.

Meeting his gaze in the mirror, I said, "You do have many promises to fulfill."

Part IV

CHAPTER FORTY-ONE

23.ONE.4005

Damien dragged a finger lazily down my spine, pulling me from a bliss-induced sleep.

"You love me," I murmured.

His finger stopped.

"Don't. That felt good."

"I didn't mean to wake you," he whispered, brushing his lips along my ear, "but I do. I love you, Eden."

Pleased, I wiggled against him, bringing his cock to attention. "How aren't you tired?" I laughed.

He dragged his thumb lightly over my nipple, sending a little shiver through me. "Because in addition to my love for you, I think you're my mate."

Rolling over, I drank in the sight of his naked body on full display: in the silver moonlight saturating the suite, his sex-mussed hair and his green eyes shone once more. I sighed internally, remembering all the ways parts of him had touched me throughout the day. "It would explain the biting and cranky pacing Isa says you do when I'm gone."

Scooting toward me, a smile tugged at his lips. "You've reduced me to my animal instincts."

I swung my leg over his waist, closing the distance further, aware that I opened myself to him as I did so. A flash of descending fang told me he knew it as well.

I planted light kisses on his collarbone. "Are you always going to be like this?"

"I've heard it's worse in the beginning. After about a decade, I've heard it slows down some."

"A decade?"

He pressed his forehead to mine. "I'll make it the best decade of your life."

Searching his lustful green eyes, heat flooded my body. "I like hearing you say that." I tapped my finger on his jaw. "Talking about our future."

"Would you let me make it the best lifetime?" he asked, hope catching in his throat.

Knowing what he wanted and how he felt might change when I was older—and not wanting to think about that—I said, "I'm yours for as long as you want me." He would be it for me. I knew it in every part of my being. But as a demi, he would have lifetimes after me.

As if knowing where my thoughts had gone, he said, "I'll never not want—"

My lips were on his in a breath, silencing him. I just wanted him and to savor the time we had. He dragged his fingers down my back, eliciting a throaty moan from me. His lips moved to my chin, to my neck. Forever exploring, devouring.

"Pack your things, and let's go to Misundre tomorrow," he murmured against my skin.

I cupped my hand at the base of his neck, trying to pull him back up to me. Couldn't this wait? "I would love to, but do you think that's a good idea? Cole will suspect something. When we return, we may have trouble waiting."

He kept his eyes steady, bringing the back of my hand to his lips. "I meant to live. Far away from this."

My heart stopped. "You want to leave?"

"That can't really come as a surprise to you. You know how I feel about Sorbis. I don't want to stay here if I don't have to," he said. "Misundre's support of the Alliance Council has been waning for years, and it's only gotten worse the last couple of months. In Misundre, we wouldn't have to hide from my brother. We could live normally and be happy together."

That sounded great, but…

The light in his eyes dimmed, his expression looking like I'd slowly sunk a butter knife into his chest. "You don't want to."

"That's not it," my voice cracked, "but I'd be lying if I said it didn't scare me. What would I do? Where would we live?"

"Whatever you want, Eden," he said, his hand squeezing mine. "I'd support you in whatever you want to do. I'd build us a house. We'll stay with my uncle until then."

Fear twisted my stomach. "You don't think Cole would come after us?"

His grip tightened. "He could try, but he'd be fighting an uphill battle."

Shoulders shuddering, I took a deep breath. "Everything I know is here."

"I know. I didn't mean to cause you distress. We don't have to if you don't want to—"

"No, it's not that—I don't know why it feels so hard to say yes." I rolled onto my back, pressing the heel of my hand between my eyes.

Damien's fingers drew a pattern across my stomach. "You've never even left Sorbis. Good or bad, leaving behind everything you've ever known isn't easy. I got too excited and dropped it on you unfairly. I had plans to do it over a nice bottle of wine."

I burst into laughter. "You were going to butter me up?"

The green of his eyes twinkled proudly. "I was going to wine you up over your favorite meal and tell you all the reasons you should live out your days with me. Isa was waiting for the sign."

"Isa knew?"

"I had to run it by her first. We are bound by blood to one another. If she didn't want to go, then it didn't matter."

"How long have you been thinking about this?"

He shrugged. "For months, in a way, but I got serious about it after the last Council meeting."

"And when were you planning on asking me?"

He ran his thumb along the curve of my breast, making me suck in a breath. "Whenever I got the courage. Before Quincy's birthday party was my self-imposed deadline."

"Q's birthday party..." I stared up at the ceiling.

The invitation had been a pleasant surprise after months of silence and ignored invitations to talk. It'd be the first time I'd seen him since...Immortals since the festival celebrating Cole's new role as acting king. My stomach shriveled. It'd also be the first time seeing Cole since that day in the market. That was in a couple of days...

Damien entertained himself by kissing his way along the plush skin of my stomach.

"Who needs wine? You make it impossible to think," I moaned.

Encouraged, he licked his way up, stopping to suck lightly at my nipple, wiping every thought from my brain. My fingers wove their way into his thick, silky hair. What had I been thinking about...

"We can leave after Quincy's birthday. I'd like to see Rho and Q one last time. That'll also give me time to pack and take care of anything I need to at Selene's House."

I was going to say goodbye, and it surprised me that it wasn't as bitter a decision as it'd seemed moments ago.

He settled his chin below my ribs, looking up at me bright-eyed through the valley of my breasts. "What—just like that? Is this a pleasure-induced decision?"

"No, it's a decision based on my love and trust in you. How much longer you'll have either if you keep teasing me is the question you should be concerned with."

Lifting my hips, the slickness between my legs slipped along the hard length of him, never too far away.

It was the only invitation he needed.

CHAPTER FORTY-TWO

27.ONE.4005

Isa eagerly packed the penthouse while Damien accepted the challenge of helping me sort through things in my apartment. Throughout the last couple of days, we'd successfully packed everything necessary, and bit by bit, it'd all quietly gone to Misundre by way of Damien, filling his Uncle Heath's spare rooms.

Heath, the first person aside Isa to know about us, Damien reported, was ecstatic about the influx of company and couldn't wait to have me.

Only the furniture and my clothes—which Damien assured me would be too warm in Misundre—remained.

Rho had been the second one to know, and because of that, there was another thing on her list she'd never let me forget. And she'd cried, not because I was leaving Sorbis, but because she was so happy I was getting laid again, even if it was with Damien Valentine.

And taking one last look around the bedroom, I realized he'd fulfilled his promise: there wasn't a surface in the home he hadn't taken me on.

Snapping my fingers, the lights went out for the last time. Smoothing my hands along the circle skirt of my pink dress, I stepped into a stripped living room, jumping half out of my skin.

Damien stood right inside the kitchen, in an all-black suit, doing a slow pan of me over the glass of water he nursed.

I clasped my stomach. "I thought you'd left."

"I'm about to, but I wanted to say goodbye to this place." He patted the granite counter, and my blood warmed, knowing why he smiled. "I'll remember it fondly. I announced myself, you know, even poked my head in, but you seemed lost in thought. I saw you gazing out the window. What were you thinking about?" Sweeping me up into his arms, he sat me on the counter and settled himself between my legs. Trapping me between the hard muscles of his chest and the cabinet. The sandalwood and cedar scent of him made my heart sigh. "I'd bet it's the same thing you're thinking about right now."

"You can't smell me," I said, more for my assurance than anything else.

He touched the strategically deodor charmed key dangling over my heart, letting his finger glide down between my breasts, drawing a shiver from me. "No, but I've become well acquainted with your body and the way you move into me when you want it. You know I'd much rather indulge you than go to this party. I've spent far too much time doing other things recently."

"You're insatiable."

He pressed a kiss to the skin beneath my ear. "I could live between your legs." His hand tapped my exposed knee. "You look beautiful in this dress, but I look forward to getting you out of it and onto your back."

"On the beach or in the woods?"

Red splintered his green eyes, his hand daring to go higher.

I stopped his hand inches shy of his destination. "You should go. I'll see you in an hour."

He stuck out his lower lip. "Scared of what I might find?

I pecked his lips and pushed him away. "You aren't going to break me, though that was a very admirable attempt."

Frowning, he obliged me, stepping back. "When did you figure me out?"

"The moment you scared me half to death."

"You let me believe it was working?"

Shrugging, I hopped down from the counter. "It was working very well. I was enjoying myself."

"Not well enough."

Slipping his hand into mine, I tugged him toward the door. "It's been months. I want to say goodbye to Quincy. He may not have responded to anything, but he'd definitely never forgive me if I left without a word."

"I'm sure he'd understand."

"If you were him, would you understand?"

He tilted his head. "You're my mate. Nothing but death would keep me from you. Or rejection—which would be its own kind of death."

"You know what I meant."

Sighing, he stopped at the door. "I do. I said goodbye to my mother and Grayden when I left the first time. But Eden, please remember—"

"Be safe. Cole will approach me, and he's crazier than ever. I remember."

He nodded, and with one quick kiss on the cheek, he left.

***

Locating a Runner took longer than expected; I arrived ten minutes before the royal family would make their usual half-hour late entrance.

Fully stocked bars and rippling chocolate fondue fountains—surrounded by trays of fruits, nuts, breads, and candies—were stationed along every wall under shining green banners bearing the concentric circles of the Valentine Insignia. Twinkly soft music arose from the orchestra pit, moving talkers to sway and couples to slow dance.

Servers bustled by carrying golden platters laden with sparkling wine in preparation for the toast. I plucked one off and put my back to the huddled groups chattering in hushed voices as they gawked at me. Formal events and high society were going on the long list of things I wouldn't miss.

Through the vast glass windows, beyond the colonnade, the rapids of the River Sorbis stirred up mist, blurring the moonlit Woodlands beyond. What people said no longer mattered. After tonight, I'd never have to see them again. In an hour, I'd find myself beyond those trees, away from all of this with Damien.

I dared one sweeping glance to the mezzanine where he'd told me he would be, finding him leaning against the railing near the stairs, speaking to Grayden.

The orchestra wound down, turning every head in the room toward the dais. A stream of Protectors came first, then Cole in his dark blue suit, his crown of golden twisted branches resting atop his combed black hair.

The crowd broke into thunderous applause, cheering *his* name like it was his birthday and not that of the hunched-over figure shuffling drunkenly behind him in a white button-down, the buttons at his throat undone, and black pants.

In the months since I'd seen Q, he'd grown out his hair—straight black hair now falling halfway down his chest. The soft flesh of his face had melted away, bringing out his high cheekbones and strong, square jawline, making him look more like his father.

Coming to a stop beside Cole, I noticed how he winced and shrank away from the light, eyes darting back and forth between the crowd and his feet as if he couldn't bear to look up. At his side, his thumb made erratic circles on his thigh.

Something was wrong. And everyone smiled as if it were *normal*.

"Good evening, everyone, and thank you for coming to celebrate my youngest brother's twenty-fourth birthday," Cole said. He raised his glass to the crowd, and everyone in the room followed suit. "Would you like to say anything, Quincy?"

Q's shifting gaze met mine at the exact moment Cole's fixed on me. Paling, the smile on Quincy's face faltered as Cole's grew—as if they were two halves giving and taking from one another.

Stopping his circles, Q pressed his fingers to the place between his eyebrows. "Ye-yeah. En-n-j-joy."

Laughing, Cole clapped him on the back, making him tense. "Looks like someone started early. You heard him—cheers, everyone. Happy birthday, Quincy."

The crowd screamed the sentiment, whooping along and clinking glasses as the music resumed.

Darting a glance at his brother—who smiled at the adoring crowd—Q slipped from the dais, making strides toward me. Cole, noticing a second late, started to follow, but a dozen people swarmed him the moment his feet touched the floor.

Thank the Immortals.

"Happy birthday, Q. I've—"

Grabbing my arm, he yanked me past a bunch of gossiping women and into one of the softly lit side rooms, dragging me toward a service entrance.

Damien was probably panicking right now.

"Let go of me, Q. What's going on with you?"

He spun on me. "Wh-wh-what are you d-doing here? You-u have to go."

Up close, there were streaks under his eyes where someone had applied make-up, and he'd rubbed it away.

"What do you mean? You invited me. Why haven't you returned any of my letters? I know you've probably been busy with Halle, and I figured you might be upset with me, but I didn't think—"

"Eden st-t-op. I didn't invite anyone. I've been in the Ground the last couple of months."

My skin chilled like he'd dumped snow down the back of my dress. "What are you talking about?"

"I hav-ven't been with Halle-e." Laughing dryly, he shook his head, eyes shifting. "That's what Cole told people. It's a long story, but you need to-o leave before—"

"She isn't going anywhere," came a cool voice.

We both looked at the doorway we had come through and the dark outline standing there. Q's hold on me went slick, body shaking. My heart shattered when, despite his fear, he dropped my hand, stepping in front of me.

"R-run, Eden."

"I'm not leaving you," I hissed. Whatever this was, I wasn't going anywhere without him.

Slinking closer, the shadow over Cole lifted like a curtain, giving definition to his slightly inclined head and the grin stretching his lips a little too thin, almost like he was baring his teeth. "Neither of you is going anywhere unless I want you to."

As if on command, the pounding of boots on marble filled the room, stomping in time to my heartbeat.

Q shifted his jaw, eyes darting to the kitchen door where a Protector had come up behind us. "Eden—"

A gloved fist came down on the crown of his head, sending my best friend to the ground in a heap.

"Q?" I screamed, falling beside him.

"Get him out of here," Cole sneered.

Two Protectors came up beside Q—shoving me aside—each grabbing one of his arms and lifting them around their shoulders.

"No, stop." I grasped at his pant legs, the fabric ripping away in my hand. Scrambling after him, I reached out again, my hand landing on a shiny black shoe.

"Get up, doll."

"What are you doing? Where are you taking him?" I spat, my hands shaking.

"I said *get up*," he growled, emphasizing each word.

Tears stinging my eyes, I looked up at him, noting the silver sparks in the green of his eyes. He had taken an aggression elixir. "Fuck off."

A sharp pain came at my scalp, forcing me to my feet. Hand tightening in my hair, he brought me within inches of his face. Come now, Eden, you wouldn't deny your king."

"What was Q talking about? What did you do to him?"

His lip curled into a snarl. "That traitor doesn't matter. We have more important things to address. Are you ready to come home?" he asked. "The people need a queen."

I forced the words through my teeth. "I told you I was done. I don't fucking love you. I'm not going to be your queen."

The corner of his eye twitched. "Did Damien tell you about what I've had to resort to since you left?" Lifting me off my feet, he moved us back into the wall. Pressing his lips to my ear, he snapped, "Or has my brother been too busy fucking you? How long have you been spreading your legs for him, doll?"

My blood roared in my ears. "I don't know what you're talking about."

He stroked the back of his hand along my cheek. "Not this again. You don't think I know? About your nightly trips up to his home?

That he's been teaching you magic. Among other things."

In a couple of words, the earth beneath my feet crumbled away. Someone had told him. It could only have been Damien or Isa or Heath or Rho. And I knew with all the precautions he took, it wasn't Damien. Just as I knew Isa would never have given us away. Nor Heath and Rho…

"Let me go," I thrashed against him, ignoring the searing pain at my scalp as I kicked at his shins, tearing at whatever I could reach with my nails. Hot tears streamed down my face.

If I could destroy him, I would, not caring about the consequences— let them throw me into the Ground, let them execute me.

Blistering pain ripped across my cheek, his hand hitting me so hard my left ear rang. "Stop that, you ungrateful bitch."

My lips parted, Damien's name on the tip of my tongue.

"Do it. Continue to fight me," he hissed, breath hot at my ear. "Call out to him. I'll have him ended right here, right now. I have Protectors and Elders standing by, waiting for my command, and I don't care who sees. It's as easy as a memory elixir."

Remembering what I'd said to Damien not even an hour ago, a fresh wave of tears wracked me, taking the last of my strength. My legs gave out, the air leaving my lungs.

Cole caught me around the waist, fingers digging into the space between my ribs. Smiling from ear to ear, he shushed me. "That's it, doll. Your time is up. The charade is over. You're coming home with me."

He dragged me through the staff door, the two remaining Protectors trailing. Someone, somewhere, screamed my name, and collapsing to the floor, as I expelled everything in my stomach, silence fell.

CHAPTER FORTY-THREE

3.TWO.4005

I stayed in near darkness. They tried exposing me the first couple of days, throwing open the drapes—a pained, angry scream meeting each attempt. Couldn't they understand the light felt like hot coals to my tear-weary eyes?

I never left the bed. I wasn't even sure I could anymore.

I ignored the food they set on the nightstand, fighting through the hunger pains until my stomach stopped trying.

They whispered around me, begging me to drink, just a sip, to which I'd roll away in answer. I knew if I lay there long enough, all those things would cease to matter. A body, even one that healed itself, could only last so long.

The end of this would come one way or another.

I soaked the silk pillows they stuffed under my head, letting the snot and tears run until I couldn't cry anymore. Until the only thing left of me was a shell.

As time wore on and exhaustion won, sleep came for me at longer intervals. It was there that I lived it again, in nightmarish color—every second. Down to the moment I'd heaved my guts in Hotel Solta's kitchen and passed out.

When I had still had my voice, I'd asked the staff about Damien, but they pretended not to hear me, making faces they thought I couldn't see in the weak light.

She's lost it.

I certainly had.

"Good morning, doll," the last voice in the world I wanted to hear whispered in my ear. "You won't be staying in bed today."

There was a quick snap of fingers, and shadows descended around me, tearing away the blanket covering me. Hands grabbed me under the arms and behind the knees, pulling me in various directions as I thrashed in protest.

Rip me apart, I would have screamed had my throat not been raw from dehydration.

The drapes flew open, drenching me in blazing light. My eyes shut against it, catching the hints of red on either side of me.

The Protectors carried me into the bathroom, tossing me into the tub —less than pleased this was their job now. Hot, soapy water splashed the creamy tile. One held my arms down, another my legs, while a member of the staff cut away my clothes and took a coarse brush to my skin.

Shocked, I barely registered the assault or when they lathered me in oils.

Silk fabric sliding across my breasts and down my hips brought me to. That and the push to the small offshoot where my vanity was.

I managed a glance at my reflection as the Protectors shoved me into the chair before the mirror. It was a silvery-white dress cut to flatter curves. It might have fit me before, but now it hung baggy like a fancy sack.

Dressed me like the pristine doll he thought I was.

A group of attendants descended on me, painting my face with a myriad of mixtures I paid no mind to, covering up the shadows of my hollowed eyes.

Couldn't have a dead-looking doll.

My hair went up in pins, and sprays of rose-scented perfume erupted around me. When the attendants dissipated, there was one girl left, clutching a glass of water.

"Drink, my lady," she whispered.

I shook my head.

"Please, my lady."

"Drink, Eden," the second-to-last voice I wanted to hear sighed. "He punishes them when you don't cooperate. You might not care about yourself, but I know you care about that."

I noticed it as he said it. Her shaking hands and the black bruises striping the insides of her wrists. I would have been sick if there had been anything in my stomach.

Taking the cup from her hands, I drank. The cool water ran across my ashy tongue and down my shriveled throat, filling the hollow inside me.

"That's what he's done in your absence," Grayden continued. Given the distraction, the girl hurried away. "Beaten the staff for not making you happy enough."

"And you stood by and let him," I croaked, "just like you did when they took Damien." Lifting my head, I glared at him in the mirror. "I saw you talking to him that night. I've thought about it a lot, lying there in that bed."

Grayden bristled.

"He would have done anything for you," I spat. "He trusted you and you did *nothing*." Immortals, where was Damien?

"That's enough." He started for me.

"Do you know what you've done? Do you?" My voice cracked as it attempted the next octave. "Where is he, and what has Cole done with him? With Quincy?"

Grayden's hand clamped down on my wrist, the hot metal of his Protector ring burning my skin.

"Don't you touch me," I spat. Using every ounce of my being, I smashed the thin glass cup into the side of his head. It didn't shatter like I hoped, but it did break.

Removing a triangle of glass from his left temple, a stream of blood ran down his face. The Protector behind him stepped forward, cinching my wrist in one hand, the remains of the cup dropping from my grasp to explode on the floor, and raising his other.

"Don't," Grayden bit out, catching the other Protector's hand inches from my face.

"Sir, she struck you. That's a capital offense—you're bleeding."

His red eyes held mine as he spoke. "You're a Protector, which means you don't strike any member of the royal family."

Royal family—like fuck. Grayden swooped me up in his arms, pinning my hands at my sides, and threw me over his shoulder. I desperately tried to fight him, but it was useless. No matter how many times my knees rammed his chest, nothing registered.

"If you know what's good for you, you'll stop that now," he muttered, entering the apartment's small dining room.

"Have trouble, cousin?" The sound of *his* voice made my blood flash cold.

"No, I slipped and busted my face on a doorknob." Grayden plunked me in the chair at the head of the dining table and turned to bow. "Your Highness, is there anything else I can do for you?"

Cole sat at the other end in a silver button-up to match my dress, partially undone at the neck, grinning from ear to ear. "You're dismissed."

"That's right, traitor, run along," I hissed, so low it was almost inaudible. I knew Grayden had heard me, though, the muscles in his neck giving him away.

I looked from him to the spread of food laid out before me. Mounds of rolls and pastries, crystal bowls of fruit, and a polished silver tea set steaming at the spout.

"I had the kitchen staff make your favorite." Cole snapped his fingers, and a staff member slipped in, carrying a silver tray.

With dramatic flair, the staff member lifted the lid, revealing a stack of pancakes as high as my head and a small pitcher of maple syrup. "I remember you commenting how much you enjoy them."

I couldn't remember the last time I'd even thought about pancakes. "Are you sure you aren't confusing me with one of your lovers? Maybe Violet?" My voice sounded like gravel being crunched together.

His nostrils flared, but his smile didn't falter. "Please eat."

Shoving the tray away, I sat back in my chair. "I'm not hungry."

"You should eat, you're ghastly thin."

"You never minded that before," I laughed, a dry wheezing sound.

"Believe it or not, I care about you, Eden, and I'm not going to let you die, which Norris tells me will happen if I let you continue as you are."

I smiled at the suggestion. "I don't see the problem."

"I thought you might feel that way, which is why Norris is on standby with an elixir that will force you to eat if you insist on behaving that way. Would you like that?" He leaned forward conspiratorially. "If the food isn't to your liking, I can let the staff know, and I can promise you they won't let you down again." The threat clear.

Glaring at him, I pointedly reached over the stack of pancakes for a roll of bread. I'd sunk my teeth in when my tongue reminded me how dry it was—how dry my throat was—forcing me to grab a glass of water to help me swallow.

"That's a good girl," he drawled, making a shiver go down my spine.

"What am I doing here?" I demanded.

He rapped a knuckle on the table. "Why don't you eat first?"

"Because I don't want to."

Sighing, he picked up his butter knife and began to twirl it, point down, on the empty white plate before him. "The first lesson my father taught me in life is that you must rule with a strong hand. I used to think he was wrong—surely the only thing a strong hand will accomplish is crushing everything it grabs." He peered up at me. "Do you know the ridicule I endured from my father, letting you do everything you wanted? Letting you continue your charade at Selene's House. Letting you go back to that shoddy apartment." He paused to take a breath. "Letting you run away from me that night."

I scoffed. "The ability to choose what I do with my life and time are not gifts you give me. Immortals, is that why you took any chance to bring me here and left me to rot while you ran off to fuck other women under the guise of work?"

His gaze flitted to the window, taking the grin with it. "There are things you don't know, things you can't know—that even my brother can't share. Things that you don't mess with, Eden. Yes, I have lovers. There are things that I crave that I would never ask of my future queen. Do you know, I've given it a lot—"

"I don't want to hear anymore. Just tell me what you want from me, Cole." In an effort to slow my heart, I grabbed the pitcher of water to refill my glass. Hands shaking, I took another bite and lifted the cup to my lips.

"I want your happiness. What can I do to make your stay at the manor more conducive to our success?"

I nearly spat out the mash of bread and water. "I'm not staying here. I don't love you, Cole. I told you I didn't want to be queen, and I still don't. I'm never going to be happy with you."

The knife on his plate made a grating sound as it came to a halt. "We're getting ahead of ourselves," he sighed. "Happiness in the home first."

"I'm not staying here. I don't love you."

Shadows darkened his eyes. "And I don't need you to. However, it would make it easier. There's no other option on the table for you. Surely that's clear."

The soft roll turned into a hard ball where I squeezed it. "I'll run away."

"And I'll hunt you down. How far do you think you'd get before my Protectors found you?" he snorted. "Where do you think you'd go that I can't find you? I am the kingdom! Now, where was I—oh, do you want to pick all the meals? Redecorate the entire place? I'll allow almost anything. It's yours to play with."

He'd gone crazy. No, he'd always been crazy. He'd just hidden it well. And in my rush to make Lupine happy, what little he'd shown, I'd excused.

I was a fool.

"You could have any woman in Solta," I whispered. "Why do you want me?"

He pushed away from the table, the heavy wooden chair scraping the wood floor. The heel of his shoes struck the floor on each step, announcing his growing proximity to me. "Because I love you, in my way. Because there's no one else in Solta who'd help me garner as much favor and respect as you do." He leaned his hip on the table's edge. "No one as beautiful with as much potential. You were promised to me."

From the corner of my eye, I watched him reach into the bowl of grapes, plucking two green ones.

"You can't make me blood bind myself to you."

The sound of his teeth cracking the skin of the grape put me on edge. "I'm prepared to come to an agreement."

I looked up at him. "I want to see Damien."

The second grape exploded under the sudden pressure of his fingers, shooting juice on my face and across his shirt.

Grabbing my cloth napkin, he wet it in my water glass and dabbed at the fabric before tossing it at me. "I'm afraid that's one thing I won't give you. I'm sure you can understand."

Straightening, he started to pull away, but I grabbed desperately for him, hooking my hand into the waist of his pants. "Please, what did you do with him?"

He was so quick I didn't even know what'd happened until I was clutching the side of my face, stars exploding in my right eye. Salt stung my dry mouth as a streak of blood ran down my cheek.

Chest heaving, Cole shook his hand, rubbing at the signet ring on his pinky as if I'd hurt it and not the other way around.

"I'm offering you everything, and you're worried about my brother," he roared. "He is in the deepest, darkest cell of the Ground where he will rot until the Alliance Council tries him."

My heart seized in my chest.

"We save that level for the worst prisoners. Would you like to know why?" He bent, leveling his gaze. "Some of the Immortal Valentine's very first monstrosities live on that level. Telepathic spiders that whisper all your fears to you. Rats the size of babies that eat everything. And I mean everything." He chuckled darkly. "I wonder what pieces of him they'll eat first." The back of his knuckle stroked my cheek, smearing the blood. "I shouldn't have done that. It's a good thing you heal."

I stared at the butter knife to the left of my plate, wondering how deep I could plunge it into his stomach before someone stopped me. "What are the charges against him?"

Cole plucked another grape, a pleased smile spreading across his face. "Conspiracy against the crown."

The honest answer: whatever pleased him. "He's your brother."

He drummed his fingers in the air. "I've never understood people's attachment to blood relations solely because they're blood. We share the same parents. That's as far as our connection goes. I've never had a particular affinity for him. His denouncing his title only made it worse."

Stretching my clenched fingers, I forced myself to relax and meet his gaze once more. "You want to make me happy?"

Cole's eyes narrowed to slits, but he inclined his head for me to go on.

"Absolve Damien of his charges, free Quincy. No more harm to either of them. Exile them to Misundre." I struggled to suck in air, my heart fighting against my next words, but I had to say them quickly before I backed out or Cole took the wrath developing in his eyes out on me. This was no longer about me or what I wanted. "Do that, and I'll agree to it—to becoming your queen on my Immortal Age day. I'll bind myself to you by blood right now. I don't care about the manor. I don't care about any of the other things you can offer me."

Cole's eyes stared deep into mine, teeth clenched. "If I won't do it?"

I didn't bat an eye, daring him to try me. "Then you know you have nothing I want, and you or Norris or whichever minion of your choosing can do anything you want to me, but I will never do what you want. I will never be your queen."

Cole's nostrils flared. I could almost see the inner workings of his mind, thoughts pouring over his options. For the briefest moment, I saw the fire in him come out in full force. That, I decided, must have been him weighing getting rid of me entirely.

"Protector Grayden," he yelled. He shifted to his feet, pacing the space beside my chair like a rabid dog. He rolled up the sleeves of his shirt to his elbows.

"Your Highness," the traitor answered.

Cole stopped, fixing his eyes on me. "Go get Master Guardian Rei and tell her to bring a dagger."

CHAPTER FORTY-FOUR
3.TWO.4005

Master Guardian Rei performed the blood bond thirty minutes later. With one cut across our palms and a couple of words, I sealed my fate.

As I watched the skin of my hand pull itself back together—the magic tingling my palm and the smear of our mixed blood remaining as evidence of what I'd done—Cole's bloody hand, shaking excitedly, slipped the sapphire and diamond ring on my left middle finger, barking out orders to those who'd borne witness.

We were to announce the news of our reunion to the people at noon.

***

The story sweeping through the city was that we'd rediscovered our love at Quincy's birthday party.

Swallowing my emotions every couple of seconds, I stood at the doors of the Capitol Building, waiting for Cole to join me for our parade, forcing myself to focus on the lie and not how much of a twisted joke it was. This display of love wouldn't last forever. I only needed to make it through this event, and I would be returned to imprisonment at the manor where I wouldn't have to fake my happiness.

"Doll, you're already here." Cole appeared from the darkened hall on my left, dressed in his regalia, crown nestled atop his thick black hair, flanked closely by the Master Guardians and Lord Faldone. "Can't wait for the good people of Sorbis to celebrate the news?" He leaned down and pressed his lips to my cheek. "Regalia suits you."

He referred to the dark green gown I'd spent the entire morning getting sewn into. It had a high neck, corseted waist, and heavy silk skirts, finished off by a dense, red cape I wore clasped in gold at the shoulders. Atop my wavy hair, making its presence known every time I moved my head, sat a tiara.

It was a look I'd seen on Lupine hundreds of times and naively idolized once.

I stayed perfectly still as he fingered the ends of my hair. "I wasn't a fan at first, but the short hair is growing on me."

Forcing myself to smile at him, I said, "Are you ready?"

"Almost. I have a gift for you."

At the sound of metal clanging, he angled us both in the direction he'd come.

Escorted by two Protectors, Damien emerged from the shadowy hall, his hair combed down and to the side, dressed in his black suit. Other than some circles under his eyes, he appeared unharmed.

Any happiness or relief I felt seeing him alive was trumped by the cold horror the anti-magic manacles on his wrists instilled in me.

My heart stopped for so long, I was sure for a moment I'd died.

A fat tear plopping onto my cheek, I stepped toward him, his name clinging to the tip of my tongue. Cole placed himself between us.

"What is this?" I choked, shoving him away. "This was not our agreement."

Norris stepped forward, hand raised. "You daft girl, you never learn."

Cole's hand shot up, catching Norris's wrist, anger flashing across his eyes. "That won't be necessary any longer." His green eyes assessed me coolly. "It's simple. I made a deal with you—your agreement to be my queen when the time came, in exchange, I'd offer my brothers exile to Misundre." He took my chin in his hand. "Quincy jumped at freedom. You'll be happy to know my broken baby brother is there now, forever indebted to you. But when it came to this one, I realized I'd gotten ahead of myself—you agreed to be my queen, but you also insist you bear no love for me, which means there is no reason for you to obey, and that is key to this working. So, I made another deal. My dearest brother could accept exile, or he could stay and work for me in a subservient capacity. Step out of line, and my brother will pay." Cole laughed to himself. "Your cunt must be gilded in gold because I've never gotten this one to bend, let alone break."

A sharp ringing cracked my ears, my whole body going numb. This couldn't be happening. Why would Damien do this?

His words from the other night echoed in my mind in answer. *Nothing but death would keep me from you.*

That's what he'd said. Why had I thought I could do one thing right? This had to be a nightmare.

Wakeupwakeupwakeup.

The smug twinkle of someone who knows they've won glittered in Cole's eyes. "That's much better." He pressed his lips once more to my cheek. "Dry your tears and smile. Everyone in the city is dying to lay their eyes upon their future queen."

***

The hour-long debut turned into the whole afternoon and part of the evening.

Thousands of people had shown up—screaming our names or crying happy tears and thanking the Immortals as they reached out to shake our hands or wrap us in hugs. A piece of me chipped away each time I forced a smile and said thank you.

By the end, nothing was left of me, which made remembering what Damien had done—how Cole planned to use him to keep me in line—as Cole and I walked the private path to the manor hand in hand, surrounded by Protectors, easier to deal with for the moment.

Expecting to go straight to his apartment, I was surprised when Cole's hand stayed firm in mine, tugging me along. "Dinner, doll," he said simply.

It was as we hit the landing leading to the lowest floor and the event rooms that I came to understand dinner wouldn't be the two of us.

Through the open double doors, the flickering orange light highlighted the state room's newly painted dark brown walls, which resembled dried blood. Every person in the room came to attention at our entrance, the boisterous chatter ending abruptly.

Gathered around the table inside were Lord Stellan Faldone, his four sons, and twelve generals, all standing erect—shoulders back and head high—dressed in red suits with bolo ties bearing the triangle insignia of the Immortal Faldone. To the side of most stood their wives and mates.

Territorial as they were, the men kept their wives secluded, and never in my life had I met one, but I'd heard stories from Lupine, and the dour women, in gowns of earthen colors covering them from their necks to their ankles, looking down their noses at me as I entered, matched her description. The wives only left the home when their husbands were going to be away for an extended period, which meant one thing to me: this was not just dinner.

We walked down the length of the room, their heads bowing to Cole as we passed, the light of the candelabras running down the center of the table catching and shifting differently in the eyes of the Charphan men who'd given over to their animal counterpart.

I smiled at them all despite the muscles in my face aching in retaliation. Despite wanting to scream and run.

Cole led me to the seat on his left, at the other end of the table, and let loose of me.

Noting who stood behind the seat across from me, I realized how big of a lie it'd been—telling myself being numb made the Damien situation easier to deal with. When it came to those I loved, there was always more to give, and his presence was a clear warning that nothing but my best behavior would be tolerated.

Dropping my gaze, I sat, content to look down for the duration of dinner.

At Cole's nod, the rest of the table sat, the shift in dynamic between men and women growing as loud as the return of the chatter.

Manor staff passed off crystal pitchers of breki to the wives—all of which had shifted behind their husbands as they'd taken their seats, heads and eyes now downcast and free hands braced over their navels —and the manor staff attended the unmated men and me.

Remembering Rho was Grayden's mate—his presence fresh in my mind as he'd taken the seat to my left—I felt sick at the thought of my free, emboldened best friend debased in such a way, and all the happier they weren't together.

The Charphans boasted of conquering the mortal rebel groups as they powered through the first three courses—tomato soup, a winter greens salad, and salt-crusted rib-eye steak—and glass after glass of breki, their wives promptly refilled. I made a show of eating a couple of bites of each, grateful the courses moved quickly, and Cole was so high on breki and enthralled in the conversation, he hadn't had time to notice. It was enough work to keep the little I'd eaten down when every other story ended in a promise of the disembowelment of every rebel.

For the most part, Damien nor Grayden ever really spoke, only when someone called on them to help rehash a story.

When dessert was served—an orange elixir in a gold-capped vial—it was set before everyone but me, Grayden, and the face I'd staunchly avoided looking toward the entire evening.

Cole wove his fingers through my hand, bringing my attention and my knuckles to his breki-slicked lips. "It's time for the gentlemen to talk now. Have a good night, doll. Grayden, cousin, thank you again for agreeing to watch my doll for the evening. Please see her to our apartment and send Protectors for my brother."

Grayden bowed his head. "An honor, Your Highness."

I forced a saccharine smile, aware of all the eyes at the table watching me as I spoke my first words of the evening. "Have a good night as well, my darling."

A condescending snicker came from the left, followed by a voice I now recognized as the youngest Faldone son, Nicho, who loved to hear his own voice. "Oh, he will. Hey Luno…"

What he said next was lost to me as standing, I made the mistake of looking into the green eyes across from me, watching me intently. My heart gave a longing sigh. Refusing to get lost in them and in hope, I tore myself away, making for the door, Grayden following half a step behind.

***

Free of my regalia and scrubbed clean by my lady's maids, I curled up on the couch before the window in Aevry's office, the moon set at the right point in the sky to fill the room with its silver light.

The highlight of my life once again being left alone in the place I disliked most in the world.

"Should you have one of your nightmares, you should wait it out in the apartment from now on if you know what's good for you," a voice said, breaking my reverie.

So much for that.

I turned to look at the shadowy figure in red haunting the doorway. "I don't need your advice. You can go."

"Cole has asked for eyes on you at home."

Hot prickling shot up my spine. "So what—you're going to watch me sleep?"

Shaking his head, Grayden stepped into the room, the moonlight shifting to highlight his red eyes and the rich brown of his skin. "Thankfully, I've been spared the bathroom and your bedroom."

I folded my arms over my chest. "I didn't invite you to come closer."

Grayden paid me no mind, shutting the door behind him.

"Did I hit you too hard on the head this morning? I said go away. Is this some kind of payback for telling Rho I didn't think you were good for her? Or maybe you're a glutton for pain? I can't imagine why you would have volunteered for this."

"Believe me, I've questioned my decision every second since I made it." His eyes went to the shelves. "I'm glad Damien helped you grow some claws—you're going to need them to survive the changes coming. However, you'll need to work on how and with whom you use them. Lupine wasn't the innocent hero you think she was—"

"She was a survivor who made the best decisions she could with what she had," I snapped, in no mood for his patronizing.

He ticked a finger. "That's one way of wording it."

Immortals go away. "Surely being high with all your family would be more entertaining."

Sighing, he put his back against the bookshelf and stared at the ceiling. "I can honestly say I'd rather be here, hearing you tell me Rho deserves better repeatedly than be with them."

I examined him closely, the loose hands at his sides and his sagging shoulders. "After seeing how Charphan men treat mates, I'm glad I encouraged her to let you go."

His eyes widened in surprise, and to my astonishment, he nodded his agreement. "I'll give you my Charphan instincts run hot and bone-deep, and I've been known to make mistakes," he met my gaze, a v forming between his brows, "but I would never willingly bring Rho around my family because of that, and if I had to, my mate would have a place at the table as my equal." A pause. "Is she okay?"

"She was the last time I saw her." Days ago now… "It's Rho, though. She's good at going with the flow."

He smiled to himself. "When I go to her again, I hope to be a worthy man."

Having nothing nice to say, I stayed quiet. Maybe he'd take the hint.

Sucking in a breath, he said, "You know I speculated for a while about you two—since the night of his arrival. After your fateful little interaction at the Eternal Tree. I warned him. I grew up with Damien. We went through everything together. He's more like a brother to me than any of my actual brothers. He and Aevry. I know him as he knows me, and I've seen him with women, and I've seen him with you."

And I'd heard enough. "Nothing romantic was going on between us before Cole's birthday. He made an Absolution Oath to Lupine that he would protect me."

"Absolution Oaths mean nothing. I know the state Damien was in when he left twenty years ago. He was broken by the war, by Aevry's death.. I know the anxiety he had coming back. He wouldn't have stayed—"

"You know nothing, Grayden. Leave."

"I know you're his mate," he blurted. Then laughed as if he couldn't believe the words. "I saw it when he ran for you that night. He'd all but said it, and I'd thought he was…high on whatever it is Cole is on when it comes to you."

My stomach cinched around the blade at its center at the thought of Damien trying to reach me. "You've always thought it was me. Cole is high on himself."

"Yes. I always stupidly thought—always hoped Cole would be better than his father. But he's worse. This slow descent—I stuck through it despite the feeling in my gut screaming it was wrong. And I can't do it any longer."

Had I heard him right? Had Grayden Faldone actually condemned the future king?

"Whether I redeem myself in anyone else's eyes, I don't care. I need to redeem myself in my own eyes, and I'm starting with you."

I laughed so loudly I surprised myself. "Am I supposed to be honored?"

He pressed the heel of his hand to the space between his eyes, looking like he couldn't tolerate much more of this. A sentiment I shared. "I understand how that came out, but—"

"What was that tonight?" I demanded.

He shook his head like I'd slammed another glass into his head. "What?"

"You want to remotely try to redeem yourself? Why don't you start by answering some questions. Why are your father and his minions here?"

He swallowed hard. "My father has been trying to make the case for an elevated position on the Alliance Council for some time—"

"You mean he wants to be king."

"—and Cole has been the perfect opportunity," he continued steadfastly. "It's been a perfect storm set in motion by King Elias. After the Queen's death, the waning relationship the Alliance Council had with Misundre all but disappeared. When you turned down his proposal, the hair-thin strings holding the loyalty of the outer city and the farmlands to the Alliance Council snapped. Quincy's working with the insurgents was an additional blow. On top of that, there have been whispers of a figure known as the Redeemer in Vivinmoor, calling for the reclaiming of the city, who has been making our Protectors and Devotees stationed there disappear, and distributing propaganda throughout to rally support. Vivinmoor's Lord Bastion doesn't seem worried, but after Roan's War, Saier has advised Cole to step in and stop it, and for that, you need—"

Slack-jawed, I shook my head. "Wait, can we go back to Quincy working with the insurgents?"

Grayden rolled his eyes. "Really, what else would have landed him in the Ground?"

"Cole's bad mood?"

The Protector snorted. "About a year ago, he met an insurgent named Halle, and she recruited him."

I sat a little straighter. "He told me he met her a couple of months ago."

He nodded. "They were taking their plans to the next level and would be seen together in public. They knew they needed to have a reason." His throat bobbed. "We got a tip about suspected rebel activity near the Northern Forest. We intercepted them and captured them. Q was part of the group. Their love, it would seem, wasn't a complete lie, though. He made a blood bond with Cole, whatever he wanted in exchange for her being spared execution and released, which is how Cole got him to perform for his birthday party."

"How do you know all of this?"

"How do you think I know all of this?" he asked, voice growing quiet. "The same way we learned about you and Damien."

I swallowed the bile creeping up my throat. "I don't know how you learned. No one knew but us—"

"You two knew about each other. Damien wouldn't have been easy to get, but you would have." He grimaced. "But we didn't need either of you when there was a third option."

"Isa wouldn't—"

"Come now, Eden," he laughed darkly. "That's nothing a truth or a compulsion and memory elixir wouldn't fix. It was my father's suggestion. He's good at that. Even better than King Elias. I saw the report on Saier's desk. There were several elixirs listed that she'd been given, ones that were unnecessary for information extraction, and a comment that after her memories were culled, she was released complaining of terrible stomach pain. There was a note in the file to monitor the situation." He shook his head. "I can't help but wonder if my father's suggestion was vengeance for her leaving when my mother released her of her bond to our family."

I got to my feet abruptly. "I'm going to kill him."

Grayden put himself between me and the door. "Let's calm down. Even if you had Damien's or my level of skill, and the manor wasn't full of bloodthirsty Charphans right now, you're nowhere close to first in line for that honor."

Hot tears stung my eyes as the reality of his words hit me. "How do they get away with this?"

Lupine. Damien. Quincy. Isa. Every citizen in the outer city and farmlands. Immortals knew who else. At some point, they had or would break us all—in some way or another.

"Because there's no one strong enough to challenge them."

CHAPTER FORTY-FIVE

6.TWO.4005

I stared at my reflection—really looked at it—as I had every night the last several. Out of my dinner attire and stripped of makeup, there was nothing to hide behind.

Under my golden eyes were gray and purple shadows minutely darkening each day, and my cheeks took on a sallow tinge, the thinning skin beginning to show the hard cut of my bones.

Running my fingers through my dull brown hair, I thought about how fading away affected everyone equally.

Believing everyone long gone, I was shaken from my stupor by a woman I'd never seen before—her wavy black hair reaching the waist of her white dress—bursting into the bathroom.

She stared, jaw slack, and blue eyes so wide they threatened to pop from her head.

Collecting herself, she bowed her head and curtsied. "My name is Gymma. I've been sent to help you get ready for tonight."

Smiling, I shook my head. "You must be mistaken. I've already been attended to for the evening."

She stepped forward, taking the hand I had resting on the white stone counter into hers, and pressed something into my palm. "Of course, I'm sorry for my confusion, my lady." The woman briefly met my eyes, something strange in them, and turned her back to me.

Confused, I looked down at a small square of paper.

My fingers fumbled at the edges, trying to unfold it. At the sight of that handwriting, a spark of hope warmed my chest for the first time in days.

Find me in the mirror at midnight.

***

Dangerous anticipation energizing every deadened nerve in my body, I dabbed some concealer under my eyes and wandered into the bedroom closet.

Grabbing a robe to match the deep pink slip I wore, I plunked down in front of the gold framed mirror embedded in the wall—at twenty past nine, I had nothing better to do than wait, and it'd be much better than standing for hours at the sink, and as wide and tall as a doorway, there was plenty to see.

I marked the passing of time by the soft chimes of the small clock I'd borrowed from Aevry's office—one for fifteen minutes past the hour, two for thirty, and so on—watching myself switch positions as I waited.

The clock chiming four times for the third time since I'd sat, I got to my feet, the sudden movement sending me stumbling forward, blood rushing to my head. I braced myself against the cool glass of the mirror.

Shaking off the gentle swaying in my head, the silver surface of the mirror darkened.

In the time it took me to blink, I went from staring at myself to looking at myself overlaying Damien, wearing the black suit Cole had him in every night at dinner.

Grinning, he pressed a finger to his lips and lifted his other hand.

Heat bloomed under my palm as his hand came to meet mine, the tips of my fingers resting beneath the top digit of his own, the silver shimmering like liquid between us.

What kind of magic was this?

The fingers of his hand interlocked with mine, tugging me forward, my hand disappearing into the mirror. Awed, I stumbled forward, passing through into a weakly lit room, the sound of drums above me loud enough to feel the vibrations in my bones.

And he was there, hand firm in mine. Shining from the inside, his green eyes were their own light. A strand of his black hair, free of the oil he had used to slick it down, rested on the lightly tanned skin of his forehead.

Immortals, he was beautiful.

I grabbed his face, running my fingers up into the lush black hair. "Did I really just walk through a mirror, or did I fall asleep, and this is a dream?"

He laughed. "It's—"

Standing on the tips of my toes, I cut him off with a kiss, deciding I didn't want to know. His lips welcomed the voracity of mine, tongue sliding into my mouth in reckless abandon. I breathed down the smell of him on each desperate inhale. Savoring the taste of him like a fine wine and only breaking apart for air when short bursts would no longer suffice.

My chest heaving, I pulled him closer again, wanting more. "I thought I'd never get to do that again."

Shrinking away, he handed me a deep golden elixir. "Before we go any further, drink this. Just a sip."

Uncorking the vial, I did as he asked. The liquid surprisingly flavorless. "What is that?"

"A more complete version of my nullify elixir. It'll nullify any elixir in your system and any given to you for the next several days. It also detects any elixirs you may have been given, so should you want to hide that you've taken it," he tucked it away in his suit pocket, "you can act like it."

He brought our joined hands to his lips, causing the light to glint off the ring Cole had given me. Not wanting to be reminded of him, I turned my attention to the room.

Shaped like a star, at each of its points were black doorways except at the one to my back, where the doorway shone like any mirror. In the center of the room, dug into the stone, was a concentric circle, at the heart of which lay a blanket and a bottle of wine.

"Where are we? What is this place?" I asked.

"Valentine's Crossroads. The Immortal Valentine's long forgotten personal version of the Hidden Halls, except far more efficient, as these entrances are mirrors that can take you all over the city."

"That explains the legends of him moving around the city without being seen."

"That door," he waved to the one I'd come through, "connects to every mirror in the manor. From what I've gathered, this transitionary room is in the earth beneath the manor on the staff quarters level."

There really were an endless number of secrets in this home, in this city—in this family. "Where do the others lead?"

"Two don't appear to work any longer, and the others I haven't figured out yet, but I'd say it's a safe bet one of them is the Capitol."

"And how do you know about this place?"

He cocked his head. "A tale for when we have more time."

More time…

I pointed my finger upward, ignoring the spark of light threatening my cautious, hopeless heart. "What is that?"

He sucked in a breath through his teeth. "That is the sound of my brother, my uncle, and all his sycophants…preoccupied for the rest of the evening, which is why I didn't come sooner. I couldn't have Cole calling on me."

I shivered, remembering what Grayden said about going on walks as I fought my brain's urge to consider what might be preoccupying them.

Bending, he knocked my legs from under me, swooping me up into his arms. "Any more questions?" he whispered, his thumb skirting along my exposed thigh.

"Was that necessary?"

Grinning, he pressed a kiss to my temple and sat down at the center of the blanket, me in his lap. "I know this isn't the most romantic place, but there will be more time for that later, and for now, it serves the need."

"I'd go anywhere—be anywhere with you, Damien Valentine." I touched the tip of my finger to his jaw. *More time.* "Later?"

"When I get you out of this Immortals forsaken place."

There was no getting out, not when Cole would hunt me down. But hearing him say it…the determination in his voice… I rested my head along the curve of his neck.

"I stopped by our home to check in on Isa and grab this," he said, holding up the bottle of wine.

Isa. My heart leapt at the mention of her name and his calling the penthouse ours. I hadn't known he thought of it that way. "Is she okay?"

Swirling his finger, the cork slowly slid up, emerging on a pop. "She's safe and unharmed. Her safety was part of my agreement with Cole."

The gratitude swelling my lungs burst like a soap bubble. The way he said it, the murderousness in his voice—he knew it was her. He knew what they'd done. The thought alone was enough to trigger reminders of all the other things Cole and Stellan had done.

Images of Damien in a dark cell accompanied by the creatures Cole had told me about filtered into my head.

Feeling suddenly sick, I crawled off his lap, grabbing the bottle of wine, and moving to a corner of the blanket.

Knees to my chest, I took several gulps. The rich, earthy wine washed down the bile creeping up my throat. "Tell me, will you," I said, the first tear falling onto my cheek, "what happened to you after Quincy's party?"

He scooted up beside me but didn't reach to hold me. "Eden, I don't think that—"

"Please?"

Brow furrowed, he inhaled deeply through his nose. "Grayden hit my drink with a knock-out elixir, but it didn't have enough time to take effect, so they physically knocked me out. I woke up in the dark with the worst headache and a lot of time to think."

I took another drink. "Cole said he put you in the deepest level of the Ground with telepathic spiders that tell you your worst fear and rats the size of babies."

"No rats." He let loose a breathy laugh. "Vanivere are real, but not scary or bad."

I looked up at him. "Vanivere?"

"The telepathic spiders. They don't tell you your fears, though, they tell you your dreams." His eyes glazed over as he tucked a strand of my hair behind my ear. "Will you tell me what's happened to you?"

Lying my head on his shoulder, I nodded. Fighting the hot tears stinging my eyes, I told him everything that'd transpired, from that cursed night, to the blood bond, to the night with Grayden. A dark laugh escaped me at the end. "And here we are, both prisoners to him. You know I'm not happy you stayed, Damien. I wanted you to leave. I wanted you to be free and safe.

He reached to wipe away a tear. "I would choose death over leaving you, period, but especially here with him."

A chill wormed its way down my spine. "Don't say that, you have —"

He shook his head. "Eden, don't. There would be nothing for me. I accomplished everything I wanted to over two decades ago. My time in Misundre wasn't bad, but it was existence. It wasn't life. You're my sun, my sky, my moon, and stars. You're my happiness and my frustration. You're my peace. You're my home, my love, my life."

Those last words were a warm hammering of love to my heart. Love I couldn't afford to receive.

"Why do you have to say beautiful things?" I sighed. Looking up at him, I dragged a finger lightly across his furrowed brow, down the bridge of his nose, along his cheekbones. I could give love, though. "I love you."

"Don't say it like that."

"Like what?"

Damien cupped my chin in his hand, pulling me close enough we shared breath. "Like it's goodbye. I have a plan. Trust in me. We're in this together."

"I do trust you," I whispered.

"But?"

Searching his eyes, I shook my head. "We've both made blood bonds, but we aren't in this together. I've made a blood bond to be his queen, and he's using you to get to me now, but when he's done with me, he'll do whatever he wants with you." A fresh batch of tears streaked my cheeks. "Fuck I hate him."

His fingers moved back and forth across my face, sweeping away tears. "I don't know the boundaries of that elixir yet, which is why I can't tell you anything, but please. Please." *Have faith in me.*

We both fell silent, the sound of the drums above filling the cavernous room.

"Let's talk about something else," I said.

"Eden…"

I traced my finger down his throat. "Maybe we can lie together and pretend…like we'd gone to Misundre and Cole never happened?"

Resigning himself, he lowered his voice to a whisper. "You only want to lie together?"

"No," I said, feeling the warmth low in my core, elevated by the wine. Climbing onto his lap, I coaxed him to lie back.

Our bodies parallel to one another, he slipped his fingers into my hair. Red cracks already splintering his eyes, he raised slightly to kiss me. "But even if you hadn't just given me an elixir to nullify all elixirs, I haven't had access to my contraceptive elixir in weeks."

"Fuck I forgot about that." His fingers knotted in my hair for a moment, considering the odds—as I was doing—and flopping onto his back in defeat.

A question came to me. One I'd wanted to ask since Union Day with Isa, and since we were pretending. "I know what you said in the past, but would you want a baby with me?"

Heat bloomed all over my skin at the feline look in his green eyes, the canyons of red widening. "I'd be lying if I said it'd ever crossed my mind, but now that it's there," he paused to touch the tip of his tongue to his elongating fangs, "I would very much like that. As many as you want."

I pressed a kiss to his jaw. "Good, because I want two, a boy and a girl."

In one swift twist of his core, he rolled us so he was on top, a low, desirous growl in his voice. "We can have two children, but I can't promise a girl. My family doesn't have a history of having girls."

I shifted my mouth to the side, adjusting my fantasy. "I guess I should be realistic." Staring up into his quickly reddening green eyes, I added. "I want our baby to look like you."

Leaning in, he grazed his fangs along my neck, his free hand running up my exposed thigh to the lacy purple underwear clinging to my hips. "Mmm, I don't know. I want our baby to have your eyes."

Hooking my leg around his waist, I scooted nearer, reaching for the snap on his jeans. I took hold of his velvety, hard cock, running my hand along the length of him. "We're being realistic, remember?"

He let out a low groan. "I want you to take it off."

"What?"

"Everything, specifically this." Pressing his forehead to mine, he flicked the key around my neck. "So I can smell your desire. I want to bury myself in you. I want to hear you moan my name. Immortals, I want everyone in this fucking place to hear you scream my name and know you're mine. I want to smell you as you come. I want your body shaking as I fill you with my seed. Fuck."

"You might not be able to smell me, but you can still taste me." I brushed my open mouth against his, inviting him in as I worked the length of him.

Damien ardently accepted the invitation, his tongue meeting mine between where our lips melded, gliding effortlessly along mine and settling deep at the back of my throat where he could worship like my mouth was his sanctuary. His grip on my waist hardened, squeezing at the flesh as if it might ground him.

I wanted him inside me so bad my body ached. Driven by need, I set the length of him free, settling him between my legs, only distantly realizing what I'd done.

"Fuck." Damien moaned into my mouth, squeezing me tighter against him, ripping down my underwear in one clean motion.

I broke the kiss abruptly. *No,* came the voice of reason, *this can't happen.* "We can—"

His fingers slipped inside of me, silencing me.

Moving in and out, palm cupping my sex, his next words were a promise. "We can't now, but we will soon. Naughty, needy thing testing my self-control like that. Thank the Immortals for those months of depriving myself, or I would have taken you."

A rush of heat pooling low in my abdomen made me shiver and clench around him.

"You would have liked that," he growled. He pressed down harder, making me arch into him, my shoulders digging into the stone floor. "Fuck Eden."

Twisting the hair at the base of his neck, I searched his feverish eyes, absent of any green. "I did say you could have me however you wanted."

The way his nostrils flared as he inhaled a steadying breath, I knew I'd inadvertently tested his willpower. He handled it the only way he could, his fingers hastening their thrust. Imagining it was his cock as I did.

It happened so fast. The explosion of lightness coursing through my body. Pressing his lips to mine, he swallowed my moan of his name.

"As much as I want the whole castle to hear," he grinned, sucking his fingers clean, "I'd rather stay here with you a little longer."

I would, too. As long as we could, but at least long enough to do what I wanted to do next. Delirious, I stroked his still erect and throbbing cock. "It's your turn."

"In a minute," he whispered. Carefully, he pried my fingers away and fixed himself in his pants. "There's something I need to do, and if I keep letting you distract me, I'll never do it."

I rolled my eyes. "Really, Damien?"

He fished around in his suit jacket for something. "I had several reasons for risking this meeting, and alas, as nice as it would be, being pleasured wasn't one of them."

Something flashed across his eyes as he found what he was looking for and held it out to me.

My heart started beating as hard and loud as the drums overhead. Clasped between his thumb and forefinger was an emerald the size of a grape and wrapped in yellow gold.

Lupine's missing Pledge Token.

I met his gaze, green eyes beckoning me to say yes to the unspoken question. Noticing for the first time he'd shifted onto one knee.

"The first time I saw you, Eden, something resonated in me—something I didn't understand and denied for a long time. I swear you were supposed to find me at the Eternal Tree. I swear my mother must have known somehow. Known you would undo me." His throat bobbed. "Known you would take the hollow, broken man I denied being and fill me with light. Whatever time I have with you is the only time I want or need. There's nothing for me after you. This isn't how I wanted to do it—none of it has been—but with everything that's happened, I don't want to wait. Will you take me as your husband and perform the Eternal Pledge with me?"

My first thought was to say no. Not the Pledge. A bond, yes, but not the Pledge. Even if I wasn't in the situation I was in, the idea of being Damien's demise when I died made me feel ill.

Then I realized how much of a hypocrite I was. When I'd believed something had happened to him, I'd been prepared to fade away. If something happened to him now, I knew it would be the same. If the situation were reversed, and he was the one who would grow old and die, I would want the Pledge, too.

There was no life without him. He was my home, my love, and my life as well.

And this had been what the Immortal Valentine had designed this bond for. For the lovers who knew losing one another was a fate worse than death.

"What about my blood bond to Cole?" I finally said, my voice a breath.

He nodded once. "We have a little over a year to figure that out, but I promise you'll never come back here to him, Eden."

For this one moment, I turned off the pessimistic, worrying voice in my head. "Damien, I love you, and everything I have, and everything I am is yours."

I got onto my knees, taking his face in my hands. Looping an arm around my waist, he pulled me flush to him, those green eyes of his searching mine in anticipation.

The warmth of him was an elixir I could lose myself in.

"Yes." I pressed my lips to his. "Yes."

CHAPTER FORTY-SIX
9.TWO.4005

Dismissing my lady's maids, I ran into my bathroom, falling to my knees before the toilet, expelling every bite I'd managed at dinner.

The gluttonous drinking and eating, the boisterous laughter, the annoying gossip. The smile I forced when they made obscene jokes. That had all been enough. Tonight, the talk of the table had regarded a successful attack against a group of rebels they'd been tracking. How they had murdered and made examples of them for the people in the farmlands.

Arms quaking, I heaved once more. Wishing I could purge the stories as I did my food.

What was worse was the look on Cole's face. The light from the candelabras dancing in his breki glossed green eyes as he listened.

I ripped at the laces on my dress, desperate to shed the suffocating second skin Cole had instructed the staff to put me in for dinner. Fingers sweat-laced, I feebly managed two laces before the sobs racked me, bringing me down to my forearms on the cold tile floor.

Damien has a plan, came a defensive voice of hope.

"Please, my lady," came a delicate voice. I looked up into the cool blue eyes of the girl—the one who had given me the first note. "There's no need to cry. Let me help you."

One hand slipped me a piece of paper while the other worked the laces down my back apart. I clutched it to me, the one lifeline I had while Damien did what he needed to do.

She tugged the laces apart, letting the dress fall away and leaving me standing in my underwear. The breath I took, free of the dress, was ecstasy. "Is there anything else I can help you with?"

I met her blue eyes in the mirror, recognizing the soft smile she offered me. Pity.

"That's all. Thank you," I said. Hoping she could hear how grateful I was for her.

Curtsying, she took her leave.

I stared at the piece of paper for a long moment. Hands shaking and heart beating hard as I unfolded it, barely gleaning the word *soon* when a tan hand gripped my wrist, squeezing my bones so hard my fingers uncurled and the note floated into the sink. The hold and pressure didn't release, pushing my bones to their max. Inhaling slowly through my nose, I gritted my teeth against the pain. I wouldn't scream, I wouldn't cry.

"What is this?" Cole snarled in my ear. "Look at me."

Letting out a whimper as bone cracked, I dropped my gaze to the floor. "Fuck you, Cole."

Fisting my hair, he yanked my head back, forcing me to look up at him. Green eyes glared at me through slits. "You know, I actually felt bad today. I'd seen the look on your face enough on my mother's when I was a boy. I remembered how it felt then, and it didn't make me feel any better now. I wanted to apologize. But I catch you with this."

Grabbing the note, he dragged me by the hair toward the door.

Screaming, I clawed at his hands. "Let me go."

"Protector Sunya," he barked, sending a shower of spittle into my face. Struggling, I caught a glimpse of the red-suited figures through the suite's open door—looking onward as if nothing was wrong. "Send someone to retrieve every maid who assisted my fiancé tonight. Interrogate them. Have them all imprisoned in the cells under Protector Headquarters on the grounds of treason. Send someone to retrieve Master Guardian Norris and instruct him to bring what I need. He'll know what that means. And send someone to retrieve my brother Damien."

My heart plummeted into my stomach. "No, Cole."

"Grayden," he roared. Silver sparks fired away in his green eyes as he leaned to hiss in my ear, "I told you what would happen if you went against me."

"I haven't gone against you."

Grayden appeared silently in the sitting room doorway, fists clenched at his side. To my surprise, he stepped forward, murder warming his red eyes.

I cast him the briefest glance, offering a single shake of my head that could easily have resulted from Cole's shaking me. No good would come for either of us if he intervened.

He dropped his gaze. "I'm here, Your Highness."

Cole paid him no mind, throwing me down onto the light blue rug in the living room. My hands and knees burned as my skin tore across it. "Tell me what this is then." He unraveled the note. "*Soon*. What's soon, Eden?"

Hope, I wanted to scream. Instead, I held my wrist—pain fading as the bones pieced themselves back together—and my tongue.

He paced the length of the carpet like a caged animal.

Protector Sunya, a tall woman with long black hair, walked into the room, her eyes forward. "I have my men rounding up the staff, and your brother is on his way. The Master Guardian of Skills is here."

Norris trudged in a beat later in his blue robe, chin folds flapping.

"How may—" he started, but noticing me in my underwear on the floor, his paper-thin lips tugged into a sneer, revealing grainy yellow teeth.

Cole stepped up to him. "Did you bring what I asked for?"

Bowing his head, he extended his hand. Two vials of pearly blue truth elixir and one vial of a putrid brown powder I'd never seen before rested in his palm.

No. Immortals no. Even if the elixir Damien gave me worked, I'd still have to play well.

Snatching them, Cole turned on his heel. I struggled to my hands and knees.

Cole's foot came down hard at the center of my back, knocking the air from my lungs and sending splintering pain through my core. I curled up, gasping. "Don't run from me, doll. It'll only make it worse for you."

Forcing me onto my back, he dropped to his knees, using them to pin me. I landed one slap on his face before he caught my hands. Laughing—the silver stars of an aggression elixir firing in his green eyes—he restrained them with one hand over my head.

Uncorking the vial, he dug his fingers firmly into the corners of my jaw. "I'm going to have to reconsider the things I said I'd never do with my queen."

I clenched my teeth hard. He smiled at me, the corners of his mouth reaching higher the harder he pushed. Fuck he enjoyed this. Unable to stand the pain any longer, my jaw gaped, and the contents hit the back of my throat. Prepared for my next move, he traded his hold of my hands for my mouth and nose.

My nails tore at his hands as my need for air increased, ripping into the flesh of his cheek. A hot drop of blood splattered onto my jaw. With no other option, my body convulsed, swallowing the sweet liquid haunting my mouth.

A single tear ran down my cheek.

"That's it," he whispered. Releasing his hold, he got to his feet, leaving me there lying on my back. "Is this the first note you received?"

Truth. The word hit me like a random thought.

I waited for the tickling sensation at the back of my throat, the one which promised the asker an honest answer, but none came. Pretending to fight, I pressed my lips together, tongue to the back of my teeth, considering which answer to give. Holding on until it felt safe to erupt in a single gasping: "Yes." I touched my shaking hands to my mouth for effect.

Cole stopped his pacing, eyes narrowing to slits. The red streak under his one eye looked like a trail left by a bloody tear. "What is soon?"

Hot drops fell like rain down my face. *Nothing now.* "I don't know."

"Has my brother made any other contact with you? Has he come to see you?"

"No," I choked. Anger made my tears burn, blurring my vision. "Immortals Cole—you have me monitored relentlessly."

For the first time since his arrival, Cole turned to look at Grayden, who stood at attention, eyes forward. "For half the day by someone known to regard your lover highly."

Face as solid and unmovable as forged steel, Grayden looked his cousin in the eye. "Are you questioning my loyalty, sir?"

Wiping the back of my hands across my eyes, a dark laugh escaped me. "All of those aggression elixirs must have fried your brain, Cole, because you're fucking crazy."

I caught sight of Norris's hand inches from my face, right before another cut in taking the smack. Cole's arm separated us—a red welt in the shape of Norris's fingers already forming.

For his part, the Master Guardian looked horrified, falling to his knees.

"I told you no, Norris."

"But Your Highness—"

"If I ever see you try that again, I'll have one of my cousins eat your hand." He ground the words out between his teeth, turning to look at me once more. "Which of your maids delivered the note?"

I said a silent prayer to the Immortal Idols for forgiveness, hoping the girl was far away from here by now, or at the very least, that she'd used a fake name. If there was a chance, I couldn't consciously let all my maids take the blame. "Gymma."

"What is it broth—" Rounding the corner into the room with a four Protector escort—dressed in a black long-sleeved shirt and cloth pants, anti-magic shackles glinting on his wrists—Damien stopped when he saw me. His face remained neutral, but his rage-filled green eyes, cracking red, betrayed him.

My heart ached like someone had it trapped between both hands, squeezing as tightly as they could. Fresh tears followed the path of their predecessors. I looked at Cole, cold, calculated anger blooming in his eyes. "Please, Cole, don't do this."

"Grayden, Norris, Sunya, and whatever your names are—stay. You're needed as both witnesses and jailers."

Damien didn't so much as blink, and he didn't take his eyes off me.

"On your knees, brother," Cole hissed.

Damien didn't move. At Cole's motion, the Protector kicked Damien, sending him onto his knees. He still didn't look away from me.

"Open your mouth, or I'll make Norris," Cole growled. I know how much you'd love that."

My mouth went dry.

Slowly, Damien turned to look up at his brother. Violence dripped from his voice as he said, "I can do it myself." He took the vial and drank it, tossing it hard against the wall where it broke into a dozen sparkling pieces.

Two of the Protectors who'd escorted him here each took an arm, pinning them behind his back.

Cole cocked his head, considering his brother. "The red is new. Do you want to kill me?"

They locked in a stare-off, Damien's jaw working. I closed my eyes to the fresh, hot tears and prayed to the Immortals.

When he finally answered, his voice dripped with venom. "Yes."

A sob wracked my chest as my hammering heart came to an abrupt stop. "Damien, no."

Cole's lips contorted into a twisted smile. "Then, really, the rest doesn't matter. Protectors, you heard him. You know what to do."

The Protectors, pinning his arms, yanked him to his feet.

As they dragged him back, Damien went calmly, smiling at me. A reassuring gleam briefly sparked in his rage-filled red and green eyes. "I love you, Eden."

It didn't matter how much I trusted Damien because I didn't trust Cole.

"No, Cole, no, please, I'll do anything." I scrambled to my knees, grabbing onto his shirt. "If you hurt him, I won't—"

Spinning on me, he struck me so hard, the ground I'd gained fell away, and my vision doubled.

Damien roared so loudly that the whole kingdom must have heard. His elbow shot back into one of the Protector's ribs, but surprisingly, their grip didn't slip. He kicked and thrashed against his captors. "I will destroy you, Cole," he screamed.

Cole shook out his hand. "That was for what you did to my face." He watched me closely as he said the next words. "I'm not worried about your threats, brother. Norris, put the mongrel down."

CHAPTER FORTY-SEVEN

9.TWO.4005

The clock on the desk chimed twice—thirty minutes to midnight.

Pillowy gray clouds blanketed the night sky, casting the frozen lawn and sparsely leaved trees beyond in steely blues and deep grays.

Everything was so still.

Soon…

As still as my heart, hanging hollow and cold in my chest.

Such a stark difference from the feeling I'd had when Damien had slipped Lupine's ring on my finger—for just a moment—before we'd parted ways that night. Despite it being nothing but a ring at the moment, the imminent bond it beckoned had everything in my body feeling warm and calm.

Soon.

The couch cushion beside me sagged. "You should try to get some rest."

Slowly, I turned to look into Grayden's red eyes. "The only way I'm ever going to sleep again in this home is if I'm dead."

His lips parted, but whatever he had to say next was lost. Down the hall, the door to the suite creaked open.

I looked to the doorway, a wisp of something sharp stirring in my chest.

Grayden stood, putting himself between me and the boots coming our way. "Stay behind me."

"What are you doing?" I hissed.

Battle magic crackled at the tip of his quickly weaving fingers. "I don't know who that is, but they've made it past the Protectors, and they aren't anyone permitted to be in Cole's apartment after sundown." He cracked his neck. "They reek of blood."

A chill surging through me, I glared at his back. "Maybe lead with the blood part next time. Shouldn't we run or hide?"

"There are only three of them by the sound of their footfall. It shouldn't be—"

Two black-clad figures—a man and a woman—stepped forth from the darkened hall, cutting him off. The man brandishing a blood-stained baton, the woman cradling a green explosion orb in her palm.

At the center of them was a third figure in a black wool coat, his black hair finger-combed back, green eyes glowing brightly. I didn't know if this was some kind of trick, and I didn't care. Leaping to my feet, I cut around Grayden, whose hand had stopped weaving, and ran into Damien's open arms.

Tears of happiness and relief sprang from my eyes.

"None of that," he smiled, holding me tight against him. "I told you what soon would mean. You said you trusted me."

I buried my face in his chest, my memories filling in for the sandalwood scent of him, the deodor charm on his signet ring hid. "I do, but I thought…"

His hand stroked my hair. "I know what you thought, but I'm here now, and I'm taking you away from all of this."

"I don't know how you did it, but I'm not surprised you found a way," Grayden said.

Damien and I both turned to look at him, Damien stiffening beside me. Grayden stood, head bowed, arms at his side, and palms outfacing in peace.

"How are we doing this, cousin?" Damien asked, voice icy.

I already knew from our conversation in Valentine's Crossroads that Damien was uninterested in Grayden's redemption arc. In his own words, there was no forgiveness for betrayal or denying one their mate.

Our uneven history together aside, I couldn't help but feel sympathy as the Protector flinched, body sagging.

"I will not fight you, but if I let you go unscathed, they'll brand me weak and a traitor to the crown, so make it look good."

Slipping his hand into mine, Damien put his back to Grayden, nodding once at the man and woman who wordlessly advanced.

We were a step beyond the doorway when Grayden said, "I'm sorry, brother."

Damien's hand tightened a fraction around mine, but he didn't slow or glance back, pulling me into a tunnel of darkness. It was only then that I noticed none of the light charms were coming on.

"Are you sure—"

He shook his head tightly—the movement barely detectable as the traces of moonlight from the office faded, and objects became slightly different shades of black—silencing me.

I reached out my free hand, feeling for the wall to orient me. We made it three more steps, and the hall clock chimed three times, denoting forty-five minutes past the hour.

A breeze whipped across my face, and I ran smack into his chest. "We need to move faster. It took longer than I expected to get in and get through to you. I'm going to need to carry you." His arm already at the back of my knees before I could protest.

Surprised at the sudden loss of ground, I tried to stabilize myself, grabbing for his shoulder and finding his hair instead, pulling him right into my chest.

"We don't have time for that right now," he chuckled.

Damien started running, my body gently bobbing into his, as we turned right into true, total darkness. What was going on?

Trying to summon the slightest modicum of light, I snapped my fingers.

"Don't. The cover of darkness is helping us," he whispered.

He turned again, and if I weren't too disoriented by my lack of sight, the next turn would be out the front door.

"How can you—" I started to ask. "Can you see in the dark?"

I could almost see the grin on his face as he said, "Yes, but it's a recent development, thanks to you. Panatats can see in the dark."

Frame splitting, the door to the manor swung open seconds before we reached it, paving the way for Damien to power through. The dry cold of the night swept up around us, cutting right through my slip.

Hitting the first step down, somewhere from up on the second floor came a clatter and then a bloodcurdling scream, followed by maniacal laughter I wouldn't forget until the day I died.

My hold on him tightened. What the fuck was happening? "Damien…"

The frantic beating of my heart matched his pace, the frozen grass crunching under each smash of his boots, pushing to put distance between the ripping of clothing and flesh and the manic cackling behind us.

His voice was a whisper. "I know."

Burrowing into the heat and safety of him, I forced myself to focus on his face.

In the soft gray light, I took in the sight of him once more. Skin blanched and black hair gleaming. His eyes glowed, looking like the lights in the Hidden Halls. A dark streak of blood glided down from the corner of his right eyebrow.

"You're bleeding."

His winced. "It's nothing."

Touching my finger lightly to his chest, I sent my magic into him. Righting the wound and any others I didn't see, dread pooling in my stomach.

"When you said it took longer than expected—what happened to everyone?"

"They've been taken care of. Most of them."

"Are they…"

A roar at the edge of the lawn silenced his response and shattered the even cadence of his steps.

"Fuck," he hissed.

Disappearing onto the private path, I caught only a glimpse of what looked like a big black bear galloping across the lawn toward us over his shoulder.

We were almost free of the wards…

Damien squeezed me a little tighter, and the yelling stopped, as did the breeze. Deadened by the buildings surrounding us. I looked up at him. A huge grin on his face. Both the calm and the happiness there lasted a mere second.

A blast of magic cracked the quiet of the night, making the hairs on my arm stand up.

Damien turned in time for us both to see a thin wall of green shimmering light unfurling from the ground, moving skyward until it disappeared into the clouds.

"What was that?" I gasped.

"Ancient magic meant to keep out unwanted guests."

As if on cue, Protectors and Devotees who'd been patrolling the area came running. They glanced at the shimmering wall and paid it no mind, charging forth.

Breathing slowly through his nose, Damien set me down, placing himself between me and the imminent onslaught, shoulders braced. The smooth cobblestones were ice cold to my bare feet, but between the sight of the green shimmering wall disappearing into the clouds and the alarmed guardians closing in quickly, I barely noticed.

They hit the wall with a dull smack and stumbled backward. The wave behind followed the first, and we stood there, watching them charge one after another to no avail. The third wave had the sense to stop. A Devotee launched a ball of crackling magic toward the wall, only to watch it backfire at them.

Damien laughed. A deep, righteous, winning laugh, so loud it echoed through the streets. He pivoted to me, grabbing me around the waist and lifting me high, spinning.

"We did it," he cheered.

I wasn't sure what we had done, but his smile and excitement were contagious, and we were free and together for the time being. Taking his face in my hands, I planted a hard kiss on his mouth.

"Go get the Master Guardians," a Protector screamed. "We're under attack."

The muscles in his back relaxing, he shifted an arm under my legs, cradling me once more, a mischievous smile on his face. "Are you ready?"

It hadn't got past me where we were.

We stood in a small square south of our home—one of the few in the city with a sanctuary at its center instead of a statue. The small wooden building big enough for a handful to worship the Immortal Idols and the retired Devotee who maintained it to live.

Butterflies danced in my stomach. "I am, but will you tell me what's going on?

"Yes, but first things first, I have a promise to keep." He kissed my cheek. "You know I made a point of meeting with you and sending you a note so you could be ready for me, yet you're in a nightgown and barefoot."

"Having watched them drag you away, I had other things on my mind."

"I'll give you, I've made planning errors in the past—"

"This evening has been traumatizing enough. Is this really what you want to talk about leading up to our Pledge ceremony?" The archway of the sanctuary appeared overhead. "I'd like to walk from here."

Eyes twinkling delightedly, he set me down at the door. Hand in hand, I let him lead me inside, tossing the ring Cole had given me into a bronze offering bowl by the door.

At the center of the small wooden building stood the sanctuary's Devotee, gray hair cut close to his scalp, placing a pillar candle in the lantern dangling from the archway at the end of the aisle. Snapping his fingers, the candle came to life.

"I implore you, sir." Damien bowed his head. "We're here to perform the Pledge."

The Devotee turned sharply—ready to contest such a request—until he saw who made it. He fell to his knees. "Your Highness. I'm sorry, but I'm unable to. It is against the law."

Damien offered his free hand to him. "You needn't worry about that law from here on. It no longer applies to you."

He stared at Damien wide-eyed, recognizing some meaning in his words that I didn't—moving to his feet. "Do you have tokens?"

We held out our respective offerings. His was the princess-cut emerald, wrapped in a gold band. Mine, my silver key necklace. The necklace I'd worn all my life. Both items bequeathed to us by our mothers on their deathbeds. The Devotee assessed them for a moment.

Maybe it was in my head, but he seemed to linger on the key. What could he be looking for in them? Was it not good enough?

Finally, he offered a stiff nod.

We stood there waiting in the archway, watching the Devotee fumble in a small trunk for his things.

Rejoining us, he motioned for us to proceed. I went first. I knew the motions well, having played them a dozen times as a child. Damien bowed his head, and I clasped the chain around his neck, brushing my fingers lightly against his collarbone as he pulled away, stopping where the key rested on his chest. It's new home forevermore.

When it came to me, there were too many options. Whatever finger I chose the ring to reside on, it would never leave as long as I lived. I presented him with my newly available left hand.

Jokingly, he started with my pinky finger. I nodded a yes when he got to my middle finger, where Cole's had been—replacing pain with beauty, hope, and love.

We smiled at each other, my heart quickening in my chest—we were really doing it.

Ready to continue, the Devotee cleared his throat. Damien held out his arms, forearms face up, and I overlaid mine atop his. Starting at the center, the magus crossed the white sash he clutched over our arms, then wound it down and around, binding our arms tightly and tucking each end into the last wrap.

Sparkling green eyes looked down at me. Warm, content, adoring eyes. Could my heart beat any faster?

"Together, whenever you're ready," the Devotee said.

Damien gave me a slight nod.

"My love, my light, my life. The earth at my feet, the air that I breathe," we said, magic filling the words. Our voices weaving together like we'd practiced this moment together a thousand times.

My eyes never left his, the magnitude of what we were doing sinking in with each word. "Who you are is who I love. What you need is what I provide. Where you are, I am. When you die, I am dead."

An infinite and unbreakable promise to one another.

The Devotee cracked his thumb against his middle finger, and all at once, the sash and the necklace around Damien's neck began to glow a uniform white light, the cloth dissolving away, leaving our joined hands—pink and tingling—behind and the glowing stone on my middle finger.

Just like that, it was done.

Arms still clutched together, Damien leaned to kiss me…

"I hear you made it out with seconds to spare," a snippy, out-of-breath voice said. Killing the moment.

We both shifted our attention to the door where an older woman entered, followed by a group of people. Damien stepped forward, his fingers weaving with mine.

"Going forward, we're going to have to discuss playing it that close to the chest."

Coming to a stop a few steps away, I realized the woman was Oona —the shop owner of Spectrum Sensations. Having traded her gray dress for a black shirt and pants and wearing her hair in a tight bun, she looked like a different person. Her gaze darted between the ring on my finger and the necklace around his neck—both still glowing—as did every pair of eyes behind her.

Her shoulders relaxed, the corners of her eyes softening. "It appears congratulations are in order. I know what I said, but I didn't expect you to do it first thing."

His thumb made slow, reassuring circles on the back of my hand. "No offense, Oona, but our deal wasn't on my mind when I phased here.

What deal? I looked up at him, but his green gaze stayed on the group before us.

"Were you able to get Isa out?" he asked.

My heart leapt at the sound of her name.

She nodded. "We have made good on our word, though it wasn't easy—your Facto was a fighter. I know what we discussed, but I think you should have told her. She'll have some choice words for you when you see her next."

I stepped up beside Damien. "Thank you so much for your help. Can you take us to her?"

Her attention shifted to me, a soft smile breaking the hard set of her lips. "Later, dear. She's been shown to a room and given something to help her sleep."

Right, it was the middle of the night.

She returned her gaze to Damien. "I hope you know we won't be able to give you the customary minimum to honor unions. As it's a new day, you'll have the rest of it and the night. That's all we can afford you. Following that, we'll need to finalize details for your coronation and next steps in regards to your broth—"

The word fell out of my mouth. "Coronation?"

CHAPTER FORTY-EIGHT

10.TWO.4005

Using a Valentine Bracelet—how had she obtained one of those?—Oona phased us to Halon Inn, located just inside the thick, lush landscape of the Northern Forest. The last stop out on this side of the city.

"Not the most romantic place in the world," Oona said, bounding up the two porch steps to the door, "but no one likes coming out here if they can help it, so you'll have privacy. It's quiet, the food's decent, baths are big and water's hot—all you could want."

The air was cold, heavy, and stagnant here, and it sank into my skin like a pebble in water. I burrowed my face into the collar of Damien's jacket, now wrapped around my shoulders, and followed her, my feet leaving impressions in the cool dirt carpet of the forest floor. Damien had happily offered to continue carrying me, but I'd refused, and I didn't care that my ego was making the decision.

I was soon to be the Queen of half of Sorbis, and I'd be damned if I would represent the people as a woman whose husband carried her around. Immortals, Damien was my husband...my Pledge. That's what he'd traded. He'd helped the insurgents secure the outer city and the farmlands from the Alliance Council in exchange for their help extracting me. They'd said yes and asked him to represent them as their leader and king—Reincimmo.

Everything he'd learned—the new nullify elixir, Valentine's Crossroads, the charm for creating the wall—he'd learned from the Vanivere during his time in the Ground. And he'd made a bond with them as well. They'd give him all their knowledge of the Immortal Valentine in turn for someone to follow once more. Several of them watched us now, glowing green eyes amidst the shadows of the trees. Their voices whispered in my head.

Our lady. Our queen. We are honored to serve.

It was all so wild and surreal that it would take me days to process it.

Oona managed one knock on the door, and as her fist went to strike again, it swung open, revealing a portly woman who regarded us in the orange light of a lantern, blue eyes wide and inches shy of an accidental strike to the face.

The innkeeper stepped forward, a wave of blistering heat accompanying her, making my cold-numbed skin tingle.

"General Oona." She bowed her head. "Prince Damien, Lady Eden, it's an honor. Please come inside."

Thinking about it all once more, I hadn't noticed everyone looking at me. Squeezing my hand, Damien nudged me in.

Oona—General Oona to the other rebels—stayed outside, rubbing her hands together, hunching her shoulders against the cold. "I won't be staying, dear, just dropping these two off for a short honeymoon before the work begins."

"Honeymoon?" The innkeeper's eyes almost bulged out of her head, gaze hungrily sweeping across us, locking in on the ring and the key, both shining preternaturally.

The idea of it must have been something. Nearly no one had seen us together, so a relationship of any kind would be surprising.

Another thing to process—come morning, our private relationship and union would be all over the city along with everything else.

"I'll have clothes delivered to you in an hour, though I imagine you won't be needing them until I return. I'll see you in a day's time." She nodded to the men and women surrounding us—our security. "Fan out. You know what to do."

Holding the lantern high, the innkeeper bounced up the stairs, gushing and showering us in congratulations. We followed quietly, offering her smiles when she looked at us. Turning down a narrow, wood-paneled hallway, it was impossible to stay side by side, so I shifted in front of Damien, expecting he'd let me go, but his fingers stayed solidly entwined with mine.

She twisted the key in the door at the end of the hall and motioned for me to go in. Pillar candles decorated the chest of drawers and the two bedside tables on either side of the king-sized bed, filling the small space. They continued flickering in the space immediately to my right, their light amplified by the bathroom mirror.

"This is coincidentally our honeymoon suite." The woman lingered outside the door. "I know it's late, but would either of you like food? I can whip something up."

Tired, I wandered into the bathroom, snapping my fingers to summon more lights. To my surprise, the tub was about as big as the one in Damien's bathroom.

"I think we're fine on food," Damien said, "but we could use some water, please, and a hot pot of tea if you wouldn't mind."

"Of course, I'll have a pitcher of water and some tea brought up. I'll put some snacks on the tray, too—just in case. Oh, and if you get cold and need extra blankets, they're in the bottom drawer."

"Thank you," my husband said, "but I'm sure we'll have no problem keeping warm."

Starting the water, I cast Damien a look over my shoulder, catching a sly smile on his lips.

"Was that necessary?" I asked as the door shut.

Kicking off his shoes by the door, he joined me. "So bashful." He pulled his sweater over his head, leaving only the necklace behind. "It's what people do quite a bit of on the night of their union," he teased. Damien swooped me up in his arms, the heat of him encouraging me to lean in.

Staying strong, I braced a hand against his abdomen.

His eyes searched mine. "I know you have questions. Will you tell me what's on your mind?"

I did. And not knowing how else to begin, I said, "You're going to be the king of Sorbis."

"I'm going to be the king of Sorbis's farmlands and parts of the outer city," he corrected.

Saying it like how much land he governed mattered. "You wanted to leave."

"I did."

"Now you can never leave."

"I know."

"I'm going to be queen."

"Yes, and I'm sorry I didn't tell you." He gathered my hands in his. "If something happened, though—if the nullify elixir failed or Immortals forbid—extracting you failed—I couldn't condemn everyone who helped. I know you didn't want to be queen. I wish I could have told you. I was trying to do anything to—"

I let him keep one hand but pressed two fingers of the other to his lips, silencing him. "You don't need to apologize. It wasn't that I didn't want to be queen, I just didn't want to be one that existed to stay silent, look pretty, and produce heirs." I dropped my hand and looked at the bathtub, filling quickly. "The only thing I am is surprised, but I think that's fair. We've lived two very different lives these past several days. I understand why you did it, and I'm not upset that it happened, but I am going to need some time to process it. I'd like to know how all this came about in detail, not today but soon."

Bringing our joined hands to his lips, he kissed the ring there. "You'll take all the time you need. I'll be here to help you process it, and I'll tell you everything, whenever you want. In however much detail you desire."

"What will we do about the bonds we made to Cole?" I sighed. Hating that this far away, with an ancient magic wall keeping him back, on what would be the happiest night of most people's lives, he was in my head.

"I made a bond to serve him. I never specified how I would do that. Regarding yours, that's a little more complicated, but I'll figure it out. There's a whole level to magic that the Vanivere have been teaching me, and there's a solution in there somewhere. I promised you, you'll never go back to him, and I meant it."

I nodded.

He considered me. "That's not all that's bothering you."

I raised an eyebrow in challenge. "What makes you think that?"

"I know you. I know when you're stuck on something. You're pretty good at hiding it, but the little purse of your lips is still stubbornly there."

Unable to look at him, I dropped my gaze, sucking in a steadying breath. "Did you want to perform the Pledge? With everything, I can't help—"

In the span of a heartbeat, his hands were on my face, green eyes bright. "Yes. Eden, yes. I meant everything I said to you in the Crossroads." His voice grew softer. "Yes, our union aided more than that desire, but having you, my mate, as my wife—my Pledge—that was the dream. I love you, Eden."

I love you, too.

The key glinted around his neck as if in recognition of my nonverbal declaration. I lay my hand over it so the ring and pendant touched, enjoying the warmth of it and his chest. Of the way the two pieces seemed to vibrate together.

With my other hand, I snapped my fingers, and my clothes and his jacket disappeared. Where they went, I hadn't mastered that yet—dismissing wasn't as straightforward as summoning—but as Oona had said, I wouldn't be needing them for the next day.

Red cracked his wide eyes. "You've been practicing."

Smiling proudly, I ran my hand up his neck and into his hair. "What do we do next, husband?"

The green of his eyes all but fell away.

Damien grabbed me around the waist and, lifting me so my thighs rested around his hips, he pushed me against the wall, positioning me perfectly between two hard places. "I have several ideas, wife."

THE END OF BOOK ONE

Demi-Immortal (aka demis): Descendants of immortals and demi-immortals. Viewed similarly to Immortal Idols since they are descendants. Don't age once they hit the Immortal Age of 25. They won't die of old age, but they are susceptible to all forms of death.

Immortal Age: the age of 25.

Immortal Idols: Beings of pure magic who created the Kingdom of Solta. See: Immortal Valentine, Immortal Faldone.

***

The Academy: During the last month of their 23rd year, every citizen of Sorbis (with few exceptions i.e., members of the royal family) is required to attend the Academy for a year and undergo testing in the four aptitudes. Those who fail to qualify remain citizens. Those who qualify become guardians and are sorted into one of the four aptitudes, typically based on which skill set they best reflect; however, those who excel in more than one can choose. Citizens of other cities are welcome to go through the Academy, but most, outside of Charph, opt not to.

The Four Guardian Aptitudes:

-Acuity: focuses on intellect. Guardians of acuity are referred to as Scholar. Represented by the color purple. Current Master Guardian of Acuity: Gillian.

-Charms: focuses on sourced magic (i.e., wards, charms, bonds, etc.). Guardians of charms are referred to as Devotees. Represented by the color yellow. Current Master Guardian of Charms: Rei.

-Combat: focuses on strength, speed, and agility. Guardians of combat are referred to as Protector. Represented by the color red. Current Master Guardian of Combat: Saier.

-Skill: focuses on inherent ability and elixirs. Guardians of skill are referred to as Elders. Represented by the color blue. Current Master Guardian of Skill: Norris.

Inherent Magic: magic that exists in the blood of a magus.

Magus: an individual with either inherent magic or the ability to access sourced magic.

Non-mage: an individual who has neither inherent magic nor the ability to access sourced magic.

Sourced Magic: magic derived from the elements.

***

The Bidding: Starting on the Crown Prince of Solta's 20th birthday, all interested women across the kingdom will vie for him before the Alliance Council. This event will take place once every 10 years on the Crown Prince's birthday and will be known as the Bidding. The Alliance Council will vote; however, the king and queen's votes carry more weight. Following a successful Bidding, the Crown Prince and the selectee are known to each other as **Bidden.** The customary length for the Crown Prince to court the selectee is a year, after which, if the courting is a success, it will end in a proposal of a blood bond (formerly the Eternal Pledge).

The Eternal Pledge: a life bond between two individuals performed by a Devotee; After Roan's War, it became an outlawed practice as it left many children orphaned. Blood bonds replaced it.

The Pledge Death: a degenerative disease that is triggered when an individual's Pledge dies (with death typically occurring within 1-2 years).

Pledge Tokens: items exchanged by individuals performing the Eternal Pledge to denote their commitment to one another.

***

The Alliance Council of the Cities of Solta: united under the Valentines of Sorbis, the Alliance Council is made up of the King of Solta and his heir, the Lord of Charph and his heir, the Misundre Five, and the Master Guardians. *Note:* Following the Allied Cities of Solta winning Roan's War, Vivinmoor became part of the Allied Cities of Solta, though to date, they do not maintain a seat on the council.

Factotum (aka facto): a woman of Charph who has chosen to stay mateless and childless, who binds themselves by blood to a family. They are given food, shelter, a weekly allowance, and all the protections of the house. In return, they care for the household and family. Typically for families of means.

The Ground: the subterranean levels of Protector Headquarters, used as a prison.

Soltans: the currency of Solta; green metal coins.

Roan's War: a war between Vivinmoor, the southernmost city of the Kingdom of Solta, and the Allied Cities of Solta that resulted in the latter winning.

Runners: Humanoid creatures created by Valentine to transport messages and people around Sorbis; like demis, they don't age but can die.

Valentine Bracelet: a silver metal cuff bracelet infused with the Immortal Valentine's blood and gifted to his Alliance Council to phase.

Acknowledgments

It takes a village and several years, if you're me, to get to this point. But here I am.

Obviously, thank you to my mom and dad—you got the dedication, didn't you?! (haha). But really, they've had to listen to me talk about this book and this series for far too long. Poor things. I bet you guys thought it'd never happen—that makes three of us :D.

Massive thanks to my editor and close friend, Stephanie Lawless. What can I say other than you're the best?! The Immortal Valentine is yours. I know I already told you that, but I'm making it official here in my acknowledgements. You have more than earned him.

My eternal gratitude to Jessica Nelson, Caroline Byrd, Barbara Lercara-Wyatt, Drew Wittenberg, Michelle Lamb, and Morgan Honeycutt, whose support in various forms was integral to the creation of this book. They gave my anxious writer heart the best gift of reading this story in its rougher states, provided me with invaluable feedback & edit suggestions, championed it, told me they wanted to read more, and asked me, "When will it finally be published?!"

Thank you to my cover artist, Anze Ban Virant - ABV atelier design. You gave my story a face, and that's pretty cool.

Thank you to my map creator, Adriano Bezerra. Your depiction of the Kingdom of Solta looks infinitely better than the scribble drawing I sent you.

Thank you, reader. If you're reading this, I'm assuming you read my book, which is pretty insane for me to think. I appreciate you and hope you enjoyed it.

And finally, thank you to my partner and best friend, Scott Rodgers. As a strictly nonfiction reader, I appreciate your attempt to follow my grand plans for this fantasy series.

About the Author

E. A. Wyatt is a schemer who loves puzzles and storytelling, which is how she wound up here. When not traveling around the world to avoid her problems, you can find her in Charlotte, NC, with her partner and their plants.

You can keep up with her on Instagram: @ea.wyatt
Or write her at: eawyatt15@gmail.com